selected short stories of
Jules Verne

maple press

SELECTED SHORT STORIES OF JULES VERNE

Published by

MAPLE PRESS PRIVATE LIMITED
office: A-63, Sector 58, Noida 201301, U.P., India
phone: +91 120 455 3581, 455 3583
email: info@maplepress.co.in
website: www.maplepress.co.in

Reprint 2021 in India

ISBN: 978-93-80005-43-0

Contents

Doctor Ox's Experiment

How it is Useless to Seek, Even on the Best Maps, for the Small Town of Quiquendone

If you try to find, on any map of Flanders, ancient or modern, the small town of Quiquendone, probably you will not succeed. Is Quiquendone, then, one of those towns which have disappeared? No. A town of the future? By no means. It exists in spite of geographies, and has done so for some eight or nine hundred years. It even numbers two thousand three hundred and ninety-three souls, allowing one soul to each inhabitant. It is situated thirteen and a half kilometres north-west of Oudenarde, and fifteen and a quarter kilometres south-east of Bruges, in the heart of Flanders. The Vaar, a small tributary of the Scheldt, passes beneath its three bridges, which are still covered with a quaint mediaeval roof, like that at Tournay. An old chateau is to be seen there, the first stone of which was laid so long ago as 1197, by Count Baldwin, afterwards Emperor of Constantinople; and there is a Town Hall, with Gothic windows, crowned by a chaplet of battlements, and surrounded by a turreted belfry, which rises three hundred and fifty-seven feet above the soil. Every hour you may hear there a chime of five octaves, a veritable aerial piano, the renown of which surpasses that of the famous chimes of Bruges. Strangers—if any ever come to Quiquendone—do not quit the curious old town until they have visited its "Stadtholder's Hall", adorned by a full-length portrait of William of Nassau, by Brandon; the loft of the Church of Saint Magloire, a masterpiece of sixteenth century architecture; the cast-iron well in the spacious Place Saint Ernuph, the admirable ornamentation of which is attributed to the artist-blacksmith, Quentin Metsys; the tomb formerly erected to Mary of Burgundy, daughter of Charles the Bold, who now reposes in the Church of Notre Dame at Bruges; and so on. The principal industry of Quiquendone is the manufacture of whipped creams and barley-sugar on a large scale. It has been governed by the Van Tricasses, from father to son, for several centuries. And yet Quiquendone is not on the map of Flanders! Have the geographers forgotten it, or is it an intentional omission? That I cannot tell; but Quiquendone really exists; with its narrow streets, its fortified walls, its Spanish-looking houses, its market, and its burgomaster—so much so, that it has recently been the theatre of some surprising phenomena, as extraordinary and incredible as they are true, which are to be recounted in the present narration.

Surely there is nothing to be said or thought against the Flemings of Western Flanders. They are a well-to-do folk, wise, prudent, sociable, with even tempers, hospitable, perhaps a little heavy in conversation as in mind; but this does not explain why one of the most interesting towns of their district has yet to appear on modern maps.

This omission is certainly to be regretted. If only history, or in default of history the chronicles, or in default of chronicles the traditions of the country, made mention of Quiquendone! But no; neither atlases, guides, nor itineraries speak of it. M. Joanne himself, that energetic hunter after small towns, says not a word of it. It might be readily conceived that this silence would injure the commerce, the industries, of the town. But let us hasten to add that Quiquendone has neither industry nor commerce, and that it does very well without them. Its barley-sugar and whipped cream are consumed on the spot; none is exported. In short, the Quiquendonians have no need of anybody. Their desires are limited, their existence is a modest one; they are calm, moderate, phlegmatic—in a word, they are Flemings; such as are still to be met with sometimes between the Scheldt and the North Sea.

In which the Burgomaster Van Tricasse and the Counsellor Niklausse Consult about the Affairs of the Town

"You think so?" asked the burgomaster.

"I—think so," replied the counsellor, after some minutes of silence.

"You see, we must not act hastily," resumed the burgomaster.

"We have been talking over this grave matter for ten years," replied the Counsellor Niklausse, "and I confess to you, my worthy Van Tricasse, that I cannot yet take it upon myself to come to a decision."

"I quite understand your hesitation," said the burgomaster, who did not speak until after a good quarter of an hour of reflection, "I quite understand it, and I fully share it. We shall do wisely to decide upon nothing without a more careful examination of the question."

"It is certain," replied Niklausse, "that this post of civil commissary is useless in so peaceful a town as Quiquendone."

"Our predecessor," said Van Tricasse gravely, "our predecessor never said, never would have dared to say, that anything is certain. Every affirmation is subject to awkward qualifications."

The counsellor nodded his head slowly in token of assent; then he remained silent for nearly half an hour. After this lapse of time, during which neither the counsellor nor the burgomaster moved so much as a finger, Niklausse asked Van Tricasse whether his predecessor—of some twenty years before—had not thought of suppressing this office of civil commissary, which each year cost the town of Quiquendone the sum of thirteen hundred and seventy-five francs and some centimes.

"I believe he did," replied the burgomaster, carrying his hand with majestic deliberation to his ample brow; "but the worthy man died without having dared to make up his mind, either as to this or any other administrative measure. He was a sage. Why should I not do as he did?"

Counsellor Niklausse was incapable of originating any objection to the burgomaster's opinion.

"The man who dies," added Van Tricasse solemnly, "without ever having decided upon anything during his life, has very nearly attained to perfection."

This said, the burgomaster pressed a bell with the end of his little finger, which gave forth a muffled sound, which seemed less a sound than a sigh. Presently some light steps glided softly across the tile floor. A mouse would not have made less noise, running over a thick carpet. The door of the room opened, turning on its well-oiled hinges. A young girl, with long blonde tresses, made her appearance. It was Suzel Van Tricasse, the burgomaster's only daughter. She handed her father a pipe, filled to the brim, and a small copper brazier, spoke not a word, and disappeared at once, making no more noise at her exit than at her entrance.

The worthy burgomaster lighted his pipe, and was soon hidden in a cloud of bluish smoke, leaving Counsellor Niklausse plunged in the most absorbing thought.

The room in which these two notable personages, charged with the government of Quiquendone, were talking, was a parlour richly adorned with carvings in dark wood. A lofty fireplace, in which an oak might have been burned or an ox roasted, occupied the whole of one of the sides of the room; opposite to it was a trellised window, the painted glass of which toned down the brightness of the sunbeams. In an antique frame above the chimney-piece appeared the portrait of some worthy man, attributed to Memling, which no doubt represented an ancestor of the Van Tricasses, whose authentic genealogy dates back to the fourteenth century, the period when the Flemings and Guy de Dampierre were engaged in wars with the Emperor Rudolph of Hapsburgh.

This parlour was the principal apartment of the burgomaster's house, which was one of the pleasantest in Quiquendone. Built in the Flemish style, with all the abruptness, quaintness, and picturesqueness of Pointed architecture, it was considered one of the most curious monuments of the town. A Carthusian convent, or a deaf and dumb asylum, was not more silent than this mansion. Noise had no existence there; people did not walk, but glided about in it; they did not speak, they murmured. There was not, however, any lack of women in the house, which, in addition to the burgomaster Van Tricasse himself, sheltered his wife, Madame Brigitte Van Tricasse, his daughter, Suzel Van Tricasse, and his domestic, Lotche Jansheu. We may also mention the burgomaster's sister, Aunt Hermance, an elderly maiden who still bore the nickname of Tatanemance, which her niece Suzel had given her when a child. But in spite of all these elements of discord and noise, the burgomaster's house was as calm as a desert.

The burgomaster was some fifty years old, neither fat nor lean, neither short nor tall, neither rubicund nor pale, neither gay nor sad, neither contented nor discontented, neither energetic nor dull, neither proud nor humble, neither good nor bad, neither generous nor miserly, neither courageous nor cowardly, neither too much nor too little of anything—a man notably moderate in all respects, whose invariable slowness of motion, slightly hanging lower jaw, prominent eyebrows, massive forehead, smooth as a copper plate and without a wrinkle, would at once have betrayed to a physiognomist that the burgomaster Van Tricasse was phlegm personified. Never, either from anger or passion, had any emotion whatever hastened the beating of this man's heart, or flushed his face; never had his pupils contracted under the influence of any irritation, however ephemeral. He invariably wore good clothes, neither too large nor too small, which he never seemed to wear out.

He was shod with large square shoes with triple soles and silver buckles, which lasted so long that his shoemaker was in despair. Upon his head he wore a large hat which dated from the period when Flanders was separated from Holland, so that this venerable masterpiece was at least forty years old. But what would you have? It is the passions which wear out body as well as soul, the clothes as well as the body; and our worthy burgomaster, apathetic, indolent, indifferent, was passionate in nothing. He wore nothing out, not even himself, and he considered himself the very man to administer the affairs of Quiquendone and its tranquil population.

The town, indeed, was not less calm than the Van Tricasse mansion. It was in this peaceful dwelling that the burgomaster reckoned on attaining the utmost limit of human existence, after having, however, seen the good Madame Brigitte Van Tricasse, his wife, precede him to the tomb, where, surely, she would not find a more profound repose than that she had enjoyed on earth for sixty years.

This demands explanation.

The Van Tricasse family might well call itself the "Jeannot family." This is why:—

Everyone knows that the knife of this typical personage is as celebrated as its proprietor, and not less incapable of wearing out, thanks to the double operation, incessantly repeated, of replacing the handle when it is worn out, and the blade when it becomes worthless. A precisely similar operation had been going on from time immemorial in the Van Tricasse family, to which Nature had lent herself with more than usual complacency. From 1340 it had invariably happened that a Van Tricasse, when left a widower, had remarried a Van Tricasse younger than himself; who, becoming in turn a widow, had married again a Van Tricasse younger than herself; and so on, without a break in the continuity, from generation to generation. Each died in his or her turn with mechanical regularity. Thus the worthy Madame Brigitte Van Tricasse had now her second husband; and, unless she violated her every duty, would precede her spouse—he being ten years younger than herself—to the other world, to make room for a new Madame Van Tricasse. Upon this the burgomaster calmly counted, that the family tradition might not be broken. Such was this mansion, peaceful and silent, of which the doors never creaked, the windows never rattled, the floors never groaned, the chimneys never roared, the weathercocks never grated, the furniture never squeaked, the locks never clanked, and the occupants never made more noise than their shadows. The god Harpocrates would certainly have chosen it for the Temple of Silence.

In which the Commissary Passauf Enters as Noisily as Unexpectedly

When the interesting conversation which has been narrated began, it was a quarter before three in the afternoon. It was at a quarter before four that Van Tricasse lighted his enormous pipe, which could hold a quart of tobacco, and it was at thirty-five minutes past five that he finished smoking it.

All this time the two comrades did not exchange a single word.

About six o'clock the counsellor, who had a habit of speaking in a very summary manner, resumed in these words,—

"So we decide—"

"To decide nothing," replied the burgomaster.

"I think, on the whole, that you are right, Van Tricasse."

"I think so too, Niklausse. We will take steps with reference to the civil commissary when we have more light on the subject—later on. There is no need for a month yet."

"Nor even for a year," replied Niklausse, unfolding his pocket-handkerchief and calmly applying it to his nose.

There was another silence of nearly a quarter of an hour. Nothing disturbed this repeated pause in the conversation; not even the appearance of the house-dog Lento, who, not less phlegmatic than his master, came to pay his respects in the parlour. Noble dog!—a model for his race. Had he been made of pasteboard, with wheels on his paws, he would not have made less noise during his stay.

Towards eight o'clock, after Lotche had brought the antique lamp of polished glass, the burgomaster said to the counsellor,—

"We have no other urgent matter to consider?"

"No, Van Tricasse; none that I know of."

"Have I not been told, though," asked the burgomaster, "that the tower of the Oudenarde gate is likely to tumble down?"

"Ah!" replied the counsellor; "really, I should not be astonished if it fell on some passer-by any day."

"Oh! before such a misfortune happens I hope we shall have come to a decision on the subject of this tower."

"I hope so, Van Tricasse."

"There are more pressing matters to decide."

"No doubt; the question of the leather-market, for instance."

"What, is it still burning?"

"Still burning, and has been for the last three weeks."

"Have we not decided in council to let it burn?"

"Yes, Van Tricasse—on your motion."

"Was not that the surest and simplest way to deal with it?"

"Without doubt."

"Well, let us wait. Is that all?"

"All," replied the counsellor, scratching his head, as if to assure himself that he had not forgotten anything important.

"Ah!" exclaimed the burgomaster, "haven't you also heard something of an escape of water which threatens to inundate the low quarter of Saint Jacques?"

"I have. It is indeed unfortunate that this escape of water did not happen above the leather-market! It would naturally have checked the fire, and would thus have saved us a good deal of discussion."

"What can you expect, Niklausse? There is nothing so illogical as accidents. They are bound by no rules, and we cannot profit by one, as we might wish, to remedy another."

It took Van Tricasse's companion some time to digest this fine observation.

"Well, but," resumed the Counsellor Niklausse, after the lapse of some moments, "we have not spoken of our great affair!"

"What great affair? Have we, then, a great affair?" asked the burgomaster.

"No doubt. About lighting the town."

"O yes. If my memory serves me, you are referring to the lighting plan of Doctor Ox."

"Precisely."

"It is going on, Niklausse," replied the burgomaster. "They are already laying the pipes, and the works are entirely completed."

"Perhaps we have hurried a little in this matter," said the counsellor, shaking his head.

"Perhaps. But our excuse is, that Doctor Ox bears the whole expense of his experiment. It will not cost us a sou."

"That, true enough, is our excuse. Moreover, we must advance with the age. If the experiment succeeds, Quiquendone will be the first town in Flanders to be lighted with the oxy—What is the gas called?"

"Oxyhydric gas."

"Well, oxyhydric gas, then."

At this moment the door opened, and Lotche came in to tell the burgomaster that his supper was ready.

Counsellor Niklausse rose to take leave of Van Tricasse, whose appetite had been stimulated by so many affairs discussed and decisions taken; and it was agreed that the council of notables should be convened after a reasonably long delay, to determine whether a decision should be provisionally arrived at with reference to the really urgent matter of the Oudenarde gate.

The two worthy administrators then directed their steps towards the street-door, the one conducting the other. The counsellor, having reached the last step, lighted a little lantern to guide him through the obscure streets of Quiquendone, which

Doctor Ox had not yet lighted. It was a dark October night, and a light fog overshadowed the town.

Niklausse's preparations for departure consumed at least a quarter of an hour; for, after having lighted his lantern, he had to put on his big cow-skin socks and his sheep-skin gloves; then he put up the furred collar of his overcoat, turned the brim of his felt hat down over his eyes, grasped his heavy crow-beaked umbrella, and got ready to start.

When Lotche, however, who was lighting her master, was about to draw the bars of the door, an unexpected noise arose outside.

Yes! Strange as the thing seems, a noise—a real noise, such as the town had certainly not heard since the taking of the donjon by the Spaniards in 1513—terrible noise, awoke the long-dormant echoes of the venerable Van Tricasse mansion.

Someone knocked heavily upon this door, hitherto virgin to brutal touch! Redoubled knocks were given with some blunt implement, probably a knotty stick, wielded by a vigorous arm. With the strokes were mingled cries and calls. These words were distinctly heard:—

"Monsieur Van Tricasse! Monsieur the burgomaster! Open, open quickly!"

The burgomaster and the counsellor, absolutely astounded, looked at each other speechless.

This passed their comprehension. If the old culverin of the chateau, which had not been used since 1385, had been let off in the parlour, the dwellers in the Van Tricasse mansion would not have been more dumbfounded.

Meanwhile, the blows and cries were redoubled. Lotche, recovering her coolness, had plucked up courage to speak.

"Who is there?"

"It is I! I! I!"

"Who are you?"

"The Commissary Passauf!"

The Commissary Passauf! The very man whose office it had been contemplated to suppress for ten years. What had happened, then? Could the Burgundians have invaded Quiquendone, as they did in the fourteenth century? No event of less importance could have so moved Commissary Passauf, who in no degree yielded the palm to the burgomaster himself for calmness and phlegm.

On a sign from Van Tricasse—for the worthy man could not have articulated a syllable—the bar was pushed back and the door opened.

Commissary Passauf flung himself into the antechamber. One would have thought there was a hurricane.

"What's the matter, Monsieur the commissary?" asked Lotche, a brave woman, who did not lose her head under the most trying circumstances.

"What's the matter!" replied Passauf, whose big round eyes expressed a genuine agitation. "The matter is that I have just come from Doctor Ox's, who has been holding a reception, and that there—"

"There?"

"There I have witnessed such an altercation as—Monsieur the burgomaster, they have been talking politics!"

"Politics!" repeated Van Tricasse, running his fingers through his wig.

"Politics!" resumed Commissary Passauf, "which has not been done for perhaps a hundred years at Quiquendone. Then the discussion got warm, and the advocate, Andre Schut, and the doctor, Dominique Custos, became so violent that it may be they will call each other out."

"Call each other out!" cried the counsellor. "A duel! A duel at Quiquendone! And what did Advocate Schut and Doctor Gustos say?"

"Just this: 'Monsieur advocate,' said the doctor to his adversary, 'you go too far, it seems to me, and you do not take sufficient care to control your words!'"

The Burgomaster Van Tricasse clasped his hands—the counsellor turned pale and let his lantern fall—the commissary shook his head. That a phrase so evidently irritating should be pronounced by two of the principal men in the country!

"This Doctor Custos," muttered Van Tricasse, "is decidedly a dangerous man—a hare-brained fellow! Come, gentlemen!"

On this, Counsellor Niklausse and the commissary accompanied the burgomaster into the parlour.

In which Doctor Ox Reveals himself as a Physiologist of the First Rank, and as an Audacious Experimentalist

Who, then, was this personage, known by the singular name of Doctor Ox?

An original character for certain, but at the same time a bold savant, a physiologist, whose works were known and highly estimated throughout learned Europe, a happy rival of the Davys, the Daltons, the Bostocks, the Menzies, the Godwins, the Vierordts—of all those noble minds who have placed physiology among the highest of modern sciences.

Doctor Ox was a man of medium size and height, aged—: but we cannot state his age, any more than his nationality. Besides, it matters little; let it suffice that he was a strange personage, impetuous and hot-blooded, a regular oddity out of one of Hoffmann's volumes, and one who contrasted amusingly enough with the good people of Quiquendone. He had an imperturbable confidence both in himself and in his doctrines. Always smiling, walking with head erect and shoulders thrown back in a free and unconstrained manner, with a steady gaze, large open nostrils, a vast mouth which inhaled the air in liberal draughts, his appearance was far from unpleasing. He was full of animation, well proportioned in all parts of his bodily mechanism, with quicksilver in his veins, and a most elastic step. He could never stop still in one place, and relieved himself with impetuous words and a superabundance of gesticulations.

Was Doctor Ox rich, then, that he should undertake to light a whole town at his expense? Probably, as he permitted himself to indulge in such extravagance,—and this is the only answer we can give to this indiscreet question.

Doctor Ox had arrived at Quiquendone five months before, accompanied by his assistant, who answered to the name of Gedeon Ygene; a tall, dried-up, thin man, haughty, but not less vivacious than his master.

And next, why had Doctor Ox made the proposition to light the town at his own expense? Why had he, of all the Flemings, selected the peaceable Quiquendonians, to endow their town with the benefits of an unheard-of system of lighting? Did he not, under this pretext, design to make some great physiological experiment by operating *in anima vili*? In short, what was this original personage about to attempt? We know not, as Doctor Ox had no confidant except his assistant Ygene, who, moreover, obeyed him blindly.

In appearance, at least, Doctor Ox had agreed to light the town, which had much need of it, "especially at night," as Commissary Passauf wittily said. Works for producing a lighting gas had accordingly been established; the gasometers were ready for use, and the main pipes, running beneath the street pavements, would soon appear in the form of burners in the public edifices and the private houses of certain friends of progress. Van Tricasse and Niklausse, in their official capacity, and some other worthies, thought they ought to allow this modern light to be introduced into their dwellings.

If the reader has not forgotten, it was said, during the long conversation of the counsellor and the burgomaster, that the lighting of the town was to be achieved, not by the combustion of common carburetted hydrogen, produced by distilling coal, but by the use of a more modern and twenty-fold more brilliant gas, oxyhydric gas, produced by mixing hydrogen and oxygen.

The doctor, who was an able chemist as well as an ingenious physiologist, knew how to obtain this gas in great quantity and of good quality, not by using manganate of soda, according to the method of M. Tessie du Motay, but by the direct decomposition of slightly acidulated water, by means of a battery made of new elements, invented by himself. Thus there were no costly materials, no platinum, no retorts, no combustibles, no delicate machinery to produce the two gases separately. An electric current was sent through large basins full of water, and the liquid was decomposed into its two constituent parts, oxygen and hydrogen. The oxygen passed off at one end; the hydrogen, of double the volume of its late associate, at the other. As a necessary precaution, they were collected in separate reservoirs, for their mixture would have produced a frightful explosion if it had become ignited. Thence the pipes were to convey them separately to the various burners, which would be so placed as to prevent all chance of explosion. Thus a remarkably brilliant flame would be obtained, whose light would rival the electric light, which, as everybody knows, is, according to Cassellmann's experiments, equal to that of eleven hundred and seventy-one wax candles,—not one more, nor one less.

It was certain that the town of Quiquendone would, by this liberal contrivance, gain a splendid lighting; but Doctor Ox and his assistant took little account of this, as will be seen in the sequel.

The day after that on which Commissary Passauf had made his noisy entrance into the burgomaster's parlour, Gedeon Ygene and Doctor Ox were talking in the laboratory which both occupied in common, on the ground-floor of the principal building of the gas-works.

"Well, Ygene, well," cried the doctor, rubbing his hands. "You saw, at my reception yesterday, the cool-bloodedness of these worthy Quiquendonians. For animation they are midway between sponges and coral! You saw them disputing and irritating each other by voice and gesture? They are already metamorphosed, morally and physically! And this is only the beginning. Wait till we treat them to a big dose!"

"Indeed, master," replied Ygene, scratching his sharp nose with the end of his forefinger, "the experiment begins well, and if I had not prudently closed the supply-tap, I know not what would have happened."

"You heard Schut, the advocate, and Custos, the doctor?" resumed Doctor Ox. "The phrase was by no means ill-natured in itself, but, in the mouth of a Quiquendonian, it is worth all the insults which the Homeric heroes hurled at each other before drawing their swords, Ah, these Flemings! You'll see what we shall do some day!"

"We shall make them ungrateful," replied Ygene, in the tone of a man who esteems the human race at its just worth.

"Bah!" said the doctor; "what matters it whether they think well or ill of us, so long as our experiment succeeds?"

"Besides," returned the assistant, smiling with a malicious expression, "is it not to be feared that, in producing such an excitement in their respiratory organs, we shall somewhat injure the lungs of these good people of Quiquendone?"

"So much the worse for them! It is in the interests of science. What would you say if the dogs or frogs refused to lend themselves to the experiments of vivisection?"

It is probable that if the frogs and dogs were consulted, they would offer some objection; but Doctor Ox imagined that he had stated an unanswerable argument, for he heaved a great sigh of satisfaction.

"After all, master, you are right," replied Ygene, as if quite convinced. "We could not have hit upon better subjects than these people of Quiquendone for our experiment."

"We—could—not," said the doctor, slowly articulating each word.

"Have you felt the pulse of any of them?"

"Some hundreds."

"And what is the average pulsation you found?"

"Not fifty per minute. See—this is a town where there has not been the shadow of a discussion for a century, where the carmen don't swear, where the coachmen don't insult each other, where horses don't run away, where the dogs don't bite, where the cats don't scratch,—a town where the police-court has nothing to do from one year's end to another,—a town where people do not grow enthusiastic about anything, either about art or business,—a town where the gendarmes are a sort of myth, and in which an indictment has not been drawn up for a hundred years,—a town, in short, where for three centuries nobody has struck a blow with his fist or so much as exchanged a slap in the face! You see, Ygene, that this cannot last, and that we must change it all."

"Perfectly! perfectly!" cried the enthusiastic assistant; "and have you analyzed the air of this town, master?"

"I have not failed to do so. Seventy-nine parts of azote and twenty-one of oxygen, carbonic acid and steam in a variable quantity. These are the ordinary proportions."

"Good, doctor, good!" replied Ygene. "The experiment will be made on a large scale, and will be decisive."

"And if it is decisive," added Doctor Ox triumphantly, "we shall reform the world!"

In which the Burgomaster and the Counsellor Pay a Visit to Doctor Ox, and what Follows

The Counsellor Niklausse and the Burgomaster Van Tricasse at last knew what it was to have an agitated night. The grave event which had taken place at Doctor Ox's house actually kept them awake. What consequences was this affair destined to bring about? They could not imagine. Would it be necessary for them to come to a decision? Would the municipal authority, whom they represented, be compelled to interfere? Would they be obliged to order arrests to be made, that so great a scandal should not be repeated? All these doubts could not but trouble these soft natures; and on that evening, before separating, the two notables had "decided" to see each other the next day.

On the next morning, then, before dinner, the Burgomaster Van Tricasse proceeded in person to the Counsellor Niklausse's house. He found his friend more calm. He himself had recovered his equanimity.

"Nothing new?" asked Van Tricasse.

"Nothing new since yesterday," replied Niklausse.

"And the doctor, Dominique Custos?"

"I have not heard anything, either of him or of the advocate, Andre Schut."

After an hour's conversation, which consisted of three remarks which it is needless to repeat, the counsellor and the burgomaster had resolved to pay a visit to Doctor Ox, so as to draw from him, without seeming to do so, some details of the affair.

Contrary to all their habits, after coming to this decision the two notables set about putting it into execution forthwith. They left the house and directed their steps towards Doctor Ox's laboratory, which was situated outside the town, near the Oudenarde gate—the gate whose tower threatened to fall in ruins.

They did not take each other's arms, but walked side by side, with a slow and solemn step, which took them forward but thirteen inches per second. This was, indeed, the ordinary gait of the Quiquendonians, who had never, within the memory of man, seen any one run across the streets of their town.

From time to time the two notables would stop at some calm and tranquil crossway, or at the end of a quiet street, to salute the passers-by.

"Good morning, Monsieur the burgomaster," said one.

"Good morning, my friend," responded Van Tricasse.

"Anything new, Monsieur the counsellor?" asked another.

"Nothing new," answered Niklausse.

But by certain agitated motions and questioning looks, it was evident that the altercation of the evening before was known throughout the town. Observing the direction taken by Van Tricasse, the most obtuse Quiquendonians guessed that the burgomaster was on his way to take some important step. The Custos and Schut affair was talked of everywhere, but the people had not yet come to the point of taking the part of one or the other. The Advocate Schut, having never had occasion to plead in a town where attorneys and bailiffs only existed in tradition, had, consequently, never lost a suit. As for the Doctor Custos, he was an honourable practitioner, who, after the example of his fellow-doctors, cured all the illnesses of his patients, except those of which they died—a habit unhappily acquired by all the members of all the faculties in whatever country they may practise.

On reaching the Oudenarde gate, the counsellor and the burgomaster prudently made a short detour, so as not to pass within reach of the tower, in case it should fall; then they turned and looked at it attentively.

"I think that it will fall," said Van Tricasse.

"I think so too," replied Niklausse.

"Unless it is propped up," added Van Tricasse. "But must it be propped up? That is the question."

"That is—in fact—the question."

Some moments after, they reached the door of the gasworks.

"Can we see Doctor Ox?" they asked.

Doctor Ox could always be seen by the first authorities of the town, and they were at once introduced into the celebrated physiologist's study.

Perhaps the two notables waited for the doctor at least an hour; at least it is reasonable to suppose so, as the burgomaster— a thing that had never before happened in his life—betrayed a certain amount of impatience, from which his companion was not exempt.

Doctor Ox came in at last, and began to excuse himself for having kept them waiting; but he had to approve a plan for the gasometer, rectify some of the machinery—But everything was going on well! The pipes intended for the oxygen were already laid. In a few months the town would be splendidly lighted. The two notables might even now see the orifices of the pipes which were laid on in the laboratory.

Then the doctor begged to know to what he was indebted for the honour of this visit.

"Only to see you, doctor; to see you," replied Van Tricasse. "It is long since we have had the pleasure. We go abroad but little in our good town of Quiquendone. We count our steps and measure our walks. We are happy when nothing disturbs the uniformity of our habits."

Niklausse looked at his friend. His friend had never said so much at once—at least, without taking time, and giving long intervals between his sentences. It seemed to him that Van Tricasse expressed himself with a certain volubility, which was by no means common with him. Niklausse himself experienced a kind of irresistible desire to talk.

As for Doctor Ox, he looked at the burgomaster with sly attention.

Van Tricasse, who never argued until he had snugly ensconced himself in a spacious armchair, had risen to his feet. I know not what nervous excitement, quite foreign to his temperament, had taken possession of him. He did not gesticulate as yet, but this could not be far off. As for the counsellor, he rubbed his legs, and breathed with slow and long gasps. His look became animated little by little, and he had "decided" to support at all hazards, if need be, his trusty friend the burgomaster.

Van Tricasse got up and took several steps; then he came back, and stood facing the doctor.

"And in how many months," he asked in a somewhat emphatic tone, "do you say that your work will be finished?"

"In three or four months, Monsieur the burgomaster," replied Doctor Ox.

"Three or four months,—it's a very long time!" said Van Tricasse.

"Altogether too long!" added Niklausse, who, not being able to keep his seat, rose also.

"This lapse of time is necessary to complete our work," returned Doctor Ox. "The workmen, whom we have had to choose in Quiquendone, are not very expeditious."

"How not expeditious?" cried the burgomaster, who seemed to take the remark as personally offensive.

"No, Monsieur Van Tricasse," replied Doctor Ox obstinately. "A French workman would do in a day what it takes ten of your workmen to do; you know, they are regular Flemings!"

"Flemings!" cried the counsellor, whose fingers closed together. "In what sense, sir, do you use that word?"

"Why, in the amiable sense in which everybody uses it," replied Doctor Ox, smiling.

"Ah, but doctor," said the burgomaster, pacing up and down the room, "I don't like these insinuations. The workmen of Quiquendone are as efficient as those of any other town in the world, you must know; and we shall go neither to Paris nor London for our models! As for your project, I beg you to hasten its execution. Our streets have been unpaved for the putting down of your conduit-pipes, and it is a hindrance to traffic. Our trade will begin to suffer, and I, being the responsible authority, do not propose to incur reproaches which will be but too just."

Worthy burgomaster! He spoke of trade, of traffic, and the wonder was that those words, to which he was quite unaccustomed, did not scorch his lips. What could be passing in his mind?

"Besides," added Niklausse, "the town cannot be deprived of light much longer."

"But," urged Doctor Ox, "a town which has been un-lighted for eight or nine hundred years—"

"All the more necessary is it," replied the burgomaster, emphasizing his words. "Times alter, manners alter! The world advances, and we do not wish to remain behind. We desire our streets to be lighted within a month, or you must pay a large indemnity for each day of delay; and what would happen if, amid the darkness, some affray should take place?"

"No doubt," cried Niklausse. "It requires but a spark to inflame a Fleming! Fleming! Flame!"

"Apropos of this," said the burgomaster, interrupting his friend, "Commissary Passauf, our chief of police, reports to us that a discussion took place in your drawing-room last evening, Doctor Ox. Was he wrong in declaring that it was a political discussion?"

"By no means, Monsieur the burgomaster," replied Doctor Ox, who with difficulty repressed a sigh of satisfaction.

"So an altercation did take place between Dominique Gustos and Andre Schut?"

"Yes, counsellor; but the words which passed were not of grave import."

"Not of grave import!" cried the burgomaster. "Not of grave import, when one man tells another that he does not measure the effect of his words! But of what stuff are you made, monsieur? Do you not know that in Quiquendone nothing more is needed to bring about extremely disastrous results? But monsieur, if you, or anyone else, presume to speak thus to me—"

"Or to me," added Niklausse.

As they pronounced these words with a menacing air, the two notables, with folded arms and bristling air, confronted Doctor Ox, ready to do him some violence, if by a gesture, or even the expression of his eye, he manifested any intention of contradicting them.

But the doctor did not budge.

"At all events, monsieur," resumed the burgomaster, "I propose to hold you responsible for what passes in your house. I am bound to insure the tranquillity of this town, and I do not wish it to be disturbed. The events of last evening must not be repeated, or I shall do my duty, sir! Do you hear? Then reply, sir."

The burgomaster, as he spoke, under the influence of extraordinary excitement, elevated his voice to the pitch of anger. He was furious, the worthy Van Tricasse, and might certainly be heard outside. At last, beside himself, and seeing that Doctor Ox did not reply to his challenge, "Come, Niklausse," said he.

And, slamming the door with a violence which shook the house, the burgomaster drew his friend after him.

Little by little, when they had taken twenty steps on their road, the worthy notables grew more calm. Their pace slackened, their gait became less feverish. The flush on their faces faded away; from being crimson, they became rosy. A quarter of an hour after quitting the gasworks, Van Tricasse said softly to Niklausse, "An amiable man, Doctor Ox! It is always a pleasure to see him!"

In which Frantz Niklausse and Suzel Van Tricasse Form Certain Projects for the Future

Our readers know that the burgomaster had a daughter, Suzel. But, shrewd as they may be, they cannot have divined that the counsellor Niklausse had a son, Frantz; and had they divined this, nothing could have led them to imagine that Frantz was the betrothed lover of Suzel. We will add that these young people were made for each other, and that they loved each other, as folks did love at Quiquendone.

It must not be thought that young hearts did not beat in this exceptional place; only they beat with a certain deliberation. There were marriages there, as in every other town in the world; but they took time about it. Betrothed couples, before engaging in these terrible bonds, wished to study each other; and these studies lasted at least ten years, as at college. It was rare that any one was "accepted" before this lapse of time.

Yes, ten years! The courtships last ten years! And is it, after all, too long, when the being bound for life is in consideration? One studies ten years to become an engineer or physician, an advocate or attorney, and should less time be spent in acquiring the knowledge to make a good husband? Is it not reasonable? and, whether due to temperament or reason with them, the Quiquendonians seem to us to be in the right in thus prolonging their courtship. When marriages in other more lively and excitable cities are seen taking place within a few months, we must shrug our shoulders, and hasten to send our boys to the schools and our daughters to the *pensions* of Quiquendone.

For half a century but a single marriage was known to have

taken place after the lapse of two years only of courtship, and that turned out badly!

Frantz Niklausse, then, loved Suzel Van Tricasse, but quietly, as a man would love when he has ten years before him in which to obtain the beloved object. Once every week, at an hour agreed upon, Frantz went to fetch Suzel, and took a walk with her along the banks of the Vaar. He took good care to carry his fishing-tackle, and Suzel never forgot her canvas, on which her pretty hands embroidered the most unlikely flowers.

Frantz was a young man of twenty-two, whose cheeks betrayed a soft, peachy down, and whose voice had scarcely a compass of one octave.

As for Suzel, she was blonde and rosy. She was seventeen, and did not dislike fishing. A singular occupation this, however, which forces you to struggle craftily with a barbel. But Frantz loved it; the pastime was congenial to his temperament. As patient as possible, content to follow with his rather dreamy eye the cork which bobbed on the top of the water, he knew how to wait; and when, after sitting for six hours, a modest barbel, taking pity on him, consented at last to be caught, he was happy—but he knew how to control his emotion.

On this day the two lovers—one might say, the two betrothed—were seated upon the verdant bank. The limpid Vaar murmured a few feet below them. Suzel quietly drew her needle across the canvas. Frantz automatically carried his line from left to right, then permitted it to descend the current from right to left. The fish made capricious rings in the water, which crossed each other around the cork, while the hook hung useless near the bottom.

From time to time Frantz would say, without raising his eyes,—

"I think I have a bite, Suzel."

"Do you think so, Frantz?" replied Suzel, who, abandoning her work for an instant, followed her lover's line with earnest eye.

"N-no," resumed Frantz; "I thought I felt a little twitch; I was mistaken."

"You *will* have a bite, Frantz," replied Suzel, in her pure, soft voice. "But do not forget to strike at the right moment. You are always a few seconds too late, and the barbel takes advantage to escape."

"Would you like to take my line, Suzel?"

"Willingly, Frantz."

"Then give me your canvas. We shall see whether I am more adroit with the needle than with the hook."

And the young girl took the line with trembling hand, while her swain plied the needle across the stitches of the embroidery. For hours together they thus exchanged soft words, and their hearts palpitated when the cork bobbed on the water. Ah, could they ever forget those charming hours, during which, seated side by side, they listened to the murmurs of the river?

The sun was fast approaching the western horizon, and despite the combined skill of Suzel and Frantz, there had not been a bite. The barbels had not shown themselves complacent, and seemed to scoff at the two young people, who were too just to bear them malice.

"We shall be more lucky another time, Frantz," said Suzel, as the young angler put up his still virgin hook.

"Let us hope so," replied Frantz.

Then walking side by side, they turned their steps towards the house, without exchanging a word, as mute as their shadows which stretched out before them. Suzel became very, very tall under the oblique rays of the setting sun. Frantz appeared very, very thin, like the long rod which he held in his hand.

They reached the burgomaster's house. Green tufts of grass bordered the shining pavement, and no one would have thought of tearing them away, for they deadened the noise made by the passers-by.

As they were about to open the door, Frantz thought it his duty to say to Suzel,—

"You know, Suzel, the great day is approaching?"

"It is indeed, Frantz," replied the young girl, with downcast eyes.

"Yes," said Frantz, "in five or six years—"

"Good-bye, Frantz," said Suzel.

"Good-bye, Suzel," replied Frantz.

And, after the door had been closed, the young man resumed the way to his father's house with a calm and equal pace.

In which the Andantes Become Allegros, and the Allegros Vivaces

The agitation caused by the Schut and Custos affair had subsided. The affair led to no serious consequences. It appeared likely that Quiquendone would return to its habitual apathy, which that unexpected event had for a moment disturbed.

Meanwhile, the laying of the pipes destined to conduct the oxyhydric gas into the principal edifices of the town was proceeding rapidly. The main pipes and branches gradually crept beneath the pavements. But the burners were still wanting; for, as it required delicate skill to make them, it was necessary that they should be fabricated abroad. Doctor Ox was here, there, and everywhere; neither he nor Ygene, his assistant, lost a moment, but they urged on the workmen, completed the delicate mechanism of the gasometer, fed day and night the immense piles which decomposed the water under the influence of a powerful electric current. Yes, the doctor was already making his gas, though the pipe-laying was not yet done; a fact which, between ourselves, might have seemed a little singular. But before long,—at least there was reason to hope so,— before long Doctor Ox would inaugurate the splendours of his invention in the theatre of the town.

For Quiquendone possessed a theatre—a really fine edifice, in truth—the interior and exterior arrangement of which combined every style of architecture. It was at once Byzantine, Roman, Gothic, Renaissance, with semicircular doors, Pointed windows, Flamboyant rose-windows, fantastic bell-turrets,—in a word, a specimen of all sorts, half a Parthenon, half a Parisian Grand Cafe. Nor was this surprising, the theatre having been commenced under the burgomaster Ludwig Van Tricasse, in 1175, and only finished in 1837, under the burgomaster Natalis Van Tricasse. It had required seven hundred years to build it, and it had, been successively adapted to the architectural style in vogue in each period. But for all that it was an imposing structure; the Roman pillars and Byzantine arches of which would appear to advantage lit up by the oxyhydric gas.

Pretty well everything was acted at the theatre of Quiquendone; but the opera and the opera comique were especially patronized. It must, however, be added that the composers would never have recognized their own works, so entirely changed were the "movements" of the music.

In short, as nothing was done in a hurry at Quiquendone, the dramatic pieces had to be performed in harmony with the peculiar temperament of the Quiquendonians. Though the doors of the theatre were regularly thrown open at four o'clock and closed again at ten, it had never been known that more than two acts were played during the six intervening hours. "Robert le Diable," "Les Huguenots," or "Guillaume Tell" usually took up three evenings, so slow was the execution of these masterpieces. The *vivaces*, at the theatre of Quiquendone, lagged like real *adagios*. The *allegros* were "long-drawn out" indeed. The demisemiquavers were scarcely equal to the ordinary semibreves of other countries. The most rapid runs, performed according to Quiquendonian taste, had the solemn march of a chant. The gayest shakes were languishing and measured, that they might not shock the ears of the *dilettanti*. To give an example, the rapid air sung by Figaro, on his entrance in the first act of "Le Barbier de Seville," lasted fifty-eight minutes—when the actor was particularly enthusiastic.

Artists from abroad, as might be supposed, were forced to conform themselves to Quiquendonian fashions; but as they were well paid, they did not complain, and willingly obeyed the leader's baton, which never beat more than eight measures to the minute in the *allegros*.

But what applause greeted these artists, who enchanted without ever wearying the audiences of Quiquendone! All hands clapped one after another at tolerably long intervals, which the papers characterized as "frantic applause;" and sometimes nothing but the lavish prodigality with which mortar and stone had been used in the twelfth century saved the roof of the hall from falling in.

Besides, the theatre had only one performance a week, that these enthusiastic Flemish folk might not be too much excited; and this enabled the actors to study their parts more thoroughly, and the spectators to digest more at leisure the beauties of the masterpieces brought out.

Such had long been the drama at Quiquendone. Foreign artists were in the habit of making engagements with the director of the town, when they wanted to rest after their exertions in other scenes; and it seemed as if nothing could ever change these inveterate customs, when, a fortnight after the Schut-Custos affair, an unlooked-for incident occurred to throw the population into fresh agitation.

It was on a Saturday, an opera day. It was not yet intended, as may well be supposed, to inaugurate the new illumination. No; the pipes had reached the hall, but, for reasons indicated above, the burners had not yet been placed, and the wax-candles still shed their soft light upon the numerous spectators who filled the theatre. The doors had been opened to the public at one o'clock, and by three the hall was half full. A queue had at one time been formed, which extended as far as the end of the Place Saint Ernuph, in front of the shop of Josse Lietrinck the apothecary. This eagerness was significant of an unusually attractive performance.

"Are you going to the theatre this evening?" inquired the counsellor the same morning of the burgomaster.

"I shall not fail to do so," returned Van Tricasse, "and I shall take Madame Van Tricasse, as well as our daughter Suzel and our dear Tatanemance, who all dote on good music."

"Mademoiselle Suzel is going then?"

"Certainly, Niklausse."

"Then my son Frantz will be one of the first to arrive," said Niklausse.

"A spirited boy, Niklausse," replied the burgomaster sententiously; "but hot-headed! He will require watching!"

"He loves, Van Tricasse,—he loves your charming Suzel."

"Well, Niklausse, he shall marry her. Now that we have agreed on this marriage, what more can he desire?"

"He desires nothing, Van Tricasse, the dear boy! But, in short—we'll say no more about it—he will not be the last to get his ticket at the box-office."

"Ah, vivacious and ardent youth!" replied the burgomaster, recalling his own past. "We have also been thus, my worthy counsellor! We have loved—we too! We have danced attendance in our day! Till to-night, then, till to-night! By-the-bye, do you know this Fiovaranti is a great artist? And what a welcome he has received among us! It will be long before he will forget the applause of Quiquendone!"

The tenor Fiovaranti was, indeed, going to sing; Fiovaranti, who, by his talents as a virtuoso, his perfect method, his melodious voice, provoked a real enthusiasm among the lovers of music in the town.

For three weeks Fiovaranti had been achieving a brilliant success in "Les Huguenots." The first act, interpreted according to the taste of the Quiquendonians, had occupied an entire evening of the first week of the month.—Another evening in the second week, prolonged by infinite *andantes*, had elicited for the celebrated singer a real ovation. His success had been still more marked in the third act of Meyerbeer's masterpiece. But now Fiovaranti was to appear in the fourth act, which was to be performed on this evening before an impatient public. Ah, the duet between Raoul and Valentine, that pathetic love-song for two voices, that strain so full of *crescendos, stringendos,* and *piu crescendos*—all this, sung slowly, compendiously, interminably! Ah, how delightful!

At four o'clock the hall was full. The boxes, the orchestra, the pit, were overflowing. In the front stalls sat the Burgomaster Van Tricasse, Mademoiselle Van Tricasse, Madame Van Tricasse, and the amiable Tatanemance in a green bonnet; not far off were the Counsellor Niklausse and his family, not forgetting the amorous Frantz. The families of Custos the doctor, of Schut the advocate, of Honore Syntax the chief judge, of Norbet Sontman the insurance director, of the banker Collaert, gone mad on German music, and himself somewhat of an amateur, and the teacher Rupp, and the master of the academy, Jerome Resh, and the civil commissary, and so many other notabilities of the town that they could not be enumerated here without wearying the reader's patience, were visible in different parts of the hall.

It was customary for the Quiquendonians, while awaiting the rise of the curtain, to sit silent, some reading the paper, others whispering low to each other, some making their way to their seats slowly and noiselessly, others casting timid looks towards the bewitching beauties in the galleries.

But on this evening a looker-on might have observed that, even before the curtain rose, there was unusual animation among the audience. People were restless who were never known to be restless before. The ladies' fans fluttered with abnormal rapidity. All appeared to be inhaling air of exceptional stimulating power. Every one breathed more freely. The eyes of some became unwontedly bright, and seemed to give forth a light equal to that of the candles, which themselves certainly threw a more brilliant light over the hall. It was evident that people saw more clearly, though the number of candles had not been increased. Ah, if Doctor Ox's experiment were being tried! But it was not being tried, as yet.

The musicians of the orchestra at last took their places. The first violin had gone to the stand to give a modest la to his colleagues. The stringed instruments, the wind instruments, the drums and cymbals, were in accord. The conductor only waited the sound of the bell to beat the first bar.

The bell sounds. The fourth act begins. The *allegro appassionato* of the inter-act is played as usual, with a majestic deliberation which would have made Meyerbeer frantic, and all the majesty of which was appreciated by the Quiquendonian *dilettanti*.

But soon the leader perceived that he was no longer master of his musicians. He found it difficult to restrain them, though usually so obedient and calm. The wind instruments betrayed a tendency to hasten the movements, and it was necessary to hold them back with a firm hand, for they would otherwise outstrip the stringed instruments; which, from a musical point of view, would have been disastrous. The bassoon himself, the son of Josse Lietrinck the apothecary, a well-bred young man, seemed to lose his self-control.

Meanwhile Valentine has begun her recitative, "I am alone," &c.; but she hurries it.

The leader and all his musicians, perhaps unconsciously, follow her in her *cantabile*, which should be taken deliberately, like a 12/8 as it is. When Raoul appears at the door at the bottom of the stage, between the moment when Valentine goes to him and that when she conceals herself in the chamber at the side, a quarter of an hour does not elapse; while formerly, according to the traditions of the Quiquendone theatre, this recitative of thirty-seven bars was wont to last just thirty-seven minutes.

Saint Bris, Nevers, Cavannes, and the Catholic nobles have appeared, somewhat prematurely, perhaps, upon the scene. The composer has marked *allergo pomposo* on the score. The orchestra and the lords proceed *allegro* indeed, but not at all *pomposo*, and at the chorus, in the famous scene of the "benediction of the poniards," they no longer keep to the enjoined *allegro*. Singers and musicians broke away impetuously. The leader does not even attempt to restrain them. Nor do the public protest; on the contrary, the people find themselves carried away, and see that they are involved in the movement, and that the movement responds to the impulses of their souls.

"Will you, with me, deliver the land,

From troubles increasing, an impious band?"

They promise, they swear. Nevers has scarcely time to protest, and to sing that "among his ancestors were many soldiers, but never an assassin." He is arrested. The police and the aldermen rush forward and rapidly swear "to strike all at once." Saint Bris shouts the recitative which summons the Catholics to vengeance. The three monks, with white scarfs, hasten in by the door at the back of Nevers's room, without making any account of the stage directions, which enjoin on them to advance slowly. Already all the artists have drawn sword or poniard, which the three monks bless in a trice. The soprani tenors, bassos, attack the *allegro furioso* with cries of rage, and of a dramatic 6/8 time they make it 6/8 quadrille time. Then they rush out, bellowing,—

"At midnight,

Noiselessly,

God wills it,

Yes,

At midnight."

At this moment the audience start to their feet. Everybody is agitated—in the boxes, the pit, the galleries. It seems as if the spectators are about to rush upon the stage, the Burgomaster Van Tricasse at their head, to join with the conspirators and annihilate the Huguenots, whose religious opinions, however, they share. They applaud, call before the curtain, make loud acclamations! Tatanemance grasps her bonnet with feverish hand. The candles throw out a lurid glow of light.

Raoul, instead of slowly raising the curtain, tears it apart with a superb gesture and finds himself confronting Valentine.

At last! It is the grand duet, and it starts off *allegro vivace*. Raoul does not wait for Valentine's pleading, and Valentine does not wait for Raoul's responses.

The fine passage beginning, "Danger is passing, time is flying," becomes one of those rapid airs which have made Offenbach famous, when he composes a dance for conspirators. The *andante amoroso*, "Thou hast said it, aye, thou lovest me," becomes a real *vivace furioso*, and the violoncello ceases to imitate the inflections of the singer's voice, as indicated in the composer's score. In vain Raoul cries, "Speak on, and prolong the ineffable slumber of my soul." Valentine cannot "prolong." It is evident that an unaccustomed fire devours her. Her *b*'s and her *c*'s above the stave were dreadfully shrill. He struggles, he gesticulates, he is all in a glow.

The alarum is heard; the bell resounds; but what a panting bell! The bell-ringer has evidently lost his self-control. It is a frightful tocsin, which violently struggles against the fury of the orchestra.

Finally the air which ends this magnificent act, beginning, "No more love, no more intoxication, O the remorse that oppresses me!" which the composer marks *allegro con moto*, becomes a wild *prestissimo*. You would say an express-train was whirling by. The alarum resounds again. Valentine falls fainting. Raoul precipitates himself from the window.

It was high time. The orchestra, really intoxicated, could not have gone on. The leader's baton is no longer anything but a broken stick on the prompter's box. The violin strings are broken, and their necks twisted. In his fury the drummer has burst his drum. The counter-bassist has perched on the top of his musical monster. The first clarionet has swallowed the reed of his instrument, and the second hautboy is chewing his reed keys. The groove of the trombone is strained, and finally the unhappy cornist cannot withdraw his hand from the bell of his horn, into which he had thrust it too far.

And the audience! The audience, panting, all in a heat, gesticulates and howls. All the faces are as red as if a fire were burning within their bodies. They crowd each other, hustle each other to get out—the men without hats, the women without mantles! They elbow each other in the corridors, crush between the doors, quarrel, fight! There are no longer any officials, any burgomaster. All are equal amid this infernal frenzy!

Some moments after, when all have reached the street, each one resumes his habitual tranquillity, and peaceably enters his house, with a confused remembrance of what he has just experienced.

The fourth act of the "Huguenots," which formerly lasted six hours, began, on this evening at half-past four, and ended at twelve minutes before five.

It had only lasted eighteen minutes!

In which the Ancient and Solemn German Waltz Becomes a Whirlwind

But if the spectators, on leaving the theatre, resumed their customary calm, if they quietly regained their homes, preserving only a sort of passing stupefaction, they had none the less undergone a remarkable exaltation, and overcome and weary as if they had committed some excess of dissipation, they fell heavily upon their beds.

The next day each Quiquendonian had a kind of recollection of what had occurred the evening before. One missed his hat, lost in the hubbub; another a coat-flap, torn in the brawl; one her delicately fashioned shoe, another her best mantle. Memory returned to these worthy people, and with it a certain shame for their unjustifiable agitation. It seemed to them an orgy in which they were the unconscious heroes and heroines. They did not speak of it; they did not wish to think of it. But the most astounded personage in the town was Van Tricasse the burgomaster.

The next morning, on waking, he could not find his wig. Lotche looked everywhere for it, but in vain. The wig had remained on the field of battle. As for having it publicly claimed by Jean Mistrol, the town-crier,—no, it would not do. It were better to lose the wig than to advertise himself thus, as he had the honour to be the first magistrate of Quiquendone.

The worthy Van Tricasse was reflecting upon this, extended beneath his sheets, with bruised body, heavy head, furred tongue, and burning breast. He felt no desire to get up; on the contrary; and his brain worked more during this morning than it had probably worked before for forty years. The worthy magistrate recalled to his mind all the incidents of the incomprehensible performance.

He connected them with the events which had taken place shortly before at Doctor Ox's reception. He tried to discover the causes of the singular excitability which, on two occasions, had betrayed itself in the best citizens of the town.

"What *can* be going on?" he asked himself. "What giddy spirit has taken possession of my peaceable town of Quiquendone? Are we about to go mad, and must we make the town one vast asylum? For yesterday we were all there, notables, counsellors, judges, advocates, physicians, schoolmasters; and ail, if my memory serves me,—all of us were assailed by this excess of furious folly! But what was there in that infernal music? It is inexplicable! Yet I certainly ate or drank nothing which could put me into such a state. No; yesterday I had for dinner a slice of overdone veal, several spoonfuls of spinach with sugar, eggs, and a little beer and water,—that couldn't get into my head! No! There is something that I cannot explain, and as, after all, I am responsible for the conduct of the citizens, I will have an investigation."

But the investigation, though decided upon by the municipal council, produced no result. If the facts were clear, the causes escaped the sagacity of the magistrates. Besides, tranquillity had been restored in the public mind, and with tranquillity, forgetfulness of the strange scenes of the theatre. The newspapers avoided speaking of them, and the account of the performance which appeared in the "Quiquendone Memorial," made no allusion to this intoxication of the entire audience.

Meanwhile, though the town resumed its habitual phlegm, and became apparently Flemish as before, it was observable that, at bottom, the character and temperament of the people changed little by little. One might have truly said, with Dominique Custos, the doctor, that "their nerves were affected."

Let us explain. This undoubted change only took place under certain conditions. When the Quiquendonians passed through the streets of the town, walked in the squares or along the Vaar, they were always the cold and methodical people of former days. So, too, when they remained at home, some working with their hands and others with their heads,—these doing nothing, those thinking nothing,—their private life was silent, inert, vegetating as before. No quarrels, no household squabbles, no acceleration in the beating of the heart, no excitement of the brain. The mean of their pulsations remained as it was of old, from fifty to fifty-two per minute.

But, strange and inexplicable phenomenon though it was, which would have defied the sagacity of the most ingenious physiologists of the day, if the inhabitants of Quiquendone did not change in their home life, they were visibly changed in their civil life and in their relations between man and man, to which it leads.

If they met together in some public edifice, it did not "work well," as Commissary Passauf expressed it. On 'change, at the town-hall, in the amphitheatre of the academy, at the sessions of the council, as well as at the reunions of the *savants*, a strange excitement seized the assembled citizens. Their relations with each other became embarrassing before they had been together an hour. In two hours the discussion degenerated into an angry dispute. Heads became heated, and personalities were used. Even at church, during the sermon, the faithful could not listen to Van Stabel, the minister, in patience, and he threw himself about in the pulpit and lectured his flock with far more than his usual severity. At last this state of things brought about altercations more grave, alas! than that between Gustos and Schut, and if they did not require the interference of the authorities, it was because the antagonists, after returning home, found there, with its calm, forgetfulness of the offences offered and received.

This peculiarity could not be observed by these minds, which were absolutely incapable of recognizing what was passing in them. One person only in the town, he whose office the council had thought of suppressing for thirty years, Michael Passauf, had remarked that this excitement, which was absent from private houses, quickly revealed itself in public edifices; and he asked himself, not without a certain anxiety, what would happen if this infection should ever develop itself in the family mansions, and if the epidemic—this was the word he used—should extend through the streets of the town. Then there would be no more forgetfulness of insults, no more tranquillity, no intermission in the delirium; but a permanent inflammation, which would inevitably bring the Quiquendonians into collision with each other.

"What would happen then?" Commissary Passauf asked himself in terror. "How could these furious savages be arrested? How check these goaded temperaments? My office would be no longer a sinecure, and the council would be obliged to double my salary—unless it should arrest me myself, for disturbing the public peace!"

These very reasonable fears began to be realized. The infection spread from 'change, the theatre, the church, the town-hall, the academy, the market, into private houses, and that in less than a fortnight after the terrible performance of the "Huguenots."

Its first symptoms appeared in the house of Collaert, the banker.

That wealthy personage gave a ball, or at least a dancing-party, to the notabilities of the town. He had issued, some months before, a loan of thirty thousand francs, three quarters of which had been subscribed; and to celebrate this financial success, he had opened his drawing-rooms, and given a party to his fellow-citizens.

Everybody knows that Flemish parties are innocent and tranquil enough, the principal expense of which is usually in beer and syrups. Some conversation on the weather, the appearance of the crops, the fine condition of the gardens, the care of flowers, and especially of tulips; a slow and measured dance, from time to time, perhaps a minuet; sometimes a waltz, but one of those German waltzes which achieve a turn and a half per minute, and during which the dancers hold each other as far apart as their arms will permit,—such is the usual fashion of the balls attended by the aristocratic society of Quiquendone. The polka, after being altered to four time, had tried to become accustomed to it; but the dancers always lagged behind the orchestra, no matter how slow the measure, and it had to be abandoned.

These peaceable reunions, in which the youths and maidens enjoyed an honest and moderate pleasure, had never been attended by any outburst of ill-nature. Why, then, on this evening at Collaert the banker's, did the syrups seem to be transformed into heady wines, into sparkling champagne, into heating punches? Why, towards the middle of the evening, did a sort of mysterious intoxication take possession of the guests? Why did the minuet become a jig? Why did the orchestra hurry with its harmonies? Why did the candles, just as at the theatre, burn with unwonted refulgence? What electric current invaded the banker's drawing-rooms? How happened it that the couples held each other so closely, and clasped each other's hands so convulsively, that the "cavaliers seuls" made themselves conspicuous by certain extraordinary steps in that figure usually so grave, so solemn, so majestic, so very proper?

Alas! what OEdipus could have answered these unsolvable questions? Commissary Passauf, who was present at the party, saw the storm coming distinctly, but he could not control it or fly from it, and he felt a kind of intoxication entering his own brain. All his physical and emotional faculties increased in intensity. He was seen, several times, to throw himself upon the confectionery and devour the dishes, as if he had just broken a long fast.

The animation of the ball was increasing all this while. A long murmur, like a dull buzzing, escaped from all breasts. They danced—really danced. The feet were agitated by increasing frenzy. The faces became as purple as those of Silenus. The eyes shone like carbuncles. The general fermentation rose to the highest pitch.

And when the orchestra thundered out the waltz in "Der Freyschuetz,"—when this waltz, so German, and with a movement so slow, was attacked with wild arms by the musicians,—ah! it was no longer a waltz, but an insensate whirlwind, a giddy rotation, a gyration worthy of being led by some Mephistopheles, beating the measure with a firebrand! Then a galop, an infernal galop, which lasted an hour without any one being able to stop it, whirled off, in its windings, across the halls, the drawing-rooms, the antechambers, by the staircases, from the cellar to the garret of the opulent mansion, the young men and young girls, the fathers and mothers, people of every age, of every weight, of both sexes; Collaert, the fat banker, and Madame Collaert, and the counsellors, and the magistrates, and the chief justice, and Niklausse, and Madame Van Tricasse, and the Burgomaster Van Tricasse, and the Commissary Passauf himself, who never could recall afterwards who had been his partner on that terrible evening.

But she did not forget! And ever since that day she has seen in her dreams the fiery commissary, enfolding her in an impassioned embrace! And "she"—was the amiable Tatanemance!

In which Doctor Ox and Ygene, his Assistant, Say a Few Words

"Well, Ygene?"

"Well, master, all is ready. The laying of the pipes is finished."

"At last! Now, then, we are going to operate on a large scale, on the masses!"

In which it will be Seen that the Epidemic Invades the Entire Town, and what Effect it Produces

During the following months the evil, in place of subsiding, became more extended. From private houses the epidemic spread into the streets. The town of Quiquendone was no longer to be recognized.

A phenomenon yet stranger than those which had already happened, now appeared; not only the animal kingdom, but the vegetable kingdom itself, became subject to the mysterious influence.

According to the ordinary course of things, epidemics are special in their operation. Those which attack humanity spare the animals, and those which attack the animals spare the vegetables. A horse was never inflicted with smallpox, nor a man with the cattle-plague, nor do sheep suffer from the potato-rot. But here all the laws of nature seemed to be overturned. Not only were the character, temperament, and ideas of the townsfolk changed, but the domestic animals—dogs and cats, horses and cows, asses and goats—suffered from this epidemic influence, as if their habitual equilibrium had been changed. The plants themselves were infected by a similar strange metamorphosis.

In the gardens and vegetable patches and orchards very curious symptoms manifested themselves. Climbing plants climbed more audaciously. Tufted plants became more tufted than ever. Shrubs became trees. Cereals, scarcely sown, showed their little green heads, and gained, in the same length of time, as much in inches as formerly, under the most favourable circumstances, they had gained in fractions. Asparagus attained the height of several feet; the artichokes swelled to the size of melons, the melons to the size of pumpkins, the pumpkins to the size of gourds, the gourds to the size of the belfry bell, which measured, in truth, nine feet in diameter. The cabbages were bushes, and the mushrooms umbrellas.

The fruits did not lag behind the vegetables. It required two persons to eat a strawberry, and four to consume a pear. The grapes also attained the enormous proportions of those so well depicted by Poussin in his "Return of the Envoys to the Promised Land."

It was the same with the flowers: immense violets spread the most penetrating perfumes through the air; exaggerated roses shone with the brightest colours; lilies formed, in a few days, impenetrable copses; geraniums, daisies, camelias, rhododendrons, invaded the garden walks, and stifled each other. And the tulips,— those dear liliaceous plants so dear to the Flemish heart, what emotion they must have caused to their zealous cultivators! The worthy Van Bistrom nearly fell over backwards, one day, on seeing in his garden an enormous "Tulipa gesneriana," a gigantic monster, whose cup afforded space to a nest for a whole family of robins!

The entire town flocked to see this floral phenomenon, and renamed it the "Tulipa quiquendonia".

But alas! if these plants, these fruits, these flowers, grew visibly to the naked eye, if all the vegetables insisted on assuming colossal proportions, if the brilliancy of their colours and perfume intoxicated the smell and the sight, they quickly withered. The air which they absorbed rapidly exhausted them, and they soon died, faded, and dried up.

Such was the fate of the famous tulip, which, after several days of splendour, became emaciated, and fell lifeless.

It was soon the same with the domestic animals, from the house-dog to the stable pig, from the canary in its cage to the turkey of the back-court. It must be said that in ordinary times these animals were not less phlegmatic than their masters. The dogs and cats vegetated rather than lived. They never betrayed a wag of pleasure nor a snarl of wrath. Their tails moved no more than if they had been made of bronze. Such a thing as a bite or scratch from any of them had not been known from time immemorial. As for mad dogs, they were looked upon as imaginary beasts, like the griffins and the rest in the menagerie of the apocalypse.

But what a change had taken place in a few months, the smallest incidents of which we are trying to reproduce! Dogs and cats began to show teeth and claws. Several executions had taken place after reiterated offences. A horse was seen, for the first time, to take his bit in his teeth and rush through the streets of Quiquendone; an ox was observed to precipitate itself, with lowered horns, upon one of his herd; an ass was seen to turn himself ever, with his legs in the air, in the Place Saint Ernuph, and bray as ass never brayed before; a sheep, actually a sheep, defended valiantly the cutlets within him from the butcher's knife.

Van Tricasse, the burgomaster, was forced to make police regulations concerning the domestic animals, as, seized with lunacy, they rendered the streets of Quiquendone unsafe.

But alas! if the animals were mad, the men were scarcely less so. No age was spared by the scourge. Babies soon became quite insupportable, though till now so easy to bring up; and for the first time Honore Syntax, the judge, was obliged to apply the rod to his youthful offspring.

There was a kind of insurrection at the high school, and the dictionaries became formidable missiles in the classes. The scholars would not submit to be shut in, and, besides, the infection took the teachers themselves, who overwhelmed the boys and girls with extravagant tasks and punishments.

Another strange phenomenon occurred. All these Quiquendonians, so sober before, whose chief food had been whipped creams, committed wild excesses in their eating and drinking. Their usual regimen no longer sufficed. Each stomach was transformed into a gulf, and it became necessary to fill this gulf by the most energetic means. The consumption of the town was trebled. Instead of two repasts they had six. Many cases of indigestion were reported. The Counsellor Niklausse could not satisfy his hunger. Van Tricasse found it impossible to assuage his thirst, and remained in a state of rabid semi-intoxication.

In short, the most alarming symptoms manifested themselves and increased from day to day. Drunken people staggered in the streets, and these were often citizens of high position.

Dominique Custos, the physician, had plenty to do with the heartburns, inflammations, and nervous affections, which proved to what a strange degree the nerves of the people had been irritated.

There were daily quarrels and altercations in the once deserted but now crowded streets of Quiquendone; for nobody could any longer stay at home. It was necessary to establish a new police force to control the disturbers of the public peace. A prison-cage was established in the Town Hall, and speedily became full, night and day, of refractory offenders. Commissary Passauf was in despair.

A marriage was concluded in less than two months,—such a thing had never been seen before. Yes, the son of Rupp, the schoolmaster, wedded the daughter of Augustine de Rovere, and that fifty-seven days only after he had petitioned for her hand and heart!

Other marriages were decided upon, which, in old times, would have remained in doubt and discussion for years. The burgomaster perceived that his own daughter, the charming Suzel, was escaping from his hands.

As for dear Tatanemance, she had dared to sound Commissary Passauf on the subject of a union, which seemed to her to combine every element of happiness, fortune, honour, youth!

At last,—to reach the depths of abomination,—a duel took place! Yes, a duel with pistols—horse-pistols—at seventy-five paces, with ball-cartridges. And between whom? Our readers will never believe!

Between M. Frantz Niklausse, the gentle angler, and young Simon Collaert, the wealthy banker's son.

And the cause of this duel was the burgomaster's daughter, for whom Simon discovered himself to be fired with passion, and whom he refused to yield to the claims of an audacious rival!

In which the Quiquendonians Adopt
a Heroic Resolution

We have seen to what a deplorable condition the people of Quiquendone were reduced. Their heads were in a ferment. They no longer knew or recognized themselves. The most peaceable citizens had become quarrelsome. If you looked at them askance, they would speedily send you a challenge. Some let their moustaches grow, and several—the most belligerent—curled them up at the ends.

This being their condition, the administration of the town and the maintenance of order in the streets became difficult tasks, for the government had not been organized for such a state of things. The burgomaster—that worthy Van Tricasse whom we have seen so placid, so dull, so incapable of coming to any decision— the burgomaster became intractable. His house resounded with the sharpness of his voice. He made twenty decisions a day, scolding his officials, and himself enforcing the regulations of his administration.

Ah, what a change! The amiable and tranquil mansion of the burgomaster, that good Flemish home—where was its former calm? What changes had taken place in your household economy! Madame Van Tricasse had become acrid, whimsical, harsh. Her husband sometimes succeeded in drowning her voice by talking louder than she, but could not silence her. The petulant humour of this worthy dame was excited by everything. Nothing went right. The servants offended her every moment. Tatanemance, her sister-in-law, who was not less irritable, replied sharply to her. M. Van Tricasse naturally supported Lotche, his servant, as is the case in all good households; and this permanently exasperated Madame, who constantly disputed, discussed, and made scenes with her husband.

"What on earth is the matter with us?" cried the unhappy burgomaster. "What is this fire that is devouring us? Are we possessed with the devil? Ah, Madame Van Tricasse, Madame Van Tricasse, you will end by making me die before you, and thus violate all the traditions of the family!"

The reader will not have forgotten the strange custom by which M. Van Tricasse would become a widower and marry again, so as not to break the chain of descent.

Meanwhile, this disposition of all minds produced other curious effects worthy of note. This excitement, the cause of which has so far escaped us, brought about unexpected physiological changes. Talents, hitherto unrecognized, betrayed themselves. Aptitudes were suddenly revealed. Artists, before common-place, displayed new ability. Politicians and authors arose. Orators proved themselves equal to the most arduous debates, and on every question inflamed audiences which were quite ready to be inflamed. From the sessions of the council, this movement spread to the public political meetings, and a club was formed at Quiquendone; whilst twenty newspapers, the "Quiquendone Signal," the "Quiquendone Impartial," the "Quiquendone Radical," and so on, written in an inflammatory style, raised the most important questions.

But what about? you will ask. Apropos of everything, and of nothing; apropos of the Oudenarde tower, which was falling, and which some wished to pull down, and others to prop up; apropos of the police regulations issued by the council, which some obstinate citizens threatened to resist; apropos of the sweeping of the gutters, repairing the sewers, and so on. Nor did the enraged orators confine themselves to the internal administration of the town. Carried on by the current they went further, and essayed to plunge their fellow-citizens into the hazards of war.

Quiquendone had had for eight or nine hundred years a *casus belli* of the best quality; but she had preciously laid it up like a relic, and there had seemed some probability that it would become effete, and no longer serviceable.

This was what had given rise to the *casus belli*.

It is not generally known that Quiquendone, in this cosy corner of Flanders, lies next to the little town of Virgamen. The territories of the two communities are contiguous.

Well, in 1185, some time before Count Baldwin's departure to the Crusades, a Virgamen cow—not a cow belonging to a citizen, but a cow which was common property, let it be observed— audaciously ventured to pasture on the territory of Quiquendone. This unfortunate beast had scarcely eaten three mouthfuls; but the offence, the abuse, the crime—whatever you will—was committed and duly indicted, for the magistrates, at that time, had already begun to know how to write.

"We will take revenge at the proper moment," said simply Natalis Van Tricasse, the thirty-second predecessor of the burgomaster of this story, "and the Virgamenians will lose nothing by waiting."

The Virgamenians were forewarned. They waited thinking, without doubt, that the remembrance of the offence would fade away with the lapse of time; and really, for several centuries, they lived on good terms with their neighbours of Quiquendone.

But they counted without their hosts, or rather without this strange epidemic, which, radically changing the character of the Quiquendonians, aroused their dormant vengeance.

It was at the club of the Rue Monstrelet that the truculent orator Schut, abruptly introducing the subject to his hearers, inflamed them with the expressions and metaphors used on such occasions. He recalled the offence, the injury which had been done to Quiquendone, and which a nation "jealous of its rights" could not admit as a precedent; he showed the insult to be still existing, the wound still bleeding: he spoke of certain special head-shakings on the part of the people of Virgamen, which indicated in what degree of contempt they regarded the people of Quiquendone; he appealed to his fellow-citizens, who, unconsciously perhaps, had supported this mortal insult for long centuries; he adjured the "children of the ancient town" to have no other purpose than to obtain a substantial reparation. And, lastly, he made an appeal to "all the living energies of the nation!"

With what enthusiasm these words, so new to Quiquendonian ears, were greeted, may be surmised, but cannot be told. All the auditors rose, and with extended arms demanded war with loud cries. Never had the Advocate Schut achieved such a success, and it must be avowed that his triumphs were not few.

The burgomaster, the counsellor, all the notabilities present at this memorable meeting, would have vainly attempted to resist the popular outburst. Besides, they had no desire to do so, and cried as loud, if not louder, than the rest,—

"To the frontier! To the frontier!"

As the frontier was but three kilometers from the walls of Quiquendone, it is certain that the Virgamenians ran a real danger, for they might easily be invaded without having had time to look about them.

Meanwhile, Josse Liefrinck, the worthy chemist, who alone had preserved his senses on this grave occasion, tried to make his fellow-citizens comprehend that guns, cannon, and generals were equally wanting to their design.

They replied to him, not without many impatient gestures, that these generals, cannons, and guns would be improvised; that the right and love of country sufficed, and rendered a people irresistible.

Hereupon the burgomaster himself came forward, and in a sublime harangue made short work of those pusillanimous people who disguise their fear under a veil of prudence, which veil he tore off with a patriotic hand.

At this sally it seemed as if the hall would fall in under the applause.

The vote was eagerly demanded, and was taken amid acclamations.

The cries of "To Virgamen! to Virgamen!" redoubled.

The burgomaster then took it upon himself to put the armies in motion, and in the name of the town he promised the honours of a triumph, such as was given in the times of the Romans to that one of its generals who should return victorious.

Meanwhile, Josse Liefrinck, who was an obstinate fellow, and did not regard himself as beaten, though he really had been, insisted on making another observation. He wished to remark that the triumph was only accorded at Rome to those victorious generals who had killed five thousand of the enemy.

"Well, well!" cried the meeting deliriously.

"And as the population of the town of Virgamen consists of but three thousand five hundred and seventy-five inhabitants, it would be difficult, unless the same person was killed several times—"

But they did not let the luckless logician finish, and he was turned out, hustled and bruised.

"Citizens," said Pulmacher the grocer, who usually sold groceries by retail, "whatever this cowardly apothecary may have said, I engage by myself to kill five thousand Virgamenians, if you will accept my services!"

"Five thousand five hundred!" cried a yet more resolute patriot.

"Six thousand six hundred!" retorted the grocer.

"Seven thousand!" cried Jean Orbideck, the confectioner of the Rue Hemling, who was on the road to a fortune by making whipped creams.

"Adjudged!" exclaimed the burgomaster Van Tricasse, on finding that no one else rose on the bid.

And this was how Jean Orbideck the confectioner became general-in-chief of the forces of Quiquendone.

In which Ygene, the Assistant, Gives a Reasonable Piece of Advice, which is Eagerly Rejected by Doctor Ox

"Well, master," said Ygene next day, as he poured the pails of sulphuric acid into the troughs of the great battery.

"Well," resumed Doctor Ox, "was I not right? See to what not only the physical developments of a whole nation, but its morality, its dignity, its talents, its political sense, have come! It is only a question of molecules."

"No doubt; but—"

"But—"

"Do you not think that matters have gone far enough, and that these poor devils should not be excited beyond measure?"

"No, no!" cried the doctor; "no! I will go on to the end!"

"As you will, master; the experiment, however, seems to me conclusive, and I think it time to—"

"To—"

"To close the valve."

"You'd better!" cried Doctor Ox. "If you attempt it, I'll throttle you!"

In which it is Once More Proved that by Taking High Ground All Human Littlenesses may be Overlooked

"You say?" asked the Burgomaster Van Tricasse of the Counsellor Niklausse.

"I say that this war is necessary," replied Niklausse, firmly, "and that the time has come to avenge this insult."

"Well, I repeat to you," replied the burgomaster, tartly, "that if the people of Quiquendone do not profit by this occasion to vindicate their rights, they will be unworthy of their name."

"And as for me, I maintain that we ought, without delay, to collect our forces and lead them to the front."

"Really, monsieur, really!" replied Van Tricasse. "And do you speak thus to *me*?"

"To yourself, monsieur the burgomaster; and you shall hear the truth, unwelcome as it may be."

"And you shall hear it yourself, counsellor," returned Van Tricasse in a passion, "for it will come better from my mouth than from yours! Yes, monsieur, yes, any delay would be dishonourable. The town of Quiquendone has waited nine hundred years for the moment to take its revenge, and whatever you may say, whether it pleases you or not, we shall march upon the enemy."

"Ah, you take it thus!" replied Niklausse harshly. "Very well, monsieur, we will march without you, if it does not please you to go."

"A burgomaster's place is in the front rank, monsieur!"

"And that of a counsellor also, monsieur."

"You insult me by thwarting all my wishes," cried the burgomaster, whose fists seemed likely to hit out before long.

"And you insult me equally by doubting my patriotism," cried Niklausse, who was equally ready for a tussle.

"I tell you, monsieur, that the army of Quiquendone shall be put in motion within two days!"

"And I repeat to you, monsieur, that forty-eight hours shall not pass before we shall have marched upon the enemy!"

It is easy to see, from this fragment of conversation, that the two speakers supported exactly the same idea. Both wished for hostilities; but as their excitement disposed them to altercation, Niklausse would not listen to Van Tricasse, nor Van Tricasse to Niklausse. Had they been of contrary opinions on this grave question, had the burgomaster favoured war and the counsellor insisted on peace, the quarrel would not have been more violent. These two old friends gazed fiercely at each other. By the quickened beating of their hearts, their red faces, their contracted pupils, the trembling of their muscles, their harsh voices, it might be conjectured that they were ready to come to blows.

But the striking of a large clock happily checked the adversaries at the moment when they seemed on the point of assaulting each other.

"At last the hour has come!" cried the burgomaster.

"What hour?" asked the counsellor.

"The hour to go to the belfry tower."

"It is true, and whether it pleases you or not, I shall go, monsieur."

"And I too."

"Let us go!"

"Let us go!"

It might have been supposed from these last words that a collision had occurred, and that the adversaries were proceeding to a duel; but it was not so. It had been agreed that the burgomaster and the counsellor, as the two principal dignitaries of the town, should repair to the Town Hall, and there show themselves on the high tower which overlooked Quiquendone; that they should examine the surrounding country, so as to make the best strategetic plan for the advance of their troops.

Though they were in accord on this subject, they did not cease to quarrel bitterly as they went. Their loud voices were heard resounding in the streets; but all the passers-by were now accustomed to this; the exasperation of the dignitaries seemed quite natural, and no one took notice of it. Under the circumstances, a calm man would have been regarded as a monster.

The burgomaster and the counsellor, having reached the porch of the belfry, were in a paroxysm of fury. They were no longer red, but pale. This terrible discussion, though they had the same idea, had produced internal spasms, and everyone knows that paleness shows that anger has reached its last limits.

At the foot of the narrow tower staircase there was a real explosion. Who should go up first? Who should first creep up the winding steps? Truth compels us to say that there was a tussle, and that the Counsellor Niklausse, forgetful of all that he owed to his superior, to the supreme magistrate of the town, pushed Van Tricasse violently back, and dashed up the staircase first.

Both ascended, denouncing and raging at each other at every step. It was to be feared that a terrible climax would occur on the summit of the tower, which rose three hundred and fifty-seven feet above the pavement.

The two enemies soon got out of breath, however, and in a little while, at the eightieth step, they began to move up heavily, breathing loud and short.

Then—was it because of their being out of breath?—their wrath subsided, or at least only betrayed itself by a succession of unseemly epithets. They became silent, and, strange to say, it seemed as if their excitement diminished as they ascended higher above the town. A sort of lull took place in their minds. Their brains became cooler, and simmered down like a coffee-pot when taken away from the fire. Why?

We cannot answer this "why;" but the truth is that, having reached a certain landing-stage, two hundred and sixty-six feet above ground, the two adversaries sat down and, really more calm, looked at each other without any anger in their faces.

"How high it is!" said the burgomaster, passing his handkerchief over his rubicund face.

"Very high!" returned the counsellor. "Do you know that we have gone fourteen feet higher than the Church of Saint Michael at Hamburg?"

"I know it," replied the burgomaster, in a tone of vanity very pardonable in the chief magistrate of Quiquendone.

The two notabilities soon resumed their ascent, casting curious glances through the loopholes pierced in the tower walls. The burgomaster had taken the head of the procession, without any remark on the part of the counsellor. It even happened that at about the three hundred and fourth step, Van Tricasse being completely tired out, Niklausse kindly pushed him from behind. The burgomaster offered no resistance to this, and, when he reached the platform of the tower, said graciously,—

"Thanks, Niklausse; I will do the same for you one day."

A little while before it had been two wild beasts, ready to tear each other to pieces, who had presented themselves at the foot of the tower; it was now two friends who reached its summit.

The weather was superb. It was the month of May. The sun had absorbed all the vapours. What a pure and limpid atmosphere! The most minute objects over a broad space might be discerned. The walls of Virgamen, glistening in their whiteness,—its red, pointed roofs, its belfries shining in the sunlight—appeared a few miles off. And this was the town that was foredoomed to all the horrors of fire and pillage!

The burgomaster and the counsellor sat down beside each other on a small stone bench, like two worthy people whose souls were in close sympathy. As they recovered breath, they looked around; then, after a brief silence,—

"How fine this is!" cried the burgomaster.

"Yes, it is admirable!" replied the counsellor. "Does it not seem to you, my good Van Tricasse, that humanity is destined to dwell rather at such heights, than to crawl about on the surface of our globe?"

"I agree with you, honest Niklausse," returned the burgomaster, "I agree with you. You seize sentiment better when you get clear of nature. You breathe it in every sense! It is at such heights that philosophers should be formed, and that sages should live, above the miseries of this world!"

"Shall we go around the platform?" asked the counsellor.

"Let us go around the platform," replied the burgomaster.

And the two friends, arm in arm, and putting, as formerly, long pauses between their questions and answers, examined every point of the horizon.

"It is at least seventeen years since I have ascended the belfry tower," said Van Tricasse.

"I do not think I ever came up before," replied Niklausse; "and I regret it, for the view from this height is sublime! Do you see, my friend, the pretty stream of the Vaar, as it winds among the trees?"

"And, beyond, the heights of Saint Hermandad! How gracefully they shut in the horizon! Observe that border of green trees, which Nature has so picturesquely arranged! Ah, Nature, Nature, Niklausse! Could the hand of man ever hope to rival her?"

"It is enchanting, my excellent friend," replied the counsellor. "See the flocks and herds lying in the verdant pastures,—the oxen, the cows, the sheep!"

"And the labourers going to the fields! You would say they were Arcadian shepherds; they only want a bagpipe!"

"And over all this fertile country the beautiful blue sky, which no vapour dims! Ah, Niklausse, one might become a poet here! I do not understand why Saint Simeon Stylites was not one of the greatest poets of the world."

"It was because, perhaps, his column was not high enough," replied the counsellor, with a gentle smile.

At this moment the chimes of Quiquendone rang out. The clear bells played one of their most melodious airs. The two friends listened in ecstasy.

Then in his calm voice, Van Tricasse said,—

"But what, friend Niklausse, did we come to the top of this tower to do?"

"In fact," replied the counsellor, "we have permitted ourselves to be carried away by our reveries—"

"What did we come here to do?" repeated the burgomaster.

"We came," said Niklausse, "to breathe this pure air, which human weaknesses have not corrupted."

"Well, shall we descend, friend Niklausse?"

"Let us descend, friend Van Tricasse."

They gave a parting glance at the splendid panorama which was spread before their eyes; then the burgomaster passed down first, and began to descend with a slow and measured pace. The counsellor followed a few steps behind. They reached the landing-stage at which they had stopped on ascending. Already their cheeks began to redden. They tarried a moment, then resumed their descent.

In a few moments Van Tricasse begged Niklausse to go more slowly, as he felt him on his heels, and it "worried him." It even did more than worry him; for twenty steps lower down he ordered the counsellor to stop, that he might get on some distance ahead.

The counsellor replied that he did not wish to remain with his leg in the air to await the good pleasure of the burgomaster, and kept on.

Van Tricasse retorted with a rude expression.

The counsellor responded by an insulting allusion to the burgomaster's age, destined as he was, by his family traditions, to marry a second time.

The burgomaster went down twenty steps more, and warned Niklausse that this should not pass thus.

Niklausse replied that, at all events, he would pass down first; and, the space being very narrow, the two dignitaries came into collision, and found themselves in utter darkness. The words "blockhead" and "booby" were the mildest which they now applied to each other.

"We shall see, stupid beast!" cried the burgomaster,—"we shall see what figure you will make in this war, and in what rank you will march!"

"In the rank that precedes yours, you silly old fool!" replied Niklausse.

Then there were other cries, and it seemed as if bodies were rolling over each other. What was going on? Why were these dispositions so quickly changed? Why were the gentle sheep of the tower's summit metamorphosed into tigers two hundred feet below it?

However this might be, the guardian of the tower, hearing the noise, opened the door, just at the moment when the two adversaries, bruised, and with protruding eyes, were in the act of tearing each other's hair,—fortunately they wore wigs.

"You shall give me satisfaction for this!" cried the burgomaster, shaking his fist under his adversary's nose.

"Whenever you please!" growled the Counsellor Niklausse, attempting to respond with a vigorous kick.

The guardian, who was himself in a passion,—I cannot say why,—thought the scene a very natural one. I know not what excitement urged him to take part in it, but he controlled himself, and went off to announce throughout the neighbourhood that a hostile meeting was about to take place between the Burgomaster Van Tricasse and the Counsellor Niklausse.

In which Matters Go so Far that the Inhabitants of Quiquendone, the Reader, and even the Author, Demand an Immediate Denouement

The last incident proves to what a pitch of excitement the Quiquendonians had been wrought. The two oldest friends in the town, and the most gentle—before the advent of the epidemic, to reach this degree of violence! And that, too, only a few minutes after their old mutual sympathy, their amiable instincts, their contemplative habit, had been restored at the summit of the tower!

On learning what was going on, Doctor Ox could not contain his joy. He resisted the arguments which Ygene, who saw what a serious turn affairs were taking, addressed to him. Besides, both of them were infected by the general fury. They were not less excited than the rest of the population, and they ended by quarrelling as violently as the burgomaster and the counsellor.

Besides, one question eclipsed all others, and the intended duels were postponed to the issue of the Virgamenian difficulty. No man had the right to shed his blood uselessly, when it belonged, to the last drop, to his country in danger. The affair was, in short, a grave one, and there was no withdrawing from it.

The Burgomaster Van Tricasse, despite the warlike ardour with which he was filled, had not thought it best to throw himself upon the enemy without warning him. He had, therefore, through the medium of the rural policeman, Hottering, sent to demand reparation of the Virgamenians for the offence committed, in 1195, on the Quiquendonian territory.

The authorities of Virgamen could not at first imagine of what the envoy spoke, and the latter, despite his official character, was conducted back to the frontier very cavalierly.

Van Tricasse then sent one of the aides-de-camp of the confectioner-general, citizen Hildevert Shuman, a manufacturer of barley-sugar, a very firm and energetic man, who carried to the authorities of Virgamen the original minute of the indictment drawn up in 1195 by order of the Burgomaster Natalis Van Tricasse.

The authorities of Virgamen burst out laughing, and served the aide-de-camp in the same manner as the rural policeman.

The burgomaster then assembled the dignitaries of the town.

A letter, remarkably and vigorously drawn up, was written as an ultimatum; the cause of quarrel was plainly stated, and a delay of twenty-four hours was accorded to the guilty city in which to repair the outrage done to Quiquendone.

The letter was sent off, and returned a few hours afterwards, torn to bits, which made so many fresh insults. The Virgamenians knew of old the forbearance and equanimity of the Quiquendonians, and made sport of them and their demand, of their *casus belli* and their *ultimatum.*

There was only one thing left to do,—to have recourse to arms, to invoke the God of battles, and, after the Prussian fashion, to hurl themselves upon the Virgamenians Before the latter could be prepared.

This decision was made by the council in solemn conclave, in which cries, objurgations, and menacing gestures were mingled with unexampled violence. An assembly of idiots, a congress of madmen, a club of maniacs, would not have been more tumultuous.

As soon as the declaration of war was known, General Jean Orbideck assembled his troops, perhaps two thousand three hundred and ninety-three combatants from a population of two thousand three hundred and ninety-three souls. The women, the children, the old men, were joined with the able-bodied males. The guns of the town had been put under requisition. Five had been found, two of which were without cocks, and these had been distributed to the advance-guard. The artillery was composed of the old culverin of the chateau, taken in 1339 at the attack on Quesnoy, one of the first occasions of the use of cannon in history, and which had not been fired off for five centuries. Happily for those who were appointed to take it in charge there were no projectiles with which to load it; but such as it was, this engine might well impose on the enemy. As for side-arms, they had been taken from the museum of antiquities,—flint hatchets, helmets, Frankish battle-axes, javelins, halberds, rapiers, and so on; and also in those domestic arsenals commonly known as "cupboards" and "kitchens." But courage, the right, hatred of the foreigner, the yearning for vengeance, were to take the place of more perfect engines, and to replace—at least it was hoped so—the modern mitrailleuses and breech-loaders.

The troops were passed in review. Not a citizen failed at the roll-call. General Orbideck, whose seat on horseback was far from firm, and whose steed was a vicious beast, was thrown three times in front of the army; but he got up again without injury, and this was regarded as a favourable omen. The burgomaster, the counsellor, the civil commissary, the chief justice, the school-teacher, the banker, the rector,—in short, all the notabilities of the town,—marched at the head. There were no tears shed, either by mothers, sisters, or daughters. They urged on their husbands, fathers, brothers, to the combat, and even followed them and formed the rear-guard, under the orders of the courageous Madame Van Tricasse.

The crier, Jean Mistrol, blew his trumpet; the army moved off, and directed itself, with ferocious cries, towards the Oudenarde gate.

At the moment when the head of the column was about to pass the walls of the town, a man threw himself before it.

"Stop! stop! Fools that you are!" he cried. "Suspend your blows! Let me shut the valve! You are not changed in nature! You are good citizens, quiet and peaceable! If you are so excited, it is my master, Doctor Ox's, fault! It is an experiment! Under the pretext of lighting your streets with oxyhydric gas, he has saturated—"

The assistant was beside himself; but he could not finish. At the instant that the doctor's secret was about to escape his lips, Doctor Ox himself pounced upon the unhappy Ygene in an indescribable rage, and shut his mouth by blows with his fist.

It was a battle. The burgomaster, the counsellor, the dignitaries, who had stopped short on Ygene's sudden appearance, carried away in turn by their exasperation, rushed upon the two strangers, without waiting to hear either the one or the other.

Doctor Ox and his assistant, beaten and lashed, were about to be dragged, by order of Van Tricasse, to the round-house, when,—

In which the Denouement Takes Place

When a formidable explosion resounded. All the atmosphere which enveloped Quiquendone seemed on fire. A flame of an intensity and vividness quite unwonted shot up into the heavens like a meteor. Had it been night, this flame would have been visible for ten leagues around.

The whole army of Quiquendone fell to the earth, like an army of monks. Happily there were no victims; a few scratches and slight hurts were the only result. The confectioner, who, as chance would have it, had not fallen from his horse this time, had his plume singed, and escaped without any further injury.

What had happened?

Something very simple, as was soon learned; the gasworks had just blown up. During the absence of the doctor and his assistant, some careless mistake had no doubt been made. It is not known how or why a communication had been established between the reservoir which contained the oxygen and that which enclosed the hydrogen. An explosive mixture had resulted from the union of these two gases, to which fire had accidentally been applied.

This changed everything; but when the army got upon its feet again, Doctor Ox and his assistant Ygene had disappeared.

In which the Intelligent Reader Sees that he has Guessed Correctly, Despite All the Author's Precautions

After the explosion, Quiquendone immediately became the peaceable, phlegmatic, and Flemish town it formerly was.

After the explosion, which indeed did not cause a very lively sensation, each one, without knowing why, mechanically took his way home, the burgomaster leaning on the counsellor's arm, the advocate Schut going arm in arm with Custos the doctor, Frantz Niklausse walking with equal familiarity with Simon Collaert, each going tranquilly, noiselessly, without even being conscious of what had happened, and having already forgotten Virgamen and their revenge. The general returned to his confections, and his aide-de-camp to the barley-sugar.

Thus everything had become calm again; the old existence had been resumed by men and beasts, beasts and plants; even by the tower of Oudenarde gate, which the explosion—these explosions are sometimes astonishing—had set upright again!

And from that time never a word was spoken more loudly than another, never a discussion took place in the town of Quiquendone. There were no more politics, no more clubs, no more trials, no more policemen! The post of the Commissary Passauf became once more a sinecure, and if his salary was not reduced, it was because the burgomaster and the counsellor could not make up their minds to decide upon it.

From time to time, indeed, Passauf flitted, without any one suspecting it, through the dreams of the inconsolable Tatanemance.

As for Frantz's rival, he generously abandoned the charming Suzel to her lover, who hastened to wed her five or six years after these events.

And as for Madame Van Tricasse, she died ten years later, at the proper time, and the burgomaster married Mademoiselle Pelagie Van Tricasse, his cousin, under excellent conditions—for the happy mortal who should succeed him.

In which Doctor Ox's Theory is Explained

What, then, had this mysterious Doctor Ox done? Tried a fantastic experiment,—nothing more.

After having laid down his gas-pipes, he had saturated, first the public buildings, then the private dwellings, finally the streets of Quiquendone, with pure oxygen, without letting in the least atom of hydrogen.

This gas, tasteless and odorless, spread in generous quantity through the atmosphere, causes, when it is breathed, serious agitation to the human organism. One who lives in an air saturated with oxygen grows excited, frantic, burns!

You scarcely return to the ordinary atmosphere before you return to your usual state. For instance, the counsellor and the burgomaster at the top of the belfry were themselves again, as the oxygen is kept, by its weight, in the lower strata of the air.

But one who lives under such conditions, breathing this gas which transforms the body physiologically as well as the soul, dies speedily, like a madman.

It was fortunate, then, for the Quiquendonians, that a providential explosion put an end to this dangerous experiment, and abolished Doctor Ox's gas-works.

To conclude: Are virtue, courage, talent, wit, imagination,—are all these qualities or faculties only a question of oxygen?

Such is Doctor Ox's theory; but we are not bound to accept it, and for ourselves we utterly reject it, in spite of the curious experiment of which the worthy old town of Quiquendone was the theatre.

Master Zacharius

A Winter Night

The city of Geneva lies at the west end of the lake of the same name. The Rhone, which passes through the town at the outlet of the lake, divides it into two sections, and is itself divided in the centre of the city by an island placed in mid-stream. A topographical feature like this is often found in the great depots of commerce and industry. No doubt the first inhabitants were influenced by the easy means of transport which the swift currents of the rivers offered them—those "roads which walk along of their own accord," as Pascal puts it. In the case of the Rhone, it would be the road that ran along.

Before new and regular buildings were constructed on this island, which was enclosed like a Dutch galley in the middle of the river, the curious mass of houses, piled one on the other, presented a delightfully confused *coup-d'oeil*. The small area of the island had compelled some of the buildings to be perched, as it were, on the piles, which were entangled in the rough currents of the river. The huge beams, blackened by time, and worn by the water, seemed like the claws of an enormous crab, and presented a fantastic appearance. The little yellow streams, which were like cobwebs stretched amid this ancient foundation, quivered in the darkness, as if they had been the leaves of some old oak forest, while the river engulfed in this forest of piles, foamed and roared most mournfully.

One of the houses of the island was striking for its curiously aged appearance. It was the dwelling of the old clockmaker, Master Zacharius, whose household consisted of his daughter Gerande, Aubert Thun, his apprentice, and his old servant Scholastique.

There was no man in Geneva to compare in interest with this Zacharius. His age was past finding out. Not the oldest inhabitant of the town could tell for how long his thin, pointed head had shaken above his shoulders, nor the day when, for the first time, he had-walked through the streets, with his long white locks floating in the wind. The man did not live; he vibrated like the pendulum of his clocks. His spare and cadaverous figure was always clothed in dark colours. Like the pictures of Leonardo di Vinci, he was sketched in black.

Gerande had the pleasantest room in the whole house, whence, through a narrow window, she had the inspiriting view of the snowy peaks of Jura; but the bedroom and workshop of the old man were a kind of cavern close on to the water, the floor of which rested on the piles.

From time immemorial Master Zacharius had never come out except at meal times, and when he went to regulate the different clocks of the town. He passed the rest of his time at his bench, which was covered with numerous clockwork instruments, most of which he had invented himself. For he was a clever man; his works were valued in all France and Germany. The best workers in Geneva readily recognized his superiority, and showed that he was an honour to the town, by saying, "To him belongs the glory of having invented the escapement." In fact, the birth of true clock-work dates from the invention which the talents of Zacharius had discovered not many years before.

After he had worked hard for a long time, Zacharius would slowly put his tools away, cover up the delicate pieces that he had been adjusting with glasses, and stop the active wheel of his lathe; then he would raise a trap-door constructed in the floor of his workshop, and, stooping down, used to inhale for hours together the thick vapours of the Rhone, as it dashed along under his eyes.

One winter's night the old servant Scholastique served the supper, which, according to old custom, she and the young mechanic shared with their master. Master Zacharius did not eat, though the food carefully prepared for him was offered him in a handsome blue and white dish. He scarcely answered the sweet words of Gerande, who evidently noticed her father's silence, and even the clatter of Scholastique herself no more struck his ear than the roar of the river, to which he paid no attention.

After the silent meal, the old clockmaker left the table without embracing his daughter, or saying his usual "Good-night" to all. He left by the narrow door leading to his den, and the staircase groaned under his heavy footsteps as he went down.

Gerande, Aubert, and Scholastique sat for some minutes without speaking. On this evening the weather was dull; the clouds dragged heavily on the Alps, and threatened rain; the severe climate of Switzerland made one feel sad, while the south wind swept round the house, and whistled ominously.

"My dear young lady," said Scholastique, at last, "do you know that our master has been out of sorts for several days? Holy Virgin! I know he has had no appetite, because his words stick in his inside, and it would take a very clever devil to drag even one out of him."

"My father has some secret cause of trouble, that I cannot even guess," replied Gerande, as a sad anxiety spread over her face.

"Mademoiselle, don't let such sadness fill your heart. You know the strange habits of Master Zacharius. Who can read his secret thoughts in his face? No doubt some fatigue has overcome him, but to-morrow he will have forgotten it, and be very sorry to have given his daughter pain."

It was Aubert who spoke thus, looking into Gerande's lovely eyes. Aubert was the first apprentice whom Master Zacharius had ever admitted to the intimacy of his labours, for he appreciated his intelligence, discretion, and goodness of heart; and this young man had attached himself to Gerande with the earnest devotion natural to a noble nature.

Gerande was eighteen years of age. Her oval face recalled that of the artless Madonnas whom veneration still displays at the street corners of the antique towns of Brittany. Her eyes betrayed an infinite simplicity. One would love her as the sweetest realization of a poet's dream. Her apparel was of modest colours, and the white linen which was folded about her shoulders had the tint and perfume peculiar to the linen of the church. She led a mystical existence in Geneva, which had not as yet been delivered over to the dryness of Calvinism.

While, night and morning, she read her Latin prayers in her iron-clasped missal, Gerande had also discovered a hidden sentiment in Aubert Thun's heart, and comprehended what a profound devotion the young workman had for her. Indeed, the whole world in his eyes was condensed into this old clockmaker's house, and he passed all his time near the young girl, when he left her father's workshop, after his work was over.

Old Scholastique saw all this, but said nothing. Her loquacity exhausted itself in preference on the evils of the times, and the little worries of the household. Nobody tried to stop its course. It was with her as with the musical snuff-boxes which they made at Geneva; once wound up, you must break them before you will prevent their playing all their airs through.

Finding Gerande absorbed in a melancholy silence, Scholastique left her old wooden chair, fixed a taper on the end of a candlestick, lit it, and placed it near a small waxen Virgin, sheltered in her niche of stone. It was the family custom to kneel before this protecting Madonna of the domestic hearth, and to beg her kindly watchfulness during the coming night; but on this evening Gerande remained silent in her seat.

"Well, well, dear demoiselle," said the astonished Scholastique, "supper is over, and it is time to go to bed. Why do you tire your eyes by sitting up late? Ah, Holy Virgin! It's much better to sleep, and to get a little comfort from happy dreams! In these detestable times in which we live, who can promise herself a fortunate day?"

"Ought we not to send for a doctor for my father?" asked Gerande.

"A doctor!" cried the old domestic. "Has Master Zacharius ever listened to their fancies and pompous sayings? He might accept medicines for the watches, but not for the body!"

"What shall we do?" murmured Gerande. "Has he gone to work, or to rest?"

"Gerande," answered Aubert softly, "some mental trouble annoys your father, that is all."

"Do you know what it is, Aubert?"

"Perhaps, Gerande"

"Tell us, then," cried Scholastique eagerly, economically extinguishing her taper.

"For several days, Gerande," said the young apprentice, "something absolutely incomprehensible has been going on. All the watches which your father has made and sold for some years have suddenly stopped. Very many of them have been brought back to him. He has carefully taken them to pieces; the springs were in good condition, and the wheels well set. He has put them together yet more carefully; but, despite his skill, they will not go."

"The devil's in it!" cried Scholastique.

"Why say you so?" asked Gerande. "It seems very natural to me. Nothing lasts forever in this world. The infinite cannot be fashioned by the hands of men."

"It is none the less true," returned Aubert, "that there is in this something very mysterious and extraordinary. I have myself been helping Master Zacharius to search for the cause of this derangement of his watches; but I have not been able to find it, and more than once I have let my tools fall from my hands in despair."

"But why undertake so vain a task?" resumed Scholastique. "Is it natural that a little copper instrument should go of itself, and mark the hours? We ought to have kept to the sun-dial!"

"You will not talk thus, Scholastique," said Aubert, "when you learn that the sun-dial was invented by Cain."

"Good heavens! what are you telling me?"

"Do you think," asked Gerande simply, "that we might pray to God to give life to my father's watches?"

"Without doubt," replied Aubert.

"Good! They will be useless prayers," muttered the old servant, "but Heaven will pardon them for their good intent."

The taper was relighted. Scholastique, Gerande, and Aubert knelt down together upon the tiles of the room. The young girl prayed for her mother's soul, for a blessing for the night, for travellers and prisoners, for the good and the wicked, and more earnestly than all for the unknown misfortunes of her father.

Then the three devout souls rose with some confidence in their hearts, because they had laid their sorrow on the bosom of God.

Aubert repaired to his own room; Gerande sat pensively by the window, whilst the last lights were disappearing from the city streets; and Scholastique, having poured a little water on the flickering embers, and shut the two enormous bolts on the door, threw herself upon her bed, where she was soon dreaming that she was dying of fright.

Meanwhile the terrors of this winter's night had increased. Sometimes, with the whirlpools of the river, the wind engulfed itself among the piles, and the whole house shivered and shook;

but the young girl, absorbed in her sadness, thought only of her father. After hearing what Aubert told her, the malady of Master Zacharius took fantastic proportions in her mind; and it seemed to her as if his existence, so dear to her, having become purely mechanical, no longer moved on its worn-out pivots without effort.

Suddenly the pent-house shutter, shaken by the squall, struck against the window of the room. Gerande shuddered and started up without understanding the cause of the noise which thus disturbed her reverie. When she became a little calmer she opened the sash. The clouds had burst, and a torrent-like rain pattered on the surrounding roofs. The young girl leaned out of the window to draw to the shutter shaken by the wind, but she feared to do so. It seemed to her that the rain and the river, confounding their tumultuous waters, were submerging the frail house, the planks of which creaked in every direction. She would have flown from her chamber, but she saw below the flickering of a light which appeared to come from Master Zacharius's retreat, and in one of those momentary calms during which the elements keep a sudden silence, her ear caught plaintive sounds. She tried to shut her window, but could not. The wind violently repelled her, like a thief who was breaking into a dwelling.

Gerande thought she would go mad with terror. What was her father doing? She opened the door, and it escaped from her hands, and slammed loudly with the force of the tempest. Gerande then found herself in the dark supper-room, succeeded in gaining, on tiptoe, the staircase which led to her father's shop, and pale and fainting, glided down.

The old watchmaker was upright in the middle of the room, which resounded with the roaring of the river. His bristling hair gave him a sinister aspect. He was talking and gesticulating, without seeing or hearing anything. Gerande stood still on the threshold.

"It is death!" said Master Zacharius, in a hollow voice; "it is death! Why should I live longer, now that I have dispersed my existence over the earth? For I, Master, Zacharius, am really the creator of all the watches that I have fashioned! It is a part of my very soul that I have shut up in each of these cases of iron, silver, or gold! Every time that one of these accursed watches stops, I feel my heart cease beating, for I have regulated them with its pulsations!"

As he spoke in this strange way, the old man cast his eyes on his bench. There lay all the pieces of a watch that he had carefully taken apart. He took up a sort of hollow cylinder, called a barrel, in which the spring is enclosed, and removed the steel spiral, but instead of relaxing itself, according to the laws of its elasticity, it remained coiled on itself like a sleeping viper. It seemed knotted, like impotent old men whose blood has long been congealed. Master Zacharius vainly essayed to uncoil it with his thin fingers, the outlines of which were exaggerated on the wall; but he tried in vain, and soon, with a terrible cry of anguish and rage, he threw it through the trap-door into the boiling Rhone. Gerande, her feet riveted to the floor, stood breathless and motionless. She wished to approach her father, but could not. Giddy hallucinations took possession of her. Suddenly she heard, in the shade, a voice murmur in her ears,—

"Gerande, dear Gerande! grief still keeps you awake. Go in again, I beg of you; the night is cold."

"Aubert!" whispered the young girl. "You!"

"Ought I not to be troubled by what troubles you?"

These soft words sent the blood back into the young girl's heart. She leaned on Aubert's arm, and said to him,—

"My father is very ill, Aubert! You alone can cure him, for this disorder of the mind would not yield to his daughter's consolings. His mind is attacked by a very natural delusion, and in working with him, repairing the watches, you will bring him back to reason.

Aubert," she continued, "it is not true, is it, that his life is mixed up with that of his watches?"

Aubert did not reply.

"But is my father's a trade condemned by God?" asked Gerande, trembling.

"I know not," returned the apprentice, warming the cold hands of the girl with his own. "But go back to your room, my poor Gerande, and with sleep recover hope!"

Gerande slowly returned to her chamber, and remained there till daylight, without sleep closing her eyelids. Meanwhile, Master Zacharius, always mute and motionless, gazed at the river as it rolled turbulently at his feet.

The Pride of Science

The severity of the Geneva merchant in business matters has become proverbial. He is rigidly honourable, and excessively just. What must, then, have been the shame of Master Zacharius, when he saw these watches, which he had so carefully constructed, returning to him from every direction?

It was certain that these watches had suddenly stopped, and without any apparent reason. The wheels were in a good condition and firmly fixed, but the springs had lost all elasticity. Vainly did the watchmaker try to replace them; the wheels remained motionless. These unaccountable derangements were greatly to the old man's discredit. His noble inventions had many times brought upon him suspicions of sorcery, which now seemed confirmed. These rumours reached Gerande, and she often trembled for her father, when she saw malicious glances directed towards him.

Yet on the morning after this night of anguish, Master Zacharius seemed to resume work with some confidence. The morning sun inspired him with some courage. Aubert hastened to join him in the shop, and received an affable "Good-day."

"I am better," said the old man. "I don't know what strange pains in the head attacked me yesterday, but the sun has quite chased them away, with the clouds of the night."

"In faith, master," returned Aubert, "I don't like the night for either of us!"

"And thou art right, Aubert. If you ever become a great man, you will understand that day is as necessary to you as food. A great savant should be always ready to receive the homage of his fellow-men."

"Master, it seems to me that the pride of science has possessed you."

"Pride, Aubert! Destroy my past, annihilate my present, dissipate my future, and then it will be permitted to me to live in obscurity! Poor boy, who comprehends not the sublime things to which my art is wholly devoted! Art thou not but a tool in my hands?"

"Yet. Master Zacharius," resumed Aubert, "I have more than once merited your praise for the manner in which I adjusted the most delicate parts of your watches and clocks."

"No doubt, Aubert; thou art a good workman, such as I love; but when thou workest, thou thinkest thou hast in thy hands but copper, silver, gold; thou dost not perceive these metals, which my genius animates, palpitating like living flesh! So that thou wilt not die, with the death of thy works!"

Master Zacharius remained silent after these words; but Aubert essayed to keep up the conversation.

"Indeed, master," said he, "I love to see you work so unceasingly! You will be ready for the festival of our corporation, for I see that the work on this crystal watch is going forward famously."

"No doubt, Aubert," cried the old watchmaker, "and it will be no slight honour for me to have been able to cut and shape the crystal to the durability of a diamond! Ah, Louis Berghem did well to perfect the art of diamond-cutting, which has enabled me to polish and pierce the hardest stones!"

Master Zacharius was holding several small watch pieces of cut crystal, and of exquisite workmanship. The wheels, pivots, and case of the watch were of the same material, and he had employed remarkable skill in this very difficult task.

"Would it not be fine," said he, his face flushing, "to see this watch palpitating beneath its transparent envelope, and to be able to count the beatings of its heart?"

"I will wager, sir," replied the young apprentice, "that it will not vary a second in a year."

"And you would wager on a certainty! Have I not imparted to it all that is purest of myself? And does my heart vary? My heart, I say?"

Aubert did not dare to lift his eyes to his master's face.

"Tell me frankly," said the old man sadly. "Have you never taken me for a madman? Do you not think me sometimes subject to dangerous folly? Yes; is it not so? In my daughter's eyes and yours, I have often read my condemnation. Oh!" he cried, as if in pain, "to be misunderstood by those whom one most loves in the world! But I will prove victoriously to thee, Aubert, that I am right! Do not shake thy head, for thou wilt be astounded. The day on which thou understandest how to listen to and comprehend me, thou wilt see that I have discovered the secrets of existence, the secrets of the mysterious union of the soul with the body!"

As he spoke thus, Master Zacharius appeared superb in his vanity. His eyes glittered with a supernatural fire, and his pride illumined every feature. And truly, if ever vanity was excusable, it was that of Master Zacharius!

The watchmaking art, indeed, down to his time, had remained almost in its infancy. From the day when Plato, four centuries before the Christian era, invented the night watch, a sort of clepsydra which indicated the hours of the night by the sound and playing of a flute, the science had continued nearly stationary. The masters paid more attention to the arts than to mechanics, and it was the period of beautiful watches of iron, copper, wood, silver, which were richly engraved, like one of Cellini's ewers. They made a masterpiece of chasing, which measured time imperfectly, but was still a masterpiece. When the artist's imagination was not directed to the perfection of modelling, it set to work to create clocks with moving figures and melodious sounds, whose appearance took all attention. Besides, who troubled himself, in those days, with regulating the advance of time? The delays of the law were not as yet invented; the physical and astronomical sciences had not as yet established their calculations on scrupulously exact measurements; there were neither establishments which were shut at a given hour, nor trains which departed at a precise moment. In the evening the curfew bell sounded; and at night the hours were cried amid the universal silence. Certainly people did not live so long, if existence is measured by the amount of business done; but they lived better. The mind was enriched with the noble sentiments born of the contemplation of chefs-d'oeuvre. They built a church in two centuries, a painter painted but few pictures in the course of his life, a poet only composed one great work; but these were so many masterpieces for after-ages to appreciate.

When the exact sciences began at last to make some progress, watch and clock making followed in their path, though it was always arrested by an insurmountable difficulty,—the regular and continuous measurement of time.

It was in the midst of this stagnation that Master Zacharius invented the escapement, which enabled him to obtain a mathematical regularity by submitting the movement of the pendulum to a sustained force. This invention had turned the old man's head. Pride, swelling in his heart, like mercury in the thermometer, had attained the height of transcendent folly. By analogy he had allowed himself to be drawn to materialistic conclusions, and as he constructed his watches, he fancied that he had discovered the secrets of the union of the soul with the body.

Thus, on this day, perceiving that Aubert listened to him attentively, he said to him in a tone of simple conviction,—

"Dost thou know what life is, my child? Hast thou comprehended the action of those springs which produce existence? Hast thou examined thyself? No. And yet, with the eyes of science, thou mightest have seen the intimate relation which exists between God's work and my own; for it is from his creature that I have copied the combinations of the wheels of my clocks."

"Master," replied Aubert eagerly, "can you compare a copper or steel machine with that breath of God which is called the soul, which animates our bodies as the breeze stirs the flowers? What mechanism could be so adjusted as to inspire us with thought?"

"That is not the question," responded Master Zacharius gently, but with all the obstinacy of a blind man walking towards an abyss. "In order to understand me, thou must recall the purpose of the escapement which I have invented. When I saw the irregular working of clocks, I understood that the movements shut up in them did not suffice, and that it was necessary to submit them to the regularity of some independent force. I then thought that the balance-wheel might accomplish this, and I succeeded in regulating the movement! Now, was it not a sublime idea that came to me, to return to it its lost force by the action of the clock itself, which it was charged with regulating?"

Aubert made a sign of assent.

"Now, Aubert," continued the old man, growing animated, "cast thine eyes upon thyself! Dost thou not understand that there are two distinct forces in us, that of the soul and that of the body—that is, a movement and a regulator? The soul is the principle of life; that is, then, the movement. Whether it is produced by a weight, by a spring, or by an immaterial influence, it is none the less in the heart. But without the body this movement would be unequal, irregular, impossible! Thus the body regulates the soul, and, like the balance-wheel, it is submitted to regular oscillations. And this is so true, that one falls ill when one's drink, food, sleep—in a word, the functions of the body—are not properly regulated; just as in my watches the soul renders to the body the force lost by its oscillations. Well, what produces this intimate union between soul and body, if not a marvellous escapement, by which the wheels of the one work into the wheels of the other? This is what I have discovered and applied; and there are no longer any secrets for me in this life, which is, after all, only an ingenious mechanism!"

Master Zacharius looked sublime in this hallucination, which carried him to the ultimate mysteries of the Infinite. But his daughter Gerande, standing on the threshold of the door, had heard all. She rushed into her father's arms, and he pressed her convulsively to his breast.

"What is the matter with thee, my daughter?" he asked.

"If I had only a spring here," said she, putting her hand on her heart, "I would not love you as I do, father."

Master Zacharius looked intently at Gerande, and did not reply. Suddenly he uttered a cry, carried his hand eagerly to his heart, and fell fainting on his old leathern chair.

"Father, what is the matter?"

"Help!" cried Aubert. "Scholastique!"

But Scholastique did not come at once. Someone was knocking at the front door; she had gone to open it, and when she returned to the shop, before she could open her mouth, the old watchmaker, having recovered his senses, spoke:—

"I divine, my old Scholastique, that you bring me still another of those accursed watches which have stopped."

"Lord, it is true enough!" replied Scholastique, handing a watch to Aubert.

"My heart could not be mistaken!" said the old man, with a sigh.

Meanwhile Aubert carefully wound up the watch, but it would not go.

A Strange Visit

Poor Gerande would have lost her life with that of her father, had it not been for the thought of Aubert, who still attached her to the world.

The old watchmaker was, little by little, passing away. His faculties evidently grew more feeble, as he concentrated them on a single thought. By a sad association of ideas, he referred everything to his monomania, and a human existence seemed to have departed from him, to give place to the extra-natural existence of the intermediate powers. Moreover, certain malicious rivals revived the sinister rumours which had spread concerning his labours.

The news of the strange derangements which his watches betrayed had a prodigious effect upon the master clockmakers of Geneva. What signified this sudden paralysis of their wheels, and why these strange relations which they seemed to have with the old man's life? These were the kind of mysteries which people never contemplate without a secret terror. In the various classes of the town, from the apprentice to the great lord who used the watches of the old horologist, there was no one who could not himself judge of the singularity of the fact. The citizens wished, but in vain, to get to see Master Zacharius. He fell very ill; and this enabled his daughter to withdraw him from those incessant visits which had degenerated into reproaches and recriminations.

Medicines and physicians were powerless in presence of this organic wasting away, the cause of which could not be discovered. It sometimes seemed as if the old man's heart had ceased to beat; then the pulsations were resumed with an alarming irregularity.

A custom existed in those days of publicly exhibiting the works of the masters. The heads of the various corporations sought to distinguish themselves by the novelty or the perfection of their productions; and it was among these that the condition of Master Zacharius excited the most lively, because most interested, commiseration. His rivals pitied him the more willingly because they feared him the less. They never forgot the old man's success, when he exhibited his magnificent clocks with moving figures, his repeaters, which provoked general admiration, and commanded such high prices in the cities of France, Switzerland, and Germany.

Meanwhile, thanks to the constant and tender care of Gerande and Aubert, his strength seemed to return a little; and in the tranquillity in which his convalescence left him, he succeeded in detaching himself from the thoughts which had absorbed him. As soon as he could walk, his daughter lured him away from the house, which was still besieged with dissatisfied customers. Aubert remained in the shop, vainly adjusting and readjusting the rebel watches; and the poor boy, completely mystified, sometimes covered his face with his hands, fearful that he, like his master, might go mad.

Gerande led her father towards the more pleasant promenades of the town. With his arm resting on hers, she conducted him sometimes through the quarter of Saint Antoine, the view from which extends towards the Cologny hill, and over the lake; on fine mornings they caught sight of the gigantic peaks of Mount Buet against the horizon. Gerande pointed out these spots to her father, who had well-nigh forgotten even their names. His memory wandered; and he took a childish interest in learning anew what had passed from his mind. Master Zacharius leaned upon his daughter; and the two heads, one white as snow and the other covered with rich golden tresses, met in the same ray of sunlight.

So it came about that the old watchmaker at last perceived that he was not alone in the world. As he looked upon his young and lovely daughter, and on himself old and broken, he reflected that after his death she would be left alone without support. Many of the young mechanics of Geneva had already sought to win Gerande's love; but none of them had succeeded in gaining access to the impenetrable retreat of the watchmaker's household. It was natural, then, that during this lucid interval, the old man's choice should fall on Aubert Thun. Once struck with this thought, he remarked to himself that this young couple had been brought up with the same ideas and the same beliefs; and the oscillations of their hearts seemed to him, as he said one day to Scholastique, "isochronous."

The old servant, literally delighted with the word, though she did not understand it, swore by her holy patron saint that the whole town should hear it within a quarter of an hour. Master Zacharius found it difficult to calm her; but made her promise to keep on this subject a silence which she never was known to observe.

So, though Gerande and Aubert were ignorant of it, all Geneva was soon talking of their speedy union. But it happened also that, while the worthy folk were gossiping, a strange chuckle was often heard, and a voice saying, "Gerande will not wed Aubert."

If the talkers turned round, they found themselves facing a little old man who was quite a stranger to them.

How old was this singular being? No one could have told. People conjectured that he must have existed for several centuries, and that was all. His big flat head rested upon shoulders the width of which was equal to the height of his body; this was not above three feet. This personage would have made a good figure to support a pendulum, for the dial would have naturally been placed on his face, and the balance-wheel would have oscillated at its ease in his chest. His nose might readily have been taken for the style of a sun-dial, for it was narrow and sharp; his teeth, far apart, resembled the cogs of a wheel, and ground themselves between his lips; his voice had the metallic sound of a bell, and you could hear his heart beat like the tick of a clock. This little man, whose arms moved like the hands on a dial, walked with jerks, without ever turning round. If anyone followed him, it was found that he walked a league an hour, and that his course was nearly circular.

This strange being had not long been seen wandering, or rather circulating, around the town; but it had already been observed that, every day, at the moment when the sun passed the meridian, he stopped before the Cathedral of Saint Pierre, and resumed his course after the twelve strokes of noon had sounded. Excepting at this precise moment, he seemed to become a part of all the conversations in which the old watchmaker was talked of; and people asked each other, in terror, what relation could exist between him and Master Zacharius. It was remarked, too, that he never lost sight of the old man and his daughter while they were taking their promenades.

One day Gerande perceived this monster looking at her with a hideous smile. She clung to her father with a frightened motion.

"What is the matter, my Gerande?" asked Master Zacharius.

"I do not know," replied the young girl.

"But thou art changed, my child. Art thou going to fall ill in thy turn? Ah, well," he added, with a sad smile, "then I must take care of thee, and I will do it tenderly."

"O father, it will be nothing. I am cold, and I imagine that it is—"

"What, Gerande?"

"The presence of that man, who always follows us," she replied in a low tone.

Master Zacharius turned towards the little old man.

"Faith, he goes well," said he, with a satisfied air, "for it is just four o'clock. Fear nothing, my child; it is not a man, it is a clock!"

Gerande looked at her father in terror. How could Master Zacharius read the hour on this strange creature's visage?

"By-the-bye," continued the old watchmaker, paying no further attention to the matter, "I have not seen Aubert for several days."

"He has not left us, however, father," said Gerande, whose thoughts turned into a gentler channel.

"What is he doing then?"

"He is working."

"Ah!" cried the old man. "He is at work repairing my watches, is he not? But he will never succeed; for it is not repair they need, but a resurrection!"

Gerande remained silent.

"I must know," added the old man, "if they have brought back any more of those accursed watches upon which the Devil has sent this epidemic!"

After these words Master Zacharius fell into complete silence, till he knocked at the door of his house, and for the first time since his convalescence descended to his shop, while Gerande sadly repaired to her chamber.

Just as Master Zacharius crossed the threshold of his shop, one of the many clocks suspended on the wall struck five o'clock. Usually the bells of these clocks—admirably regulated as they were—struck simultaneously, and this rejoiced the old man's heart; but on this day the bells struck one after another, so that for a quarter of an hour the ear was deafened by the successive noises. Master Zacharius suffered acutely; he could not remain still, but went from one clock to the other, and beat the time to them, like a conductor who no longer has control over his musicians.

When the last had ceased striking, the door of the shop opened, and Master Zacharius shuddered from head to foot to see before him the little old man, who looked fixedly at him and said,—

"Master, may I not speak with you a few moments?"

"Who are you?" asked the watchmaker abruptly.

"A colleague. It is my business to regulate the sun."

"Ah, you regulate the sun?" replied Master Zacharius eagerly, without wincing. "I can scarcely compliment you upon it. Your sun goes badly, and in order to make ourselves agree with it, we have to keep putting our clocks forward so much or back so much."

"And by the cloven foot," cried this weird personage, "you are right, my master! My sun does not always mark noon at the same moment as your clocks; but some day it will be known that this is because of the inequality of the earth's transfer, and a mean noon will be invented which will regulate this irregularity!"

"Shall I live till then?" asked the old man, with glistening eyes.

"Without doubt," replied the little old man, laughing. "Can you believe that you will ever die?"

"Alas! I am very ill now."

"Ah, let us talk of that. By Beelzebub! that will lead to just what I wish to speak to you about."

Saying this, the strange being leaped upon the old leather chair, and carried his legs one under the other, after the fashion of the bones which the painters of funeral hangings cross beneath death's heads. Then he resumed, in an ironical tone,—

"Let us see, Master Zacharius, what is going on in this good town of Geneva? They say that your health is failing, that your watches have need of a doctor!"

"Ah, do you believe that there is an intimate relation between their existence and mine?" cried Master Zacharius.

"Why, I imagine that these watches have faults, even vices. If these wantons do not preserve a regular conduct, it is right that they should bear the consequences of their irregularity. It seems to me that they have need of reforming a little!"

"What do you call faults?" asked Master Zacharius, reddening at the sarcastic tone in which these words were uttered. "Have they not a right to be proud of their origin?"

"Not too proud, not too proud," replied the little old man. "They bear a celebrated name, and an illustrious signature is graven on their cases, it is true, and theirs is the exclusive privilege of being introduced among the noblest families; but for some time they have got out of order, and you can do nothing in the matter, Master Zacharius; and the stupidest apprentice in Geneva could prove it to you!"

"To me, to me,—Master Zacharius!" cried the old man, with a flush of outraged pride.

"To you, Master Zacharius,—you, who cannot restore life to your watches!"

"But it is because I have a fever, and so have they also!" replied the old man, as a cold sweat broke out upon him.

"Very well, they will die with you, since you cannot impart a little elasticity to their springs."

"Die! No, for you yourself have said it! I cannot die,—I, the first watchmaker in the world; I, who, by means of these pieces and diverse wheels, have been able to regulate the movement with absolute precision! Have I not subjected time to exact laws, and can I not dispose of it like a despot? Before a sublime genius had arranged these wandering hours regularly, in what vast uncertainty was human destiny plunged? At what certain moment could the acts of life be connected with each other? But you, man or devil, whatever you may be, have never considered the magnificence of my art, which calls every science to its aid! No, no! I, Master Zacharius, cannot die, for, as I have regulated time, time would end with me! It would return to the infinite, whence my genius has rescued it, and it would lose itself irreparably in the abyss of nothingness! No, I can no more die than the Creator of this universe, that submitted to His laws! I have become His equal, and I have partaken of His power! If God has created eternity, Master Zacharius has created time!"

The old watchmaker now resembled the fallen angel, defiant in the presence of the Creator. The little old man gazed at him, and even seemed to breathe into him this impious transport.

"Well said, master," he replied. "Beelzebub had less right than you to compare himself with God! Your glory must not perish! So your servant here desires to give you the method of controlling these rebellious watches."

"What is it? what is it?" cried Master Zacharius.

"You shall know on the day after that on which you have given me your daughter's hand."

"My Gerande?"

"Herself!"

"My daughter's heart is not free," replied Master Zacharius, who seemed neither astonished nor shocked at the strange demand.

"Bah! She is not the least beautiful of watches; but she will end by stopping also—"

"My daughter,—my Gerande! No!"

"Well, return to your watches, Master Zacharius. Adjust and readjust them. Get ready the marriage of your daughter and your apprentice. Temper your springs with your best steel. Bless Aubert and the pretty Gerande. But remember, your watches will never go, and Gerande will not wed Aubert!"

Thereupon the little old man disappeared, but not so quickly that Master Zacharius could not hear six o'clock strike in his breast.

The Church of Saint Pierre

Meanwhile Master Zacharius became more feeble in mind and body every day. An unusual excitement, indeed, impelled him to continue his work more eagerly than ever, nor could his daughter entice him from it.

His pride was still more aroused after the crisis to which his strange visitor had hurried him so treacherously, and he resolved to overcome, by the force of genius, the malign influence which weighed upon his work and himself. He first repaired to the various clocks of the town which were confided to his care. He made sure, by a scrupulous examination, that the wheels were in good condition, the pivots firm, the weights exactly balanced. Every part, even to the bells, was examined with the minute attention of a physician studying the breast of a patient. Nothing indicated that these clocks were on the point of being affected by inactivity.

Gerande and Aubert often accompanied the old man on these visits. He would no doubt have been pleased to see them eager to go with him, and certainly he would not have been so much absorbed in his approaching end, had he thought that his existence was to be prolonged by that of these cherished ones, and had he understood that something of the life of a father always remains in his children.

The old watchmaker, on returning home, resumed his labours with feverish zeal. Though persuaded that he would not succeed, it yet seemed to him impossible that this could be so, and he unceasingly took to pieces the watches which were brought to his shop, and put them together again.

Aubert tortured his mind in vain to discover the causes of the evil.

"Master," said he, "this can only come from the wear of the pivots and gearing."

"Do you want, then, to kill me, little by little?" replied Master Zacharius passionately. "Are these watches child's work? Was it lest I should hurt my fingers that I worked the surface of these copper pieces in the lathe? Have I not forged these pieces of copper myself, so as to obtain a greater strength? Are not these springs tempered to a rare perfection? Could anybody have used finer oils than mine? You must yourself agree that it is impossible, and you avow, in short, that the devil is in it!"

From morning till night discontented purchasers besieged the house, and they got access to the old watchmaker himself, who knew not which of them to listen to.

"This watch loses, and I cannot succeed in regulating it," said one.

"This," said another, "is absolutely obstinate, and stands still, as did Joshua's sun."

"If it is true," said most of them, "that your health has an influence on that of your watches, Master Zacharius, get well as soon as possible."

The old man gazed at these people with haggard eyes, and only replied by shaking his head, or by a few sad words,—

"Wait till the first fine weather, my friends. The season is coming which revives existence in wearied bodies. We want the sun to warm us all!"

"A fine thing, if my watches are to be ill through the winter!" said one of the most angry. "Do you know, Master Zacharius, that your name is inscribed in full on their faces? By the Virgin, you do little honour to your signature!"

JULES VERNE

It happened at last that the old man, abashed by these reproaches, took some pieces of gold from his old trunk, and began to buy back the damaged watches. At news of this, the customers came in a crowd, and the poor watchmaker's money fast melted away; but his honesty remained intact. Gerande warmly praised his delicacy, which was leading him straight towards ruin; and Aubert soon offered his own savings to his master.

"What will become of my daughter?" said Master Zacharius, clinging now and then in the shipwreck to his paternal love.

Aubert dared not answer that he was full of hope for the future, and of deep devotion to Gerande. Master Zacharius would have that day called him his son-in-law, and thus refuted the sad prophecy, which still buzzed in his ears,—

"Gerande will not wed Aubert."

By this plan the watchmaker at last succeeded in entirely despoiling himself. His antique vases passed into the hands of strangers; he deprived himself of the richly-carved panels which adorned the walls of his house; some primitive pictures of the early Flemish painters soon ceased to please his daughter's eyes, and everything, even the precious tools that his genius had invented, were sold to indemnify the clamorous customers.

Scholastique alone refused to listen to reason on the subject; but her efforts failed to prevent the unwelcome visitors from reaching her master, and from soon departing with some valuable object. Then her chattering was heard in all the streets of the neighbourhood, where she had long been known. She eagerly denied the rumours of sorcery and magic on the part of Master Zacharius, which gained currency; but as at bottom she was persuaded of their truth, she said her prayers over and over again to redeem her pious falsehoods.

It had been noticed that for some time the old watchmaker had neglected his religious duties. Time was, when he had accompanied

Gerande to church, and had seemed to find in prayer the intellectual charm which it imparts to thoughtful minds, since it is the most sublime exercise of the imagination. This voluntary neglect of holy practices, added to the secret habits of his life, had in some sort confirmed the accusations levelled against his labours. So, with the double purpose of drawing her father back to God, and to the world, Gerande resolved to call religion to her aid. She thought that it might give some vitality to his dying soul; but the dogmas of faith and humility had to combat, in the soul of Master Zacharius, an insurmountable pride, and came into collision with that vanity of science which connects everything with itself, without rising to the infinite source whence first principles flow.

It was under these circumstances that the young girl undertook her father's conversion; and her influence was so effective that the old watchmaker promised to attend high mass at the cathedral on the following Sunday. Gerande was in an ecstasy, as if heaven had opened to her view. Old Scholastique could not contain her joy, and at last found irrefutable arguments' against the gossiping tongues which accused her master of impiety. She spoke of it to her neighbours, her friends, her enemies, to those whom she knew not as well as to those whom she knew.

"In faith, we scarcely believe what you tell us, dame Scholastique," they replied; "Master Zacharius has always acted in concert with the devil!"

"You haven't counted, then," replied the old servant, "the fine bells which strike for my master's clocks? How many times they have struck the hours of prayer and the mass!"

"No doubt," they would reply. "But has he not invented machines which go all by themselves, and which actually do the work of a real man?"

"Could a child of the devil," exclaimed dame Scholastique wrathfully, "have executed the fine iron clock of the chateau of

Andernatt, which the town of Geneva was not rich enough to buy? A pious motto appeared at each hour, and a Christian who obeyed them, would have gone straight to Paradise! Is that the work of the devil?"

This masterpiece, made twenty years before, had carried Master Zacharius's fame to its acme; but even then there had been accusations of sorcery against him. But at least the old man's visit to the Cathedral ought to reduce malicious tongues to silence.

Master Zacharius, having doubtless forgotten the promise made to his daughter, had returned to his shop. After being convinced of his powerlessness to give life to his watches, he resolved to try if he could not make some new ones. He abandoned all those useless works, and devoted himself to the completion of the crystal watch, which he intended to be his masterpiece; but in vain did he use his most perfect tools, and employ rubies and diamonds for resisting friction. The watch fell from his hands the first time that he attempted to wind it up!

The old man concealed this circumstance from everyone, even from his daughter; but from that time his health rapidly declined. There were only the last oscillations of a pendulum, which goes slower when nothing restores its original force. It seemed as if the laws of gravity, acting directly upon him, were dragging him irresistibly down to the grave.

The Sunday so ardently anticipated by Gerande at last arrived. The weather was fine, and the temperature inspiriting. The people of Geneva were passing quietly through the streets, gaily chatting about the return of spring. Gerande, tenderly taking the old man's arm, directed her steps towards the cathedral, while Scholastique followed behind with the prayer-books. People looked curiously at them as they passed. The old watchmaker permitted himself to be led like a child, or rather like a blind man. The faithful of Saint Pierre were almost frightened when they saw him cross the threshold, and shrank back at his approach.

The chants of high mass were already resounding through the church. Gerande went to her accustomed bench, and kneeled with profound and simple reverence. Master Zacharius remained standing upright beside her.

The ceremonies continued with the majestic solemnity of that faithful age, but the old man had no faith. He did not implore the pity of Heaven with cries of anguish of the "Kyrie;" he did not, with the "Gloria in Excelsis," sing the splendours of the heavenly heights; the reading of the Testament did not draw him from his materialistic reverie, and he forgot to join in the homage of the "Credo." This proud old man remained motionless, as insensible and silent as a stone statue; and even at the solemn moment when the bell announced the miracle of transubstantiation, he did not bow his head, but gazed directly at the sacred host which the priest raised above the heads of the faithful. Gerande looked at her father, and a flood of tears moistened her missal. At this moment the clock of Saint Pierre struck half-past eleven. Master Zacharius turned quickly towards this ancient clock which still spoke. It seemed to him as if its face was gazing steadily at him; the figures of the hours shone as if they had been engraved in lines of fire, and the hands shot forth electric sparks from their sharp points.

The mass ended. It was customary for the "Angelus" to be said at noon, and the priests, before leaving the altar, waited for the clock to strike the hour of twelve. In a few moments this prayer would ascend to the feet of the Virgin.

But suddenly a harsh noise was heard. Master Zacharius uttered a piercing cry.

The large hand of the clock, having reached twelve, had abruptly stopped, and the clock did not strike the hour.

Gerande hastened to her father's aid. He had fallen down motionless, and they carried him outside the church.

"It is the death-blow!" murmured Gerande, sobbing.

When he had been borne home, Master Zacharius lay upon his bed utterly crushed. Life seemed only to still exist on the surface of his body, like the last whiffs of smoke about a lamp just extinguished. When he came to his senses, Aubert and Gerande were leaning over him. In these last moments the future took in his eyes the shape of the present. He saw his daughter alone, without a protector.

"My son," said he to Aubert, "I give my daughter to thee."

So saying, he stretched out his hands towards his two children, who were thus united at his death-bed.

But soon Master Zacharius lifted himself up in a paroxysm of rage. The words of the little old man recurred to his mind.

"I do not wish to die!" he cried; "I cannot die! I, Master Zacharius, ought not to die! My books—my accounts!—"

With these words he sprang from his bed towards a book in which the names of his customers and the articles which had been sold to them were inscribed. He seized it and rapidly turned over its leaves, and his emaciated finger fixed itself on one of the pages.

"There!" he cried, "there! this old iron clock, sold to Pittonaccio! It is the only one that has not been returned to me! It still exists—it goes—it lives! Ah, I wish for it—I must find it! I will take such care of it that death will no longer seek me!"

And he fainted away.

Aubert and Gerande knelt by the old man's bed-side and prayed together.

The Hour of Death

Several days passed, and Master Zacharius, though almost dead, rose from his bed and returned to active life under a supernatural excitement. He lived by pride. But Gerande did not deceive herself; her father's body and soul were for ever lost.

The old man got together his last remaining resources, without thought of those who were dependent upon him. He betrayed an incredible energy, walking, ferreting about, and mumbling strange, incomprehensible words.

One morning Gerande went down to his shop. Master Zacharius was not there. She waited for him all day. Master Zacharius did not return.

Gerande wept bitterly, but her father did not reappear.

Aubert searched everywhere through the town, and soon came to the sad conviction that the old man had left it.

"Let us find my father!" cried Gerande, when the young apprentice told her this sad news.

"Where can he be?" Aubert asked himself.

An inspiration suddenly came to his mind. He remembered the last words which Master Zacharius had spoken. The old man only lived now in the old iron clock that had not been returned! Master Zacharius must have gone in search of it.

Aubert spoke of this to Gerande.

"Let us look at my father's book," she replied.

They descended to the shop. The book was open on the bench. All the watches or clocks made by the old man, and which had been returned to him because they were out of order, were stricken out excepting one:—

"Sold to M. Pittonaccio, an iron clock, with bell and moving figures; sent to his chateau at Andernatt."

It was this "moral" clock of which Scholastique had spoken with so much enthusiasm.

"My father is there!" cried Gerande.

"Let us hasten thither," replied Aubert. "We may still save him!"

"Not for this life," murmured Gerande, "but at least for the other."

"By the mercy of God, Gerande! The chateau of Andernatt stands in the gorge of the 'Dents-du-Midi' twenty hours from Geneva. Let us go!"

That very evening Aubert and Gerande, followed by the old servant, set out on foot by the road which skirts Lake Leman. They accomplished five leagues during the night, stopping neither at Bessinge nor at Ermance, where rises the famous chateau of the Mayors. They with difficulty forded the torrent of the Dranse, and everywhere they went they inquired for Master Zacharius, and were soon convinced that they were on his track.

The next morning, at daybreak, having passed Thonon, they reached Evian, whence the Swiss territory may be seen extended over twelve leagues. But the two betrothed did not even perceive the enchanting prospect. They went straight forward, urged on by a supernatural force. Aubert, leaning on a knotty stick, offered his arm alternately to Gerande and to Scholastique, and he made the greatest efforts to sustain his companions. All three talked of their sorrow, of their hopes, and thus passed along the beautiful road by the water-side, and across the narrow plateau which unites the borders of the lake with the heights of the Chalais. They soon reached Bouveret, where the Rhone enters the Lake of Geneva.

On leaving this town they diverged from the lake, and their weariness increased amid these mountain districts. Vionnaz, Chesset, Collombay, half lost villages, were soon left behind.

Meanwhile their knees shook, their feet were lacerated by the sharp points which covered the ground like a brushwood of granite;—but no trace of Master Zacharius!

He must be found, however, and the two young people did not seek repose either in the isolated hamlets or at the chateau of Monthay, which, with its dependencies, formed the appanage of Margaret of Savoy. At last, late in the day, and half dead with fatigue, they reached the hermitage of Notre-Dame-du-Sex, which is situated at the base of the Dents-du-Midi, six hundred feet above the Rhone.

The hermit received the three wanderers as night was falling. They could not have gone another step, and here they must needs rest.

The hermit could give them no news of Master Zacharius. They could scarcely hope to find him still living amid these sad solitudes. The night was dark, the wind howled amid the mountains, and the avalanches roared down from the summits of the broken crags.

Aubert and Gerande, crouching before the hermit's hearth, told him their melancholy tale. Their mantles, covered with snow, were drying in a corner; and without, the hermit's dog barked lugubriously, and mingled his voice with that of the tempest.

"Pride," said the hermit to his guests, "has destroyed an angel created for good. It is the stumbling-block against which the destinies of man strike. You cannot reason with pride, the principal of all the vices, since, by its very nature, the proud man refuses to listen to it. It only remains, then, to pray for your father!"

All four knelt down, when the barking of the dog redoubled, and someone knocked at the door of the hermitage.

"Open, in the devil's name!"

The door yielded under the blows, and a dishevelled, haggard, ill-clothed man appeared.

"My father!" cried Gerande.

It was Master Zacharius.

"Where am I?" said he. "In eternity! Time is ended—the hours no longer strike—the hands have stopped!"

"Father!" returned Gerande, with so piteous an emotion that the old man seemed to return to the world of the living.

"Thou here, Gerande?" he cried; "and thou, Aubert? Ah, my dear betrothed ones, you are going to be married in our old church!"

"Father," said Gerande, seizing him by the arm, "come home to Geneva,—come with us!"

The old man tore away from his daughter's embrace and hurried towards the door, on the threshold of which the snow was falling in large flakes.

"Do not abandon your children!" cried Aubert.

"Why return," replied the old man sadly, "to those places which my life has already quitted, and where a part of myself is forever buried?"

"Your soul is not dead," said the hermit solemnly.

"My soul? O no,—its wheels are good! I perceive it beating regularly—"

"Your soul is immaterial,—your soul is immortal!" replied the hermit sternly.

"Yes—like my glory! But it is shut up in the chateau of Andernatt, and I wish to see it again!"

The hermit crossed himself; Scholastique became almost inanimate. Aubert held Gerande in his arms.

"The chateau of Andernatt is inhabited by one who is lost," said the hermit, "one who does not salute the cross of my hermitage."

"My father, go not thither!"

"I want my soul! My soul is mine—"

"Hold him! Hold my father!" cried Gerande.

But the old man had leaped across the threshold, and plunged into the night, crying, "Mine, mine, my soul!"

Gerande, Aubert, and Scholastique hastened after him. They went by difficult paths, across which Master Zacharius sped like a tempest, urged by an irresistible force. The snow raged around them, and mingled its white flakes with the froth of the swollen torrents.

As they passed the chapel erected in memory of the massacre of the Theban legion, they hurriedly crossed themselves. Master Zacharius was not to be seen.

At last the village of Evionnaz appeared in the midst of this sterile region. The hardest heart would have been moved to see this hamlet, lost among these horrible solitudes. The old man sped on, and plunged into the deepest gorge of the Dents-du-Midi, which pierce the sky with their sharp peaks.

Soon a ruin, old and gloomy as the rocks at its base, rose before him.

"It is there—there!" he cried, hastening his pace still more frantically.

The chateau of Andernatt was a ruin even then. A thick, crumbling tower rose above it, and seemed to menace with its downfall the old gables which reared themselves below. The vast piles of jagged stones were gloomy to look on. Several dark halls appeared amid the debris, with caved-in ceilings, now become the abode of vipers.

A low and narrow postern, opening upon a ditch choked with rubbish, gave access to the chateau. Who had dwelt there none knew. No doubt some margrave, half lord, half brigand, had sojourned in it; to the margrave had succeeded bandits or counterfeit coiners, who had been hanged on the scene of their crime. The legend went that, on winter nights, Satan came to lead his diabolical dances on the slope of the deep gorges in which the shadow of these ruins was engulfed.

But Master Zacharius was not dismayed by their sinister aspect. He reached the postern. No one forbade him to pass. A spacious and gloomy court presented itself to his eyes; no one forbade him to cross it. He passed along the kind of inclined plane which conducted to one of the long corridors, whose arches seemed to banish daylight from beneath their heavy springings. His advance was unresisted. Gerande, Aubert, and Scholastique closely followed him.

Master Zacharius, as if guided by an irresistible hand, seemed sure of his way, and strode along with rapid step. He reached an old worm-eaten door, which fell before his blows, whilst the bats described oblique circles around his head.

An immense hall, better preserved than the rest, was soon reached. High sculptured panels, on which serpents, ghouls, and other strange figures seemed to disport themselves confusedly, covered its walls. Several long and narrow windows, like loopholes, shivered beneath the bursts of the tempest.

Master Zacharius, on reaching the middle of this hall, uttered a cry of joy.

On an iron support, fastened to the wall, stood the clock in which now resided his entire life. This unequalled masterpiece represented an ancient Roman church, with buttresses of wrought iron, with its heavy bell-tower, where there was a complete chime for the anthem of the day, the "Angelus," the mass, vespers, compline, and the benediction. Above the church door, which opened at the hour of the services, was placed a "rose," in the centre of which two hands moved, and the archivault of which reproduced the twelve hours of the face sculptured in relief. Between the door and the rose, just as Scholastique had said, a maxim, relative to the employment of every moment of the day, appeared on a copper plate. Master

Zacharius had once regulated this succession of devices with a really Christian solicitude; the hours of prayer, of work, of repast, of recreation, and of repose, followed each other according to the religious discipline, and were to infallibly insure salvation to him who scrupulously observed their commands.

Master Zacharius, intoxicated with joy, went forward to take possession of the clock, when a frightful roar of laughter resounded behind him.

He turned, and by the light of a smoky lamp recognized the little old man of Geneva.

"You here?" cried he.

Gerande was afraid. She drew closer to Aubert.

"Good-day, Master Zacharius," said the monster.

"Who are you?"

"Signor Pittonaccio, at your service! You have come to give me your daughter! You have remembered my words, 'Gerande will not wed Aubert.'"

The young apprentice rushed upon Pittonaccio, who escaped from him like a shadow.

"Stop, Aubert!" cried Master Zacharius.

"Good-night," said Pittonaccio, and he disappeared.

"My father, let us fly from this hateful place!" cried Gerande. "My father!"

Master Zacharius was no longer there. He was pursuing the phantom of Pittonaccio across the rickety corridors. Scholastique, Gerande, and Aubert remained, speechless and fainting, in the large gloomy hall. The young girl had fallen upon a stone seat; the old servant knelt beside her, and prayed; Aubert remained erect, watching his betrothed. Pale lights wandered in the darkness, and the silence was only broken by the movements of the little animals which live in old wood, and the noise of which marks the hours of "death watch."

When daylight came, they ventured upon the endless staircase which wound beneath these ruined masses; for two hours they wandered thus without meeting a living soul, and hearing only a far-off echo responding to their cries. Sometimes they found themselves buried a hundred feet below the ground, and sometimes they reached places whence they could overlook the wild mountains.

Chance brought them at last back again to the vast hall, which had sheltered them during this night of anguish. It was no longer empty. Master Zacharius and Pittonaccio were talking there together, the one upright and rigid as a corpse, the other crouching over a marble table.

Master Zacharius, when he perceived Gerande, went forward and took her by the hand, and led her towards Pittonaccio, saying, "Behold your lord and master, my daughter. Gerande, behold your husband!"

Gerande shuddered from head to foot.

"Never!" cried Aubert, "for she is my betrothed."

"Never!" responded Gerande, like a plaintive echo.

Pittonaccio began to laugh.

"You wish me to die, then!" exclaimed the old man. "There, in that clock, the last which goes of all which have gone from my hands, my life is shut up; and this man tells me, 'When I have thy daughter, this clock shall belong to thee.' And this man will not rewind it. He can break it, and plunge me into chaos. Ah, my daughter, you no longer love me!"

"My father!" murmured Gerande, recovering consciousness.

"If you knew what I have suffered, far away from this principle of my existence!" resumed the old man. "Perhaps no one looked after this timepiece. Perhaps its springs were left to wear out, its wheels to get clogged. But now, in my own hands, I can nourish this health so dear, for I must not die,—I, the great watchmaker of Geneva. Look, my daughter, how these hands advance with certain step. See, five o'clock is about to strike. Listen well, and look at the maxim which is about to be revealed."

Five o'clock struck with a noise which resounded sadly in Gerande's soul, and these words appeared in red letters:

"YOU MUST EAT OF THE FRUITS OF THE TREE OF SCIENCE."

Aubert and Gerande looked at each other stupefied. These were no longer the pious sayings of the Catholic watchmaker. The breath of Satan must have passed over it. But Zacharius paid no attention to this, and resumed—

"Dost thou hear, my Gerande? I live, I still live! Listen to my breathing,—see the blood circulating in my veins! No, thou wouldst not kill thy father, and thou wilt accept this man for thy husband, so that I may become immortal, and at last attain the power of God!"

At these blasphemous words old Scholastique crossed herself, and Pittonaccio laughed aloud with joy.

"And then, Gerande, thou wilt be happy with him. See this man,—he is Time! Thy existence will be regulated with absolute precision. Gerande, since I gave thee life, give life to thy father!"

"Gerande," murmured Aubert, "I am thy betrothed."

"He is my father!" replied Gerande, fainting.

"She is thine!" said Master Zacharius. "Pittonaccio, them wilt keep thy promise!"

"Here is the key of the clock," replied the horrible man.

Master Zacharius seized the long key, which resembled an uncoiled snake, and ran to the clock, which he hastened to wind up with fantastic rapidity. The creaking of the spring jarred upon the nerves. The old watchmaker wound and wound the key, without stopping a moment, and it seemed as if the movement were beyond his control. He wound more and more quickly, with strange contortions, until he fell from sheer weariness.

"There, it is wound up for a century!" he cried.

Aubert rushed from the hall as if he were mad. After long wandering, he found the outlet of the hateful chateau, and hastened into the open air. He returned to the hermitage of Notre-Dame-du-Sex, and talked so despairingly to the holy recluse, that the latter consented to return with him to the chateau of Andernatt.

If, during these hours of anguish, Gerande had not wept, it was because her tears were exhausted.

Master Zacharius had not left the hall. He ran every moment to listen to the regular beating of the old clock.

Meanwhile the clock had struck, and to Scholastique's great terror, these words had appeared on the silver face:—"MAN OUGHT TO BECOME THE EQUAL OF GOD."

The old man had not only not been shocked by these impious maxims, but read them deliriously, and flattered himself with thoughts of pride, whilst Pittonaccio kept close by him.

The marriage-contract was to be signed at midnight. Gerande, almost unconscious, saw or heard nothing. The silence was only broken by the old man's words, and the chuckling of Pittonaccio.

Eleven o'clock struck. Master Zacharius shuddered, and read in a loud voice:—

"MAN SHOULD BE THE SLAVE OF SCIENCE, AND
SACRIFICE TO IT RELATIVES AND FAMILY."

"Yes!" he cried, "there is nothing but science in this world!"

The hands slipped over the face of the clock with the hiss of a serpent, and the pendulum beat with accelerated strokes.

Master Zacharius no longer spoke. He had fallen to the floor, his throat rattled, and from his oppressed bosom came only these half-broken words: "Life—science!"

The scene had now two new witnesses, the hermit and Aubert. Master Zacharius lay upon the floor; Gerande was praying beside him, more dead than alive.

Of a sudden a dry, hard noise was heard, which preceded the strike.

Master Zacharius sprang up.

"Midnight!" he cried.

The hermit stretched out his hand towards the old clock,—and midnight did not sound.

Master Zacharius uttered a terrible cry, which must have been heard in hell, when these words appeared:—

"WHO EVER SHALL ATTEMPT TO MAKE HIMSELF THE EQUAL OF GOD, SHALL BE FOR EVER DAMNED!"

The old clock burst with a noise like thunder, and the spring, escaping, leaped across the hall with a thousand fantastic contortions; the old man rose, ran after it, trying in vain to seize it, and exclaiming, "My soul,—my soul!"

The spring bounded before him, first on one side, then on the other, and he could not reach it.

At last Pittonaccio seized it, and, uttering a horrible blasphemy, ingulfed himself in the earth.

The old watchmaker was buried in the midst of the peaks of Andernatt.

Then Aubert and Gerande returned to Geneva, and during the long life which God accorded to them, they made it a duty to redeem by prayer the soul of the castaway of science.

A Drama in the Air

A Drama in the Air

In the month of September, 185—, I arrived at Frankfort-on-the-Maine. My passage through the principal German cities had been brilliantly marked by balloon ascents; but as yet no German had accompanied me in my car, and the fine experiments made at Paris by MM. Green, Eugene Godard, and Poitevin had not tempted the grave Teutons to essay aerial voyages.

But scarcely had the news of my approaching ascent spread through Frankfort, than three of the principal citizens begged the favour of being allowed to ascend with me. Two days afterwards we were to start from the Place de la Comedie. I began at once to get my balloon ready. It was of silk, prepared with gutta percha, a substance impermeable by acids or gasses; and its volume, which was three thousand cubic yards, enabled it to ascend to the loftiest heights.

The day of the ascent was that of the great September fair, which attracts so many people to Frankfort. Lighting gas, of a perfect quality and of great lifting power, had been furnished to me in excellent condition, and about eleven o'clock the balloon was filled; but only three-quarters filled,—an indispensable precaution, for, as one rises, the atmosphere diminishes in density, and the fluid enclosed within the balloon, acquiring more elasticity, might burst its sides. My calculations had furnished me with exactly the quantity of gas necessary to carry up my companions and myself.

We were to start at noon. The impatient crowd which pressed around the enclosed space, filling the enclosed square, overflowing into the contiguous streets, and covering the houses from the ground-floor to the slated gables, presented a striking scene. The high winds of the preceding days had subsided. An oppressive heat fell from the cloudless sky. Scarcely a breath animated the atmosphere. In such weather, one might descend again upon the very spot whence he had risen.

I carried three hundred pounds of ballast in bags; the car, quite round, four feet in diameter, was comfortably arranged; the hempen cords which supported it stretched symmetrically over the upper hemisphere of the balloon; the compass was in place, the barometer suspended in the circle which united the supporting cords, and the anchor carefully put in order. All was now ready for the ascent.

Among those who pressed around the enclosure, I remarked a young man with a pale face and agitated features. The sight of him impressed me. He was an eager spectator of my ascents, whom I had already met in several German cities. With an uneasy air, he closely watched the curious machine, as it lay motionless a few feet above the ground; and he remained silent among those about him.

Twelve o'clock came. The moment had arrived, but my travelling companions did not appear.

I sent to their houses, and learnt that one had left for Hamburg, another for Vienna, and the third for London. Their courage had failed them at the moment of undertaking one of those excursions which, thanks to the ability of living aeronauts, are free from all danger. As they formed, in some sort, a part of the programme of the day, the fear had seized them that they might be forced to execute it faithfully, and they had fled far from the scene at the instant when the balloon was being filled. Their courage was evidently the inverse ratio of their speed—in decamping.

The multitude, half deceived, showed not a little ill-humour. I did not hesitate to ascend alone. In order to re-establish the equilibrium between the specific gravity of the balloon and the weight which had thus proved wanting, I replaced my companions by more sacks of sand, and got into the car. The twelve men who held the balloon by twelve cords fastened to the equatorial circle, let them slip a little between their fingers, and the balloon rose several feet higher. There was not a breath of wind, and the atmosphere was so leaden that it seemed to forbid the ascent.

"Is everything ready?" I cried.

The men put themselves in readiness. A last glance told me that I might go.

"Attention!"

There was a movement in the crowd, which seemed to be invading the enclosure.

"Let go!"

The balloon rose slowly, but I experienced a shock which threw me to the bottom of the car.

When I got up, I found myself face to face with an unexpected fellow-voyager,—the pale young man.

"Monsieur, I salute you," said he, with the utmost coolness.

"By what right—"

"Am I here? By the right which the impossibility of your getting rid of me confers."

I was amazed! His calmness put me out of countenance, and I had nothing to reply. I looked at the intruder, but he took no notice of my astonishment.

"Does my weight disarrange your equilibrium, monsieur?" he asked. "You will permit me—"

And without waiting for my consent, he relieved the balloon of two bags, which he threw into space.

"Monsieur," said I, taking the only course now possible, "you have come; very well, you will remain; but to me alone belongs the management of the balloon."

"Monsieur," said he, "your urbanity is French all over: it comes from my own country. I morally press the hand you refuse me. Make all precautions, and act as seems best to you. I will wait till you have done—"

"For what?"

"To talk with you."

The barometer had fallen to twenty-six inches. We were nearly six hundred yards above the city; but nothing betrayed the horizontal displacement of the balloon, for the mass of air in which it is enclosed goes forward with it. A sort of confused glow enveloped the objects spread out under us, and unfortunately obscured their outline.

I examined my companion afresh.

He was a man of thirty years, simply clad. The sharpness of his features betrayed an indomitable energy, and he seemed very muscular. Indifferent to the astonishment he created, he remained motionless, trying to distinguish the objects which were vaguely confused below us.

"Miserable mist!" said he, after a few moments.

I did not reply.

"You owe me a grudge?" he went on. "Bah! I could not pay for my journey, and it was necessary to take you by surprise."

"Nobody asks you to descend, monsieur!"

"Eh, do you not know, then, that the same thing happened to the Counts of Laurencin and Dampierre, when they ascended at Lyons, on the 15th of January, 1784? A young merchant, named Fontaine, scaled the gallery, at the risk of capsizing the machine. He accomplished the journey, and nobody died of it!"

"Once on the ground, we will have an explanation," replied I, piqued at the light tone in which he spoke.

"Bah! Do not let us think of our return."

"Do you think, then, that I shall not hasten to descend?"

"Descend!" said he, in surprise. "Descend? Let us begin by first ascending."

And before I could prevent it, two more bags had been thrown over the car, without even having been emptied.

"Monsieur!" cried I, in a rage.

"I know your ability," replied the unknown quietly, "and your fine ascents are famous. But if Experience is the sister of Practice, she is also a cousin of Theory, and I have studied the aerial art long. It has got into my head!" he added sadly, falling into a silent reverie.

The balloon, having risen some distance farther, now became stationary. The unknown consulted the barometer, and said,—

"Here we are, at eight hundred yards. Men are like insects. See! I think we should always contemplate them from this height, to judge correctly of their proportions. The Place de la Comedie is transformed into an immense ant-hill. Observe the crowd which is gathered on the quays; and the mountains also get smaller and smaller. We are over the Cathedral. The Main is only a line, cutting the city in two, and the bridge seems a thread thrown between the two banks of the river."

The atmosphere became somewhat chilly.

"There is nothing I would not do for you, my host," said the unknown. "If you are cold, I will take off my coat and lend it to you."

"Thanks," said I dryly.

"Bah! Necessity makes law. Give me your hand. I am your fellow-countryman; you will learn something in my company, and my conversation will indemnify you for the trouble I have given you."

I sat down, without replying, at the opposite extremity of the car. The young man had taken a voluminous manuscript from his great-coat. It was an essay on ballooning.

"I possess," said he, "the most curious collection of engravings and caricatures extant concerning aerial manias. How people admired and scoffed at the same time at this precious discovery! We are happily no longer in the age in which Montgolfier tried to make artificial clouds with steam, or a gas having electrical properties, produced by the combustion of moist straw and chopped-up wool."

"Do you wish to depreciate the talent of the inventors?" I asked, for I had resolved to enter into the adventure. "Was it not good to have proved by experience the possibility of rising in the air?"

"Ah, monsieur, who denies the glory of the first aerial navigators? It required immense courage to rise by means of those frail envelopes which only contained heated air. But I ask you, has the aerial science made great progress since Blanchard's ascensions, that is, since nearly a century ago? Look here, monsieur."

The unknown took an engraving from his portfolio.

"Here," said he, "is the first aerial voyage undertaken by Pilatre des Rosiers and the Marquis d'Arlandes, four months after the discovery of balloons. Louis XVI refused to consent to the venture, and two men who were condemned to death were the first to attempt the aerial ascent. Pilatre des Rosiers became indignant at this injustice, and, by means of intrigues, obtained permission to make the experiment. The car, which renders the management easy, had not then been invented, and a circular gallery was placed around the lower and contracted part of the Montgolfier balloon. The two aeronauts must then remain motionless at each extremity of this gallery, for the moist straw which filled it forbade them all motion. A chafing-dish with fire was suspended below the orifice of the balloon; when the aeronauts wished to rise, they threw straw upon this brazier, at the risk of setting fire to the balloon, and the air, more heated, gave it fresh ascending power. The two bold travellers rose, on the 21st of November, 1783, from the Muette Gardens, which the dauphin had put at their disposal. The balloon went up majestically, passed over the Isle of Swans, crossed the Seine at the Conference barrier, and, drifting between the dome of the Invalides and the Military School, approached the Church of Saint Sulpice. Then the aeronauts added to the fire, crossed the Boulevard, and descended beyond the Enfer barrier. As it touched the soil, the balloon collapsed, and for a few moments buried Pilatre des Rosiers under its folds."

"Unlucky augury," I said, interested in the story, which affected me nearly.

"An augury of the catastrophe which was later to cost this unfortunate man his life," replied the unknown sadly. "Have you never experienced anything like it?"

"Never."

"Bah! Misfortunes sometimes occur unforeshadowed!" added my companion.

He then remained silent.

Meanwhile we were advancing southward, and Frankfort had already passed from beneath us.

"Perhaps we shall have a storm," said the young man.

"We shall descend before that," I replied.

"Indeed! It is better to ascend. We shall escape it more surely."

And two more bags of sand were hurled into space.

The balloon rose rapidly, and stopped at twelve hundred yards. I became colder; and yet the sun's rays, falling upon the surface, expanded the gas within, and gave it a greater ascending force.

"Fear nothing," said the unknown. "We have still three thousand five hundred fathoms of breathing air. Besides, do not trouble yourself about what I do."

I would have risen, but a vigorous hand held me to my seat.

"Your name?" I asked.

"My name? What matters it to you?"

"I demand your name!"

"My name is Erostratus or Empedocles, whichever you choose!"

This reply was far from reassuring.

The unknown, besides, talked with such strange coolness that I anxiously asked myself whom I had to deal with.

"Monsieur," he continued, "nothing original has been imagined since the physicist Charles. Four months after the discovery of balloons, this able man had invented the valve, which permits the gas to escape when the balloon is too full, or when you wish to descend; the car, which aids the management of the machine; the netting, which holds the envelope of the balloon, and divides the weight over its whole surface; the ballast, which enables you to ascend, and to choose the place of your landing; the India-rubber coating, which renders the tissue impermeable; the barometer, which shows the height attained. Lastly, Charles used hydrogen, which, fourteen times lighter than air, permits you to penetrate to the highest atmospheric regions, and does not expose you to the dangers of a combustion in the air. On the 1st of December, 1783, three hundred thousand spectators were crowded around the Tuileries. Charles rose, and the soldiers presented arms to him. He travelled nine leagues in the air, conducting his balloon with an ability not surpassed by modern aeronauts. The king awarded him a pension of two thousand livres; for then they encouraged new inventions."

The unknown now seemed to be under the influence of considerable agitation.

"Monsieur," he resumed, "I have studied this, and I am convinced that the first aeronauts guided their balloons. Without speaking of Blanchard, whose assertions may be received with doubt, Guyton-Morveaux, by the aid of oars and rudder, made his machine answer to the helm, and take the direction he determined on. More recently, M. Julien, a watchmaker, made some convincing experiments at the Hippodrome, in Paris; for, by a special mechanism, his aerial apparatus, oblong in form, went visibly against the wind. It occurred to M. Petin to place four hydrogen balloons together; and, by means of sails hung horizontally and partly folded, he hopes to be able to disturb the equilibrium, and, thus inclining the apparatus, to convey it in an oblique direction. They speak, also, of forces to overcome the resistance of currents,—for instance, the screw; but the screw, working on a moveable centre, will give no result. I, monsieur, have discovered the only means of guiding balloons; and no academy has come to my aid, no city has filled up subscriptions for me, no government has thought fit to listen to me! It is infamous!"

The unknown gesticulated fiercely, and the car underwent violent oscillations. I had much trouble in calming him.

Meanwhile the balloon had entered a more rapid current, and we advanced south, at fifteen hundred yards above the earth.

"See, there is Darmstadt," said my companion, leaning over the car. "Do you perceive the chateau? Not very distinctly, eh? What would you have? The heat of the storm makes the outline of objects waver, and you must have a skilled eye to recognize localities."

"Are you certain it is Darmstadt?" I asked.

"I am sure of it. We are now six leagues from Frankfort."

"Then we must descend."

"Descend! You would not go down, on the steeples," said the unknown, with a chuckle.

"No, but in the suburbs of the city."

"Well, let us avoid the steeples!"

So speaking, my companion seized some bags of ballast. I hastened to prevent him; but he overthrew me with one hand, and the unballasted balloon ascended to two thousand yards.

"Rest easy," said he, "and do not forget that Brioschi, Biot, Gay-Lussac, Bixio, and Barral ascended to still greater heights to make their scientific experiments."

"Monsieur, we must descend," I resumed, trying to persuade him by gentleness. "The storm is gathering around us. It would be more prudent—"

"Bah! We will mount higher than the storm, and then we shall no longer fear it!" cried my companion. "What is nobler than to overlook the clouds which oppress the earth? Is it not an honour thus to navigate on aerial billows? The greatest men have travelled as we are doing. The Marchioness and Countess de Montalembert, the Countess of Podenas, Mademoiselle la Garde, the Marquis de Montalembert, rose from the Faubourg Saint-Antoine for these unknown regions, and the Duke de Chartres exhibited much skill and presence of mind in his ascent on the 15th of July, 1784. At Lyons, the Counts of Laurencin and Dampierre; at Nantes, M. de Luynes; at Bordeaux, D'Arbelet des Granges; in Italy, the Chevalier Andreani; in our own time, the Duke of Brunswick,—have all left the traces of their glory in the air. To equal these great personages, we must penetrate still higher than they into the celestial depths! To approach the infinite is to comprehend it!"

The rarefaction of the air was fast expanding the hydrogen in the balloon, and I saw its lower part, purposely left empty, swell out, so that it was absolutely necessary to open the valve; but my companion did not seem to intend that I should manage the balloon as I wished. I then resolved to pull the valve cord secretly, as he was excitedly talking; for I feared to guess with whom I had to deal. It would have been too horrible! It was nearly a quarter before one. We had been gone forty minutes from Frankfort; heavy clouds were coming against the wind from the south, and seemed about to burst upon us.

"Have you lost all hope of succeeding in your project?" I asked with anxious interest.

"All hope!" exclaimed the unknown in a low voice. "Wounded by slights and caricatures, these asses' kicks have finished me! It is the eternal punishment reserved for innovators! Look at these caricatures of all periods, of which my portfolio is full."

While my companion was fumbling with his papers, I had seized the valve-cord without his perceiving it. I feared, however, that he might hear the hissing noise, like a water-course, which the gas makes in escaping.

"How many jokes were made about the Abbe Miolan!" said he. "He was to go up with Janninet and Bredin. During the filling their balloon caught fire, and the ignorant populace tore it in pieces! Then this caricature of 'curious animals' appeared, giving each of them a punning nickname."

I pulled the valve-cord, and the barometer began to ascend. It was time. Some far-off rumblings were heard in the south.

"Here is another engraving," resumed the unknown, not suspecting what I was doing. "It is an immense balloon carrying a ship, strong castles, houses, and so on. The caricaturists did not suspect that their follies would one day become truths. It is complete, this large vessel. On the left is its helm, with the pilot's box; at the prow are pleasure-houses, an immense organ, and a cannon to call the attention of the inhabitants of the earth or the moon; above the poop there are the observatory and the balloon long-boat; in the equatorial circle, the army barrack; on the left, the funnel; then the upper galleries for promenading, sails, pinions; below, the cafes and general storehouse. Observe this pompous announcement: 'Invented for the happiness of the human race, this globe will depart at once for the ports of the Levant, and on its return the programme of its voyages to the two poles and the extreme west will be announced. No one need furnish himself with anything; everything is foreseen, and all will prosper. There will be a uniform price for all places of destination, but it will be the same for the most distant countries of our hemisphere—that is to say, a thousand louis for one of any of the said journeys. And it must be confessed that this sum is very moderate, when the speed, comfort, and arrangements which will be enjoyed on the balloon are considered—arrangements which are not to be found on land, while on the balloon each passenger may consult his own habits and tastes. This is so true that in the same place some will be dancing, others standing; some will be enjoying delicacies; others fasting. Whoever desires the society of wits may satisfy himself; whoever is stupid may find stupid people to keep him company. Thus pleasure will be the soul of the aerial company.' All this provoked laughter; but before long, if I am not cut off, they will see it all realized."

We were visibly descending. He did not perceive it!

"This kind of 'game at balloons,'" he resumed, spreading out before me some of the engravings of his valuable collection, "this game contains the entire history of the aerostatic art. It is used by elevated minds, and is played with dice and counters, with whatever stakes you like, to be paid or received according to where the player arrives."

"Why," said I, "you seem to have studied the science of aerostation profoundly."

"Yes, monsieur, yes! From Phaethon, Icarus, Architas, I have searched for, examined, learnt everything. I could render immense services to the world in this art, if God granted me life. But that will not be!"

"Why?"

"Because my name is Empedocles, or Erostratus."

Meanwhile, the balloon was happily approaching the earth; but when one is falling, the danger is as great at a hundred feet as at five thousand.

"Do you recall the battle of Fleurus?" resumed my companion, whose face became more and more animated. "It was at that battle that Contello, by order of the Government, organized a company of balloonists. At the siege of Manbenge General Jourdan derived so much service from this new method of observation that Contello ascended twice a day with the general himself. The communications between the aeronaut and his agents who held the balloon were made by means of small white, red, and yellow flags. Often the gun and cannon shot were directed upon the balloon when he ascended, but without result. When General Jourdan was preparing to invest Charleroi, Contello went into the vicinity, ascended from the plain of Jumet, and continued his observations for seven or eight hours with General Morlot, and this no doubt aided in giving us the victory of Fleurus. General Jourdan publicly acknowledged the help which the aeronautical observations had afforded him. Well, despite the services rendered on that occasion and during the Belgian campaign, the year which had seen the beginning of the military career of balloons saw also its end. The school of Meudon, founded by the Government, was closed by Buonaparte on his return from Egypt. And now, what can you expect from the new-born infant? as Franklin said. The infant was born alive; it should not be stifled!"

The unknown bowed his head in his hands, and reflected for some moments; then raising his head, he said,—

"Despite my prohibition, monsieur, you have opened the valve."

I dropped the cord.

"Happily," he resumed, "we have still three hundred pounds of ballast."

"What is your purpose?" said I.

"Have you ever crossed the seas?" he asked.

I turned pale.

"It is unfortunate," he went on, "that we are being driven towards the Adriatic. That is only a stream; but higher up we may find other currents."

And, without taking any notice of me, he threw over several bags of sand; then, in a menacing voice, he said,—

"I let you open the valve because the expansion of the gas threatened to burst the balloon; but do not do it again!"

Then he went on as follows:—

"You remember the voyage of Blanchard and Jeffries from Dover to Calais? It was magnificent! On the 7th of January, 1785, there being a north-west wind, their balloon was inflated with gas on the Dover coast. A mistake of equilibrium, just as they were ascending, forced them to throw out their ballast so that they might not go down again, and they only kept thirty pounds. It was too little; for, as the wind did not freshen, they only advanced very slowly towards the French coast. Besides, the permeability of the tissue served to reduce the inflation little by little, and in an hour and a half the aeronauts perceived that they were descending.

"'What shall we do?' said Jeffries.

"'We are only one quarter of the way over,' replied Blanchard, 'and very low down. On rising, we shall perhaps meet more favourable winds.'

"'Let us throw out the rest of the sand.'

"The balloon acquired some ascending force, but it soon began to descend again. Towards the middle of the transit the aeronauts threw over their books and tools. A quarter of an hour after, Blanchard said to Jeffries,—

"'The barometer?'

"'It is going up! We are lost, and yet there is the French coast.'

"A loud noise was heard.

"'Has the balloon burst?' asked Jeffries.

"'No. The loss of the gas has reduced the inflation of the lower part of the balloon. But we are still descending. We are lost! Out with everything useless!'

"Provisions, oars, and rudder were thrown into the sea. The aeronauts were only one hundred yards high.

"'We are going up again,' said the doctor.

"'No. It is the spurt caused by the diminution of the weight, and not a ship in sight, not a bark on the horizon! To the sea with our clothing!'

"The unfortunates stripped themselves, but the balloon continued to descend.

"'Blanchard,' said Jeffries, 'you should have made this voyage alone; you consented to take me; I will sacrifice myself! I am going to throw myself into the water, and the balloon, relieved of my weight, will mount again.'

"'No, no! It is frightful!'

"The balloon became less and less inflated, and as it doubled up its concavity pressed the gas against the sides, and hastened its downward course.

"'Adieu, my friend,' said the doctor. 'God preserve you!'

"He was about to throw himself over, when Blanchard held him back.

"'There is one more chance,' said he. 'We can cut the cords which hold the car, and cling to the net! Perhaps the balloon will rise. Let us hold ourselves ready. But—the barometer is going down! The wind is freshening! We are saved!'

"The aeronauts perceived Calais. Their joy was delirious. A few moments more, and they had fallen in the forest of Guines. I do not doubt," added the unknown, "that, under similar circumstances, you would have followed Doctor Jeffries' example!"

The clouds rolled in glittering masses beneath us. The balloon threw large shadows on this heap of clouds, and was surrounded as by an aureola. The thunder rumbled below the car. All this was terrifying.

"Let us descend!" I cried.

"Descend, when the sun is up there, waiting for us? Out with more bags!"

And more than fifty pounds of ballast were cast over.

At a height of three thousand five hundred yards we remained stationary.

The unknown talked unceasingly. I was in a state of complete prostration, while he seemed to be in his element.

"With a good wind, we shall go far," he cried. "In the Antilles there are currents of air which have a speed of a hundred leagues an hour. When Napoleon was crowned, Garnerin sent up a balloon with coloured lamps, at eleven o'clock at night. The wind was blowing north-north-west. The next morning, at daybreak, the inhabitants of Rome greeted its passage over the dome of St. Peter's. We shall go farther and higher!"

I scarcely heard him. Everything whirled around me. An opening appeared in the clouds.

"See that city," said the unknown. "It is Spires!"

I leaned over the car and perceived a small blackish mass. It was Spires. The Rhine, which is so large, seemed an unrolled ribbon. The sky was a deep blue over our heads. The birds had long abandoned us, for in that rarefied air they could not have flown. We were alone in space, and I in presence of this unknown!

"It is useless for you to know whither I am leading you," he said, as he threw the compass among the clouds. "Ah! a fall is a grand thing! You know that but few victims of ballooning are to be reckoned, from Pilatre des Rosiers to Lieutenant Gale, and that the accidents have always been the result of imprudence. Pilatre des Rosiers set out with Romain of Boulogne, on the 13th of June, 1785. To his gas balloon he had affixed a Montgolfier apparatus of hot air, so as to dispense, no doubt, with the necessity of losing gas or throwing out ballast. It was putting a torch under a powder-barrel. When they had ascended four hundred yards, and were taken by opposing winds, they were driven over the open sea. Pilatre, in order to descend, essayed to open the valve, but the valve-cord became entangled in the balloon, and tore it so badly that it became empty in an instant. It fell upon the Montgolfier apparatus, overturned it, and dragged down the unfortunates, who were soon shattered to pieces! It is frightful, is it not?"

I could only reply, "For pity's sake, let us descend!"

The clouds gathered around us on every side, and dreadful detonations, which reverberated in the cavity of the balloon, took place beneath us.

"You provoke me," cried the unknown, "and you shall no longer know whether we are rising or falling!"

The barometer went the way of the compass, accompanied by several more bags of sand. We must have been 5000 yards high. Some icicles had already attached themselves to the sides of the car, and a kind of fine snow seemed to penetrate to my very bones. Meanwhile a frightful tempest was raging under us, but we were above it.

"Do not be afraid," said the unknown. "It is only the imprudent who are lost. Olivari, who perished at Orleans, rose in a paper 'Montgolfier;' his car, suspended below the chafing-dish, and ballasted with combustible materials, caught fire; Olivari fell, and was killed! Mosment rose, at Lille, on a light tray; an oscillation disturbed his equilibrium; Mosment fell, and was killed! Bittorf, at Mannheim, saw his balloon catch fire in the air; and he, too, fell, and was killed! Harris rose in a badly constructed balloon, the valve of which was too large and would not shut; Harris fell, and was killed! Sadler, deprived of ballast by his long sojourn in the air, was dragged over the town of Boston and dashed against the chimneys; Sadler fell, and was killed! Cokling descended with a convex parachute which he pretended to have perfected; Cokling fell, and was killed! Well, I love them, these victims of their own imprudence, and I shall die as they did. Higher! still higher!"

All the phantoms of this necrology passed before my eyes. The rarefaction of the air and the sun's rays added to the expansion of the gas, and the balloon continued to mount. I tried mechanically to open the valve, but the unknown cut the cord several feet above my head. I was lost!

"Did you see Madame Blanchard fall?" said he. "I saw her; yes, I! I was at Tivoli on the 6th of July, 1819. Madame Blanchard rose in a small sized balloon, to avoid the expense of filling, and she was forced to entirely inflate it. The gas leaked out below, and left a regular train of hydrogen in its path. She carried with her a sort of pyrotechnic aureola, suspended below her car by a wire, which she was to set off in the air. This she had done many times before. On this day she also carried up a small parachute ballasted by a firework contrivance, that would go off in a shower of silver. She was to start this contrivance after having lighted it with a port-fire made on purpose. She set out; the night was gloomy. At the moment of lighting her fireworks she was so imprudent as to pass the taper under the column of hydrogen which was leaking from the balloon. My eyes were fixed upon her. Suddenly an unexpected gleam lit up the darkness. I thought she was preparing a surprise. The light flashed out, suddenly disappeared and reappeared, and gave the summit of the balloon the shape of an immense jet of ignited gas. This sinister glow shed itself over the Boulevard and the whole Montmartre quarter. Then I saw the unhappy woman rise, try twice to close the appendage of the balloon, so as to put out the fire, then sit down in her car and try to guide her descent; for she did not fall. The combustion of the gas lasted for several minutes. The balloon, becoming gradually less, continued to descend, but it was not a fall. The wind blew from the north-west and drove it towards Paris. There were then some large gardens just by the house No. 16, Rue de Provence. Madame Blanchard essayed to fall there without danger: but the balloon and the car struck on the roof of the house with a light shock. 'Save me!' cried the wretched woman. I got into the street at this moment. The car slid along the roof, and encountered an iron cramp. At this concussion, Madame Blanchard was thrown out of her car and precipitated upon the pavement. She was killed!"

These stories froze me with horror. The unknown was standing with bare head, dishevelled hair, haggard eyes!

There was no longer any illusion possible. I at last recognized the horrible truth. I was in the presence of a madman!

He threw out the rest of the ballast, and we must have now reached a height of at least nine thousand yards. Blood spurted from my nose and mouth!

"Who are nobler than the martyrs of science?" cried the lunatic. "They are canonized by posterity."

But I no longer heard him. He looked about him, and, bending down to my ear, muttered,—

"And have you forgotten Zambecarri's catastrophe? Listen. On the 7th of October, 1804, the clouds seemed to lift a little. On the preceding days, the wind and rain had not ceased; but the announced ascension of Zambecarri could not be postponed. His enemies were already bantering him. It was necessary to ascend, to save the science and himself from becoming a public jest. It was at Boulogne. No one helped him to inflate his balloon.

"He rose at midnight, accompanied by Andreoli and Grossetti. The balloon mounted slowly, for it had been perforated by the rain, and the gas was leaking out. The three intrepid aeronauts could only observe the state of the barometer by aid of a dark lantern. Zambecarri had eaten nothing for twenty-four hours. Grossetti was also fasting.

"'My friends,' said Zambecarri, 'I am overcome by cold, and exhausted. I am dying.'

"He fell inanimate in the gallery. It was the same with Grossetti. Andreoli alone remained conscious. After long efforts, he succeeded in reviving Zambecarri.

"'What news? Whither are we going? How is the wind? What time is it?'

"'It is two o'clock.'

"'Where is the compass?'

"'Upset!'

"'Great God! The lantern has gone out!'

"'It cannot burn in this rarefied air,' said Zambecarri.

"The moon had not risen, and the atmosphere was plunged in murky darkness.

"'I am cold, Andreoli. What shall I do?'

"They slowly descended through a layer of whitish clouds.

"'Sh!' said Andreoli. 'Do you hear?'

"'What?' asked Zambecarri.

"'A strange noise.'

"'You are mistaken.'

"'No.'

"Consider these travellers, in the middle of the night, listening to that unaccountable noise! Are they going to knock against a tower? Are they about to be precipitated on the roofs?

"'Do you hear? One would say it was the noise of the sea.'

"'Impossible!'

"'It is the groaning of the waves!'

"'It is true.'

"'Light! light!'

"After five fruitless attempts, Andreoli succeeded in obtaining light. It was three o'clock.

"The voice of violent waves was heard. They were almost touching the surface of the sea!

"'We are lost!' cried Zambecarri, seizing a large bag of sand.

"'Help!' cried Andreoli.

"The car touched the water, and the waves came up to their breasts.

"'Throw out the instruments, clothes, money!'

"The aeronauts completely stripped themselves. The balloon, relieved, rose with frightful rapidity. Zambecarri was taken with vomiting. Grossetti bled profusely. The unfortunate men could not speak, so short was their breathing. They were taken with cold, and they were soon crusted over with ice. The moon looked as red as blood.

"After traversing the high regions for a half-hour, the balloon again fell into the sea. It was four in the morning. They were half submerged in the water, and the balloon dragged them along, as if under sail, for several hours.

"At daybreak they found themselves opposite Pesaro, four miles from the coast. They were about to reach it, when a gale blew them back into the open sea. They were lost! The frightened boats fled at their approach. Happily, a more intelligent boatman accosted them, hoisted them on board, and they landed at Ferrada.

"A frightful journey, was it not? But Zambecarri was a brave and energetic man. Scarcely recovered from his sufferings, he resumed his ascensions. During one of them he struck against a tree; his spirit-lamp was broken on his clothes; he was enveloped in fire, his balloon began to catch the flames, and he came down half consumed.

"At last, on the 21st of September, 1812, he made another ascension at Boulogne. The balloon clung to a tree, and his lamp again set it on fire. Zambecarri fell, and was killed! And in presence of these facts, we would still hesitate! No. The higher we go, the more glorious will be our death!"

The balloon being now entirely relieved of ballast and of all it contained, we were carried to an enormous height. It vibrated in the atmosphere. The least noise resounded in the vaults of heaven. Our globe, the only object which caught my view in immensity, seemed ready to be annihilated, and above us the depths of the starry skies were lost in thick darkness.

I saw my companion rise up before me.

"The hour is come!" he said. "We must die. We are rejected of men. They despise us. Let us crush them!"

"Mercy!" I cried.

"Let us cut these cords! Let this car be abandoned in space. The attractive force will change its direction, and we shall approach the sun!"

Despair galvanized me. I threw myself upon the madman, we struggled together, and a terrible conflict took place. But I was thrown down, and while he held me under his knee, the madman was cutting the cords of the car.

"One!" he cried.

"My God!"

"Two! Three!"

I made a superhuman effort, rose up, and violently repulsed the madman.

"Four!"

The car fell, but I instinctively clung to the cords and hoisted myself into the meshes of the netting.

The madman disappeared in space!

The balloon was raised to an immeasurable height. A horrible cracking was heard. The gas, too much dilated, had burst the balloon. I shut my eyes—

Some instants after, a damp warmth revived me. I was in the midst of clouds on fire. The balloon turned over with dizzy velocity.

Taken by the wind, it made a hundred leagues an hour in a horizontal course, the lightning flashing around it.

Meanwhile my fall was not a very rapid one. When I opened my eyes, I saw the country. I was two miles from the sea, and the tempest was driving me violently towards it, when an abrupt shock forced me to loosen my hold. My hands opened, a cord slipped swiftly between my fingers, and I found myself on the solid earth!

It was the cord of the anchor, which, sweeping along the surface of the ground, was caught in a crevice; and my balloon, unballasted for the last time, careered off to lose itself beyond the sea.

When I came to myself, I was in bed in a peasant's cottage, at Harderwick, a village of La Gueldre, fifteen leagues from Amsterdam, on the shores of the Zuyder-Zee.

A miracle had saved my life, but my voyage had been a series of imprudences, committed by a lunatic, and I had not been able to prevent them.

May this terrible narrative, though instructing those who read it, not discourage the explorers of the air.

The Blockade Runners

The Dolphin

The Clyde was the first river whose waters were lashed into foam by a steam-boat. It was in 1812 when the steamer called the Comet ran between Glasgow and Greenock, at the speed of six miles an hour. Since that time more than a million of steamers or packet-boats have plied this Scotch river, and the inhabitants of Glasgow must be as familiar as any people with the wonders of steam navigation.

However, on the 3rd of December, 1862, an immense crowd, composed of shipowners, merchants, manufacturers, workmen, sailors, women and children, thronged the muddy streets of Glasgow, all going in the direction of Kelvin Dock, the large shipbuilding premises belonging to Messrs. Tod & MacGregor. This last name especially proves that the descendants of the famous Highlanders have become manufacturers, and that they have made workmen of all the vassals of the old clan chieftains.

Kelvin Dock is situated a few minutes walk from the town, on the right bank of the Clyde. Soon the immense timber-yards were thronged with spectators; not a part of the quay, not a wall of the wharf, not a factory roof showed an unoccupied place; the river itself was covered with craft of all descriptions, and the heights of Govan, on the left bank, swarmed with spectators.

There was, however, nothing extraordinary in the event about to take place; it was nothing but the launching of a ship, and this was an everyday affair with the people of Glasgow. Had the Dolphin, then, for that was the name of the ship built by Messrs. Tod & MacGregor, "some special peculiarity?" To tell the truth, it had none.

It was a large ship, about 1,500 tons, in which everything combined to obtain superior speed. Her engines, of 500 horse-power, were from the workshops of Lancefield Forge; they worked two screws, one on either side the stern-post, completely independent of each other. As for the depth of water the Dolphin would draw, it must be very inconsiderable; connoisseurs were not deceived, and they concluded rightly that this ship was destined for shallow straits. But all these particulars could not in any way justify the eagerness of the people: taken altogether, the Dolphin was nothing more or less than an ordinary ship. Would her launching present some mechanical difficulty to be overcome? Not any more than usual. The Clyde had received many a ship of heavier tonnage, and the launching of the Dolphin would take place in the usual manner.

In fact, when the water was calm, the moment the ebb-tide set in, the workmen began to operate. Their mallets kept perfect time falling on the wedges meant to raise the ship's keel: soon a shudder ran through the whole of her massive structure; although she had only been slightly raised, one could see that she shook, and then gradually began to glide down the well greased wedges, and in a few moments she plunged into the Clyde. Her stern struck the muddy bed of the river, then she raised herself on the top of a gigantic wave, and, carried forward by her start, would have been dashed against the quay of the Govan timber-yards, if her anchors had not restrained her.

The launch had been perfectly successful, the Dolphin swayed quietly on the waters of the Clyde, all the spectators clapped their hands when she took possession of her natural element, and loud hurrahs arose from either bank.

But wherefore these cries and this applause? Undoubtedly the most eager of the spectators would have been at a loss to explain the reason of his enthusiasm. What was the cause, then, of the lively interest excited by this ship? Simply the mystery which shrouded her destination; it was not known to what kind of commerce she was to be appropriated, and in questioning different groups the diversity of opinion on this important subject was indeed astonishing.

However, the best informed, at least those who pretended to be so, agreed in saying that the steamer was going to take part in the terrible war which was then ravaging the United States of America, but more than this they did not know, and whether the Dolphin was a privateer, a transport ship, or an addition to the Federal marine was what no one could tell.

"Hurrah!" cried one, affirming that the Dolphin had been built for the Southern States.

"Hip! hip! hip!" cried another, swearing that never had a faster boat crossed to the American coasts.

Thus its destination was unknown, and in order to obtain any reliable information one must be an intimate friend, or, at any rate, an acquaintance of Vincent Playfair & Co., of Glasgow.

A rich, powerful, intelligent house of business was that of Vincent Playfair & Co., in a social sense, an old and honourable family, descended from those tobacco lords who built the finest quarters of the town. These clever merchants, by an act of the Union, had founded the first Glasgow warehouse for dealing in tobacco from Virginia and Maryland. Immense fortunes were realised; mills and foundries sprang up in all parts, and in a few years the prosperity of the city attained its height.

The house of Playfair remained faithful to the enterprising spirit of its ancestors, it entered into the most daring schemes, and maintained the honour of English commerce. The principal, Vincent Playfair, a man of fifty, with a temperament essentially practical and decided, although somewhat daring, was a genuine shipowner. Nothing affected him beyond commercial questions, not even the political side of the transactions, otherwise he was a perfectly loyal and honest man.

However, he could not lay claim to the idea of building and fitting up the Dolphin; she belonged to his nephew, James Playfair, a fine young man of thirty, the boldest skipper of the British merchant marine.

It was one day at the Tontine coffee-room under the arcades of the town hall, that James Playfair, after having impatiently scanned the American journal, disclosed to his uncle an adventurous scheme.

"Uncle Vincent," said he, coming to the point at once, "there are two millions of pounds to be gained in less than a month."

"And what to risk?" asked Uncle Vincent.

"A ship and a cargo."

"Nothing else?"

"Nothing, except the crew and the captain, and that does not reckon for much."

"Let us see," said Uncle Vincent.

"It is all seen," replied James Playfair. "You have read the Tribune, the New York Herald, The Times, the Richmond Inquirer, the American Review?"

"Scores of times, nephew."

"You believe, like me, that the war of the United States will last a long time still?"

"A very long time."

"You know how much this struggle will affect the interests of England, and especially those of Glasgow?"

"And more especially still the house of Playfair & Co.," replied Uncle Vincent.

"Theirs especially," added the young Captain.

"I worry myself about it every day, James, and I cannot think without terror of the commercial disasters which this war may produce; not but that the house of Playfair is firmly established, nephew; at the same time it has correspondents which may fail. Ah! those Americans, slave-holders or Abolitionists, I have no faith in them!"

If Vincent Playfair was wrong in thus speaking with respect to the great principles of humanity, always and everywhere superior to personal interests, he was, nevertheless, right from a commercial point of view. The most important material was failing at Glasgow, the cotton famine became every day more threatening, thousands of workmen were reduced to living upon public charity. Glasgow possessed 25,000 looms, by which 625,000 yards of cotton were spun daily; that is to say, fifty millions of pounds yearly. From these numbers it may be guessed what disturbances were caused in the commercial part of the town when the raw material failed altogether. Failures were hourly taking place, the manufactories were closed, and the workmen were dying of starvation.

It was the sight of this great misery which had put the idea of his bold enterprise into James Playfair's head.

"I will go for cotton, and will get it, cost what it may."

But, as he also was a merchant as well as his uncle Vincent, he resolved to carry out his plan by way of exchange, and to make his proposition under the guise of a commercial enterprise.

"Uncle Vincent," said he, "this is my idea."

"Well, James?"

"It is simply this: we will have a ship built of superior sailing qualities and great bulk."

"That is quite possible."

"We will load her with ammunition of war, provisions, and clothes."

"Just so."

"I will take the command of this steamer, I will defy all the ships of the Federal marine for speed, and I will run the blockade of one of the southern ports."

"You must make a good bargain for your cargo with the Confederates, who will be in need of it," said his uncle.

"And I shall return laden with cotton."

"Which they will give you for nothing."

"As you say, Uncle. Will it answer?"

"It will; but shall you be able to get there?"

"I shall, if I have a good ship."

"One can be made on purpose. But the crew?"

"Oh, I will find them. I do not want many men; enough to work with, that is all. It is not a question of fighting with the Federals, but distancing them."

"They shall be distanced," said Uncle Vincent, in a peremptory tone; "but now, tell me, James, to what port of the American coast do you think of going?"

"Up to now, Uncle, ships have run the blockade of New Orleans, Wilmington, and Savannah, but I think of going straight to Charleston; no English boat has yet been able to penetrate into the harbour, except the Bermuda. I will do like her, and, if my ship draws but very little water, I shall be able to go where the Federalists will not be able to follow."

"The fact is," said Uncle Vincent, "Charleston is overwhelmed with cotton; they are even burning it to get rid of it."

"Yes," replied James; "besides, the town is almost invested; Beauregard is running short of provisions, and he will pay me a golden price for my cargo!"

"Well, nephew, and when will you start?"

"In six months; I must have the long winter nights to aid me."

"It shall be as you wish, nephew."

"It is settled, then, Uncle?"

"Settled!"

"Shall it be kept quiet?"

"Yes; better so."

And this is how it was that five months later the steamer Dolphin was launched from the Kelvin Dock timber-yards, and no one knew her real destination.

Getting under Sail

The Dolphin was rapidly equipped, her rigging was ready, and there was nothing to do but fit her up. She carried three schooner-masts, an almost useless luxury; in fact, the Dolphin did not rely on the wind to escape the Federalists, but rather on her powerful engines.

Towards the end of December a trial of the steamer was made in the gulf of the Clyde. Which was the more satisfied, builder or captain, it is impossible to say. The new steamer shot along wonderfully, and the patent log showed a speed of seventeen miles an hour, a speed which as yet no English, French, or American boat had ever obtained. The Dolphin would certainly have gained by several lengths in a sailing match with the fastest opponent.

The loading was begun on the 25th of December, the steamer having ranged along the steamboat-quay a little below Glasgow Bridge, the last which stretches across the Clyde before its mouth. Here the wharfs were heaped with a heavy cargo of clothes, ammunition, and provisions which were rapidly carried to the hold of the Dolphin. The nature of this cargo betrayed the mysterious destination of the ship, and the house of Playfair could no longer keep it secret; besides, the Dolphin must not be long before she started. No American cruiser had been signalled in English waters; and, then, when the question of getting the crew came, how was it possible to keep silent any longer? They could not embark them, even, without informing the men whither they were bound, for, after all, it was a matter of life and death, and when one risks one's life, at least it is satisfactory to know how and wherefore.

However, this prospect hindered no one; the pay was good, and everyone had a share in the speculation, so that a great number of the finest sailors soon presented themselves. James Playfair was only embarrassed which to choose, but he chose well, and in twenty-four hours his muster-roll bore the names of thirty sailors who would have done honour to her Majesty's yacht.

The departure was settled for the 3rd of January; on the 31st of December the Dolphin was ready, her hold full of ammunition and provisions, and nothing was keeping her now.

The skipper went on board on the 2nd of January, and was giving a last look round his ship with a captain's eye, when a man presented himself at the fore part of the Dolphin, and asked to speak with the Captain. One of the sailors led him on to the poop.

He was a strong, hearty-looking fellow, with broad shoulders and ruddy face, the simple expression of which ill-concealed a depth of wit and mirth. He did not seem to be accustomed to a seafaring life, and looked about him with the air of a man little used to being on board a ship; however, he assumed the manner of a Jack-tar, looking up at the rigging of the Dolphin, and waddling in true sailor fashion.

When he had reached the Captain, he looked fixedly at him, and said, "Captain James Playfair?"

"The same," replied the skipper. "What do you want with me?"

"To join your ship."

"There is no room; the crew is already complete."

"Oh, one man, more or less, will not be in the way; quite the contrary."

"You think so?" said James Playfair, giving a sidelong glance at his questioner.

"I am sure of it," replied the sailor.

"But who are you?" asked the Captain.

"A rough sailor, with two strong arms, which, I can tell you, are not to be despised on board a ship, and which I now have the honour of putting at your service."

"But there are other ships besides the Dolphin, and other captains besides James Playfair. Why do you come here?"

"Because it is on board the Dolphin that I wish to serve, and under the orders of Captain James Playfair."

"I do not want you."

"There is always need of a strong man, and if to prove my strength you will try me with three or four of the strongest fellows of your crew, I am ready."

"That will do," replied James Playfair. "And what is your name?"

"Crockston, at your service."

The Captain made a few steps backwards in order to get a better view of the giant who presented himself in this odd fashion. The height, the build, and the look of the sailor did not deny his pretensions to strength.

"Where have you sailed?" asked Playfair of him.

"A little everywhere."

"And do you know where the Dolphin is bound for?"

"Yes; and that is what tempts me."

"Ah, well! I have no mind to let a fellow of your stamp escape me. Go and find the first mate, and get him to enrol you."

Having said this, the Captain expected to see the man turn on his heels and run to the bows, but he was mistaken. Crockston did not stir.

"Well! did you hear me?" asked the Captain.

"Yes, but it is not all," replied the sailor. "I have something else to ask you."

"Ah! You are wasting my time," replied James, sharply; "I have not a moment to lose in talking."

"I shall not keep you long," replied Crockston; "two words more and that is all; I was going to tell you that I have a nephew."

"He has a fine uncle, then," interrupted James Playfair.

"Hah! Hah!" laughed Crockston.

"Have you finished?" asked the Captain, very impatiently.

"Well, this is what I have to say, when one takes the uncle, the nephew comes into the bargain."

"Ah! indeed!"

"Yes, that is the custom, the one does not go without the other."

"And what is this nephew of yours?"

"A lad of fifteen whom I am going to train to the sea; he is willing to learn, and will make a fine sailor some day."

"How now, Master Crockston," cried James Playfair; "do you think the Dolphin is a training-school for cabin-boys?"

"Don't let us speak ill of cabin-boys: there was one of them who became Admiral Nelson, and another Admiral Franklin."

"Upon my honour, friend," replied James Playfair, "you have a way of speaking which I like; bring your nephew, but if I don't find the uncle the hearty fellow he pretends to be, he will have some business with me. Go, and be back in an hour."

Crockston did not want to be told twice; be bowed awkwardly to the Captain of the Dolphin, and went on to the quay. An hour afterwards he came on board with his nephew, a boy of fourteen or fifteen, rather delicate and weakly looking, with a timid and astonished air, which showed that he did not possess his uncle's self-possession and vigorous corporeal qualities. Crockston was even obliged to encourage him by such words as these:

"Come," said he, "don't be frightened, they are not going to eat us, besides, there is yet time to return."

"No, no," replied the young man, "and may God protect us!"

The same day the sailor Crockston and his nephew were inscribed in the muster-roll of the Dolphin.

The next morning, at five o'clock, the fires of the steamer were well fed, the deck trembled under the vibrations of the boiler, and the steam rushed hissing through the escape-pipes. The hour of departure had arrived.

A considerable crowd, in spite of the early hour, flocked on the quays and on Glasgow Bridge; they had come to salute the bold steamer for the last time. Vincent Playfair was there to say good-bye to Captain James, but he conducted himself on this occasion like a Roman of the good old times. His was a heroic countenance, and the two loud kisses with which he gratified his nephew were the indication of a strong mind.

"Go, James," said he to the young Captain, "go quickly, and come back quicker still; above all, don't abuse your position. Sell at a good price, make a good bargain, and you will have your uncle's esteem."

On this recommendation, borrowed from the manual of the perfect merchant, the uncle and nephew separated, and all the visitors left the boat.

At this moment Crockston and John Stiggs stood together on the forecastle, while the former remarked to his nephew, "This is well, this is well; before two o'clock we shall be at sea, and I have a good opinion of a voyage which begins like this."

For reply the novice pressed Crockston's hand.

James Playfair then gave the orders for departure.

"Have we pressure on?" he asked of his mate.

"Yes, Captain," replied Mr. Mathew.

"Well, then, weigh anchor."

This was immediately done, and the screws began to move. The Dolphin trembled, passed between the ships in the port, and soon disappeared from the sight of the people, who shouted their last hurrahs.

The descent of the Clyde was easily accomplished, one might almost say that this river had been made by the hand of man, and even by the hand of a master. For sixty years, thanks to the dredges and constant dragging, it has gained fifteen feet in depth, and its breadth has been tripled between the quays and the town. Soon the forests of masts and chimneys were lost in the smoke and fog; the noise of the foundry hammers and the hatchets of the timber-yards grew fainter in the distance. After the village of Partick had been passed the factories gave way to country houses and villas. The Dolphin, slackening her speed, sailed between the dykes which carry the river above the shores, and often through a very narrow channel, which, however, is only a small inconvenience for a navigable river, for, after all, depth is of more importance than width. The steamer, guided by one of those excellent pilots from the Irish sea, passed without hesitation between floating buoys, stone columns, and biggings, surmounted with lighthouses, which mark the entrance to the channel. Beyond the town of Renfrew, at the foot of Kilpatrick hills, the Clyde grew wider. Then came Bouling Bay, at the end of which opens the mouth of the canal which joints Edinburgh to Glasgow. Lastly, at the height of four hundred feet from the ground, was seen the outline of Dumbarton Castle, almost indiscernible through the mists, and soon the harbour-boats of Glasgow were rocked on the waves which the Dolphin caused. Some miles farther on Greenock, the birthplace of James Watt, was passed: the Dolphin now found herself at the mouth of the Clyde, and at the entrance of the gulf by which it empties its waters into the Northern Ocean. Here the first undulations of the sea were felt, and the steamer ranged along the picturesque coast of the Isle of Arran. At last the promontory of Cantyre, which runs out into the channel, was doubled; the Isle of Rattelin was hailed, the pilot returned by a shore-boat to his cutter, which was cruising in the open sea; the Dolphin, returning to her Captain's authority, took a less frequented route round the north of Ireland, and soon, having lost sight of the last European land, found herself in the open ocean.

Things are not what they Seem

The Dolphin had a good crew, not fighting men, or boarding sailors, but good working men, and that was all she wanted. These brave, determined fellows were all, more or less, merchants; they sought a fortune rather than glory; they had no flag to display, no colours to defend with cannon; in fact, all the artillery on board consisted of two small swivel signal-guns.

The Dolphin shot bravely across the water, and fulfilled the utmost expectations of both builder and captain. Soon she passed the limit of British seas; there was not a ship in sight; the great ocean route was free; besides, no ship of the Federal marine would have a right to attack her beneath the English flag. Followed she might be, and prevented from forcing the blockade, and precisely for this reason had James Playfair sacrificed everything to the speed of his ship, in order not to be pursued.

Howbeit a careful watch was kept on board, and, in spite of the extreme cold, a man was always in the rigging ready to signal the smallest sail that appeared on the horizon. When evening came, Captain James gave the most precise orders to Mr. Mathew.

"Don't leave the man on watch too long in the rigging; the cold may seize him, and in that case it is impossible to keep a good look-out; change your men often."

"I understand, Captain," replied Mr. Mathew.

"Try Crockston for that work; the fellow pretends to have excellent sight; it must be put to trial; put him on the morning watch, he will have the morning mists to see through. If anything particular happens call me."

This said, James Playfair went to his cabin. Mr. Mathew called Crockston, and told him the Captain's orders.

"To-morrow, at six o'clock," said he, "you are to relieve watch of the main masthead."

For reply, Crockston gave a decided grunt, but Mr. Mathew had hardly turned his back when the sailor muttered some incomprehensible words, and then cried:

"What on earth did he say about the mainmast?"

At this moment his nephew, John Stiggs, joined him on the forecastle.

"Well, my good Crockston," said he.

"It's all right, all right," said the seaman, with a forced smile; "there is only one thing, this wretched boat shakes herself like a dog coming out of the water, and it makes my head confused."

"Dear Crockston, and it is for my sake."

"For you and him," replied Crockston, "but not a word about that, John. Trust in God, and He will not forsake you."

So saying, John Stiggs and Crockston went to the sailor's berth, but the sailor did not lie down before he had seen the young novice comfortably settled in the narrow cabin which he had got for him.

The next day, at six o'clock in the morning, Crockston got up to go to his place; he went on deck, where the first officer ordered him to go up into the rigging, and keep good watch.

At these words the sailor seemed undecided what to do; then, making up his mind, he went towards the bows of the Dolphin.

"Well, where are you off to now?" cried Mr. Mathew.

"Where you sent me," answered Crockston.

"I told you to go to the mainmast."

"And I am going there," replied the sailor, in an unconcerned tone, continuing his way to the poop.

"Are you a fool?" cried Mr. Mathew, impatiently; "you are looking for the bars of the main on the foremast. You are like a cockney, who doesn't know how to twist a cat-o'-nine-tails, or make a splice. On board what ship can you have been, man? The mainmast, stupid, the mainmast!"

The sailors who had run up to hear what was going on burst out laughing when they saw Crockston's disconcerted look, as he went back to the forecastle.

"So," said he, looking up the mast, the top of which was quite invisible through the morning mists; "so, am I to climb up here?"

"Yes," replied Mr. Mathew, "and hurry yourself! By St. Patrick, a Federal ship would have time to get her bowsprit fast in our rigging before that lazy fellow could get to his post. Will you go up?"

Without a word, Crockston got on the bulwarks with some difficulty; then he began to climb the rigging with most visible awkwardness, like a man who did not know how to make use of his hands or feet. When he had reached the topgallant, instead of springing lightly on to it, he remained motionless, clinging to the ropes, as if he had been seized with giddiness. Mr. Mathew, irritated by his stupidity, ordered him to come down immediately.

"That fellow there," said he to the boatswain, "has never been a sailor in his life. Johnston, just go and see what he has in his bundle."

The boatswain made haste to the sailor's berth.

In the meantime Crockston was with difficulty coming down again, but, his foot having slipped, he slid down the rope he had hold of, and fell heavily on the deck.

"Clumsy blockhead! land-lubber!" cried Mr. Mathew, by way of consolation. "What did you come to do on board the Dolphin! Ah! you entered as an able seaman, and you cannot even distinguish the main from the foremast! I shall have a little talk with you."

Crockston made no attempt to speak; he bent his back like a man resigned to anything he might have to bear; just then the boatswain returned.

"This," said he to the first officer, "is all that I have found; a suspicious portfolio with letters."

"Give them here," said Mr. Mathew. "Letters with Federal stamps! Mr. Halliburtt, of Boston! An Abolitionist! a Federalist! Wretch! you are nothing but a traitor, and have sneaked on board to betray us! Never mind, you will be paid for your trouble with the cat-o'-nine-tails! Boatswain, call the Captain, and you others just keep an eye on that rogue there."

Crockston received these compliments with a hideous grimace, but he did not open his lips. They had fastened him to the capstan, and he could move neither hand nor foot.

A few minutes later James Playfair came out of his cabin and went to the forecastle, where Mr. Mathew immediately acquainted him with the details of the case.

"What have you to say?" asked James Playfair, scarcely able to restrain his anger.

"Nothing," replied Crockston.

"And what did you come on board my ship for?"

"Nothing."

"And what do you expect from me now?"

"Nothing."

"Who are you? An American, as letters seem to prove?" Crockston did not answer.

"Boatswain," said James Playfair, "fifty lashes with the cat-o'-nine-tails to loosen his tongue. Will that be enough, Crockston?"

"It will remain to be seen," replied John Stiggs" uncle without moving a muscle.

"Now then, come along, men," said the boatswain.

At this order, two strong sailors stripped Crockston of his woollen jersey; they had already seized the formidable weapon, and laid it across the prisoner's shoulders, when the novice, John Stiggs, pale and agitated, hurried on deck.

"Captain!" exclaimed he.

"Ah! the nephew!" remarked James Playfair.

"Captain," repeated the novice, with a violent effort to steady his voice, "I will tell you what Crockston does not want to say. I will hide it no longer; yes, he is American, and so am I; we are both enemies of the slave-holders, but not traitors come on board to betray the Dolphin into the hands of the Federalists."

"What did you come to do, then?" asked the Captain, in a severe tone, examining the novice attentively. The latter hesitated a few seconds before replying, then he said, "Captain, I should like to speak to you in private."

Whilst John Stiggs made this request, James Playfair did not cease to look carefully at him; the sweet young face of the novice, his peculiarly gentle voice, the delicacy and whiteness of his hands, hardly disguised by paint, the large eyes, the animation of which could not bide their tenderness all this together gave rise to a certain suspicion in the Captain's mind. When John Stiggs had made his request, Playfair glanced fixedly at Crockston, who shrugged his shoulders; then he fastened a questioning look on the novice, which the latter could not withstand, and said simply to him, "Come."

John Stiggs followed the Captain on to the poop, and then James Playfair, opening the door of his cabin, said to the novice, whose cheeks were pale with emotion, "Be so kind as to walk in, miss."

John, thus addressed, blushed violently, and two tears rolled involuntarily down his cheeks.

"Don't be alarmed, miss," said James Playfair, in a gentle voice, "but be so good as to tell me how I come to have the honour of having you on board?"

The young girl hesitated a moment, then, reassured by the Captain's look, she made up her mind to speak.

"Sir," said she, "I wanted to join my father at Charleston; the town is besieged by land and blockaded by sea. I knew not how to get there, when I heard that the Dolphin meant to force the blockade. I came on board your ship, and I beg you to forgive me if I acted without your consent, which you would have refused me."

"Certainly," said James Playfair.

"I did well, then, not to ask you," resumed the young girl, with a firmer voice.

The Captain crossed his arms, walked round his cabin, and then came back.

"What is your name?" said he.

"Jenny Halliburtt."

"Your father, if I remember rightly the address on the letters, is he not from Boston?"

"Yes, sir."

"And a Northerner is thus in a southern town in the thickest of the war?"

"My father is a prisoner; he was at Charleston when the first shot of the Civil War was fired, and the troops of the Union driven from Fort Sumter by the Confederates. My father's opinions exposed him to the hatred of the slavist part, and by the order of General Beauregard he was imprisoned. I was then in England, living with a relation who has just died, and left alone, with no help but that of Crockston, our faithful servant, I wished to go to my father and share his prison with him."

"What was Mr. Halliburtt, then?" asked James Playfair.

"A loyal and brave journalist," replied Jenny proudly, one of the noblest editors of the Tribune, and the one who was the boldest in defending the cause of the negroes.

"An Abolitionist," cried the Captain angrily; "one of those men who, under the vain pretence of abolishing slavery, have deluged their country with blood and ruin."

"Sir!" replied Jenny Halliburtt, growing pale, "you are insulting my father; you must not forget that I stand alone to defend him."

The young Captain blushed scarlet; anger mingled with shame struggled in his breast; perhaps he would have answered the young girl, but he succeeded in restraining himself, and, opening the door of the cabin, he called "Boatswain!"

The boatswain came to him directly.

"This cabin will henceforward belong to Miss Jenny Halliburtt. Have a cot made ready for me at the end of the poop; that's all I want."

The boatswain looked with a stupefied stare at the young novice addressed in a feminine name, but on a sign from James Playfair he went out.

"And now, miss, you are at home," said the young Captain of the Dolphin. Then he retired.

Crockston's Trick

It was not long before the whole crew knew Miss Halliburtt's story, which Crockston was no longer hindered from telling. By the Captain's orders he was released from the capstan, and the cat-o'-nine-tails returned to its Place.

"A pretty animal," said Crockston, "especially when it shows its velvety paws."

As soon as he was free, he went down to the sailors' berths, found a small portmanteau, and carried it to Miss Jenny; the young girl was now able to resume her feminine attire, but she remained in her cabin, and did not again appear on deck.

As for Crockston, it was well and duly agreed that, as he was no more a sailor than a horse-guard, he should be exempt from all duty on board.

In the meanwhile the Dolphin, with her twin screws cutting the waves, sped rapidly across the Atlantic, and there was nothing now to do but keep a strict look-out. The day following the discovery of Miss Jenny's identity, James Playfair paced the deck at the poop with a rapid step; he had made no attempt to see the young girl and resume the conversation of the day before.

Whilst he was walking to and fro, Crockston passed him several times, looking at him askant with a satisfied grin. He evidently wanted to speak to the Captain, and at last his persistent manner attracted the attention of the latter, who said to him, somewhat impatiently:

"How now, what do you want? You are turning round me like a swimmer round a buoy: when are you going to leave off?"

"Excuse me, Captain," answered Crockston, winking, "I wanted to speak to you."

"Speak, then."

"Oh, it is nothing very much. I only wanted to tell you frankly that you are a good fellow at bottom."

"Why at bottom?"

"At bottom and surface also."

"I don't want your compliments."

"I am not complimenting you. I shall wait to do that when you have gone to the end."

"To what end?"

"To the end of your task."

"Ah! I have a task to fulfil?"

"Decidedly, you have taken the young girl and myself on board; good! You have given up your cabin to Miss Halliburtt; good! You released me from the cat-o'-nine-tails; nothing could be better. You are going to take us straight to Charleston; that's delightful, but it is not all."

"How not all?" cried James Playfair, amazed at Crockston's boldness.

"No, certainly not," replied the latter, with a knowing look, "the father is prisoner there."

"Well, what about that?"

"Well, the father must be rescued."

"Rescue Miss Halliburtt's father?"

"Most certainly, and it is worth risking something for such a noble man and courageous citizen as he."

"Master Crockston," said James Playfair, frowning, "I am not in the humour for your jokes, so have a care what you say."

"You misunderstand me, Captain," said the American. "I am not joking in the least, but speaking quite seriously. What I have proposed may at first seem very absurd to you; when you have thought it over, you will see that you cannot do otherwise."

"What, do you mean that I must deliver Mr. Halliburtt?"

"Just so. You can demand his release of General Beauregard, who will not refuse you."

"But if he does refuse me?"

"In that case," replied Crockston, in a deliberate tone, "we must use stronger measures, and carry off the prisoner by force."

"So," cried James Playfair, who was beginning to get angry, "so, not content with passing through the Federal fleets and forcing the blockade of Charleston, I must run out to sea again from under the cannon of the forts, and this to deliver a gentleman I know nothing of, one of those Abolitionists whom I detest, one of those journalists who shed ink instead of their blood!"

"Oh, it is but a cannon-shot more or less!" added Crockston.

"Master Crockston," said James Playfair, "mind what I say: if ever you mention this affair again to me, I will send you to the hold for the rest of the passage, to teach you manners."

Thus saying, the Captain dismissed the American, who went off murmuring, "Ah, well, I am not altogether displeased with this conversation: at any rate, the affair is broached; it will do, it will do!"

James Playfair had hardly meant it when he said an Abolitionist whom I detest; he did not in the least side with the Federals, but he did not wish to admit that the question of slavery was the predominant reason for the civil war of the United States, in spite of President Lincoln's formal declaration. Did he, then, think that the Southern States, eight out of thirty-six, were right in separating when they had been voluntarily united? Not so; he detested the Northerners, and that was all; he detested them as brothers separated from the common family "true Englishmen" who had thought it right to do what he, James Playfair, disapproved of with regard to the United States: these were the political opinions of the Captain of the Dolphin. But, more than this, the American war interfered with him personally, and he had a grudge against those who had caused this war; one can understand, then, how he would receive a proposition to deliver an Abolitionist, thus bringing down on him the Confederates, with whom he pretended to do business.

However, Crockston's insinuation did not fail to disturb him; he cast the thought from him, but it returned unceasingly to his mind, and when Miss Jenny came on deck the next day for a few minutes, he dared not look her in the face.

And really it was a great pity, for this young girl, with the fair hair and sweet, intelligent face, deserved to be looked at by a young man of thirty. But James felt embarrassed in her presence; he felt that this charming creature who had been educated in the school of misfortune possessed a strong and generous soul; he understood that his silence towards her inferred a refusal to acquiesce in her dearest wishes; besides, Miss Jenny never looked out for James Playfair, neither did she avoid him. Thus for the first few days they spoke little or not at all to each other. Miss Halliburtt scarcely ever left her cabin, and it is certain she would never have addressed herself to the Captain of the Dolphin if it had not been for Crockston's strategy, which brought both parties together.

The worthy American was a faithful servant of the Halliburtt family; he had been brought up in his master's house, and his devotion knew no bounds. His good sense equalled his courage and energy, and, as has been seen, he had a way of looking things straight in the face. He was very seldom discouraged, and could generally find a way out of the most intricate dangers with a wonderful skill.

This honest fellow had taken it into his head to deliver Mr. Halliburtt, to employ the Captain's ship, and the Captain himself for this purpose, and to return with him to England. Such was his intention, so long as the young girl had no other object than to rejoin her father and share his captivity. It was this

Crockston tried to make the Captain understand, as we have seen, but the enemy had not yet surrendered; on the contrary.

"Now," said he, "it is absolutely necessary that Miss Jenny and the Captain come to an understanding; if they are going to be sulky like this all the passage we shall get nothing done. They must speak, discuss; let them dispute even, so long as they talk, and I'll be hanged if during their conversation James Playfair does not propose himself what he refused me to-day."

But when Crockston saw that the young girl and the young man avoided each other, he began to be perplexed.

"We must look sharp," said he to himself, and the morning of the fourth day he entered Miss Halliburtt's cabin, rubbing his hands with an air of perfect satisfaction.

"Good news!" cried he, "good news! You will never guess what the Captain has proposed to me. A very noble young man he is. Now try."

"Ah!" replied Jenny, whose heart beat violently, "has he proposed to?"

"To deliver Mr. Halliburtt, to carry him off from the Confederates, and bring him to England."

"Is it true?" cried Jenny.

"It is as I say, miss. What a good-hearted man this James Playfair is! These English are either all good or all bad. Ah! he may reckon on my gratitude, and I am ready to cut myself in pieces if it would please him."

Jenny's joy was profound on hearing Crockston's words. Deliver her father! She had never dared to think of such a plan, and the Captain of the Dolphin was going to risk his ship and crew!

"That's what he is," added Crockston; "and this, Miss Jenny, is well worth an acknowledgment from you."

"More than an acknowledgment," cried the young girl; "a lasting friendship!"

And immediately she left the cabin to find James Playfair, and express to him the sentiments which flowed from her heart.

"Getting on by degrees," muttered the American.

James Playfair was pacing to and fro on the poop, and, as may be thought, he was very much surprised, not to say amazed, to see the young girl come up to him, her eyes moist with grateful tears, and, holding out her hand to him, saying:

"Thank you, sir, thank you for your kindness, which I should never have dared to expect from a stranger."

"Miss," replied the Captain, as if he understood nothing of what she was talking, and could not understand, "I do not know."

"Nevertheless, sir, you are going to brave many dangers, perhaps compromise your interests for me, and you have done so much already in offering me on board an hospitality to which I have no right whatever?"

"Pardon me, Miss Jenny," interrupted James Playfair, "but I protest again I do not understand your words. I have acted towards you as any well-bred man would towards a lady, and my conduct deserves neither so many thanks nor so much gratitude."

"Mr. Playfair," said Jenny, "it is useless to pretend any longer; Crockston has told me all!"

"Ah!" said the Captain, "Crockston has told you all; then I understand less than ever the reason for your leaving your cabin, and saying these words which?"

Whilst speaking the Captain felt very much embarrassed; he remembered the rough way in which he had received the American's overtures, but Jenny, fortunately for him, did not give him time for further explanation; she interrupted him, holding out her hand and saying:

"Mr. James, I had no other object in coming on board your ship except to go to Charleston, and there, however cruel the slave-holders may be, they will not refuse to let a poor girl share her father's prison; that was all. I had never thought of a return as possible; but, since you are so generous as to wish for my father's deliverance, since you will attempt everything to save him, be assured you have my deepest gratitude."

James did not know what to do or what part to assume; he bit his lip; he dared not take the hand offered him; he saw perfectly that Crockston had compromised him, so that escape was impossible. At the same time he had no thoughts of delivering Mr. Halliburtt, and getting complicated in a disagreeable business: but how dash to the ground the hope which had arisen in this poor girl's heart? How refuse the hand which she held out to him with a feeling of such profound friendship? How change to tears of grief the tears of gratitude which filled her eyes?

So the young man tried to reply evasively, in a manner which would ensure his liberty of action for the future.

"Miss Jenny," said he, "rest assured I will do everything in my power for?"

And he took the little hand in both of his, but with the gentle pressure he felt his heart melt and his head grow confused: words to express his thoughts failed him. He stammered out some incoherent words:

"Miss, Miss Jenny for you?"

Crockston, who was watching him, rubbed his hands, grinning and repeating to himself:

"It will come! it will come! it has come!"

How James Playfair would have managed to extricate himself from his embarrassing position no one knows, but fortunately for him, if not for the Dolphin, the man on watch was heard crying:

"Ahoy, officer of the watch!"

"What now?" asked Mr. Mathew.

"A sail to windward!"

James Playfair, leaving the young girl, immediately sprang to the shrouds of the mainmast.

The Shot from the Iroquois, and Miss Jenny's Arguments

Until now the navigation of the Dolphin had been very fortunate. Not one ship had been signalled before the sail hailed by the man on watch.

The Dolphin was then in 32° 51° lat., and 57° 43° W. longitude. For forty-eight hours a fog, which now began to rise, had covered the ocean. If this mist favoured the Dolphin by hiding her course, it also prevented any observations at a distance being made, and, without being aware of it, she might be sailing side by side, so to speak, with the ships she wished most to avoid.

Now this is just what had happened, and when the ship was signalled she was only three miles to windward.

When James Playfair had reached the cross-trees, he saw distinctly, through an opening in the mist, a large Federal corvette in full pursuit of the Dolphin.

After having carefully examined her, the Captain came down on deck again, and called to the first officer.

"Mr. Mathew," said he, "what do you think of this ship?"

"I think, Captain, that it is a Federal cruiser, which suspects our intentions."

"There is no possible doubt of her nationality," said James Playfair. "Look!"

At this moment the starry flag of the North United States appeared on the gaff-yards of the corvette, and the latter asserted her colours with a cannon-shot.

"An invitation to show ours," said Mr. Mathew. "Well, let us show them; there is nothing to be ashamed of."

"What's the good?" replied James Playfair. "Our flag will hardly protect us, and it will not hinder those people from paying us a visit. No; let us go ahead."

"And go quickly," replied Mr. Mathew, "for, if my eyes do not deceive me, I have already seen that corvette lying off Liverpool, where she went to watch the ships in building: my name is not Mathew, if that is not the Iroquois on her taffrail."

"And is she fast?"

"One of the fastest vessels of the Federal marine."

"What guns does she carry?"

"Eight."

"Pooh!"

"Oh, don't shrug your shoulders, Captain," said Mr. Mathew, in a serious tone; "two out of those eight guns are rifled, one is a sixty-pounder on the forecastle, and the other a hundred-pounder on deck."

"Upon my soul!" exclaimed James Playfair, "they are Parrott's, and will carry three miles."

"Yes, and farther than that, Captain."

"Ah, well! Mr. Mathew, let their guns be sixty or only four-pounders, and let them carry three miles or five hundred yards, it is all the same if we can go fast enough to avoid their shot. We will show this Iroquois how a ship can go when she is built on purpose to go. Have the fires drawn forward, Mr. Mathew."

The first officer gave the Captain's orders to the engineer, and soon volumes of black smoke curled from the steamer's chimneys.

This proceeding did not seem to please the corvette, for she made the Dolphin the signal to lie to, but James Playfair paid no attention to this warning, and did not change his ship's course.

"Now," said he, "we shall see what the Iroquois will do; here is a fine opportunity for her to try her guns. Go ahead full speed!"

"Good!" exclaimed Mr. Mathew; "she will not be long in saluting us."

Returning to the poop, the Captain saw Miss Halliburtt sitting quietly near the bulwarks.

"Miss Jenny," said he, "we shall probably be chased by that corvette you see to windward, and as she will speak to us with shot, I beg to offer you my arm to take you to your cabin again."

"Thank you, very much, Mr. Playfair," replied the young girl, looking at him, "but I am not afraid of cannon-shots."

"However, miss, in spite of the distance, there may be some danger."

"Oh, I was not brought up to be fearful; they accustom us to everything in America, and I assure you that the shot from the Iroquois will not make me lower my head."

"You are brave, Miss Jenny."

"Let us admit, then, that I am brave, and allow me to stay by you."

"I can refuse you nothing, Miss Halliburtt," replied the Captain, looking at the young girl's calm face.

These words were hardly uttered when they saw a line of white smoke issue from the bulwarks of the corvette; before the report had reached the Dolphin a projectile whizzed through the air in the direction of the steamer.

At about twenty fathoms from the Dolphin the shot, the speed of which had sensibly lessened, skimmed over the surface of the waves, marking its passage by a series of water-jets; then, with another burst, it rebounded to a certain height, passed over the Dolphin, grazing the mizzen-yards on the starboard side, fell at thirty fathoms beyond, and was buried in the waves.

"By Jove!" exclaimed James Playfair, "we must get along; another slap like that is not to be waited for."

"Oh!" exclaimed Mr. Mathew, "they will take some time to reload such pieces."

"Upon my honour, it is an interesting sight," said Crockston, who, with arms crossed, stood perfectly at his ease looking at the scene.

"Ah! that's you," cried James Playfair, scanning the American from head to foot.

"It is me, Captain," replied the American, undisturbed. "I have come to see how these brave Federals fire; not badly, in truth, not badly."

The Captain was going to answer Crockston sharply, but at this moment a second shot struck the sea on the starboard side.

"Good!" cried James Playfair, "we have already gained two cables on this Iroquois. Your friends sail like a buoy; do you hear, Master Crockston?"

"I will not say they don't," replied the American, "and for the first time in my life it does not fail to please me."

A third shot fell still farther astern, and in less than ten minutes the Dolphin was out of range of the corvette's guns.

"So much for patent-logs, Mr. Mathew," said James Playfair; "thanks to those shot we know how to rate our speed. Now have the fires lowered; it is not worthwhile to waste our coal uselessly."

"It is a good ship that you command," said Miss Halliburtt to the young Captain.

"Yes, Miss Jenny, my good Dolphin makes her seventeen knots, and before the day is over we shall have lost sight of that corvette."

James Playfair did not exaggerate the sailing qualities of his ship, and the sun had not set before the masts of the American ship had disappeared below the horizon.

This incident allowed the Captain to see Miss Halliburtt's character in a new light; besides, the ice was broken, henceforward, during the whole of the voyage; the interviews between the Captain and his passenger were frequent and prolonged; be found her to be a young girl, calm, strong, thoughtful, and intelligent, speaking with great ease, having her own ideas about everything, and expressing her thoughts with a conviction which unconsciously penetrated James Playfair's heart.

She loved her country, she was zealous in the great cause of the Union, and expressed herself on the civil war in the United States with an enthusiasm of which no other woman would have been capable. Thus it happened, more than once, that James Playfair found it difficult to answer her, even when questions purely mercantile arose in connection with the war: Miss Jenny attacked them none the less vigorously, and would come to no other terms whatever. At first James argued a great deal, and tried to uphold the Confederates against the Federals, to prove that the Secessionists were in the right, and that if the people were united voluntarily they might separate in the same manner. But the young girl would not yield on this point; she demonstrated that the question of slavery was predominant in the struggle between the North and South Americans, that it was far more a war in the cause of morals and humanity than politics, and James could make no answer. Besides, during these discussions, which he listened to attentively, it is difficult to say whether he was more touched by Miss Halliburtt's arguments or the charming manner in which she spoke; but at last he was obliged to acknowledge, among other things, that slavery was the principal feature in the war, that it must be put an end to decisively, and the last horrors of barbarous times abolished.

It has been said that the political opinions of the Captain did not trouble him much. He would have sacrificed his most serious opinion before such enticing arguments and under like circumstances; he made a good bargain of his ideas for the same reason, but at last he was attacked in his tenderest point; this was the question of the traffic in which the Dolphin was being employed, and, consequently, the ammunition which was being carried to the Confederates.

"Yes, Mr. James," said Miss Halliburtt, "gratitude does not hinder me from speaking with perfect frankness; on the contrary, you are a brave seaman, a clever merchant, the house of Playfair is noted for its respectability; but in this case it fails in its principles, and follows a trade unworthy of it."

"How!" cried James, "the house of Playfair ought not to attempt such a commercial enterprise?"

"No! it is taking ammunition to the unhappy creatures in revolt against the government of their country, and it is lending arms to a bad cause."

"Upon my honour, Miss Jenny, I will not discuss the right of the Confederates with you; I will only answer you with one word: I am a merchant, and as such I only occupy myself with the interests of my house; I look for gain wherever there is an opportunity of getting it."

"That is precisely what is to be blamed, Mr. James," replied the young girl; "profit does not excuse it; thus, when you supply arms to the Southerners, with which to continue a criminal war, you are quite as guilty as when you sell opium to the Chinese, which stupefies them."

"Oh, for once, Miss Jenny, this is too much, and I cannot admit?"

"No; what I say is just, and when you consider it, when you understand the part you are playing, when you think of the results for which you are responsible, you will yield to me in this point, as in so many others."

James Playfair was dumfounded at these words; he left the young girl, a prey to angry thoughts, for he felt his powerlessness to answer; then he sulked like a child for half an hour, and an hour later he returned to the singular young girl who could overwhelm him with convincing arguments with quite a pleasant smile.

In short, however it may have come about, and although he would not acknowledge it to himself, Captain James Playfair belonged to himself no longer; he was no longer commander-in-chief on board his own ship.

Thus, to Crockston's great joy, Mr. Halliburtt's affairs appeared to be in a good way; the Captain seemed to have decided to undertake everything in his power to deliver Miss Jenny's father, and for this he would be obliged to compromise the Dolphin, his cargo, his crew, and incur the displeasure of his worthy Uncle Vincent.

Sullivan Island Channel

Two days after the meeting with the Iroquois, the Dolphin found herself abreast of the Bermudas, where she was assailed by a violent squall. These isles are frequently visited by hurricanes, and are celebrated for shipwrecks. It is here that Shakespeare has placed the exciting scene of his drama, *The Tempest*, in which Ariel and Caliban dispute for the empire of the floods.

The squall was frightful; James Playfair thought once of running for one of the Bermudas, where the English had a military post: it would have been a sad waste of time, and therefore especially to be regretted; happily the Dolphin behaved herself wonderfully well in the storm, and, after flying a whole day before the tempest, she was able to resume her course towards the American coast.

But if James Playfair had been pleased with his ship, he had not been less delighted with the young girl's bravery; Miss Halliburtt had passed the worst hours of the storm at his side, and James knew that a profound, imperious, irresistible love had taken possession of his whole being.

"Yes," said he, "this brave girl is mistress on board; she turns me like the sea a ship in distress." I feel that I am foundering! What will Uncle Vincent say? Ah! poor nature, I am sure that if Jenny asked me to throw all this cursed cargo into the sea, I should do it without hesitating, for love of her.

Happily for the firm of Playfair & Co., Miss Halliburtt did not demand this sacrifice; nevertheless, the poor Captain had been taken captive, and Crockston, who read his heart like an open book, rubbed his hands gleefully.

"We will hold him fast!" he muttered to himself, "and before a week has passed my master will be quietly installed in one of the best cabins of the Dolphin."

As for Miss Jenny, did she perceive the feelings which she inspired? Did she allow herself to share them? No one could say, and James Playfair least of all; the young girl kept a perfect reserve, and her secret remained deeply buried in her heart.

But whilst love was making such progress in the heart of the young Captain, the Dolphin sped with no less rapidity towards Charleston.

On the 13th of January, the watch signalled land ten miles to the west. It was a low-lying coast, and almost blended with the line of the sea in the distance. Crockston was examining the horizon attentively, and about nine o'clock in the morning he cried:

"Charleston lighthouse!"

Now that the bearings of the Dolphin were set, James Playfair had but one thing to do, to decide by which channel he would run into Charleston Bay.

"If we meet with no obstacles," said he, "before three o'clock we shall be in safety in the docks of the port."

The town of Charleston is situated on the banks of an estuary seven miles long and two broad, called Charleston Harbour, the entrance to which is rather difficult. It is enclosed between Morris Island on the south and Sullivan Island on the north. At the time when the Dolphin attempted to force the blockade Morris Island already belonged to the Federal troops, and General Gillmore had caused batteries to be erected overlooking the harbour. Sullivan Island, on the contrary, was in the hands of the Confederates, who were also in possession of Moultrie Fort, situated at the extremity of the island; therefore it would be advantageous to the Dolphin to go as close as possible to the northern shores to avoid the firing from the forts on Morris Island.

Five channels led into the estuary, Sullivan Island Channel, the Northern Channel, the Overall Channel, the Principal Channel, and lastly, the Lawford Channel; but it was useless for strangers, unless they had skilful pilots on board, or ships drawing less than seven feet of water, to attempt this last; as for Northern and Overall Channels, they were in range of the Federalist batteries, so that it was no good thinking of them. If James Playfair could have had his choice, he would have taken his steamer through the Principal Channel, which was the best, and the bearings of which were easy to follow; but it was necessary to yield to circumstances, and to decide according to the event. Besides, the Captain of the Dolphin knew perfectly all the secrets of this bay, its dangers, the depths of its water at low tide, and its currents, so that he was able to steer his ship with the greatest safety as soon as he entered one of these narrow straits. The great question was to get there.

Now this work demanded an experienced seaman, and one who knew exactly the qualities of the Dolphin.

In fact, two Federal frigates were now cruising in the Charleston waters. Mr. Mathew soon drew James Playfair's attention to them.

"They are preparing to ask us what we want on these shores," said he.

"Ah, well! we won't answer them," replied the Captain, "and they will not get their curiosity satisfied."

In the meanwhile the cruisers were coming on full steam towards the Dolphin, who continued her course, taking care to keep out of range of their guns. But in order to gain time James Playfair made for the south-west, wishing to put the enemies' ships off their guard; the latter must have thought that the Dolphin intended to make for Morris Island Channel. Now there they had batteries and guns, a single shot from which would have been enough to sink the English ship; so the Federals allowed the Dolphin to run towards the south-west, contenting themselves by observing her without following closely.

Thus for an hour the respective situations of the ships did not change, for James Playfair, wishing to deceive the cruisers as to the course of the Dolphin, had caused the fires to be moderated, so that the speed was decreased. However, from the thick volumes of smoke which escaped from the chimneys, it might have been thought that he was trying to get his maximum pressure, and, consequently his maximum of rapidity.

"They will be slightly astonished presently," said James Playfair, "when they see us slip through their fingers!"

In fact, when the Captain saw that he was near enough to Morris Island, and before a line of guns, the range of which he did not know, he turned his rudder quickly, and the ship resumed her northerly course, leaving the cruisers two miles to windward of her; the latter, seeing this manoeuvre, understood the steamer's object, and began to pursue her in earnest, but it was too late. The Dolphin doubled her speed under the action of the screws, and distanced them rapidly. Going nearer to the coast, a few shell were sent after her as an acquittal of conscience, but the Federals were outdone, for their projectiles did not reach half-way. At eleven o'clock in the morning, the steamer ranging near Sullivan Island, thanks to her small draft, entered the narrow strait full steam; there she was in safety, for no Federalist cruiser dared follow her in this channel, the depth of which, on an average, was only eleven feet at low tide.

"How!" cried Crockston, "and is that the only difficulty?"

"Oh! oh! Master Crockston," said James Playfair, "the difficulty is not in entering, but in getting out again."

"Nonsense!" replied the American, "that does not make me at all uneasy; with a boat like the Dolphin and a Captain like Mr. James Playfair, one can go where one likes, and come out in the same manner."

Nevertheless, James Playfair, with telescope in his hand, was attentively examining the route to be followed. He had before him excellent coasting guides, with which he could go ahead without any difficulty or hesitation.

Once his ship was safely in the narrow channel which runs the length of Sullivan Island, James steered bearing towards the middle of Fort Moultrie as far as the Pickney Castle, situated on the isolated island of Shute's Folly; on the other side rose Fort Johnson, a little way to the north of Fort Sumter.

At this moment the steamer was saluted by some shot which did not reach her, from the batteries on Morris Island. She continued her course without any deviation, passed before Moultrieville, situated at the extremity of Sullivan Island, and entered the bay.

Soon Fort Sumter on the left protected her from the batteries of the Federalists.

This fort, so celebrated in the civil war, is situated three miles and a half from Charleston, and about a mile from each side of the bay: it is nearly pentagonal in form, built on an artificial island of Massachusetts granite; it took ten years to construct and cost more than 900,000 dollars.

It was from this fort, on the 13th of April, 1861, that Anderson and the Federal troops were driven, and it was against it that the first shot of the Confederates was fired. It is impossible to estimate the quantity of iron and lead which the Federals showered down upon it. However, it resisted for almost three years, but a few months after the passage of the Dolphin it fell beneath General Gillmore's three hundred-pounders on Morris Island.

But at this time it was in all its strength, and the Confederate flag floated proudly above it.

Once past the fort, the town of Charleston appeared, lying between Ashley and Cooper Rivers.

James Playfair threaded his way through the buoys which mark the entrance of the channel, leaving behind the Charleston lighthouse, visible above Morris Island. He had hoisted the English flag, and made his way with wonderful rapidity through the narrow channels. When he had passed the quarantine buoy, he advanced freely into the centre of the bay. Miss Halliburtt was standing on the poop, looking at the town where her father was kept prisoner, and her eyes filled with tears.

At last the steamer's speed was moderated by the Captain's orders; the Dolphin ranged along the end of the south and east batteries, and was soon moored at the quay of the North Commercial Wharf.

A Southern General

The Dolphin, on arriving at the Charleston quay, had been saluted by the cheers of a large crowd. The inhabitants of this town, strictly blockaded by sea, were not accustomed to visits from European ships. They asked each other, not without astonishment, what this great steamer, proudly bearing the English flag, had come to do in their waters; but when they learned the object of her voyage, and why she had just forced the passage Sullivan, when the report spread that she carried a cargo of smuggled ammunition, the cheers and joyful cries were redoubled.

James Playfair, without losing a moment, entered into negotiation with General Beauregard, the military commander of the town. The latter eagerly received the young Captain of the Dolphin, who had arrived in time to provide the soldiers with the clothes and ammunition they were so much in want of. It was agreed that the unloading of the ship should take place immediately, and numerous hands came to help the English sailors.

Before quitting his ship James Playfair had received from Miss Halliburtt the most pressing injunctions with regard to her father, and the Captain had placed himself entirely at the young girl's service.

"Miss Jenny," he had said, "you may rely on me; I will do the utmost in my power to save your father, but I hope this business will not present many difficulties. I shall go and see General Beauregard to-day, and, without asking him at once for Mr. Halliburtt's liberty, I shall learn in what situation he is, whether he is on bail or a prisoner."

"My poor father!" replied Jenny, sighing; "he little thinks his daughter is so near him. Oh that I could fly into his arms!"

"A little patience, Miss Jenny; you will soon embrace your father. Rely upon my acting with the most entire devotion, but also with prudence and consideration."

This is why James Playfair, after having delivered the cargo of the Dolphin up to the General, and bargained for an immense stock of cotton, faithful to his promise, turned the conversation to the events of the day.

"So," said he, "you believe in the triumph of the slave-holders?"

"I do not for a moment doubt of our final success, and, as regards Charleston, Lee's army will soon relieve it: besides, what do you expect from the Abolitionists? Admitting that which will never be, that the commercial towns of Virginia, the two Carolinas, Georgia, Alabama, fall under their power, what then? Will they be masters of a country they can never occupy? No, certainly not; and for my part, if they are ever victorious, they shall pay dearly for it."

"And you are quite sure of your soldiers?" asked the Captain. "You are not afraid that Charleston will grow weary of a siege which is ruining her?"

"No, I do not fear treason; besides, the traitors would be punished remorselessly, and I would destroy the town itself by sword or fire if I discovered the least Unionist movement. Jefferson Davis confided Charleston to me, and you may be sure that Charleston is in safe hands."

"Have you any Federal prisoners?" asked James Playfair, coming to the interesting object of the conversation.

"Yes, Captain," replied the General, "it was at Charleston that the first shot of separation was fired. The Abolitionists who were here attempted to resist, and, after being defeated, they have been kept as prisoners of war."

"And have you many?"

"About a hundred."

"Free in the town?"

"They were until I discovered a plot formed by them: their chief succeeded in establishing a communication with the besiegers, who were thus informed of the situation of affairs in the town. I was then obliged to lock up these dangerous guests, and several of them will only leave their prison to ascend the slope of the citadel, where ten confederate balls will reward them for their federalism."

"What! To be shot!" cried the young man, shuddering involuntarily.

"Yes, and their chief first of all. He is a very dangerous man to have in a besieged town. I have sent his letters to the President at Richmond, and before a week is passed his sentence will be irrevocably passed."

"Who is this man you speak of?" asked James Playfair, with an assumed carelessness.

"A journalist from Boston, a violent Abolitionist with the confunded spirit of Lincoln."

"And his name?"

"Jonathan Halliburtt."

"Poor wretch!" exclaimed James, suppressing his emotion. "Whatever he may have done, one cannot help pitying him. And you think that he will be shot?"

"I am sure of it," replied Beauregard. "What can you expect? War is war; one must defend oneself as best one can."

"Well, it is nothing to me," said the Captain. "I shall be far enough away when this execution takes place."

"What! you are thinking of going away already."

"Yes, General, business must be attended to; as soon as my cargo of cotton is on board I shall be out to sea again. I was fortunate enough to enter the bay, but the difficulty is in getting out again. The Dolphin is a good ship; she can beat any of the Federal vessels for speed, but she does not pretend to distance cannon-balls, and a shell in her hull or engine would seriously affect my enterprise."

"As you please, Captain," replied Beauregard; "I have no advice to give you under such circumstances. You are doing your business, and you are right. I should act in the same manner were I in your place; besides, a stay at Charleston is not very pleasant, and a harbour where shells are falling three days out of four is not a safe shelter for your ship; so you will set sail when you please; but can you tell me what is the number and the force of the Federal vessels cruising before Charleston?"

James Playfair did his best to answer the General, and took leave of him on the best of terms; then he returned to the Dolphin very thoughtful and very depressed from what he had just heard.

"What shall I say to Miss Jenny? Ought I to tell her of Mr. Halliburtt's terrible situation? Or would it be better to keep her in ignorance of the trial which is awaiting her? Poor child!"

He had not gone fifty steps from the governor's house when he ran against Crockston. The worthy American had been watching for him since his departure.

"Well, Captain?"

James Playfair looked steadily at Crockston, and the latter soon understood he had no favourable news to give him.

"Have you seen Beauregard?" he asked.

"Yes," replied James Playfair.

"And have you spoken to him about Mr. Halliburtt?"

"No, it was he who spoke to me about him."

"Well, Captain?"

"Well, I may as well tell you everything, Crockston."

"Everything, Captain."

"General Beauregard has told me that your master will be shot within a week."

At this news anyone else but Crockston would have grown furious or given way to bursts of grief, but the American, who feared nothing, only said, with almost a smile on his lips:

"Pooh! what does it matter?"

"How! what does it matter?" cried James Playfair. "I tell you that Mr. Halliburtt will be shot within a week, and you answer, what does it matter?"

"And I mean it? If in six days he is on board the Dolphin, and if in seven days the Dolphin is on the open sea."

"Right!" exclaimed the Captain, pressing Crockston's hand. "I understand, my good fellow, you have got some pluck; and for myself, in spite of Uncle Vincent, I would throw myself overboard for Miss Jenny."

"No one need be thrown overboard," replied the American, "only the fish would gain by that: the most important business now is to deliver Mr. Halliburtt."

"But you must know that it will be difficult to do so."

"Pooh!" exclaimed Crockston.

"It is a question of communicating with a prisoner strictly guarded."

"Certainly."

"And to bring about an almost miraculous escape."

"Nonsense," exclaimed Crockston; "a prisoner thinks more of escaping than his guardian thinks of keeping him; that's why, thanks to our help, Mr. Halliburtt will be saved."

"You are right, Crockston."

"Always right."

"But now what will you do? There must be some plan: and there are precautions to be taken."

"I will think about it."

"But when Miss Jenny learns that her father is condemned to death, and that the order for his execution may come any day?"

"She will know nothing about it, that is all."

"Yes, it will be better for her and for us to tell her nothing."

"Where is Mr. Halliburtt imprisoned?" asked Crockston.

"In the citadel," replied James Playfair.

"Just so!... On board now?"

"On board, Crockston!"

The Escape

Miss Jenny, sitting at the poop of the Dolphin, was anxiously waiting the Captain's return; when the latter went up to her she could not utter a word, but her eyes questioned James Playfair more eagerly than her lips could have done. The latter, with Crockston's help, informed the young girl of the facts relating to her father's imprisonment. He said that he had carefully broached the subject of the prisoners of war to Beauregard, but, as the General did not seem disposed at all in their favour, he had thought it better to say no more about it, but think the matter over again.

"Since Mr. Halliburtt is not free in the town, his escape will be more difficult; but I will finish my task, and I promise you, Miss Jenny, that the Dolphin shall not leave Charleston without having your father on board."

"Thank you, Mr. James; I thank you with my whole heart."

At these words James Playfair felt a thrill of joy through his whole being.

He approached the young girl with moist eyes and quivering lips; perhaps he was going to make an avowal of the sentiments he could no longer repress, when Crockston interfered:

"This is no time for grieving," said he; "we must go to work, and consider what to do."

"Have you any plan, Crockston?" asked the young girl.

"I always have a plan," replied the American: "it is my peculiarity."

"But a good one?" said James Playfair.

"Excellent! and all the ministers in Washington could not

devise a better; it is almost as good as if Mr. Halliburtt was already on board."

Crockston spoke with such perfect assurance, at the same time with such simplicity, that it must have been the most incredulous person who could doubt his words.

"We are listening, Crockston," said James Playfair.

"Good! You, Captain, will go to General Beauregard, and ask a favour of him which he will not refuse you."

"And what is that?"

"You will tell him that you have on board a tiresome subject, a scamp who has been very troublesome during the voyage, and excited the crew to revolt. You will ask of him permission to shut him up in the citadel; at the same time, on the condition that he shall return to the ship on her departure, in order to be taken back to England, to be delivered over to the justice of his country."

"Good!" said James Playfair, half smiling, "I will do all that, and Beauregard will grant my request very willingly."

"I am perfectly sure of it," replied the American.

"But," resumed Playfair, "one thing is wanting."

"What is that?"

"The scamp."

"He is before you, Captain."

"What, the rebellious subject?"

"Is myself; don't trouble yourself about that."

"Oh! you brave, generous heart," cried Jenny, pressing the American's rough hands between her small white palms.

"Go, Crockston," said James Playfair; "I understand you, my friend; and I only regret one thing, that is, that I cannot take your place."

"Everyone his part," replied Crockston; "if you put yourself in my place you would be very much embarrassed, which I shall not be; you will have enough to do later on to get out of the harbour under the fire of the Feds and Rebs, which, for my part, I should manage very badly."

"Well, Crockston, go on."

"Once in the citadel, I know it, I shall see what to do, and rest assured I shall do my best; in the meanwhile, you will be getting your cargo on board."

"Oh, business is now a very unimportant detail," said the Captain.

"Not at all! And what would your Uncle Vincent say to that? We must join sentiment with work; it will prevent suspicion; but do it quickly. Can you be ready in six days?"

"Yes."

"Well, let the Dolphin be ready to start on the 22nd."

"She shall be ready."

"On the evening of the 22nd of January, you understand, send a gig with your best men to White Point, at the end of the town; wait there till nine o'clock, and then you will see Mr. Halliburtt and your servant."

"But how will you manage to effect Mr. Halliburtt's deliverance, and also escape yourself?"

"That's my look-out."

"Dear Crockston, you are going to risk your life then, to save my father!"

"Don't be uneasy, Miss Jenny, I shall risk absolutely nothing, you may believe me."

"Well," asked James Playfair, "when must I have you locked up?"

"To-day, you understand, I demoralise your crew; there is no time to be lost."

"Would you like any money? It may be of use to you in the citadel."

"Money to buy the gaoler! Oh, no, it would be a poor bargain; when one goes there the gaoler keeps the money and the prisoner! No, I have surer means than that; however, a few dollars may be useful; one must be able to drink, if needs be."

"And intoxicate the gaoler."

"No, an intoxicated gaoler would spoil everything. No, I tell you I have an idea; let me work it out."

"Here, my good fellow, are ten dollars."

"It is too much, but I will return what is over."

"Well, then, are you ready?"

"Quite ready to be a downright rogue."

"Let us go to work, then."

"Crockston," said the young girl, in a faltering voice, "you are the best man on earth."

"I know it," replied the American, laughing good-humouredly. "By the by, Captain, an important item."

"What is that?"

"If the General proposes to hang your rebel? You know that military men like sharp work?"

"Well, Crockston?"

"Well, you will say that you must think about it."

"I promise you I will."

The same day, to the great astonishment of the crew, who were not in the secret, Crockston, with his feet and hands in irons, was taken on shore by a dozen sailors, and half an hour after, by Captain James Playfair's request, he was led through the streets of the town, and, in spite of his resistance, was imprisoned in the citadel.

During this and the following days the unloading of the Dolphin was rapidly accomplished; the steam cranes lifted out the European cargo to make room for the native goods. The people of

Charleston, who were present at this interesting work, helped the sailors, whom they held in great respect, but the Captain did not leave the brave fellows much time for receiving compliments; he was constantly behind them, and urged them on with a feverish activity, the reason of which the sailors could not suspect.

Three days later, on the 18th of January, the first bales of cotton began to be packed in the hold; although James Playfair troubled himself no more about it, the firm of Playfair and Co. were making an excellent bargain, having obtained the cotton which encumbered the Charleston wharves at very far less than its value.

In the meantime no news had been heard of Crockston. Jenny, without saying anything about it, was a prey to incessant fears; her pale face spoke for her, and James Playfair endeavoured his utmost to ease her mind.

"I have all confidence in Crockston," said he; "he is a devoted servant, as you must know better than I do, Miss Jenny. You must make yourself quite at ease; believe me, in three days you will be folded in your father's arms."

"Ah! Mr. James," cried the young girl, "how can I ever repay you for such devotion? How shall we ever be able to thank you?"

"I will tell you when we are in English seas," replied the young Captain.

Jenny raised her tearful face to him for a moment, then her eyelids drooped, and she went back to her cabin.

James Playfair hoped that the young girl would know nothing of her father's terrible situation until he was in safety, but she was apprised of the truth by the involuntary indiscretion of a sailor.

The reply from the Richmond cabinet had arrived by a courier who had been able to pass the line of outposts; the reply contained Jonathan Halliburtt's death-warrant. The news of the approaching execution was not long in spreading through the town, and it was brought on board by one of the sailors of the Dolphin; the man told the Captain, without thinking that Miss Halliburtt was within hearing; the young girl uttered a piercing cry, and fell unconscious on the deck. James Playfair carried her to her cabin, but the most assiduous care was necessary to restore her to life.

When she opened her eyes again, she saw the young Captain, who, with a finger on his lips, enjoined absolute silence. With difficulty she repressed the outburst of her grief, and James Playfair, leaning towards her, said gently:

"Jenny, in two hours your father will be in safety near you, or I shall have perished in endeavouring to save him!"

Then he left the cabin, saying to himself, "And now he must be carried off at any price, since I must pay for his liberty with my own life and those of my crew."

The hour for action had arrived, the loading of the cotton cargo had been finished since morning; in two hours the ship would be ready to start.

James Playfair had left the North Commercial Wharf and gone into the roadstead, so that he was ready to make use of the tide, which would be high at nine o'clock in the evening.

It was seven o'clock when James left the young girl, and began to make preparations for departure. Until the present time the secret had been strictly kept between himself, Crockston, and Jenny; but now he thought it wise to inform Mr. Mathew of the situation of affairs, and he did so immediately.

"Very well, sir," replied Mr. Mathew, without making the least remark, "and nine o'clock is the time?"

"Nine o'clock, and have the fires lit immediately, and the steam got up."

"It shall be done, Captain."

"The Dolphin may remain at anchor; we will cut our moorings and sheer off, without losing a moment."

"Just so."

"Have a lantern placed at the mainmast-head; the night is dark, and will be foggy; we must not risk losing our way in returning. You had better have the bell for starting rung at nine o'clock."

"Your orders shall be punctually attended to, Captain."

"And now, Mr. Mathew, have a shore-boat manned with six of our best men. I am going to set out directly for White Point. I leave Miss Jenny in your charge, and may God protect us!"

"May God protect us!" repeated the first officer.

Then he immediately gave the necessary orders for the fires to be lighted, and the shore-boat provided with men. In a few minutes the boat was ready, and James Playfair, after bidding Jenny good-bye, stepped into it, whilst at the same time he saw volumes of black smoke issuing from the chimneys of the ship, and losing itself in the fog.

The darkness was profound; the wind had fallen, and in the perfect silence the waters seemed to slumber in the immense harbour, whilst a few uncertain lights glimmered through the mist. James Playfair had taken his place at the rudder, and with a steady hand he guided his boat towards White Point. It was a distance of about two miles; during the day James had taken his bearings perfectly, so that he was able to make direct for Charleston Point.

Eight o'clock struck from the church of St. Philip when the shore-boat ran aground at White Point.

There was an hour to wait before the exact time fixed by Crockston; the quay was deserted, with the exception of the sentinel pacing to and fro on the south and east batteries. James Playfair grew impatient, and the minutes seemed hours to him.

At half-past eight he heard the sound of approaching steps; he left his men with their oars clear and ready to start, and went himself to see who it was; but he had not gone ten feet when he met a band of coastguards, in all about twenty men. James drew his revolver from his waist, deciding to make use of it, if needs be; but what could he do against these soldiers, who were coming on to the quay?

The leader came up to him, and, seeing the boat, asked:

"Whose craft is that?"

"It is a gig belonging to the Dolphin," replied the young man.

"And who are you?"

"Captain James Playfair."

"I thought you had already started, and were now in the Charleston channels."

"I am ready to start. I ought even now to be on my way but?"

"But?" persisted the coastguard.

A bright idea shot through James's mind, and he answered:

"One of my sailors is locked up in the citadel, and, to tell the truth, I had almost forgotten him; fortunately I thought of him in time, and I have sent my men to bring him."

"Ah! that troublesome fellow; you wish to take him back to England?"

"Yes."

"He might as well be hung here as there," said the coast-guard, laughing at his joke.

"So I think," said James Playfair, "but it is better to have the thing done in the regular way."

"Not much chance of that, Captain, when you have to face the Morris Island batteries."

"Don't alarm yourself. I got in and I'll get out again."

"Prosperous voyage to you!"

"Thank you."

With this the men went off, and the shore was left silent.

At this moment nine o'clock struck; it was the appointed moment. James felt his heart beat violently; a whistle was heard; he replied to it, then he waited, listening, with his hand up to enjoin perfect silence on the sailors. A man appeared enveloped in a large cloak, and looking from one side to another. James ran up to him.

"Mr. Halliburtt?"

"I am he," replied the man with the cloak.

"God be praised!" cried James Playfair. "Embark without losing a minute. Where is Crockston?"

"Crockston!" exclaimed Mr. Halliburtt, amazed. "What do you mean?"

"The man who has saved you and brought you here was your servant Crockston."

"The man who came with me was the gaoler from the citadel," replied Mr. Halliburtt.

"The gaoler!" cried James Playfair.

Evidently he knew nothing about it, and a thousand fears crowded in his mind.

"Quite right, the gaoler," cried a well-known voice. "The gaoler is sleeping like a top in my cell."

"Crockston! you! Can it be you?" exclaimed Mr. Halliburtt.

"No time to talk now, master; we will explain everything to you afterwards. It is a question of life or death. Get in quick!"

The three men took their places in the boat.

"Push off!" cried the captain.

Immediately the six oars dipped into the water; the boat darted like a fish through the waters of Charleston Harbour.

Between Two Fires

The boat, pulled by six robust oarsmen, flew over the water. The fog was growing dense, and it was with difficulty that James Playfair succeeded in keeping to the line of his bearings. Crockston sat at the bows, and Mr. Halliburtt at the stern, next the Captain. The prisoner, only now informed of the presence of his servant, wished to speak to him, but the latter enjoined silence.

However, a few minutes later, when they were in the middle of the harbour, Crockston determined to speak, knowing what thoughts were uppermost in Mr. Halliburtt's mind.

"Yes, my dear master," said he, "the gaoler is in my place in the cell, where I gave him two smart blows, one on the head and the other on the stomach, to act as a sleeping draught, and this when he was bringing me my supper; there is gratitude for you. I took his clothes and his keys, found you, and let you out of the citadel, under the soldiers' noses. That is all I have done."

"But my daughter?" asked Mr. Halliburtt.

"Is on board the ship which is going to take you to England."

"My daughter there! there!" cried the American, springing from his seat.

"Silence!" replied Crockston, "a few minutes, and we shall be saved."

The boat flew through the darkness, but James Playfair was obliged to steer rather by guess, as the lanterns of the Dolphin were no longer visible through the fog. He was undecided what direction to follow, and the darkness was so great that the rowers could not even see to the end of their oars.

"Well, Mr. James?" said Crockston.

"We must have made more than a mile and a half," replied the Captain. "You don't see anything, Crockston?"

"Nothing; nevertheless, I have good eyes; but we shall get there all right. They don't suspect anything out there."

These words were hardly finished when the flash of a gun gleamed for an instant through the darkness, and vanished in the mist.

"A signal!" cried James Playfair.

"Whew!" exclaimed Crockston. "It must have come from the citadel. Let us wait."

A second, then a third shot was fired in the direction of the first, and almost the same signal was repeated a mile in front of the gig.

"That is from Fort Sumter," cried Crockston, "and it is the signal of escape. Urge on the men; everything is discovered."

"Pull for your lives, my men!" cried James Playfair, urging on the sailors, "those gun-shots cleared my route. The Dolphin is eight hundred yards ahead of us. Stop! I hear the bell on board. Hurrah, there it is again! Twenty pounds for you if we are back in five minutes!"

The boat skimmed over the waves under the sailors' powerful oars. A cannon boomed in the direction of the town. Crockston heard a ball whiz past them.

The bell on the Dolphin was ringing loudly. A few more strokes and the boat was alongside. A few more seconds and Jenny fell into her father's arms.

The gig was immediately raised, and James Playfair sprang on to the poop.

"Is the steam up, Mr. Mathew?"

"Yes, Captain."

"Have the moorings cut at once."

A few minutes later the two screws carried the steamer towards the principal channel, away from Fort Sumter.

"Mr. Mathew," said James, "we must not think of taking the Sullivan Island channel; we should run directly under the Confederate guns. Let us go as near as possible to the right side of the harbour out of range of the Federal batteries. Have you a safe man at the helm?"

"Yes, Captain."

"Have the lanterns and the fires on deck extinguished; there is a great deal too much light, but we cannot help the reflection from the engine-rooms."

During this conversation the Dolphin was going at a great speed; but in altering her course to keep to the right side of the Charleston Harbour she was obliged to enter a channel which took her for a moment near Fort Sumter; and when scarcely half a mile off all the guns bearing on her were discharged at the same time, and a shower of shot and shell passed in front of the Dolphin with a thundering report.

"Too soon, stupids," cried James Playfair, with a burst of laughter. "Make haste, make haste, Mr. Engineer! We shall get between two fires."

The stokers fed the furnaces, and the Dolphin trembled all over with the effort of the engine as if she was on the point of exploding.

At this moment a second report was heard, and another shower of balls whizzed behind the Dolphin.

"Too late, stupids," cried the young Captain, with a regular roar.

Then Crockston, who was standing on the poop, cried, "That's one passed. A few minutes more, and we shall have done with the Rebs."

"Then do you think we have nothing more to fear from Fort Sumter?" asked James.

"Nothing at all, but everything from Fort Moultrie, at the end of Sullivan Island; but they will only get a chance at us for half a minute, and then they must choose their time well, and shoot straight if they want to reach us. We are getting near."

"Right; the position of Fort Moultrie will allow us to go straight for the principal channel. Fire away then, fire away!"

At the same moment, and as if in obedience to James Playfair, the fort was illuminated by a triple line of lightning. A frightful crash was heard; then a crackling sound on board the steamer.

"Touched this time!" exclaimed Crockston.

"Mr. Mathew!" cried the Captain to his second, who was stationed at the bows, "what has been damaged?"

"The bowsprit broken."

"Any wounded?"

"No, Captain."

"Well, then, the masts may go to Jericho. Straight into the pass! Straight! and steer towards the island."

"We have passed the Rebs!" cried Crockston; "and, if we must have balls in our hull, I would much rather have the Northerners; they are more easily digested."

In fact, the Dolphin could not yet consider herself out of danger; for, if Morris Island was not fortified with the formidable pieces of artillery which were placed there a few months later, nevertheless its guns and mortars could easily have sunk a ship like the Dolphin.

The alarm had been given to the Federals on the island, and to the blockading squadron, by the firing from Forts Sumter and Moultrie. The besiegers could not make out the reason of this night attack; it did not seem to be directed against them. However, they were obliged to consider it so, and were ready to reply.

It occupied James Playfair's thoughts whilst making towards the passes of Morris Island; and he had reason to fear, for in a quarter of an hour's time lights gleamed rapidly through the darkness. A shower of small shell fell round the steamer, scattering the water over her bulwarks; some of them even struck the deck of the Dolphin, but not on their points, which saved the ship from certain ruin. In fact, these shell, as it was afterwards discovered, could break into a hundred fragments, and each cover a superficial area of a hundred and twenty square feet with Greek fire, which would burn for twenty minutes, and nothing could extinguish it. One of these shell alone could set a ship on fire. Fortunately for the Dolphin, they were a new invention, and as yet far from perfect. Once thrown into the air, a false rotary movement kept them inclined, and, when falling, instead of striking on their points, where is the percussion apparatus, they fell flat. This defect in construction alone saved the Dolphin. The falling of these shells did her little harm, and under the pressure of her over-heated boilers she continued to advance into the pass.

At this moment, and in spite of his orders, Mr. Halliburtt and his daughter went to James Playfair on the poop; the latter urged them to return to their cabins, but Jenny declared that she would remain by the Captain. As for Mr. Halliburtt, who had just learnt all the noble conduct of his deliverer, he pressed his hand without being able to utter a word.

The Dolphin was speeding rapidly towards the open sea. There were only three miles more before she would be in the waters of the Atlantic; if the pass was free at its entrance, she was saved. James Playfair was wonderfully well acquainted with all the secrets of Charleston Bay, and he guided his ship through the darkness with an unerring hand. He was beginning to think his daring enterprise successful, when a sailor on the forecastle cried:

"A ship!"

"A ship?" cried James.

"Yes, on the larboard side."

The fog had cleared off, and a large frigate was seen making towards the pass, in order to obstruct the passage of the Dolphin. It was necessary, cost what it might, to distance her, and urge the steam-engine to an increase of speed, or all was lost.

"Port the helm at once!" cried the Captain.

Then he sprang on to the bridge above the engine. By his orders one of the screws was stopped, and under the action of the other the Dolphin, veering with an extraordinary rapidity, avoided running foul of the frigate, and advanced like her to the entrance of the pass. It was now a question of speed.

James Playfair understood that in this lay his own safety, Miss Jenny's, her father's, and that of all his crew.

The frigate was considerably in advance of the Dolphin. It was evident from the volumes of black smoke issuing from her chimneys that she was getting up her steam. James Playfair was not the man to be left in the background.

"How are the engines?" cried he to the engineer.

"At the maximum speed," replied the latter; "the steam is escaping by all the valves."

"Fasten them down," ordered the Captain.

And his orders were executed at the risk of blowing up the ship.

The Dolphin again increased her speed; the pistons worked with frightful rapidity; the metal plates on which the engine was placed trembled under the terrific force of their blows. It was a sight to make the boldest shudder.

"More pressure!" cried James Playfair; "put on more pressure!"

"Impossible!" replied the engineer. "The valves are tightly closed; our furnaces are full up to the mouths."

"What difference! Fill them with cotton soaked in spirits; we must pass that frigate at any price."

At these words the most daring of the sailors looked at each other, but did not hesitate. Some bales of cotton were thrown into the engine-room, a barrel of spirits broached over them, and this expensive fuel placed, not without danger, in the red-hot furnaces. The stokers could no longer hear each other speak for the roaring of the flames. Soon the metal plates of the furnaces became red-hot; the pistons worked like the pistons of a locomotive; the steamgauge showed a frightful tension; the steamer flew over the water; her boards creaked, and her chimneys threw out volumes of smoke mingled with flames. She was going at a headlong speed, but, nevertheless, she was gaining on the frigate' passed her, distanced her, and in ten minutes was out of the channel.

"Saved!" cried the Captain.

"Saved!" echoed the crew, clapping their hands.

Already the Charleston beacon was disappearing in the south-west; the sound of firing from the batteries grew fainter, and it might with reason be thought that the danger was all past, when a shell from a gun-boat cruising at large was hurled whizzing through the air. It was easy to trace its course, thanks to the line of fire which followed it.

Then was a moment of anxiety impossible to describe; everyone was silent, and each watched fearfully the arch described by the projectile. Nothing could be done to escape it, and in a few seconds it fell with a frightful noise on the fore-deck of the Dolphin.

The terrified sailors crowded to the stern, and no one dared move a step, whilst the shell was burning with a brisk crackle.

But one brave man alone among them ran up to the formidable weapon of destruction. It was Crockston; he took the shell in his strong arms, whilst showers of sparks were falling from it; then, with a superhuman effort, he threw it overboard.

Hardly had the shell reached the surface of the water when it burst with a frightful report.

"Hurrah! hurrah!" cried the whole crew of the Dolphin unanimously, whilst Crockston rubbed his hands.

Some time later the steamer sped rapidly through the waters of the Atlantic; the American coast disappeared in the darkness, and the distant lights which shot across the horizon indicated that the attack was general between the batteries of Morris Island and the forts of Charleston Harbour.

St. Mungo

The next day at sunrise the American coast had disappeared; not a ship was visible on the horizon, and the Dolphin, moderating the frightful rapidity of her speed, made quietly towards the Bermudas.

It is useless to recount the passage across the Atlantic, which was marked by no accidents, and ten days after the departure from Queenstown the French coast was hailed.

What passed between the Captain and the young girl may be imagined, even by the least observant individuals. How could Mr. Halliburtt acknowledge the devotion and courage of his deliverer, if it was not by making him the happiest of men? James Playfair did not wait for English seas to declare to the father and daughter the sentiments which overflowed his heart, and, if Crockston is to be believed, Miss Jenny received his confession with a happiness she did not try to conceal.

Thus it happened that on the 14th of February, a numerous crowd was collected in the dim aisles of St. Mungo, the old cathedral of Glasgow. There were seamen, merchants, manufacturers, magistrates, and some of every denomination gathered here. There was Miss Jenny in bridal array and beside her the worthy Crockston, resplendent in apple-green clothes, with gold buttons, whilst Uncle Vincent stood proudly by his nephew.

In short, they were celebrating the marriage of James Playfair, of the firm of Vincent Playfair & Co., of Glasgow, with Miss Jenny Halliburtt, of Boston.

The ceremony was accomplished amidst great pomp. Everyone knew the history of the Dolphin, and everyone thought the young

Captain well recompensed for his devotion. He alone said that his reward was greater than he deserved.

In the evening there was a grand ball and banquet at Uncle Vincent's house, with a large distribution of shillings to the crowd collected in Gordon Street. Crockston did ample justice to this memorable feast, while keeping himself perfectly within bounds.

Everyone was happy at this wedding; some at their own happiness, and others at the happiness around them, which is not always the case at ceremonies of this kind.

Late in the evening, when the guests had retired, James Playfair took his uncle's hand.

"Well, Uncle Vincent," said he to him.

"Well, Nephew James?"

"Are you pleased with the charming cargo I brought you on board the Dolphin?" continued Captain Playfair, showing him his brave young wife.

"I am quite satisfied," replied the worthy merchant; "I have sold my cotton at three hundred and seventy-five per cent profit."

Frritt–Flacc

I

Swish! It is the wind, let loose.

Swash! It is the rain, falling in torrents.

This shrieking squall bends down the trees of the Volsinian coast, and hurries on, flinging itself against the sides of the mountains of Crimma. Along the whole length of the littoral are high rocks, gnawed by the billows of the vast Sea of Megalocrida.

Swish! swash!

Down by the harbour nestles the little town of Luktrop; perhaps a hundred houses, with green palings, which defend them indifferently from the wild wind; four or five hilly streets - ravines rather than streets - paved with pebbles and strewn with ashes thrown from the active cones in the background. The volcano is not far distant; it is called the Vauglor. During the day it sends forth sulphurous vapours; at night, from time to time, great outpourings of flame. Like a lighthouse carrying a hundred and fifty kertzes, the Vauglor indicates the port of Luktrop to the coasters, felzans, verliches, and balanzes, whose keels furrow the waters of Megalocrida.

On the other side of the town are ruins dating from the Crimmarian era. Then a suburb, Arab in appearance, much like a casbah, with white walls, domed roofs, and sun-scorched terraces, which are all nothing but accumulations of square stones thrown together at random. Veritable dice are these, whose numbers will never be effaced by the rust of Time.

Among others we notice the Six-four, a name given to a curious erection, having six openings on one side and four on the other.

A belfry overlooks the town, the square belfry of Saint Philfilena, with bells hung in the thickness of the walls, which sometimes a hurricane will set in motion. That is a bad sign; the people tremble when they hear it.

Such is Luktrop. Then come the scattered habitations in the country, set amid heath and broom, as in Brittany. But this is not Brittany. Is it in France? I do not know. Is it in Europe? I cannot tell. At all events, do not look for Luktrop on any map.

II

RAT-TAT! A discreet knock is struck upon the narrow door of Six-four, at the left corner of the Rue Messagliere. This is one of the most comfortable houses in Luktrop - if such a word is known there - one of the richest, if gaining some millions of fretzers, by hook or by crook, constitutes riches.

The rat-tat is answered by a savage bark, in which is much a lupine howl, as if a wolf should bark. Then a window is opened above the door of Six-four, and an ill-tempered voice says, "Deuce take people who come bothering here!"

A young girl, shivering in the rain wrapped in a thin cloak, asks if Dr. Trifulgas is at home.

"He is, or he is not, according to circumstances."

"I want him to come to my father, who is dying."

"Where is he dying?"

"At Val Karnion, four kertzes from here."

"And his name?"

"Vort Kartif."

"Vort Kartif, the herring-salter?"

"Yes; and if Dr. Trifulgas…"

"Dr. Trifulgas is not at home."

And the window is closed with a slam, while the swishes of the wind and the swashes of the rain mingle in a deafening uproar.

III

A hard man, this Dr. Trifulgas, with little compassion, and attending no one unless paid cash in advance. His old Hurzof, a mongrel of bulldog and spaniel, would have had more feeling than he. The house called Six-four admitted no poor, and opened only to the rich. Further, it had a regular tariff: so much for a typhoid fever, so much for a fit, so much for a pericarditis, and for other complaints which doctors invent by the dozen. Now, Vort Kartif, the herring-salter, was a poor man, and of low degree. Why should Dr. Trifulgas have taken any trouble, and on such a night?

"Is it nothing that I should have had to get up?" he murmured, as he went back to bed; "that alone is worth ten fretzers."

Hardly twenty minutes had passed, when the iron hammer was again struck on the door of Six-four.

Much against his inclination the doctor left his bed, and leaned out of his window.

"Who is there?" he cried.

"I am the wife of Vort Kartif."

"The herring-salter of Val Karnion?"

"Yes; and if you refuse to come, he will die."

"All right; you will be a widow."

"Here are twenty fretzers."

"Twenty fretzers for going to Val Karnion, four kertzes from here! Thank you! Be off with you!"

And the window was closed again. Twenty fretzers! A grand fee! Risk a cold or lumbago for twenty fretzers, especially when to-morrow one has to go to Kiltreno to visit the rich Edzingov, laid up with gout, which is valued at fifty fretzers the visit! With this agreeable prospect before him, Dr. Trifulgas slept more soundly than before.

Swish! Swash! and then rat-tat! rat-tat! rat-tat! To the noises of the squall were now added three blows of the knocker, struck by a more decided hand. The doctor slept. He woke, but in a fearful humour. When he opened the window the storm came in like a charge of shot.

"I am come about the herring-salter."

"That wretched herring-salter again!"

"I am his mother."

"May his mother, his wife, and his daughter perish with him!"

"He has had an attack..."

"Let him defend himself."

"Some money has been paid us," continued the old woman, "an instalment on the house sold to the camondeur Doutrup, of the Rue Messagliere. If you do not come, my granddaughter will no longer have a father, my daughter-in-law a husband, myself a son."

It was piteous and terrible to hear the old woman's voice - to know that the wind was freezing the blood in her veins, that the rain was soaking her very bones beneath her thin flesh.

"A fit! why, that would be two hundred fretzers!" replied the heartless Trifulgas.

"We have only a hundred and twenty."

"Good-night," and the window was again closed. But, after due reflection, it appeared that a hundred and twenty fretzers for an hour and a half on the road, plus half an hour of visit, made a fretzer a minute. A small profit, but still, not to be despised.

Instead of going to bed again, the doctor slipped into his coat of valveter, went down in his wading boots, stowed himself away in his great coat of lurtaine, with his sourouet on his head, and his mufflers on his hands. He left his lamp lighted close to the pharmacopoeia, open at page 197. Then, pulling the door of Six-four, he paused on the threshold. The old woman was there, leaning on her stick, bowed down by her eighty years of misery.

"The hundred and twenty fretzers."

"Here is the money; and may God multiply it for you a hundredfold!"

"God! Who ever saw the colour of his money?"

The doctor whistled for Hurzof, gave him a small lantern to carry, and took the road towards the sea. The old woman followed.

IV

What swishy-swashy weather! The bells of St. Philfilena are all swinging by reason of the gale. A bad sign! But Dr. Trifulgas is not superstitious. He believes in nothing - not even in his own science, except for what it brings him in. What weather, and also what a road! Pebbles and ashes; the pebbles slippery with seaweed, the ashes crackling with iron refuse. No other light than that from Hurzof's lantern, vague and uncertain. At times jets of flame from Vauglor uprear themselves, and in the midst of them appear great comical silhouettes. In truth no one knows what is in the depths of those unfathomable craters. Perhaps spirits of the other world, which volatilise themselves as they come forth.

The doctor and the old woman follow the curves of the little bays of the littoral. The sea is white with livid whiteness - a mourning white. It sparkles as it throws off the crests of the surf, which seem like outpourings of glow-worms.

These two persons go on thus as far as the turn in the road between sand-hills, where the brooms and the reeds clash together with a shock like that of bayonets.

The dog had drawn near to his master, and seemed to say to him, "Come, come! a hundred and twenty fretzers for the strong box! That is the way to make a fortune. Another rood added to the vineyard; another dish added to our supper; another meat pie for the faithful Hurzof. Let us look after the rich invalids, and look after them - according to their purses!"

At that spot the old woman pauses. With her trembling finger she points out among the shadows a reddish light. There is the house of Vort Kartif, the herring-salter.

"There?" said the doctor.

"Yes," said the old woman.

"Hurrah!" cries the dog Hurzof.

A sudden explosion from the Vauglor, shaken to its very base. A sheaf of lurid flame springs up to the zenith, forcing its way through the clouds. Dr. Trifulgas is hurled to the ground. He swears roundly, picks himself up, and looks about him.

The old woman is no longer there. Has she disappeared through some fissure of the earth, or has she flown away on the wings of the mist? As for the dog, he is there still, standing on his hind legs, his jaws apart, his lantern extinguished.

"Nevertheless, we will go on," mutters Dr. Trifulgas. The honest man has been paid his hundred and twenty fretzers, and he must earn them.

V

Only a luminous speck at the distance of half a kertz. It is the lamp of the dying -perhaps the dead. Of course, it is the herring-salter's house; the old woman pointed to it with her finger; no mistake is possible. Through the whistling swishes and the dashing swashes, through the uproar of the tempest, Dr. Trifulgas tramps on with hurried steps. As he advances, the house becomes more distinct, being isolated in the midst of the landscape.

It is very remarkable how much it resembles that of Dr. Trifulgas, the Six-four of Luktrop. The same arrangement of windows, the same little arched door. Dr. Trifulgas hastens on as fast as the gale allows him. The door is ajar; he has but to push it. He pushes it, he enters, and the wind roughly closes it behind him. The dog Hurzof, left outside, howls, with intervals of silence.

Strange! One would have said that Dr. Trifulgas had come back to his own house. And yet he has not wandered; he has not even taken a turning. He is at Val Karnion, not at Luktrop. And yet, here is the same low, vaulted passage, the same wooden staircase, with high banisters, worn away by the constant rubbing of hands.

He ascends. He reaches the landing. Beneath the door a faint light filters through, as in Six-four. Is it a delusion? In the dimness he recognises his room - the yellow sofa, on the right the old chest of pearwood, on the left the brass-bound strong box, in which he intended to deposit his hundred and twenty fretzers. There is his armchair, with the leathern cushions; there is his table, with its twisted legs, and on it, close to the expiring lamp, his pharmacopoeia, open at page 197.

"What is the matter with me?" he murmurs.

What is the matter with him? Fear! His pupils are dilated; his body is contracted, shrivelled; an icy perspiration freezes his skin - every hair stands on end.

But hasten! For want of oil, the lamp expires; and also the dying man! Yes, there is the bed - his own bed - with posts and canopy; as wide as it is long, shut in by heavy curtains. Is it possible that this is the pallet of a wretched herring-salter? With a quaking hand Dr. Trifulgas seizes the curtains; he opens them; he looks in.

The dying man, his head uncovered, is motionless, as if at his last breath. The doctor leans over him...

Ah! what a cry, to which, outside, responds an unearthly howl from the dog.

The dying man is not the herring-salter, Vort Kartif - it is Dr. Trifulgas; it is he, whom congestion has attacked - he himself! Cerebral apoplexy, with sudden accumulation of serosity on the cavities of the brain, with paralysis of the body on the side opposite that of the seat of the lesion.

Yes, it is he, who was sent for, and for whom a hundred and twenty fretzers have been paid. He who, from hardness of heart, refused to attend the herring-salter - he who was dying.

Dr. Trifulgas is like a madman, he knows himself lost. At each moment the symptoms increase. Not only all the functions of the organs slacken, but the lungs and the heart cease to act. And yet he has not quite lost consciousness. What can be done? Bleed! If he hesitates, Dr. Trifulgas is dead. In those days they still bled; and then, as now, medical men cured all those apoplectic patients who were not going to die.

Dr. Trifulgas seizes his case, takes out his lancet, opens a vein in the arm of his double. The blood does not flow. He rubs his chest violently - his own breathing grows slower. He warms his feet with hot bricks - his own grow cold.

Then his double lifts himself, falls back, and draws one last breath. Dr. Trifulgas, notwithstanding all that his science has taught him to do, dies beneath his own hands.

VI

In the morning a corpse was found in the house Six-four - that of Dr. Trifulgas. They put him in a coffin, and carried him with much pomp to the cemetery of Luktrop, wither he had sent so many others - in a professional manner.

As to old Hurzof, it is said that, to this day, he haunts the country with his lantern alight, and howling like a lost dog. I do not know if that be true; but strange things happen in Volsinia, especially in the neighbourhood of Luktrop.

And, again, I warn you not to hunt for that town on the map. The best geographers have not yet agreed as to its latitude - not even as to its longitude.

The Pearl of Lima
A Story of True Love

The Plaza-Mayor

The sun had disappeared behind the snowy peaks of the Cordilleras; but the beautiful Peruvian sky long retains, through the transparent veil of night, the reflection of his rays; the atmosphere is impregnated with a refreshing coolness, which in these burning latitudes affords freedom of breath; it is the hour in which one can live a European life, and seek without on the verandas some cooling gentle zephyr; it seems as if a metallic roof was then interposed between the sun and the earth, which, retaining the heat and suffering only the light to pass, offers beneath its shelter a reparative repose.

This much desired hour had at last sounded from the clock of the cathedral. While the earliest stars were rising above the horizon, the numerous promenaders were traversing the streets of Lima, wrapped in their light mantles, and conversing gravely on the most trivial affairs. There was a great movement of the populace on the Plaza-Mayor, that forum of the ancient city of kings; artisans were profiting by the coolness to quit their daily labors; they circulated actively among the crowd, crying their various merchandise; the ladies of Lima, carefully enveloped in the mantillas which mask their countenances, with the exception of the right eye, darted stealthy glances on the surrounding masses; they undulated through the groups of smokers, like foam at the will of the waves; other señoras, in ball costume, coiffed only with their abundant hair or some natural flowers, passed in large calêches, throwing on the caballeros nonchalant regards.

But these glances were not bestowed indiscriminately upon the young cavaliers; the thoughts of the noble ladies could rest only on aristocratic heights. The Indians passed without lifting their eyes upon them, knowing themselves to be beneath their notice; betraying by no gesture or word, the bitter envy of their hearts. They contrasted strongly with the half-breeds, or mestizoes, who, repulsed like the former, vented their indignation in cries and protestations.

The proud descendants of Pizarro marched with heads high, as in the times when their ancestors founded the city of kings; their traditional scorn rested alike on the Indians whom they had conquered, and the mestizoes, born of their relations with the natives of the New World. The Indians, on the contrary, were constantly struggling to break their chains, and cherished alike aversion toward the conquerors of the ancient empire of the Incas and their haughty and insolent descendants.

But the mestizoes, Spanish in their contempt for the Indians, and Indian in their hatred which they had vowed against the Spaniards, burned with both these vivid and impassioned sentiments.

A group of these young people stood near the pretty fountain in the centre of the Plaza-Mayor. Clad in their poncho, a piece of cloth or cotton in the form of a parallelogram, with an opening in the middle to give passage to the head, in large pantaloons, striped with a thousand colors, coiffed with broad-brimmed hats of Guayaquil straw, they were talking, declaiming, gesticulating.

"You are right, André," said a very obsequious young man, whom they called Milleflores.

This was the friend, the parasite of André Certa, a young mestizo of swarthy complexion, whose thin beard gave a singular appearance to his countenance.

André Certa, the son of a rich merchant killed in the last émeute of the conspirator Lafuente, had inherited a large fortune; this he freely scattered among his friends, whose humble salutations he demanded in exchange for handfuls of gold.

"Of what use are these changes in government, these eternal pronunciamentos which disturb Peru to gratify private ambition?" resumed André, in a loud voice; "what is it to me whether Gambarra or Santa Cruz rule, if there is no equality."

"Well said," exclaimed Milleflores, who, under the most republican government, could never have been the equal of a man of sense.

"How is it," resumed André Certa, "that I, the son of a merchant, can ride only in a calêche drawn by mules? Have not my ships brought wealth and prosperity to the country? Is not the aristocracy of piasters worth all the titles of Spain?"

"It is a shame!" resumed the young mestizo. "There is Don Fernand, who passes in his carriage drawn by two horses! Don Fernand d'Aiquillo! He has scarcely property enough to feed his coachman and horses, and he must come to parade himself proudly about the square. And, hold! here is another! the Marquis Don Vegal!"

A magnificent carriage, drawn by four fine horses, at that moment entered the Plaza-Mayor; its only occupant was a man of proud mien, mingled with sadness; he gazed, without seeming to see them, on the multitude assembled to breathe the coolness of the evening. This man was the Marquis Don Vegal, knight of Alcantara, of Malta, and of Charles III. He had a right to appear in this pompous equipage; the viceroy and the archbishop could alone take precedence of him; but this great nobleman came here from ennui and not from ostentation; his thoughts were not depicted on his countenance, they were concentrated beneath his bent brow; he received no impression from exterior objects, on which he bestowed not a look, and heard not the envious reflections of the mestizoes, when his four horses made their way through the crowd.

"I hate that man," said André Certa.

"You will not hate him long."

"I know it! All these nobles are displaying the last splendors of their luxury; I can tell where their silver and their family jewels go."

"You have not your entrée with the Jew Samuel for nothing."

"Certainly not! On his account-books are inscribed aristocratic creditors; in his strong-box are piled the wrecks of great fortunes; and in the day when the Spaniards shall be as ragged as their Cæsar de Bazan, we will have fine sport."

"Yes, we will have fine sport, dear André, mounted on your millions, on a golden pedestal! And you are about to double your fortune! When are you to marry the beautiful young daughter of old Samuel, a Limanienne to the end of her nails, with nothing Jewish about her but her name of Sarah?"

"In a month," replied André Certa, proudly, "there will be no fortune in Peru which can compete with mine."

"But why," asked some one, "do you not espouse some Spanish girl of high descent?"

"I despise these people as much as I hate them."

André Certa concealed the fact of his having been repulsed by several noble families, into which he had sought to introduce himself.

His interlocutor still wore an expression of doubt, and the brow of the mestizo had contracted, when the latter was rudely elbowed by a man of tall stature, whose gray hairs proclaimed him to be at least fifty, while the muscular force of his firmly knit limbs seemed undiminished by age.

This man was clad in a brown vest, through which appeared a coarse shirt with a broad collar; his short breeches, striped with green, were fastened by red garters to stockings of clay-color; on his feet were sandals made of ojotas, ox-hide prepared for this purpose; beneath his high-pointed hat gleamed large ear-rings. His complexion was dark. After having jostled André Certa, he looked at him fixedly, but with no particular expression.

"Miserable Indian!" exclaimed the mestizo, raising his hand upon him.

His companions restrained him. Milleflores, whose face was pale with terror, exclaimed:

"André! André! take care."

"A vile slave! to presume to elbow me!"

"It is a madman! it is the Sambo!"

The Sambo, as the name indicated, was an Indian of the mountains; he continued to fix his eyes on the mestizo, whom he had intentionally jostled. The latter, whose anger was unbounded, had seized a poignard at his girdle, and was about to have rushed on the impassable aggressor, when a guttural cry, like that of the cilguero, (a kind of linnet of Peru,) re-echoed in the midst of the tumult of promenaders, and the Sambo disappeared.

"Brutal and cowardly!" exclaimed André.

"Control yourself," said Milleflores, softly. "Let us leave the Plaza-Mayor; the Limanienne ladies are too haughty here."

As he said these words, the brave Milleflores looked cautiously around to see whether he was not within reach of the foot or arm of some Indian in the neighborhood.

"In an hour, I must be at the house of Jew Samuel," said André.

"In an hour! we have time to pass to the Calle del Peligro; you can offer some oranges or ananas to the charming tapadas who promenade there. Shall we go, gentlemen?"

The group directed their steps toward the extremity of the square, and began to descend the street of Danger, where

Milleflores hoped his good looks would be appreciated; but it was nightfall, and the young Limaniennes merited better than ever their name of tapadas(hidden), for they drew their mantles more closely over their countenances.

The Plaza-Mayor was all alive; the cries and the tumult were redoubled; the guards on horseback, stationed before the central portico of the viceroy's palace, situated on the north side of the square, could scarcely maintain their position amid the shifting crowd; there were merchants for all customers and customers for all merchants. The greatest variety of trades seemed to be congregated there, and from the Portal de Escribanos to the Portal de Botoneros, there was one immense display of articles of every kind, the Plaza-Mayor serving at once as promenade, bazaar, market and fair. The ground-floor of the viceroy's palace is occupied by shops; along the first story runs an immense gallery where the crowd can promenade on days of public rejoicing; on the east side of the square rises the cathedral, with its steeples and light balustrades, proudly adorning its two towers; the basement story of the edifice being ten feet high, and containing warehouses full of the products of tropical climates.

In the centre of this square is situated the beautiful fountain, constructed in 1653, by the orders of the viceroy, the Comte de Salvatierra. From the top of the pillar, which rises in the middle of the fountain and is surmounted with a statue of Fame, the water falls in sheets, and is discharged into a basin beneath through the mouths of lions. It is here that the water-carriers (aguadores) load their mules with barrels, attach a bell to a hoop, and mount behind their liquid merchandise.

This square is therefore noisy from morning till evening, and when the stars of night rise above the snowy summits of the Cordilleras, the tumult of the élite of Lima equals the matinal hubbub of the merchants.

Nevertheless, when the oracion (evening angelus) sounds from the bell of the cathedral, all this noise suddenly ceases; to the clamor of pleasure succeeds the murmur of prayer; the women pause in their walk and put their hands on their rosaries, invoking the Virgin Mary. Then, not a merchant dares sell his merchandise, not a customer thinks of buying, and this square, so recently animated, seems to have become a vast solitude.

While the Limanians paused and knelt at the sound of the angelus, a young girl, carefully surrounded by her discreet mantle, sought to pass through the praying multitude; she was followed by a mestizo woman, a sort of duenna, who watched every glance and step. The duenna, as if she had not understood the warning bell, continued her way through the devout populace: to the general surprise succeeded harsh epithets. The young girl would have stopped, but the duenna kept on.

"Do you see that daughter of Satan?" said someone near her.

"Who is that balarina—that impious dancer?"

"It is one of the Carcaman women." (A reproachful name bestowed upon Europeans.)

The young girl at last stopped, blushing and confused.

Suddenly a gaucho, a merchant of mules, seized her by the shoulder, and would have compelled her to kneel; but he had scarcely laid his hand upon her when a vigorous arm rudely felled him to the ground. This scene, rapid as lightning, was followed by a moment of confusion.

"Save yourself, miss," said a gentle and respectful voice in the ear of the young girl.

The latter turned, pale with terror, and saw a young Indian of tall stature, who, with his arms tranquilly folded, was awaiting with firm foot the attack of his adversary.

"We are lost!" exclaimed the duenna; "niña, niña, let us go, for the love of God!" and she seized the arm of the young girl, who disappeared, while the crowd rose and dispersed.

The gaucho had risen, bruised with his fall, and thinking it not prudent to seek revenge, rejoined his mules, muttering threats.

Evening in the Streets of Lima

Night had succeeded, almost without intervening twilight, the glare of day. The two women quickened their pace, for it was late; the young girl, still under the influence of strong emotion, maintained silence, while the duenna murmured some mysterious paternosters—they walked rapidly through one of the sloping streets leading from the Plaza-Mayor.

This place is situated more than four hundred feet above the level of the sea, and about a hundred and fifty rods from the bridge thrown over the river Rimac, which forms the diameter of the city of Lima, arranged in a semicircle.

The city of Lima lies in the valley of the Rimac, nine leagues from its mouth; at the north and east commence the first undulations of ground which form a part of the great chain of the Andes: the valley of Lungaucho, formed by the mountains of San Cristoval and the Amancaës, which rise behind Lima, terminates in its suburbs. The city lies on one bank of the river; the other is occupied by the suburb of San Lazaro, and is united to the city by a bridge of five arches, the upper piers of which are triangular to break the force of the current; while the lower ones present to the promenaders circular benches, on which the fashionables may lounge during the summer evenings, and where they can contemplate a pretty cascade.

The city is two miles long from east to west, and only a mile and a quarter wide from the bridge to the walls; the latter, twelve feet in height, ten feet thick at their base, are built of adobes, a kind of brick dried in the sun, and made of potter's clay mingled with a great quantity of chopped straw: these walls are calculated to resist earthquakes; the enclosure, pierced with seven gates and three posterns, terminates at its south-east extremity by the little citadel of Santa Caterina.

Such is the ancient city of kings, founded in 1534 by Pizarro, on the day of Epiphany; it has been and is still the theatre of constantly renewed revolutions. Lima, situated three miles from the sea, was formerly the principal storehouse of America on the Pacific Ocean, thanks to its Port of Callao, built in 1779, in a singular manner. An old vessel, filled with stones, sand, and rubbish of all sorts, was wrecked on the shore; piles of the mangrove-tree, brought from Guayaquil and impervious to water, were driven around this as a centre, which became the immovable base on which rose the mole of Callao.

The climate, milder and more temperate than that of Carthagena or Bahia, situated on the opposite side of America, makes Lima one of the most agreeable cities of the New World: the wind has two directions from which it never varies; either it blows from the south-east, and becomes cool by crossing the Pacific Ocean; or it comes from the south-west, impregnated with the mild atmosphere of the forests and the freshness which it has derived from the icy summits of the Cordilleras.

The nights beneath tropical latitudes are very beautiful and very clear; they mysteriously prepare that beneficent dew which fertilizes a soil exposed to the rays of a cloudless sky—so the inhabitants of Lima prolong their nocturnal conversations and receptions; household labors are quietly finished in the dwellings refreshed by the shadows, and the streets are soon deserted; scarcely is some pulperia still haunted by the drinkers of chica or quarapo.

These, the young girl, whom we have seen, carefully avoided; crossing in the middle of the numerous squares scattered about the city, she arrived, without interruption, at the bridge of the

Rimac, listening to catch the slightest sound—which her emotion exaggerated, and hearing only the bells of a train of mules conducted by its arriero, or the joyous stribillo of some Indian.

This young girl was called Sarah, and was returning to the house of the Jew Samuel, her father; she was clad in a saya of satin—a kind of petticoat of a dark color, plaited in elastic folds, and very narrow at the bottom, which compelled her to take short steps, and gave her that graceful delicacy peculiar to the Limanienne ladies; this petticoat, ornamented with lace and flowers, was in part covered with a silk mantle, which was raised above the head and enveloped it like a hood; stockings of exquisite fineness and little satin shoes peeped out beneath the graceful saya; bracelets of great value encircled the arms of the young girl, whose rich toilet was of exquisite taste, and her whole person redolent of that charm so well expressed by the Spanish word donaire.

Milleflores might well say to André Certa that his betrothed had nothing of the Jewess but the name, for she was a faithful specimen of those admirable señoras whose beauty is above all praise.

The duenna, an old Jewess, whose countenance was expressive of avarice and cupidity, was a devoted servant of Samuel, who paid her liberally.

At the moment when these two women entered the suburb of San Lazaro, a man, clad in the robe of a monk, and with his head covered with a cowl, passed near them and looked at them attentively. This man, of tall stature, possessed a countenance expressive of gentleness and benevolence; it was Padre Joachim de Camarones; he threw a glance of intelligence on Sarah, who immediately looked at her follower.

The latter was still grumbling, muttering and whining, which prevented her seeing anything; the young girl turned toward the good father and made a graceful sign with her hand.

"Well, señora," said the old woman, sharply, "is it not enough to have been insulted by these Christians, that you should stop to look at a priest?"

Sarah did not reply.

"Shall we see you one day, with rosary in hand, engaged in the ceremonies of the church?"

The ceremonies of the church—las funciones de iglesia—are the great business of the Limanian ladies.

"You make strange suppositions," replied the young girl, blushing.

"Strange as your conduct! What would my master Samuel say, if he knew what had taken place this evening?"

"Am I to blame because a brutal muleteer chose to address me?"

"I understand, señora," said the old woman, shaking her head, "and will not speak of the gaucho."

"Then the young man did wrong in defending me from the abuse of the populace?"

"Is it the first time the Indian has thrown himself in your way?"

The countenance of the young girl was fortunately sheltered by her mantle, for the darkness would not have sufficed to conceal her emotion from the inquisitive glance of the duenna.

"But let us leave the Indian where he is," resumed the old woman, "it is not my business to watch him. What I complain of is, that in order not to disturb these Christians, you wished to remain among them! Had you not some desire to kneel with them? Ah, señora, your father would soon dismiss me if I were guilty of such apostasy."

But the young girl no longer heard; the remark of the old woman on the subject of the young Indian had inspired her with sweeter thoughts; it seemed to her that the intervention of this young man was providential; and she turned several times to see if he had not followed her in the shadow. Sarah had in her heart a certain natural confidence which became her wonderfully; she felt herself to be the child of these warm latitudes, which the sun decorates with surprising vegetation; proud as a Spaniard, if she had fixed her regards on this man, it was because he had stood proudly in the presence of her pride, and had not begged a glance as a reward of his protection.

In imagining that the Indian was near her, Sarah was not mistaken; Martin Paz, after having come to the assistance of the young girl, wished to ensure her safe retreat; so when the promenaders had dispersed, he followed her, without being perceived by her, but without concealing himself; the darkness alone favoring his pursuit.

This Martin Paz was a handsome young man, wearing with unparalleled nobility the national costume of the Indian of the mountains; from his broad-brimmed straw hat escaped fine black hair, whose curls harmonized with the bronze of his manly face. His eyes shone with infinite sweetness, like the transparent atmosphere of starry nights; his well-formed nose surmounted a pretty mouth, unlike that of most of his race. He was one of the noblest descendants of Manco-Capac, and his veins were full of that ardent blood which leads men to the accomplishment of lofty deeds.

He was proudly draped in his poncho of brilliant colors; at his girdle hung one of those Malay poignards, so terrible in a practiced hand, for they seem to be riveted to the arm which strikes. In North America, on the shores of Lake Ontario, Martin Paz would have been a great chief among those wandering tribes which have fought with the English so many heroic combats.

Martin Paz knew that Sarah was the daughter of the wealthy Samuel; he knew her to be the most charming woman in Lima; he knew her to be betrothed to the opulent mestizo André Certa; he knew that by her birth, her position and her wealth she was beyond the reach of his heart; but he forgot all these impossibilities in his all-absorbing passion. It seemed to him that this beautiful young girl belonged to him, as the llama to the Peruvian forests, as the eagle to the depths of immensity.

Plunged in his reflections, Martin Paz hastened his steps to see the saya of the young girl sweep the threshold of the paternal dwelling; and Sarah herself, half-opening then her mantilla, cast on him a bewildering glance of gratitude.

He was quickly joined by two Indians of the species of zambos, pillagers and robbers, who walked beside him.

"Martin Paz," said one of them to him, "you ought this very evening to meet our brethren in the mountains."

"I shall be there," coldly replied the other.

"The schooner Annonciation has appeared in sight from Callao, tacked for a few moments, then, protected by the point, rapidly disappeared. She will undoubtedly approach the land near the mouth of the Rimac, and our bark canoes must be there to relieve her of her merchandise. We shall need your presence."

"You are losing time by your observations. Martin Paz knows his duty and he will do it."

"It is in the name of the Sambo that we speak to you here."

"It is in my own name that I speak to you."

"Do you not fear that he will find your presence in the suburb of San Lazaro at this hour unaccountable?"

"I am where my fancy and my will have brought me."

"Before the house of the Jew?"

"Those of my brethren who are disposed to find fault can meet me to-night in the mountain."

The eyes of the three men sparkled, and this was all. The zambos regained the bank of the Rimac, and the sound of their footsteps died away in the darkness.

Martin Paz had hastily approached the house of the Jew. This house, like all those of Lima, had but two stories; the ground floor, built of bricks, was surmounted with walls formed of canes tied together and covered with plaster; all this part of the building, constructed to resist earthquakes, imitated, by a skillful painting, the bricks of the lower story; the square roof, called asoetas, was covered with flowers, and formed a terrace full of perfumes and pretty points of view.

A vast gate, placed between two pavilions, gave access to a court; but as usual, these pavilions had no window opening upon the street.

The clock of the parish church was striking eleven when Martin Paz stopped before the dwelling of Sarah. Profound silence reigned around; a flickering light within proved that the saloon of the Jew Samuel was still occupied.

Why does the Indian stand motionless before these silent walls? The cool atmosphere woos him with its transparency and its perfumes; the radiant stars send down upon the sleeping earth rays of diaphanous mildness; the white constellations illumine the darkness with their enchanting light; his heart believes in those sympathetic communications which brave time and distance.

A white form appears upon the terrace amid the flowers to which night has only left a vague outline, without diminishing their delicious perfumes; the dahlias mingle with the mentzelias, with the helianthus, and, beneath the occidental breeze, form a waving basket which surrounds Sarah, the young and beautiful Jewess.

Martin Paz involuntarily raises his hands and clasps them with adoration. Suddenly the white form sinks down, as if terrified.

Martin Paz turns, and finds himself face to face with André Certa.

"Since when do the Indians pass their nights in contemplation?" André Certa spoke angrily.

"Since the Indians have trodden the soil of their ancestors."

"Have they no longer, on the mountain side, some yaravis to chant, some boleros to dance with the girls of their caste?"

"The cholos," replied the Indian, in a high voice, "bestow their devotion where it is merited; the Indians love according to their hearts."

André Certa became pale with anger; he advanced a step toward his immovable rival.

"Wretch! will you quit this place?"

"Rather quit it yourself," shouted Martin Paz; and two poignards gleamed in the two right hands of the adversaries; they were of equal stature, they seemed of equal strength, and the lightnings of their eyes were reflected in the steel of their arms.

André Certa rapidly raised his arm, which he dropped still more quickly. But his poignard had encountered the Malay poignard of the Indian; at the fire which flashed from this shock, André saw the arm of Martin Paz suspended over his head, and immediately rolled on the earth, his arm pierced through.

"Help, help!" he exclaimed.

The door of the Jew's house opened at his cries. Some mestizoes ran from a neighboring house; some pursued the Indian, who fled rapidly; others raised the wounded man. He had swooned.

"Who is this man?" said one of them. "If he is a sailor, take him to the hospital of Spiritu Santo; if an Indian, to the hospital of Santa Anna."

An old man advanced toward the wounded youth; he had scarcely looked upon him when he exclaimed:

"Let the poor young man be carried into my house. This is a strange mischance."

This man was the Jew Samuel; he had just recognized the betrothed of his daughter.

Martin Paz, thanks to the darkness and the rapidity of his flight, may hope to escape his pursuers; he has risked his life; an Indian assassin of a mestizo! If he can gain the open country he is safe, but he knows that the gates of the city are closed at eleven o'clock in the evening, not to be re-opened till four in the morning.

He reaches at last the stone bridge which he had already crossed. The Indians, and some soldiers who had joined them, pursue him closely; he springs upon the bridge. Unfortunately a patrol appears at the opposite extremity; Martin Paz can neither advance nor retrace his steps; without hesitation he clears the parapet and leaps into the rapid current which breaks against the corners of the stones.

The pursuers spring upon the banks below the bridge to seize the swimmer at his landing.

But it is in vain; Martin Paz does not re-appear.

The Jew Every where a Jew

André Certa, once introduced into the house of Samuel, and laid in a bed hastily prepared, recovered his senses and pressed the hand of the old Jew. The physician, summoned by one of the domestics, was promptly in attendance. The wound appeared to be a slight one; the shoulder of the mestizo had been pierced in such a manner that the steel had only glided among the flesh. In a few days, André Certa might be once more upon his feet.

When Samuel was left alone with André, the latter said to him:

"You would do well to wall up the gate which leads to your terrace, Master Samuel."

"What fear you, André?"

"I fear lest Sarah should present herself there to the contemplation of the Indians. It was not a robber who attacked me; it was a rival, from whom I have escaped but by miracle!"

"By the holy tables, it is a task to bring up young girls!" exclaimed the Jew. "But you are mistaken, señor," he resumed, "Sarah will be a dutiful spouse. I spare no pains that she may do you honor."

André Certa half raised himself on his elbow.

"Master Samuel, there is one thing which you do not enough remember, that I pay you for the hand of Sarah a hundred thousand piasters."

"Señor," replied the Jew, with a miserly chuckle, "I remember it so well, that I am ready now to exchange this receipt for the money."

As he said this, Samuel drew from his pocket-book a paper which André Certa repulsed with his hand.

"The bargain is not complete until Sarah has become my wife, and she will never be such if her hand is to be disputed by such an adversary. You know, Master Samuel, what is my object; in espousing Sarah, I wish to be the equal of this nobility which casts such scornful glances upon us."

"And you will, señor, for you see the proudest grandees of Spain throng our saloons, around the pearl of Lima."

"Where has Sarah been this evening?"

"To the Israelitish temple, with old Ammon."

"Why should Sarah attend your religious rites?"

"I am a Jew, señor," replied Samuel proudly, "and would Sarah be my daughter if she did not fulfill the duties of my religion?"

The old Jew remained sad and silent for several minutes. His bent brow rested on one of his withered hands. His face usually bronze, was now almost pale; beneath a brown cap appeared locks of an indescribable color. He was clad in a sort of great-coat fastened around the waist.

This old man trafficked everywhere and in everything; he might have been a descendant of the Judas who sold his Master for thirty pieces of silver. He had been a resident of Lima ten years; his taste and his economy had led him to choose his dwelling at the extremity of the suburb of San Lazaro, and from thence he entered into various speculations to make money. By degrees, Samuel assumed a luxury uncommon in misers; his house was sumptuously furnished; his numerous domestics, his splendid equipages betokened immense revenues. Sarah was then eight years of age. Already graceful and charming, she pleased all, and was the idol of the Jew. All her inclinations were unhesitatingly gratified. Always elegantly dressed, she attracted the eyes of the most fastidious, of which her father seemed strangely careless. It will readily be understood how the mestizo, André Certa, became enamored of the beautiful Jewess. What would have appeared inexplicable to the public, was the hundred thousand piasters, the price of her hand; but this bargain was secret.

And besides, Samuel trafficked in sentiments as in native productions. A banker, usurer, merchant, ship-owner, he had the talent to do business with everybody. The schooner Annonciation, which was hovering about the mouth of the Rimac, belonged to the Jew Samuel.

Amid this life of business and speculation this man fulfilled the duties of his religion with scrupulous punctuality; his daughter had been carefully instructed in the Israelitish faith and practices.

So, when the mestizo had manifested his displeasure on this subject, the old man remained mute and pensive, and André Certa broke the silence, saying:

"Do you forget that the motive for which I espouse Sarah will compel her to become a convert to Catholicism? It is not my fault," added the mestizo; "but in spite of you, in spite of me, in spite of herself, it will be so."

"You are right," said the Jew sadly; "but, by the Bible, Sarah shall be a Jewess as long as she is my daughter."

At this moment the door of the chamber opened, and the major-domo of the Jew Samuel respectfully entered.

"Is the murderer arrested?" asked the old man.

"We have reason to believe he is dead!"

"Dead!" repeated André, with a joyful exclamation.

"Caught between us and a company of soldiers," replied the major-domo, "he was obliged to leap over the parapet of the bridge."

"He has thrown himself into the Rimac!" exclaimed André.

"And how do you know that he has not reached the shore?" asked Samuel.

"The melting of the snow has made the current rapid at that spot; besides, we stationed ourselves on each side of the river, and he did not re-appear. I have left sentinels who will pass the night in watching the banks."

"It is well," said the old man; "he has met with a just fate. Did you recognize him in his flight?"

"Perfectly, sir; it was Martin Paz, the Indian of the mountains."

"Has this man been observing Sarah for some time past?"

"I do not know," replied the servant.

"Summon old Ammon."

The major-domo withdrew.

"These Indians," said the old man, "have secret understandings among themselves; I must know whether the pursuit of this man dates from a distant period."

The duenna entered, and remained standing before her master.

"Does my daughter," asked Samuel, "know anything of what has taken place this morning?"

"When the cries of your servants awoke me, I ran to the chamber of the señora, and found her almost motionless and of a mortal paleness."

"Fatality!" said Samuel; "continue," added he, seeing that the mestizo was apparently asleep.

"To my urgent inquiries as to the cause of her agitation, the señora would not reply; she retired without accepting my services, and I withdrew."

"Has this Indian often thrown himself in her way?"

"I do not know, master; nevertheless I have often met him in the streets of San Lazaro."

"And you have told me nothing of this?"

"He came to her assistance this evening on the Plaza-Mayor," added the old duenna.

"Her assistance! how?"

The old woman related the scene with downcast head.

"Ah! my daughter wish to kneel among these Christians!"

exclaimed the Jew, angrily; "and I knew nothing of all this! You deserve that I should dismiss you."

The duenna went out of the room in confusion.

"Do you not see that the marriage should take place soon?" said André Certa. "I am not asleep, Master Samuel! But I need rest, now, and I will dream of our espousals."

At these words, the old man slowly retired. Before regaining his room, he wished to assure himself of the condition of his daughter, and softly entered the chamber of Sarah.

The young girl was in an agitated slumber, in the midst of the rich silk drapery around her; a watch-lamp of alabaster, suspended from the arabesques of the ceiling, shed its soft light upon her beautiful countenance; the half-open window admitted, through lowercd blinds, the quiet coolness of the air, impregnated with the penetrating perfumes of the aloes and magnolia; creole luxury was displayed in the thousand objects of art which good taste and grace had dispersed on richly carved étagères; and, beneath the vague and placid rays of night, it seemed as if the soul of the child was sporting amid these wonders.

The old man approached the bed of Sarah: he bent over her to listen. The beautiful Jewess seemed disturbed by sorrowful thoughts, and more than once the name of Martin Paz escaped her lips.

Samuel regained his chamber, uttering maledictions.

At the first rays of morning, Sarah hastily arose. Liberta, a full-blooded Indian attached to her service, hastened to her; and, in pursuance of her orders, saddled a mule for his mistress and a horse for himself.

Sarah was accustomed to take morning-rides, accompanied by this Indian, who was entirely devoted to her.

She was clad in a saya of a brown color, and a mantle of cashmere with long tassels; her head was not covered with the usual hood, but sheltered beneath the broad brim of a straw hat, which left her long black tresses to float over her shoulders; and to conceal any unusual pre-occupation, she held between her lips a cigarette of perfumed tobacco.

Liberta, clad like an Indian of the mountains, prepared to accompany his mistress.

"Liberta," said the young girl to him, "remember to be blind and dumb."

Once in the saddle, Sarah left the city as usual, and began to ride through the country; she directed her way toward Callao. The port was in full animation: there had been a conflict during the night between the revenue-officers and a schooner, whose undecided movements betrayed a fraudulent speculation. The Annonciation seemed to have been awaiting some suspicious barks near the mouth of the Rimac; but before the latter could reach her, she had been compelled to flee before the custom-house boats, which had boldly given her chase.

Various rumors were in circulation respecting the destination of this vessel—which bore no name on her stern. According to some, this schooner, laden with Colombian troops, was seeking to seize the principal vessels of Callao; for Bolivar had it in his heart to revenge the affront given to the soldiers left by him in Peru, and who had been driven from it in disgrace.

According to others, the schooner was simply a smuggler of European goods.

Without troubling herself about these rumors, more or less important, Sarah, whose ride to the port had been only a pretext, returned toward Lima, which she reached near the banks of the Rimac.

She ascended them toward the bridge: numbers of soldiers, mestizoes, and Indians, were stationed at various points on the shore.

JULES VERNE

Liberta had acquainted the young girl with the events of the night. In compliance with her orders, he interrogated some Indians leaning over the parapet, and learned that although Martin Paz had been undoubtedly drowned, his body had not yet been recovered.

Sarah was pale and almost fainting; it required all her strength of soul not to abandon herself to her grief.

Among the people wandering on the banks, she remarked an Indian with ferocious features—the Sambo! He was crouched on the bank, and seemed a prey to despair.

As Sarah passed near the old mountaineer, she heard these words, full of gloomy anger:

"Wo! wo! They have killed the son of the Sambo! They have killed my son!"

The young girl resolutely drew herself up, made a sign to Liberta to follow her; and this time, without caring whether she was observed or not, went directly to the church of Santa Anna; left her mule in charge of the Indian, entered the Catholic temple, and asking for the good Father Joachim, knelt on the stone steps, praying to Jesus and Mary for the soul of Martin Paz.

A Spanish Grandee

Any other than the Indian, Martin Paz, would have, indeed, perished in the waters of the Rimac; to escape death, his surprising strength, his insurmountable will, and especially his sublime coolness, one of the privileges of the free hordes of the pampas of the New World, had all been found necessary.

Martin knew that his pursuers would concentrate their efforts to seize him below the bridge; it seemed impossible for him to overcome the current, and that the Indian must be carried down; but by vigorous strokes he succeeded in stemming the torrent; he dived repeatedly, and finding the under-currents less strong, at last ventured to land, and concealed himself behind a thicket of mangrove-trees.

But what was to become of him? Retreat was perilous; the soldiers might change their plans and ascend the river; the Indian must then inevitably be captured; he would lose his life, and, worse yet, Sarah. His decision was rapidly made; through the narrow streets and deserted squares he plunged into the heart of the city; but it was important that he should be supposed dead; he therefore avoided being seen, since his garments, dripping with water and covered with sea-weed, would have betrayed him.

To avoid the indiscreet glances of some belated inhabitants, Martin Paz was obliged to pass through one of the widest streets of the city; a house still brilliantly illuminated presented itself: the port-cochere was open to give passage to the elegant equipages which were issuing from the court, and conveying to their respective dwellings the nobles of the Spanish aristocracy.

The Indian adroitly glided into this magnificent dwelling; he could not remain in the street, where curious zambos were thronging around, attracted by the carriages. The gates of the hotel were soon carefully closed, and the Indian found flight impossible.

Some lacqueys were going to and fro in the court; Martin Paz rapidly passed up a rich stairway of cedar-wood, ornamented with valuable tapestry; the saloons, still illuminated, presented no convenient place of refuge; he crossed them with the rapidity of lightning, and disappeared in a room filled with protecting darkness.

The last lustres were quickly extinguished, and the house became profoundly silent.

The Indian Paz, as a man of energy to whom moments are precious, hastened to reconnoitre the place, and to find the surest means of evasion; the windows of this chamber opened on an interior garden; flight was practicable, and Martin Paz was about to spring from them, when he heard these words:

"Señor, you have forgotten to take the diamonds which I had left on that table!"

Martin Paz turned. A man of noble stature and of great pride of countenance was pointing to a jewel-case.

At this insult Martin Paz laid his hand on his poignard. He approached the Spaniard, who stood unmoved, and, in a first impulse of indignation, raised his arm to strike him; but turning his weapon against himself, said, in a deep tone,

"Señor, if you repeat such words, I will kill myself at your feet."

The Spaniard, astonished, looked at the Indian more attentively, and through his tangled and dripping locks perceived so lofty a frankness, that he felt a strange sympathy fill his heart. He went toward the window, gently closed it, and returned toward the Indian, whose poignard had fallen to the ground.

"Who are you?" said he to him.

"The Indian, Martin Paz. I am pursued by soldiers for having defended myself against a mestizo who attacked me, and levelled him to the ground with a blow from my poignard. This mestizo is the betrothed of a young girl whom I love. Now, señor, you can deliver me to my enemies, if you judge it noble and right."

"Sir," replied the Spaniard, gravely, "I depart to-morrow for the Baths of Chorillos; if you please to accompany me, you will be for the present safe from pursuit, and will never have reason to complain of the hospitality of the Marquis Don Vegal."

Martin Paz bent coldly without manifesting any emotion.

"You can rest until morning on this bed," resumed Don Vegal; "no one here will suspect your retreat. Good-night, señor!"

The Spaniard went out of the room, and left the Indian, moved to tears by a confidence so generous; he yielded himself entirely to the protection of the marquis, and without thinking that his slumbers might be taken advantage of to seize him, slept with peaceful security.

The next day, at sunrise, the marquis gave the last orders for his departure, and summoned the Jew Samuel to come to him; in the meantime he attended the morning mass.

This was a custom generally observed by the aristocracy. From its very foundation Lima had been essentially Catholic. Besides its numerous churches, it numbered twenty-two convents, seventeen monasteries, and four beaterios, or houses of retreat for females who did not take the vows. Each of these establishments possessed a chapel, so that there were at Lima more than a hundred edifices for worship, where eight hundred secular or regular priests, three hundred religieuses, lay-brothers and sisters, performed the duties of religion.

As Don Vegal entered the church of Santa Anna, he noticed a young girl kneeling in prayer and in tears. There was so much of grief in her depression, that the marquis could not look at her without emotion; and he was preparing to console her by some kind words, when Father Joachim de Camarones approached him, saying in a low voice:

"Señor Don Vegal, pray do not approach her."

Then he made a sign to Sarah, who followed him to an obscure and deserted chapel.

Don Vegal directed his steps to the altar and listened to the mass; then, as he was returning, he thought involuntarily of the deep sadness of the kneeling maiden. Her image followed him to his hotel, and remained deeply engraven in his soul.

Don Vegal found in his saloon the Jew Samuel, who had come in compliance with his request. Samuel seemed to have forgotten the events of the night; the hope of gain animated his countenance with a natural gayety.

"What is your lordship's will?" asked he of the Spaniard.

"I must have thirty thousand piasters within an hour."

"Thirty thousand piasters! And who has them! By the holy king David, my lord, I am far from being able to furnish such a sum."

"Here are some jewels of great value," resumed Don Vegal, without noticing the language of the Jew; "besides I can sell you at a low price a considerable estate near Cusco."

"Ah! señor, lands ruin us—we have not arms enough left to cultivate them; the Indians have withdrawn to the mountains, and our harvests do not pay us for the trouble they cost."

"At what value do you estimate these diamonds?"

Samuel drew from his pocket a little pair of scales and began to weigh the stones with scrupulous skill. As he did this, he continued to talk, and, as was his custom, depreciated the pledges offered him.

"Diamonds! a poor investment! What would they bring? One might as well bury money! You will notice, señor, that this is not of the purest water. Do you know that I do not find a ready market for these costly ornaments? I am obliged to send such merchandise to the United Provinces! The Americans would buy them, undoubtedly, but to give them up to the sons of Albion. They wish besides, and it is very just, to gain an honest percentage, so that the depreciation falls upon me. I think that ten thousand piasters should satisfy your lordship. It is little, I know; but——"

"Have I not said," resumed the Spaniard, with a sovereign air of scorn, "that ten thousand piasters would not suffice?"

"Señor, I cannot give you a half real more!"

"Take away these caskets and bring me the sum I ask for. To complete the thirty thousand piasters which I need, you will take a mortgage on this house. Does it seem to you to be solid?"

"Ah, señor, in this city, subject to earthquakes, one knows not who lives or dies, who stands or falls."

And, as he said this, Samuel let himself fall on his heels several times to test the solidity of the floors.

"Well, to oblige your lordship, I will furnish you with the required sum; although, at this moment I ought not to part with money; for I am about to marry my daughter to the caballero André Certa. Do you know him, sir?"

"I do not know him, and I beg of you to send me this instant, the sum agreed upon. Take away these jewels."

"Will you have a receipt for them?" asked the Jew.

Don Vegal passed into the adjoining room, without replying.

"Proud Spaniard!" muttered Samuel, "I will crush thy insolence, as I disperse thy riches! By Solomon! I am a skillful man, since my interests keep pace with my sentiments."

Don Vegal, on leaving the Jew, had found Martin Paz in profound dejection of spirits, mingled with mortification.

"What is the matter?" he asked affectionately.

"Señor, it is the daughter of the Jew whom I love."

"A Jewess!" exclaimed Don Vegal, with disgust.

But seeing the sadness of the Indian, he added:

"Let us go, amigo, we will talk of these things afterward!"

An hour later, Martin Paz, clad in Spanish costume, left the city, accompanied by Don Vegal, who took none of his people with him.

The Baths of Chorillos are situated at two leagues from Lima. This Indian parish possesses a pretty church; during the hot season it is the rendezvous of the fashionable Limanian society. Public games, interdicted at Lima, are permitted at Chorillos during the whole summer. The señoras there display unwonted ardor, and, in decorating himself for these pretty partners, more than one rich cavalier has seen his fortune dissipated in a few nights.

Chorillos was still little frequented; so Don Vegal and Martin Paz retired to a pretty cottage, built on the sea-shore, could live in quiet contemplation of the vast plains of the Pacific Ocean.

The Marquis Don Vegal, belonging to one of the most ancient families of Peru, saw about to terminate in himself the noble line of which he was justly proud; so his countenance bore the impress of profound sadness. After having mingled for some time in political affairs, he had felt an inexpressible disgust for the incessant revolutions brought about to gratify personal ambition; he had withdrawn into a sort of solitude, interrupted only at rare intervals by the duties of strict politeness.

His immense fortune was daily diminishing. The neglect into which his vast domains had fallen for want of laborers, had compelled him to borrow at a disadvantage; but the prospect of approaching mediocrity did not alarm him; that carelessness natural to the Spanish race, joined to the ennui of a useless existence, had rendered him insensible to the menaces of the future. Formerly the husband of an adored wife, the father of a charming little girl, he had seen himself deprived, by a horrible event, of both these objects of his love. Since then, no bond of affection had attached him to earth, and he suffered his life to float at the will of events.

Don Vegal had thought his heart to be indeed dead, when he felt it palpitate at contact with that of Martin Paz. This ardent nature awoke fire beneath the ashes; the proud bearing of the Indian suited the chivalric hidalgo; and then, weary of the Spanish nobles, in whom he no longer had confidence, disgusted with the selfish mestizoes, who wished to aggrandize themselves at his expense, he took a pleasure in turning to that primitive race, who have disputed so valiantly the American soil with the soldiers of Pizarro.

According to the intelligence received by the marquis, the Indian passed for dead at Lima; but, looking on his attachment for the Jewess as worse than death itself, the Spaniard resolved doubly to save his guest, by leaving the daughter of Samuel to marry André Certa.

While Martin Paz felt an infinite sadness pervade his heart, Don Vegal avoided all allusion to the past, and conversed with the young Indian on indifferent subjects.

Meanwhile, one day, saddened by his gloomy preoccupations, the Spaniard said to him:

"Why, my friend, do you lower the nobility of your nature by a sentiment so much beneath you? Was not that bold Manco-Capac, whom his patriotism placed in the rank of heroes, your ancestor? There is a noble part left for a valiant man, who will not suffer himself to be overcome by an unworthy passion. Have you no heart to regain your independence?"

"We are laboring for this, señor," said the Indian; "and the day when my brethren shall rise en masse is perhaps not far distant."

"I understand you; you allude to the war for which your brethren are preparing among their mountains; at a signal they will descend on the city, arms in hand—and will be conquered as they have always been! See how your interests will disappear amid these perpetual revolutions of which Peru is the theatre, and which will ruin it entirely, Indians and Spaniards, to the profit of the mestizoes, who are neither."

"We will save it ourselves," exclaimed Martin Paz.

"Yes, you will save it if you understand how to play your part! Listen to me, Paz, you whom I love from day to day as a son! I say it with grief; but, we Spaniards, the degenerate sons of a powerful race, no longer have the energy necessary to elevate and govern a state. It is therefore yours to triumph over that unhappy Americanism, which tends to reject European colonization. Yes, know that only European emigration can save the old Peruvian empire. Instead of this intestine war which tends to exclude all castes, with the exception of one, frankly extend your hands to the industrious population of the Old World."

"The Indians, señor, will always see in strangers an enemy, and will never suffer them to breathe with impunity the air of their mountains. The kind of dominion which I exercise over them will be without effect on the day when I do not swear death to their oppressors, whoever they may be! And, besides, what am I now?" added Martin Paz, with great sadness; "a fugitive who would not have three hours to live in the streets of Lima."

"Paz, you must promise me that you will not return thither."

"How can I promise you this, Don Vegal? I speak only the truth, and I should perjure myself were I to take an oath to that effect."

Don Vegal was silent. The passion of the young Indian increased from day to day; the marquis trembled to see him incur certain death by re-appearing at Lima. He hastened by all his desires, he would have hastened by all his efforts, the marriage of the Jewess!

To ascertain himself the state of things he quitted Chorillos one morning, returned to the city, and learned that André Certa had recovered from his wound. His approaching marriage was the topic of general conversation.

Don Vegal wished to see this woman whose image troubled the mind of Martin Paz. He repaired, at evening, to the Plaza-Mayor. The crowd was always numerous there. There he met Father Joachim de Camarones, his confessor and his oldest friend; he acquainted him with his mode of life. What was the astonishment of the good father to learn the existence of Martin Paz. He promised Don Vegal to watch also himself over the young Indian, and to convey to the marquis any intelligence of importance.

Suddenly the glances of Don Vegal rested on a young girl, enveloped in a black mantle, reclining in a calêche.

"Who is that beautiful person?" asked he of the father.

"It is the betrothed of André Certa, the daughter of the Jew Samuel."

"She! the daughter of the Jew!"

The marquis could hardly suppress his astonishment, and, pressing the hand of Father Joachim, pensively took the road to Chorillos.

He had just recognized in Sarah, the pretended Jewess, the young girl whom he had seen praying with such Christian fervor, at the church of Santa Anna.

The Hatred of the Indians

Since the Colombian troops, confided by Bolivar to the orders of General Santa Cruz, had been driven from lower Peru, this country, which had been incessantly agitated by pronunciamentos, military revolts, had recovered some calmness and tranquillity.

In fact, private ambition no longer had anything to expect; the president Gambarra seemed immovable in his palace of the Plaza-Mayor. In this direction there was nothing to fear; but the true danger, concealed, imminent, was not from these rebellions, as promptly extinguished as kindled, and which seemed to flatter the taste of the Americans for military parades.

This unknown peril escaped the eyes of the Spaniards, too lofty to perceive it, and the attention of the mestizoes, who never wished to look beneath them.

And yet there was an unusual agitation among the Indians of the city; they often mingled with the serranos, the inhabitants of the mountains; these people seemed to have shaken off their natural apathy. Instead of rolling themselves in their ponchos, with their feet turned to the spring sun, they were scattered throughout the country, stopping one another, exchanging private signals, and haunting the least frequented pulperias, in which they could converse without danger.

This movement was principally to be observed on one of the squares remote from the centre of the city. At the corner of a street stood a house, of only one story, whose wretched appearance struck the eye disagreeably.

A tavern of the lowest order, a chingana, kept by an old Indian woman, offered to the lowest zambos the chica, beer of fermented maize, and the quarapo, a beverage made of the sugar-cane.

The concourse of Indians on this square took place only at certain hours, and principally when a long pole was raised on the roof of the inn as a signal of assemblage, then the zambos of every profession, the capataz, the arrieros, muleteers, the carreteros, carters, entered the chingana, one by one, and immediately disappeared in the great hall; the padrona (hostess) seemed very busy, and leaving to her servant the care of the shop, hastened to serve herself her usual customers.

A few days after the disappearance of Martin Paz, there was a numerous assembly in the hall of the inn; one could scarcely through the darkness, rendered still more obscure by the tobacco-smoke, distinguish the frequenters of this tavern. Fifty Indians were ranged around a long table; some were chewing the coca, a kind of tea-leaf, mingled with a little piece of fragrant earth called manubi; others were drinking from large pots of fermented maize; but these occupations did not distract their attention, and they were closely listening to the speech of an Indian.

This was the Sambo, whose fixed eyes were strangely wild. He was clad as on the Plaza-Mayor.

After having carefully observed his auditors, the Sambo commenced in these terms:

"The children of the Sun can converse on grave affairs; there is no perfidious ear to hear them; on the square, some of our friends, disguised as street-singers, will attract the attention of the passers-by, and we shall enjoy entire liberty."

In fact the tones of a mandoline and of a viguela were echoing without.

The Indians within, knowing themselves in safety, lent therefore close attention to the words of the Sambo, in whom they placed entire confidence.

"What news can the Sambo give us of Martin Paz?" asked an Indian.

"None—is he dead or not? The Great Spirit only knows. I am expecting some of our brethren, who have descended the river to its mouth, perhaps they will have found the body of Martin Paz."

"He was a good chief," said Manangani, a ferocious Indian, much dreaded; "but why was he not at his post on the day when the schooner brought us arms?"

The Sambo cast down his head without reply.

"Did not my brethren know," resumed Manangani, "that there was an exchange of shots between the Annonciation and the custom-house officers, and that the capture of the vessel would have ruined our projects of conspiracy?"

A murmur of approbation received the words of the Indian.

"Those of my brethren who will wait before they judge will be the beloved of my heart," resumed the Sambo; "who knows whether my son Martin Paz will not one day re-appear? Listen now; the arms which have been sent us from Sechura are in our power; they are concealed in the mountains of the Cordilleras, and ready to do their office when you shall be prepared to do your duty."

"And what delays us?" said a young Indian; "we have sharpened our knives and are waiting."

"Let the hour come," said the Sambo; "do my brethren know what enemy their arms should strike first?"

"Those mestizoes who treat us as slaves, and strike us with the hand and whip, like restive mules."

"These are the monopolizers of the riches of the soil, who will not suffer us to purchase a little comfort for our old age."

"You are mistaken; and your first blows must be struck elsewhere," said the Sambo, growing animated; "these are not the men who have dared for three hundred years past to tread the soil of our ancestors; it is not these rich men gorged with gold who have dragged to the tomb the sons of Manco-Capac; no, it is these proud Spaniards whom Fate has thrust on our independent shores! These are the true conquerors of whom you are the true slaves! If they have no longer wealth, they have authority; and, in spite of Peruvian emancipation, they crush and trample upon our natural rights. Let us forget what we are, to remember what our fathers have been!"

"Anda! anda!" exclaimed the assembly, with stamps of approbation.

After a few moments of silence, the Sambo assured himself, by interrogating various conspirators, that the friends of Cusco and of all Bolivia were ready to strike as a single man.

Then, resuming with fire:

"And our brethren of the mountains, brave Manangani, if they have all a heart of hatred equal to thine, a courage equal to thine, they will fall on Lima like an avalanche from the summit of the Cordilleras."

"The Sambo shall not complain of their boldness on the day appointed. Let the Indian leave the city, he shall not go far without seeing throng around him zambos burning for vengeance! In the gorges of San Cristoval and the Amancaës, more than one is couched on his poncho, with his poignard at his girdle, waiting until a long carbine shall be confided to his skillful hand. They also have not forgotten that they have to revenge on the vain Spaniards the defeat of Manco-Capac."

"Well said! Manangani; it is the god of hatred who speaks from thy mouth. My brethren shall know before long him whom their chiefs have chosen to lead this great vengeance. President Gambarra is seeking only to consolidate his power; Bolivar is afar, Santa Cruz has been driven away; we can act with certainty. In a few days, the fête of the Amancaës will summon our oppressors to pleasure; then, let each be ready to march, and let the news be carried to the most remote villages of Bolivia."

At this moment three Indians entered the great hall. The Sambo hastened to meet them.

"Well?" said he to them.

"The body of Martin Paz has not been recovered; we have sounded the river in every direction; our most skillful divers have explored it with religious care, and the son of the Sambo cannot have perished in the waters of the Rimac."

"Have they killed him? What has become of him? Oh! wo, wo to them if they have killed my son! Let my brethren separate in silence; let each return to his post, look, watch and wait!"

The Indians went out and dispersed; the Sambo alone remained with Manangani, who asked him:

"Does the Sambo know what sentiment conducted his son to San Lazaro? The Sambo, I trust, is sure of his son?"

The eyes of the Indian flashed, and the blood mounted to his cheek. The ferocious Manangani recoiled.

But the Indian controlled himself, and said:

"If Martin Paz has betrayed his brethren, I will first kill all those to whom he has given his friendship, all those to whom he has given his love! Then I will kill him, and myself afterward, that nothing may be left beneath the sun of an infamous, and dishonored race."

At this moment, the padrona opened the door of the room, advanced toward the Sambo, and handed him a billet directed to his address.

"Who gave you this?" said he.

"I do not know; this paper may have been designedly forgotten by a chica-drinker. I found it on the table."

"Have there been any but Indians here?"

"There have been none but Indians."

The padrona went out; the Sambo unfolded the billet, and read aloud:

"A young girl has prayed for the return of Martin Paz, for she has not forgotten that the young Indian protected her and risked his life for her. If the Sambo has any news of his poor son, or any hope of finding him, let him surround his arm with a red handkerchief; there are eyes which see him pass daily."

The Sambo crushed the billet in his hand.

"The unhappy boy," said he, "has suffered himself to be caught by the eyes of a woman."

"Who is this woman?" asked Manangani.

"It is not an Indian," replied the Sambo, observing the billet; "it is some young girl of the other classes. Martin Paz, I no longer know thee!"

"Shall you do what this woman requests?"

"No," replied the Indian, violently; "let her lose all hope of seeing him again; let her die, if she will."

And the Sambo tore the billet in a rage.

"It must have been an Indian who brought this billet," observed Manangani.

"Oh, it cannot have been one of ours! He must have known that I often came to this inn, but I will set my foot in it no more. We have occupied ourselves long enough with trifling affairs," resumed he, coldly; "let my brother return to the mountains; I will remain to watch over the city. We shall see whether the fête of the Amancaës will be joyous for the oppressors or the oppressed!"

The two Indians separated.

The plan of the conspiracy was well conceived and the hour of its execution well chosen. Peru, almost depopulated, counted only a small number of Spaniards and mestizoes. The invasion of the Indians, gathered from every direction, from the forests of Brazil, as well as the mountains of Chili and the plains of La Plata, would cover the theatre of war with a formidable army. The great cities, like Lima, Cusco, Puña, might be utterly destroyed; and it was not to be expected that the Colombian troops, so recently driven away by the Peruvian government, would come to the assistance of their enemies in peril.

This social overturn might therefore have succeeded, if the secret had remained buried in the hearts of the Indians, and there surely could not be traitors among them?

But they were ignorant that a man had obtained private audience of the President Gambarra. This man informed him that the schooner Annonciation had been captured from him by Indian pirates! That it had been laden with arms of all sorts; that canoes had unloaded it at the mouth of the Rimac; and he claimed a high indemnity for the service he thus rendered to the Peruvian government.

And yet this man had let his vessel to the agents of the Sambo; he had received for it a considerable sum, and had come to sell the secret which he had surprised.

By these traits the reader will recognize the Jew Samuel.

The Betrothal

André Certa, entirely recovered, sure of the death of Martin Paz, pressed his marriage: he was impatient to parade the young and beautiful Jewess through the streets of Lima.

Sarah constantly manifested toward him a haughty indifference; but he cared not for it, considering her as an article of sale, for which he had paid a hundred thousand piasters.

And yet André Certa suspected the Jew, and with good reason; if the contract was dishonorable, the contractors were still more so. So the mestizo wished to have a secret interview with Samuel, and took him one day to the Baths of Chorillos.

He was not sorry, besides, to try the chances of play before his wedding: public gaming, prohibited at Lima, is perfectly tolerated elsewhere. The passion of the Limanian ladies and gentlemen for this hazardous amusement is singular and irresistible.

The games were open some days before the arrival of the Marquis Don Vegal; thenceforth there was a perpetual movement of the populace on the road from Lima: some came on foot, who returned in carriages; others were about to risk and lose the last remnants of their fortunes.

Don Vegal and Martin Paz took no part in these exciting pleasures. The reveries of the young Indian had more noble causes; he was thinking of Sarah and of his benefactor.

The concourse of the Limanians to the Baths of Chorillos was without danger for him; little known by the inhabitants of the city, like all the mountain Indians he easily concealed himself from all eyes.

After his evening walk with the marquis, Martin Paz would return to his room, and leaning his elbow on the window, pass long hours in allowing his tumultuous thoughts to wander over the Pacific Ocean. Don Vegal lodged in a neighboring chamber, and guarded him with paternal tenderness.

The Spaniard always remembered the daughter of Samuel, whom he had so unexpectedly seen at prayer in the Catholic temple. But he had not dared to confide this important secret to Martin Paz while instructing him by degrees in Christian truths; he feared to re-animate sentiments which he wished to extinguish—for the poor Indian, unknown and proscribed, must renounce all hope of happiness! Father Joachim kept Don Vegal informed of the progress of affairs: the police had at last ceased to trouble themselves about Martin Paz; and with time and the influence of his protector, the Indian, become a man of merit and capable of great things, might one day take rank in the highest Peruvian society.

Weary of the uncertainty into which his incognito plunged him, Paz resolved to know what had become of the young Jewess. Thanks to his Spanish costume, he could glide into a gaming-saloon, and listen to the conversation of its various frequenters. André Certa was a man of so much importance, that his marriage, if it was approaching, would be the subject of conversation.

One evening, instead of directing his steps toward the sea, the Indian climbed over the high rocks on which the principal habitations of Chorillos are built; a house, fronted by broad stone steps, struck his eyes—he entered it without noise.

The day had been hard for many of the wealthy Limanians; some among them, exhausted with the fatigues of the preceding night, were reposing on the ground, wrapped in their ponchos.

Other players were seated before a large green table, divided into four compartments by two lines, which intersected each other at the centre in right angles; on each of these compartments were the first letters of the words azar and suerte (chance and fate), A and S.

At this moment, the parties of the monte were animated; a mestizo was pursuing the unfavorable chance with feverish ardor.

"Two thousand piasters!" exclaimed he.

The banker shook the dice, and the player burst into imprecations.

"Four thousand piasters!" said he, again. And he lost once more.

Martin Paz, protected by the obscurity of the saloon, could look the player in the face, and he turned pale.

It was André Certa!

Near him, was standing the Jew Samuel.

"You have played enough, Señor André," said Samuel to him; "the luck is not for you."

"What business is it of yours?" replied the mestizo, roughly.

Samuel bent down to his ear.

"If it is not my business, it is your business to break off these habits during the days which precede your marriage."

"Eight thousand piasters!" resumed André Certa.

He lost again: the mestizo suppressed a curse and the banker resumed—"Play on!"

André Certa, drawing from his pocket some bills, was about to have hazarded a considerable sum; he had even deposited it on one of the tables, and the banker, shaking his dice, was about to have decided its fate, when a sign from Samuel stopped him short. The Jew bent again to the ear of the mestizo, and said—

"If nothing remains to you to conclude our bargain, it shall be broken off this evening!"

André Certa shrugged his shoulders, took up his money, and went out.

"Continue now," said Samuel to the banker; "you may ruin this gentleman after his marriage."

The banker bowed submissively. The Jew Samuel was the founder and proprietor of the games of Chorillos. Wherever there was a real to be made this man was to be met with.

He followed the mestizo; and finding him on the stone steps, said to him—

"I have secrets of importance to communicate. Where can we converse in safety?"

"Wherever you please," replied Certa, roughly.

"Señor, let not your passions ruin your prospects. I would neither confide my secret to the most carefully closed chambers, nor the most lonely plains. If you pay me dearly for it, it is because it is worth telling and worth keeping."

As they spoke thus, these two men had reached the sea, near the cabins destined for the use of the bathers. They knew not that they were seen, heard and watched by Martin Paz, who glided like a serpent in the shadow.

"Let us take a canoe," said André, "and go out into the open sea; the sharks may, perhaps, show themselves discreet."

André detached from the shore a little boat, and threw some money to its guardian. Samuel embarked with him, and the mestizo pushed off. He vigorously plied two flexible oars, which soon took them a mile from the shore.

But as he saw the canoe put off, Martin Paz, concealed in a crevice of the rock, hastily undressed, and precipitating himself into the sea, swam vigorously toward the boat.

The sun had just buried his last rays in the waves of the ocean, and darkness hovered over the crests of the waves.

Martin Paz had not once reflected that sharks of the most dangerous species frequented these fatal shores. He stopped not far from the boat of the mestizo, and listened.

"But what proof of the identity of the daughter shall I carry to the father?" asked André Certa of the Jew.

"You will recall to him the circumstances under which he lost her."

"What were these circumstances?"

Martin Paz, now scarcely above the waves, listened without understanding. In a girdle attached to his body, he had a poignard; he waited.

"Her father," said the Jew, "lived at Concencion, in Chili: he was then the great nobleman he is now; only his fortune equalled his nobility. Obliged to come to Lima on business, he set out alone, leaving at Concencion his wife, and child aged fifteen months. The climate of Peru agreed with him, and he sent for the marchioness to rejoin him. She embarked on the San-José of Valparaiso, with her confidential servants.

"I was going to Peru in the same ship. The San-José was about to enter the harbor of Lima; but, near Juan Fernandez, was struck by a terrific hurricane, which disabled her and threw her on her side—it was the affair of half an hour. The San-José filled with water and was slowly sinking; the passengers and crew took refuge in the boat, but at sight of the furious waves, the marchioness refused to enter it; she pressed her infant in her arms, and remained in the ship. I remained with her—the boat was swallowed up at a hundred fathoms from the San-José, with all her crew. We were alone—the tempest blew with increasing violence. As my fortune was not on board, I had nothing to lose. The San-José, having five feet of water in her hold, drifted on the rocks of the shore, where she broke to pieces. The young woman was thrown into the sea with her daughter: fortunately, for me," said the Jew, with a gloomy smile, "I could seize the child, and reach the shore with it."

"All these details are exact?"

"Perfectly so. The father will recognize them. I had done a good day's work, señor; since she is worth to me the hundred thousand piasters which you are about to pay me. Now, let the marriage take place to-morrow."

"What does this mean?" asked Martin Paz of himself, still swimming in the shadow.

"Here is my pocket-book, with the hundred thousand piasters—take it, Master Samuel," replied André Certa to the Jew.

"Thanks, Señor André," said the Israelite, seizing the treasure; "take this receipt in exchange—I pledge myself to restore you double this sum, if you do not become a member of one of the proudest families of Spain."

But the Indian had not heard this last sentence; he had dived to avoid the approach of the boat, and his eyes could see a shapeless mass gliding rapidly toward him. He thought it was the canoe—he was mistaken.

It was a tintorea; a shark of the most ferocious species.

Martin Paz did not quail, or he would have been lost. The animal approached him—the Indian dived; but he was obliged to come up, in order to breathe.... He looked at the sky, as if he was never to behold it again. The stars sparkled above his head; the tintorea continued to approach. A vigorous blow with his tail struck the swimmer; Martin Paz felt his slimy scales brush his breast. The shark, in order to snatch at him, turned on his back and opened his jaws, armed with a triple row of teeth. Martin Paz saw the white belly of the animal gleam beneath the wave, and with a rapid hand struck it with his poignard.

Suddenly he found the waters around him red with blood. He dived—came up again at ten fathoms' distance—thought of the daughter of Samuel; and seeing nothing more of the boat of the mestizo, regained the shore in a few strokes, already forgetting that he had just escaped death.

He quickly rejoined Don Vegal. The latter, not having found him on his return, was anxiously awaiting him. Paz made no allusion to his recent adventures; but seemed to take a lively pleasure in his conversation.

But the next day Martin Paz had left Chorillos, and Don Vegal, tortured with anxiety, hastily returned to Lima.

The marriage of André Certa with the daughter of the wealthy Samuel, was an important event. The beautiful señoras had not given themselves a moment's rest; they had exhausted their ingenuity to invent some pretty corsage or novel head-dress; they had wearied themselves in trying without cessation the most varied toilets.

Numerous preparations were also going on in the house of Samuel; it was a part of the Jew's plan to give great publicity to the marriage of Sarah. The frescoes which adorned his dwelling according to the Spanish custom, had been newly painted; the richest hangings fell in large folds at the windows and doors of the habitation. Furniture carved in the latest fashion, of precious or fragrant wood, was crowded in vast saloons, impregnated with a delicious coolness. Rare shrubs, the productions of warm countries, seized the eye with their splendid colors, and one would have thought Spring had stolen along the balconies and terraces, to inundate them with flowers and perfumes.

Meanwhile, amid these smiling marvels, the young girl was weeping; Sarah no longer had hope, since the Sambo had none; and the Sambo had no hope, since he wore no sign of hope! The negro Liberta had watched the steps of the old Indian; he had seen nothing. Ah! if the poor child could have followed the impulses of her heart, she would have immured herself in one of those tranquil beaterios, to die there amid tears and prayer.

Urged by an irresistible attraction to the doctrines of Catholicism, the young Jewess had been secretly converted; by the cares of the good Father Joachim, she had been won over to a religion more in accordance with her feelings than that in which she had been educated. If Samuel had destined her for a Jew, she would have avowed her faith; but, about to espouse a Catholic, she reserved for her husband the secret of her conversion.

Father Joachim, in order to avoid scandal, and besides, better read in his breviary than in the human heart, had suffered Sarah to believe in the death of Martin Paz. The conversion of the young girl was the most important thing to him; he saw it assured by her union with André Certa, and he sought to accustom her to the idea of this marriage, the conditions of which he was far from respecting.

At last the day so joyous for some, so sad for others, had arrived. André Certa had invited the entire city to his nuptials; his invitations were refused by the noble families, who excused themselves on various pretexts. The mestizo, meanwhile, proudly held up his head, and scarcely looked at those of his own class. The little Milleflores in vain essayed his humblest vows; but he consoled himself with the idea that he was about to figure as an active party in the repast which was to follow.

In the meantime, the young mestizoes were discoursing with him in the brilliant saloons of the Jew, and the crowd of guests thronged around André Certa, who proudly displayed the splendors of his toilet.

The contract was soon to be signed; the sun had long been set, and the young girl had not appeared.

Doubtless she was discussing with her duenna and her maids the place of a ribbon or the choice of an ornament. Perhaps, that enchanting timidity which so beautifully adorns the cheeks of a young girl, detained her still from their inquisitive regards.

The Jew Samuel seemed a prey to secret uneasiness; André Certa bent his brow in an impatient manner; a sort of embarrassment was depicted on the countenance of more than one guest, while the thousand of wax-lights, reflected by the mirrors, filled the saloon with dazzling splendor.

Without, a man was wandering in mortal anxiety; it was the Marquis Don Vegal.

All Interests at Stake

Meanwhile, Sarah was left alone, alone with her anguish and her grief! She was about to give up her whole life to a man whom she did not love! She leaned over the perfumed balcony of her chamber, which overlooked the interior gardens. Through the green jalousies, her ear listened to the sounds of the slumbering country. Her lace mantle, gliding over her arms, revealed a profusion of diamonds sparkling on her shoulders. Her sorrow, proud and majestic, appeared through all her ornaments, and she might have been taken for one of those beautiful Greek slaves, nobly draped in their antique garments.

Suddenly her glance rested on a man who was gliding silently among the avenues of the magnolia; she recognized him; it was Liberta, her servant. He seemed to be watching some invisible enemy, now sheltering himself behind a statue, now crouching on the ground.

Sarah was afraid, and looked around her. She was alone, entirely alone. Her eyes rested on the gardens, and she became pale, paler still! Before her was transpiring a terrible scene. Liberta was in the grasp of a man of tall stature, who had thrown him down; stifled sighs proved that a robust hand was pressing the lips of the Indian.

The young girl, summoning all her courage, was about to cry out, when she saw the two men rise! The negro was looking fixedly at his adversary.

"It is you, then! it is you!" exclaimed he.

And he followed this man in a strange stupefaction. They arrived beneath the balcony of Sarah. Suddenly, before she had time to utter a cry, Martin Paz appeared to her, like a phantom from another world; and, like the negro when overthrown by the Indian, the young girl, bending before the glance of Martin Paz, could in her turn only repeat these words,

"It is you, then! it is you!"

The young Indian fixed on her his motionless eyes, and said:

"Does the betrothed hear the sound of the festival? The guests are thronging into the saloons to see happiness radiate from her countenance! Is it then a victim, prepared for the sacrifice, who is about to present herself to their impatient eyes? Is it with these features, pale with sorrow, with eyes in which sparkle bitter tears, that the young girl is to appear herself before her betrothed?"

Martin Paz spoke thus, in a tone full of sympathizing sadness, and Sarah listened vaguely as to those harmonies which we hear in dreams!

The young Indian resumed with infinite sweetness:

"Since the soul of the young girl is in mourning, let her look beyond the house of her father, beyond the city where she suffers and weeps; beyond the mountains, the palm-trees lift up their heads in freedom, the birds strike the air with an independent wing; men have immensity to live in, and the young girls may unfold their spirits and their hearts!"

Sarah raised her head toward Martin Paz. The Indian had drawn himself up to his full height, and with his arm extended toward the summits of the Cordilleras, was pointing out to the young girl the path to liberty.

Sarah felt herself constrained by an irresistible force. Already the sound of voices reached her; they approached her chamber; her father was undoubtedly about to enter; perhaps her lover would accompany him! The Indian suddenly extinguished the lamp suspended above his head. A whistling, similar to the cry of the cilguero, and reminding one of that heard on the Plaza-Mayor, pierced the silent darkness of night; the young girl swooned.

The door opened hastily; Samuel and André Certa entered. The darkness was profound; some servants ran with torches. The chamber was empty.

"Death and fury!" exclaimed the mestizo.

"Where is she?" asked Samuel.

"You are responsible for her," said André, brutally.

At these words, the Jew felt a cold sweat freeze even his bones.

"Help! help!" he exclaimed.

And, followed by his domestics, he sprang out of the house.

Martin Paz fled rapidly through the streets of the city. The negro Liberta followed him; but did not appear disposed to dispute with him the possession of the young girl.

At two hundred paces from the dwelling of the Jew, Paz found some Indians of his companions, who had assembled at the whistle uttered by him.

"To our mountain ranchos!" exclaimed he.

"To the house of the Marquis Don Vegal!" said another voice behind him.

Martin Paz turned; the Spaniard was at his side.

"Will you not confide this young girl to me?" asked the marquis.

The Indian bent his head, and said in a low voice to his companions:

"To the dwelling of the Marquis Don Vegal!"

They turned their steps in this direction.

An extreme confusion reigned then in the saloons of the Jew. The news of Sarah's disappearance was a thunderbolt; the friends of André hastened to follow him. The faubourg of San Lazaro was explored, hastily searched; but nothing could be discovered. Samuel tore his hair in despair. During the whole night the most active research was useless.

"Martin Paz is living!" exclaimed André Certa, in a moment of fury.

And the presentiment quickly acquired confirmation. The police were immediately informed of the elopement; its most active agents bestirred themselves; the Indians were closely watched, and if the retreat of the young girl was not discovered, evident proofs of an approaching revolt came to light, which accorded with the denunciations of the Jew.

André Certa lavished gold freely, but could learn nothing. Meanwhile, the gate-keepers declared that they had seen no person leave Lima; the young girl must therefore be concealed in the city.

Liberta, who returned to his master, was often interrogated; but no person seemed more astonished than himself at the elopement of Sarah.

Meanwhile, one man besides André Certa had seen in the disappearance of the young Jewess, a proof of the existence of Martin Paz; it was the Sambo. He was wandering in the streets of Lima, when the cry uttered by the Indian fixed his attention; it was a signal of rally well known to him! The Sambo was therefore a spectator of the capture of the young girl, and followed her to the dwelling of the marquis.

The Spaniard entered by a secret door, of which he alone had the key; so that his domestics suspected nothing. Martin Paz carried the young girl in his arms and laid her on a bed.

When Don Vegal, who had returned to re-enter by the principal door, reached the chamber where Sarah was reposing, he found Martin Paz kneeling beside her. The marquis was about to reproach the Indian with his conduct, when the latter said to him:

"You see, my father, whether I love you! Ah! why did you throw yourself in my way? We should have been already free in our mountains. But how, should I not have obeyed your words?"

Don Vegal knew not what to reply, his heart was seized with a powerful emotion. He felt how much he was beloved by Martin Paz.

"The day on which Sarah shall quit your dwelling to be restored to her father and her betrothed," sighed the Indian, "you will have a son and a friend less in the world."

As he said these last words, Paz moistened with his tears the hand of Don Vegal. They were the first tears this man had shed!

The reproaches of Don Vegal died away before this respectful submission. The young girl had become his guest; she was sacred! He could not help admiring Sarah, still in a swoon; he was prepared to love her, of whose conversion he had been a witness, and whom he would have been pleased to bestow as a companion upon the young Indian.

It was then that, on opening her eyes, Sarah found herself in the presence of a stranger.

"Where am I?" said she, with a sentiment of terror.

"With a generous man who has permitted me to call him my father," replied Martin Paz, pointing to the Spaniard.

The young girl, restored by the voice of the Indian to a consciousness of her position, covered her face with her trembling hands, and began to sob.

"Withdraw, friend," said Don Vegal to the young man; "withdraw."

Martin Paz slowly left the room, not without having pressed the hand of the Spaniard, and cast on Sarah a lingering look.

Then Don Vegal bestowed upon this poor child consolations of exquisite delicacy; he conveyed in suitable language his sentiments of nobility and honor. Attentive and resigned, the young girl comprehended what danger she had escaped; and she confided her future happiness to the care of the Spaniard. But amid phrases interrupted by sighs and mingled with tears, Don Vegal perceived the intense attachment of this simple heart for him whom she called her deliverer. He induced Sarah to take some repose, and watched over her with the solicitude of a father.

Martin Paz comprehended the duties that honor required of him, and, in spite of perils and dangers, would not pass the night beneath the roof of Don Vegal.

He therefore went out; his head was burning, his blood was boiling with fever in his veins.

He had not gone a hundred paces in the street, when five or six men threw themselves upon him, and, notwithstanding his obstinate defense, succeeded in binding him. Martin Paz uttered a cry of despair, which was lost in the night. He believed himself in the power of his enemies, and gave a last thought to the young girl.

A short time afterward the Indian was deposited in a room. The bandage which had covered his eyes was taken off. He looked around him, and saw himself in the lower hall of that tavern where his brethren had organized their approaching revolt.

The Sambo, Manangani, and others, surrounded him. A gleam of indignation flashed from his eyes, which was reciprocated by his captors.

"My son had then no pity on my tears," said the Sambo, "since he suffered me for so long a time to believe in his death?"

"Is it on the eve before a revolt that Martin Paz, our chief, should be found in the camp of our enemies?"

Martin Paz replied neither to his father, nor to Manangani.

"So our most important interests have been sacrificed to a woman!"

As he spoke thus, Manangani had approached Martin Paz; a poignard was gleaming in his hand. Martin Paz did not even look at him.

"Let us first speak," said the Sambo; "we will act afterward. If my son fails to conduct his brethren to the combat, I shall know now on whom to avenge his treason. Let him take care! the daughter of the Jew Samuel is not so well concealed that she can escape our hatred. My son will reflect. Struck with a mortal condemnation, proscribed, wandering among our masters, he will not have a stone on which to rest his sorrows. If, on the contrary, we resume our ancient country and our ancient power, Martin Paz, the chief of numerous tribes, may bestow upon his betrothed both happiness and glory."

Martin Paz remained silent; but a terrific conflict was going on within him. The Sambo had roused the most sensitive chords of his proud nature to vibrate; placed between a life of fatigues, of dangers, of despair, and an existence happy, honored, illustrious, he could not hesitate. But should he then abandon the Marquis Don Vegal, whose noble hopes destined him as the deliverer of Peru!

"Oh!" thought he, as he looked at his father, "they will kill Sarah, if I forsake them."

"What does my son reply to us?" imperiously demanded the Sambo.

"That Martin Paz is indispensable to your projects; that he enjoys a supreme authority over the Indians of the city; that he leads them at his will, and, at a sign, could have them dragged to death. He must therefore resume his place in the revolt, in order to ensure victory."

The bonds which still enchained him were detached by order of the Sambo; Martin Paz arose free among his brethren.

"My son," said the Indian, who was observing him attentively, "to-morrow, during the fête of the Amancaës, our brethren will fall like an avalanche on the unarmed Limanians. There is the road to the Cordilleras, there is the road to the city; you will go wherever your good pleasure shall lead you. To-morrow! to-morrow! you will find more than one mestizo breast to break your poignard against. You are free."

"To the mountains!" exclaimed Martin Paz, with a stern voice.

The Indian had again become an Indian amid the hatred which surrounded him.

"To the mountains," repeated he, "and wo to our enemies, wo!"

And the rising sun illumined with its earliest rays the council of the Indian chiefs in the heart of the Cordilleras.

These rays were joyless to the heart of the poor young girl, who wept and prayed. The marquis had summoned Father Joachim; and the worthy man had there met his beloved penitent. What happiness was it for her to kneel at the feet of the old priest, and to pour out her anguish and her afflictions.

But Sarah could no longer remain in the dwelling of the Spaniard. Father Joachim suggested this to Don Vegal, who knew not what part to take, for he was a prey to extreme anxiety. What had become of Martin Paz? He had fled the house. Was he in the power of his enemies? Oh! how the Spaniard regretted having suffered him to leave it during that night of alarms! He sought him with the ardor, with the affection of a father; he found him not.

"My old friend," said he to Joachim, "the young girl is in safety near you; do not leave her during this fatal night."

"But her father, who seeks her—her betrothed, who awaits her?"

"One day—one single day! You know not whose existence is bound to that of this child. One day—one single day! at least until I find Martin Paz, he whom my heart and God have named my son!"

Father Joachim returned to the young girl; Don Vegal went out and traversed the streets of Lima.

The Spaniard was surprised at the noise, the commotion, the agitation of the city. It was that the great fête of the Amancaës, forgotten by him alone, the 24th of June, the day of St. John, had arrived. The neighboring mountains were covered with verdure and flowers; the inhabitants, on foot, on horseback, in carriages, were repairing to a celebrated table-land, situated at half a league from Lima, where the spectators enjoyed an admirable prospect; mestizoes and Indians mingled in the common fête; they walked gayly by groups of relatives or friends; each group, calling itself by the name of partida, carried its provisions, and was preceded by a player on the guitar, who chanted, accompanying himself, the most popular yaravis and llantos. These joyous promenaders advanced with cries, sports, endless jests, through the fields of maize and of alfalfa, through the groves of banana, whose fruits hung to the ground; they traversed those beautiful alamedas, planted with willows, and forests of citron, and orange-trees, whose intoxicating perfumes were mingled with the wild fragrance from the mountains. All along the road, traveling cabarets offered to the promenaders the brandy of pisco and the chica, whose copious libations excited to laughter and clamor; cavaliers made their horses caracole in the midst of the throng, and rivaled each other in swiftness, address, and dexterity; all the dances in vogue, from the loudon to the mismis, from the boleros to the zamacuecas, agitated and hurried on the caballeros and black-eyed sambas. The sounds of the viguela were soon no longer sufficient for the disordered movements of the dancers; the musicians uttered wild cries, which stimulated them to delirium; the spectators beat the measure with their feet and hands, and the exhausted couples sunk one after another to the ground.

There reigned in this fête, which derives its name from the little mountain-flowers, an inconceivable transport and freedom; and yet no private brawl mingled among the cries of public rejoicing; a few lancers on horseback, ornamented with their shining cuirasses, maintained here and there order among the populace.

The various classes of Limanian society mingled in these rejoicings, which are repeated every day throughout the month of July. Pretty tapadas laughingly elbow beautiful girls, who bravely come, with uncovered faces, to meet joyous cavaliers; and when at last this multitude arrive at the plateau of the Amancaës, an immense clamor of admiration is repeated by the mountain echoes.

At the feet of the spectators extends the ancient city of kings, proudly lifting toward heaven its towers and its steeples, whose bells are ringing joyous peals. San Pedro, Saint Augustine, the Cathedral, attract the eye to their roofs, resplendent with the rays of the sun. San Domingo, the rich church, the Madonna of which is never clad in the same garments two days in succession, raises above her neighbors her tapering spire; on the right, the vast plains of the Pacific Ocean are undulating to the breath of the occidental breeze, and the eye, as it roves from Callao to Lima, rests on those funereal chulpas, the last remains of the great dynasty of the Incas; at the horizon, Cape Morro-Solar frames, with its sloping hills, the wonderful splendors of this picture.

So the Limanians are never satisfied with these admirable prospects, and their noisy approbation deafens every year the echoes of San Cristoval and the Amancaës.

Now, while they fearlessly enjoyed these picturesque views, and were giving themselves up to an irresistible delight, a gloomy bloody funereal drama was preparing on the snowy summits of the Cordilleras.

Conquerors and Conquered

A prey to his blind grief, Don Vegal walked at random. After having lost his daughter, the hope of his race and of his love, was he about to see himself also deprived of the child of his adoption whom he had wrested from death? Don Vegal had forgotten Sarah, to think only of Martin Paz.

He was struck with the great number of Indians, of zambos, of chiños, who were wandering about the streets; these men, who usually took an active part in the sports of the Amancaës, were now walking silently with singular pre-occupation. Often some busy chief gave them a secret order, and went on his way; and all, notwithstanding their detours, were assembling by degrees in the wealthiest quarters of Lima, in proportion as the Limanians were scattered abroad in the country.

Don Vegal, absorbed in his own researches, soon forgot this singular state of things. He traversed San Lazaro throughout, saw André Certa there, enraged and armed, and the Jew Samuel, in the extremity of distress, not for the loss of his daughter, but for the loss of his hundred thousand piasters; but he found not Martin Paz, whom he was impatiently seeking. He ran to the consistorial prison. Nothing! He returned home. Nothing! He mounted his horse and hastened to Chorillos. Nothing! He returned at last, exhausted with fatigue, to Lima; the clock of the cathedral was striking four.

Don Vegal remarked some groups of Indians before his dwelling; but he could not, without compromising the man of whom he was in search, ask them—

"Where is Martin Paz?"

He re-entered, more despairing than ever.

Immediately a man emerged from a neighboring alley, and came directly to the Indians. This man was the Sambo.

"The Spaniard has returned," said he to them; "you know him now; he is one of the representatives of the race which crushes us— wo to him!"

"And when shall we strike?"

"When five o'clock sounds, and the tocsin from the mountain gives the signal of vengeance."

Then the Sambo marched with hasty steps to the chingana, and rejoined the chief of the revolt.

Meanwhile the sun had begun to sink beneath the horizon; it was the hour in which the Limanian aristocracy went in its turn to the Amancaës; the richest toilets shone in the equipages which defiled to the right and left beneath the trees along the road; there was an inextricable mêlée of foot-passengers, carriages, horses; a confusion of cries, songs, instruments, and vociferations.

The clock on the tower of the cathedral suddenly struck five! and a shrill funereal sound vibrated through the air; the tocsin thundered over the crowd, frozen in its delirium.

An immense cry resounded in the city. From every square, every street, every house issued the Indians, with arms in their hands, and fury in their eyes. The principal places of the city were thronged with these men, some of whom shook above their heads burning torches!

"Death to the Spaniards! death to the oppressors!" such was the watch-word of the rebels.

Those who attempted to return to Lima must have recoiled before these masses; but the summits of the hills were quickly covered with other enemies, and all retreat was impossible; the zambos precipitated themselves like a thunderbolt on this crowd, exhausted with the fatigues of the festival, while the mountain

Indians cleared for themselves a bloody path to rejoin their brethren of the city.

Imagine the aspect presented by Lima at this terrible moment. The rebels had left the square of the tavern, and were scattered in all quarters; at the head of one of the columns, Martin Paz was waving the black flag—the flag of independence; while the Indians in the other streets were attacking the houses appointed to ruin, Martin Paz took possession of the Plaza-Mayor with his company; near him, Manangani was uttering ferocious yells, and proudly displaying his bloody arms.

But the soldiers of the government, forewarned of the revolt, were ranged in battle array before the palace of the president; a frightful fusillade greeted the insurgents at their entrance on the square; surprised by this unexpected discharge, which extended a goodly number of them on the ground, they sprang upon the troops with insurmountable impatience; a horrible mêlée followed, in which men fought body to body. Martin Paz and Manangani performed prodigies of valor, and escaped death only by miracle.

It was necessary at all hazards that the palace should be taken and occupied by their men.

"Forward!" cried Martin Paz, and his voice led the Indians to the assault. Although they were crushed in every direction, they succeeded in making the body of troops around the palace recoil. Already had Manangani sprang on the first steps; but he suddenly stopped as the opening ranks of soldiers unmasked two pieces of cannon ready to fire on the assailants.

There was not a moment to lose; the battery must be seized before it could be discharged.

"On!" cried Manangani, addressing himself to Martin Paz.

But the young Indian had just stooped and no longer heard him, for an Indian had whispered these words in his ear:

"They are pillaging the house of Don Vegal, perhaps assassinating him!"

At these words Martin Paz recoiled. Manangani seized him by the arm; but, repulsing him with a vigorous hand, the Indian darted toward the square.

"Traitor! infamous traitor!" exclaimed Manangani, discharging his pistols at Martin Paz.

At this moment the cannons were fired, and the grape swept the Indians on the steps.

"This way, brethren," cried Martin Paz, and a few fugitives, his devoted companions, joined him; with this little company he could make his way through the soldiers.

This flight had all the consequences of treason; the Indians believed themselves abandoned by their chief. Manangani in vain attempted to bring them back to the combat; a rapid fusillade sent among them a shower of balls; thenceforth it was no longer possible to rally them; the confusion was at its height and the rout complete. The flames which arose in certain quarters attracted some fugitives to pillage; but the conquering soldiers pursued them with the sword, and killed a great number without mercy.

Meanwhile, Martin Paz had gained the house of Don Vegal; it was the theatre of a bloody struggle, headed by the Sambo himself; he had a double interest in being there; while contending with the Spanish noblemen, he wished to seize Sarah, as a pledge of the fidelity of his son.

On seeing Martin Paz return, he no longer doubted his treason, and turned his brethren against him.

The overthrown gate and walls of the court revealed Don Vegal, sword in hand, surrounded by his faithful servants, and contending with an invading mass. This man's courage and pride were sublime; he was the first to present himself to mortal blows, and his formidable arm had surrounded him with corpses.

But what could be done against this crowd of Indians, which was then increasing with all the conquered of the Plaza-Mayor. Don Vegal felt that his defenders were becoming exhausted, and nothing remained for him but death, when Martin Paz arrived, rapid as the thunderbolt, charged the aggressors from behind, forced them to turn against him, and, amid balls, poignard-strokes and maledictions, reached Don Vegal, to whom he made a rampart of his body. Courage revived in the hearts of the besieged.

"Well done, my son, well done!" said Don Vegal to Martin Paz, pressing his hand.

But the young Indian was gloomy.

"Well done! Martin Paz," exclaimed another voice which went to his very soul; he recognized Sarah, and his arm traced a bloody circle around him.

The company of Sambo gave way in its turn. Twenty times had this modern Brutus directed his blows against his son, without being able to reach him, and twenty times Martin had turned away the weapon about to strike his father.

Suddenly the ferocious Manangani, covered with blood, appeared beside the Sambo.

"Thou hast sworn," said he, "to avenge the treason of a wretch on his kindred, on his friends, on himself. Well, it is time! the soldiers are coming; the mestizo, André Certa, is with them."

"Come then," said the Sambo, with a ferocious laugh: "come then, for our vengeance approaches."

And both abandoned the house of Don Vegal, while their companions were being killed there. They went directly to the company who were arriving. The latter aimed at them; but without being intimidated, the Sambo approached the mestizo.

"You are André Certa," said he; "well, your betrothed is in the house of Don Vegal, and Martin Paz is about to carry her to the mountains."

This said, the Indians disappeared. Thus the Sambo had put face to face two mortal enemies, and, deceived by the presence of Martin Paz in the house of Don Vegal, the soldiers rushed upon the dwelling of the marquis.

André Certa was intoxicated with rage. As soon as he perceived Martin Paz, he rushed upon him.

"Here!" exclaimed the young Indian, and quitting the stone steps which he had so valiantly defended, he joined the mestizo. Meanwhile the companions of Martin Paz were repulsing the soldiers body to body.

Martin Paz had seized André Certa with his powerful hand, and clasped him so closely that the mestizo could not use his pistols. They were there, foot against foot, breast against breast, their faces touched, and their glances mingled in a single gleam; their movements became rapid, even invisible; neither friends nor enemies could approach them; in this terrible embrace respiration failed, both fell. André Certa raised himself above Martin Paz, whose poignard had escaped his grasp. The mestizo raised his arm, but the Indian succeeded in seizing it before it had struck. The moment was horrible. André Certa in vain attempted to disengage himself; Martin Paz, with supernatural strength, turned against the mestizo the poignard and the arm which held it, and plunged it into his heart.

Martin Paz arose all bloody. The place was free, the soldiers flying in every direction. Martin Paz might have conquered had he remained on the Plaza-Mayor. He fell into the arms of Don Vegal.

"To the mountains, my son; flee to the mountains! now I command it."

"Is my enemy indeed dead?" said Martin Paz, returning to the corpse of André Certa.

A man was that moment searching it, and held a pocket-book which he had taken from it. Martin Paz sprang on this man and overthrew him; it was the Jew Samuel.

The Indian picked up the pocket-book, opened it hastily, searched it, uttered a cry of joy, and springing toward the marquis, put in his hand a paper on which were written these words:

"Received of the Señor André Certa the sum of 100,000 piasters; I pledge myself to restore this sum doubled, if Sarah, whom I saved from the shipwreck of the San-José, and whom he is about to espouse, is not the daughter and only heir of the Marquis Don Vegal.

"SAMUEL."

"My daughter! my daughter!" exclaimed the Spaniard, and he fell into the arms of Martin Paz, who carried him to the chamber of Sarah.

Alas! the young girl was no longer there; Father Joachim, bathed in his own blood, could articulate only these words:

"The Sambo!—carried off!—toward the river of Madeira!—"

And he fainted.

The Cataracts of the Madeira

"On! on!" Martin Paz had exclaimed. And without saying a word, Don Vegal followed the Indian. His daughter!—he must find again his daughter! Mules were brought, prepared for a long journey among the Cordilleras; the two men mounted them, wrapped in their ponchos; large gaiters were attached by thongs above their knees; immense stirrups, armed with long spurs, surrounded their feet, and broad-brimmed Guayaquil hats sheltered their heads. Arms filled the holsters of each saddle; a carbine, formidable in the hands of Don Vegal, was suspended at his side. Martin Paz had encircled himself with his lasso, one extremity of which was fixed to the harness of his mule.

The Spaniard and the Indian spurred their horses to their utmost speed. At the moment of leaving the walls of the city they were joined by an Indian equipped like themselves. It was Liberta— Don Vegal recognized him; the faithful servant wished to share in their pursuit.

Martin Paz knew all the plains, all the mountains, which they were to traverse; he knew among what savage tribes, into what desert country the Sambo had conveyed his betrothed. His betrothed! he no longer dared give this name to the daughter of Don Vegal.

"My son," said the latter, "have you any hope in your heart?"

"As much as hatred and tenderness."

"The daughter of the Jew, in becoming my blood, has not ceased to be thine."

"Let us press on!" hastily replied Martin Paz.

On their way the travelers saw a great number of Indians flying to regain their ranchos amid the mountains. The defection of Martin Paz had been followed by defeat. If the émeute had triumphed in some places, it had received its death-blow at Lima.

The three cavaliers traveled rapidly, having but one idea, one object. They soon buried themselves among the almost impracticable passes of the Cordilleras. Difficult pathways circulated through these reddish masses, planted here and there with cocoanut and pine trees; the cedars, cotton-trees, and aloes were left behind them, with the plains covered with maize and lucerne; some thorny cactuses sometimes pricked their mules, and made them hesitate on the verge of precipices.

It was a difficult task to traverse the Cordilleras during these summer months; the melting of snows beneath the sun of June often made unforeseen cataracts spout from beneath the steps of the traveler; often frightful masses, detaching themselves from the summits of the peaks, were engulfed near them in fathomless abysses!

But they continued their march, fearing neither the hurricane nor the cold of these high solitudes; they traveled day and night, finding neither cities nor dwellings where they might for a moment repose; happy if in some deserted hut they found a mat of tortora upon which to extend their wearied limbs, some pieces of meat dried in the sun, some calabashes full of muddy water.

They reached at last the summit of the Andes, 14,000 feet above the level of the sea. There, no more trees, no more vegetation; sometimes an oso or ucuman, a sort of enormous black bear, came to meet them. Often, during the afternoon, they were enveloped in those formidable storms of the Cordilleras, which raise whirlwinds of snow from the loftiest summits. Don Vegal sometimes paused, unaccustomed to these frightful perils. Martin Paz then supported him in his arms, and sheltered him against the drifting snow. And yet lightnings flashed from the clouds, and thunders broke over these barren peaks, and filled the mountain recesses with their terrific roar.

At this point, the most elevated of the Andes, the travelers were seized with a malady called by the Indians soroche, which deprives the most intrepid man of his courage and his strength. A superhuman will is then necessary to keep one from falling motionless on the stones of the road, and being devoured by those immense condors which display above their vast wings! These three men spoke little; each wrapped himself in the silence which these vast deserts inspired.

On the eastern slope of the Cordilleras, they hoped to find traces of their enemies; they therefore traveled on, and were at last descending the chain of mountains; but the Andes are composed of a great number of salient peaks, so that inaccessible precipices were constantly rising before them.

Nevertheless they soon found the trees of inferior levels; the llamas, the vigonias, which feed on the thin grass, announced the neighborhood of men. Sometimes they met gauchos conducting their arias of mules; and more than one capataz (leader of a convoy) exchanged fresh animals for their exhausted ones.

In this manner they reached the immense virgin forests which cover the plains situated between Peru and Brazil; they began thenceforth to recover traces of the captors; and it was in the midst of these inextricable woods that Martin Paz recovered all his Indian sagacity.

Courage returned to the Spaniard, strength returned to Liberta, when a half-extinct fire and prints of footsteps proved the proximity of their enemies. Martin Paz noted all and studied all, the breaking of the little branches, the nature of the vestiges.

Don Vegal feared lest his unfortunate daughter should have been dragged on foot through the stones and thorns; but the Indian showed him some pebbles strongly imbedded in the earth, which indicated the pressure of an animal's foot; above, branches had been pushed aside in the same direction, which could have been reached only by a person on horseback. The poor father comforted himself and recovered life and hope, and then Martin Paz was so confident, so skillful, so strong, that there were for him neither impassable obstacles nor insurmountable perils.

Nevertheless immense forests contracted the horizon around them, and trees multiplied incessantly before their fatigued eyes.

One evening, while the darkness was gathering beneath the opaque foliage, Martin Paz, Liberta and Don Vegal were compelled by fatigue to stop. They had reached the banks of a river; it was the river Madeira, which the Indian recognized perfectly; immense mangrove trees bent above the sleeping wave and were united to the trees on the opposite shore by capricious lianes (vines), on which were balancing the titipaying and the concoulies.

Had the captors ascended the banks? had they descended the course of the river? had they crossed it in a direct line? Such were the questions with which Martin Paz puzzled himself. He stepped a little aside from his companions, following with infinite difficulty some fugitive tracks; these brought him to a clearing a little less gloomy. Some footsteps indicated that a company of men had, perhaps, crossed the river at this spot, which was the opinion of the Indian, although he found around him no proof of the construction of a canoe; he knew that the Sambo might have cut down some tree in the middle of the forest, and having spoiled it of its bark, made of it a boat, which could have been carried on the arms of men to the shores of the Madeira. Nevertheless, he was still hesitating, when he saw a sort of black mass move near a thicket; he quickly prepared his lasso and made ready for an attack; he advanced a few paces, and perceived an animal lying on the ground, a prey to the final convulsions—it was a mule. The poor, expiring beast had been struck at a distance from the spot whither it had been dragged, leaving long traces of blood on its passage. Martin Paz no longer doubted that the Indians, unable to induce it to cross the river, had killed it with the stroke of a poignard, as a deep wound indicated. From this moment he felt certain of the direction of his enemies; and returned to his companions, who were already uneasy at his long absence.

"To-morrow, perhaps, we shall see the young girl!" said he to them.

"My daughter! Oh! my son! let us set out this instant," said the Spaniard; "I am no longer fatigued, and strength returns with hope—let us go!"

"But we must cross this river, and we cannot lose time in constructing a canoe."

"We will swim across."

"Courage, then, my father! Liberta and myself will sustain you."

All three laid aside their garments, which Martin Paz carried in a bundle upon his head; and all three glided silently into the water, for fear of awakening some of these dangerous caïmans so numerous in the rivers of Brazil and Peru.

They arrived safely at the opposite shore: the first care of Martin Paz was to recover traces of the Indians; but in vain did he scrutinize the smallest leaves, the smallest pebbles—he could discover nothing; as the rapid current had carried them down in crossing, he ascended the bank of the river to the spot opposite that where he had found the mule, but nothing indicated the direction taken by the captors. It must have been that these, that their tracks might be entirely lost, had descended the river for several miles, in order to land far from the spot of their embarkation.

Martin Paz, that his companions might not be discouraged, did not communicate to them his fears; he said not even a word to Don Vegal respecting the mule, for fear of saddening him still more with the thought that his daughter must now be dragged through these difficult passes.

When he returned to the Spaniard, he found him asleep— fatigue had prevailed over grief and resolution; Martin Paz was careful not to awaken him; a little sleep might do him much good; but, while he himself watched, resting the head of Don Vegal on his knees and piercing with his quick glances the surrounding shadows, he sent Liberta to seek below on the river some trace which might guide them at the first rays of the sun.

The Indian departed in the direction indicated, gliding like a serpent between the high brush with which the shores were bristling, and the sound of his footsteps was soon lost in the distance.

Thenceforth Martin Paz remained alone amid these gloomy solitudes: the Spaniard was sleeping peacefully; the names of his daughter and the Indian sometimes mingled in his dreams, and alone disturbed the silence of these obscure forests.

The young Indian was not mistaken; the Sambo had descended the Madeira three miles, then had landed with the young girl and his numerous companions, among whom might be numbered Manangani, still covered with hideous wounds.

The company of Sambo had increased during the journey. The Indians of the plains and the mountains had awaited with impatience the triumph of the revolt; on learning the failure of their brethren, they fell a prey to a gloomy despair; hearing that they had been betrayed by Martin Paz, they uttered yells of rage; when they saw that they had a victim to be sacrificed to their anger, they burst forth in cries of joy and followed the company of the old Indian.

They marched thus to the approaching sacrifice, devouring the young girl with sanguinary glances—it was the betrothed, the beloved of Martin Paz whom they were about to put to death; abuse was heaped upon her, and more than once the Sambo, who wished his revenge to be public, with difficulty wrested Sarah from their fury.

The young girl, pale, languishing, was without thought and almost without life amid this frightful horde; she had no longer the sentiment of motion, of will, of existence—she advanced, because bloody hands urged her onward; they might have abandoned her in the midst of these great solitudes—she could not have taken a step to have escaped death. Sometimes the remembrance of her father and of the young Indian passed before her eyes, but like a gleam of lightning bewildering her; then she fell again an inert mass on the neck of the poor mule, whose wounded feet could no longer sustain her. When beyond the river she was compelled to follow her captors on foot, two Indians taking her by the arm dragged her rapidly along, and a trace of blood marked on the sand and dead leaves her painful passage.

But the Sambo was no longer afraid of pursuit; he cared little that this blood betrayed the direction he had taken—he was approaching the termination of his journey, and soon the cataracts which abound in the currents of the great river sent up their deafening clamor.

The numerous company of Indians arrived at a sort of village, composed of a hundred huts, made of reeds interlaced and clay; at their approach, a multitude of women and children darted toward them with loud cries of joy—more than one found there his anxious family—more than one wife missed the father of her children!

These women soon learned the defeat of their party; their sadness was transformed into rage on learning the defection of Martin Paz, and on seeing his betrothed devoted to death.

Sarah remained immovable before these enemies and looked at them with a dim eye; all these hideous faces were making grimaces around her, and the most terrific threats were uttered in her ears— the poor child might have thought herself delivered over to the torturers of the infernal regions.

"Where is my husband?" said one; "it is thou who hast caused him to be killed!"

"And my brother, who will never again return to the cabin— what hast thou done with him? Death! death! Let each of us have a piece of her flesh! let each of us have a pain to make her suffer! Death! death!"

And these women, with dishevelled hair, brandishing knives, waving flaming brands, bearing enormous stones, approached the young girl, surrounded her, pressed her, crushed her.

"Back!" cried the Sambo, "back! and let all await the decision of their chiefs! This girl must disarm the anger of the Great Spirit, which has rested upon our arms; and she shall not serve for private revenge alone!"

The women obeyed the words of the old Indian, casting frightful glances on the young girl; the latter, covered with blood, remained extended on the pebbly shore.

Above this village, plunges, from a height of more than a hundred feet, a foaming cataract, which breaks against sharp rocks; the Madeira, contracted into a deep bed, precipitates this dense mass of water with frightful rapidity; a cloud of mist is eternally suspended above this torrent, whose fall sends its formidable and thundering roar afar.

It was in the midst of this foaming tempest that the unfortunate young girl was destined to die; at the first rays of the sun, exposed in a bark canoe above the cataract, she was to be precipitated with the mass of waters on the rude rocks against which the Madeira broke.

So the council of chiefs had decided; and they had delayed until the morrow the punishment of their victim, to give her a night of anguish, of torment, and of terror.

When the sentence was made known, cries of joy welcomed it, and a furious delirium seized the Indians.

It was a night of orgies—a night of blood and of horror; brandy increased the excitement of these wild natives; dances, accompanied with perpetual yells, surrounded the young girl, and wound their fantastic chains about the stake to which she was fastened.

Sometimes the circle narrowed, and enlaced her in its furious whirls: the Indians ran through the uncultivated fields, brandishing blazing pine-branches, and surrounding the victim with light.

And it was thus until sunrise, and worse yet when its first rays illuminated the scene. The young girl was detached from the stake, and a hundred arms were stretched out to drag her to execution, when the name of Martin Paz involuntarily escaped her lips, and cries of hatred and of vengeance responded.

It was necessary to climb by steep paths the immense pile of rocks which led to the upper level of the river, and the victim arrived there all bloody; a canoe of bark awaited her a hundred paces above the fall; she was deposited in it, and fastened by bonds which entered her flesh.

"Vengeance and death!" exclaimed the whole tribe, with one voice.

The canoe was hurried on with increasing rapidity and began to whirl.

Suddenly a man appeared on the opposite shore— It is Martin Paz! Beside him, are Don Vegal and Liberta.

"My daughter! my daughter!" exclaims the father, kneeling on the shore.

"My father!" replied Sarah, raising herself up with superhuman strength.

The scene was indescribable. The canoe was rapidly hastening to the cataract, in whose foam it was already enveloped.

Martin Paz, standing on a rock, balanced his lasso which whistled around his head. At the instant the boat was about to be precipitated, the long leathern thong unfolded from above the head of the Indian, and surrounded the canoe with its noose.

"My daughter! my daughter!" exclaimed Don Vegal.

"My betrothed! my beloved!" cried Martin Paz.

"Death!" yelled the savage multitude.

Meanwhile Martin Paz redoubles his efforts; the canoe remains suspended over the abyss; the current cannot prevail over the strength of the young Indian; the canoe is drawn to him; the enemies are far on the opposite shore; the young girl is saved.

Suddenly an arrow whistles through the air, and pierces the heart of Martin Paz. He falls forward in the bark of the victim; and, re-descending the current of the river in her arms, is engulfed with Sarah in the vortex of the cataract.

A yell of triumph is heard above the sound of the torrent.

Liberta bore off the Spaniard amid a cloud of arrows, and disappeared with him.

Don Vegal regained Lima, where he died with grief and exhaustion.

The Sambo, who remained among his sanguinary tribes, was never heard of more.

The Jew Samuel kept the hundred thousand piasters he had received, and continued his usuries at the expense of the Limanian nobles.

Martin Paz and Sarah were, in their brief and final re-union, betrothed for eternity.

The Mutineers of
the Bounty

Turned Adrift

Not a breath of wind, not a ripple on the surface of the ocean, not a cloud in the sky. The splendid constellations of the Southern Hemisphere shone with exquisite brilliancy. The Bounty lay motionless, with drooping sails, as the night wore on; and the moon, turning pale at the approach of dawn, filled the air with dim and uncertain light.

The Bounty, a vessel of two hundred and fifteen tons burden, manned by a crew of forty-six, had left Spithead on the 23rd of December, 1787, under the command of Captain Bligh, a rough, but experienced seaman, who had accompanied Captain Cook on his last voyage of discovery.

The special object of this voyage of the Bounty was to obtain plants of the bread-fruit tree, which grows in profusion in the Tahitian Archipelago, and to carry them to the Antilles.

After remaining for six months in the Bay of Matavai, Captain Bligh, with a cargo of a thousand bread-fruit trees, set sail for the West Indies, stopping at the Friendly Islands for a short time.

The suspicious and passionate character of the captain had repeatedly occasioned disagreeable scenes between him and his officers; but, when the sun rose on the morning of the 28th of April, 1789, the perfect tranquility which prevailed on board the Bounty, was disturbed by no token of the serious events about to take place.

By-and-by the apparent tranquility was broken by unwonted animation among the crew: the seamen met, exchanged two or three words in whispers, and then separated quietly. What could be going on?

"Above all things, make no noise, friends," said Fletcher Christian, the second officer of the Bounty. "Load your pistol, Bob; but do not fire till I give the word. Churchill, take a hatchet to burst open the lock of the captain's cabin door, and, mark me, I must have him alive."

Followed by a dozen seamen, armed with sabres, cutlasses, and pistols, Christian glided between decks, where he placed two sentinels before the cabins of Stewart and Peter Heywood, the one the boatswain, the other a midshipman of the Bounty, and then, passing on, he stopped at the captain's door.

"Come, lads!" he cried, "one good shove all together!" The door yielded to their vigorous blows, and the seamen rushed into the cabin.

Confused by the darkness, and, perhaps, reflecting on the serious nature of the step they had taken, they hesitated for a moment.

"Hullo! What's the matter? Who dares --?" exclaimed the captain, jumping out of his cot.

"Silence, Captain Bligh!" answered Churchill. "Silence, and do not attempt to resist, or I will gag you!"

"You needn't trouble yourself to dress," added Bob; "you will cut quite a good enough figure as you are when you are dangling at the yard-arm!"

"Lash his hands behind his back, Churchill," said Christian, "and hoist him up on deck!"

"The most tyrannical captains need be feared no longer, when one knows how to set about dealing with them," remarked John Smith, the philosopher of the crew.

Then, without caring whether or not they awoke the rest of the crew, they returned on deck.

It was a regular mutiny. Of the officers on board besides Christian, Young alone, one of the midshipmen, had made common cause with the mutineers.

As to the crew, those who hesitated at first had been obliged to give in, whilst the other officers, without arms, and without a leader, remained spectators of the drama which was being acted before their eyes.

All were drawn up in silence on the deck, and gazed at their captain, who, half-naked, held his head high in the midst of these men, who usually trembled before him.

"Captain Bligh," said Christian, roughly, "you are deprived of your command."

"I do not recognise your right," replied the captain.

"Do not waste time in useless protestations," interrupted Christian. "I now speak the sentiments of the Bounty's crew. We had scarcely left England when we had already reason to complain of your insulting suspicions, your brutal proceedings. When I say we, I mean the officers as well as the seamen. We not only could not obtain the satisfaction which was our due, but you set aside our complaints with contempt! Are we dogs, that we should be abused on every occasion? Scoundrels, ruffians, liars, thieves, you had no expression strong enough, no abuse coarse enough for us! Indeed, had we patiently borne such a life, we should have been unworthy to be called men! And I, I your countryman, who know your family, and have already made two voyages under you, have you spared me? Did you not accuse me, only yesterday, of stealing some wretched fruit? And the men, they are put in irons when guiltless of a fault. For a trifle they are condemned to receive two dozen lashes. Well, everything is paid for in this world! You have been too liberal with us, Bligh! It is our turn now! You are about to expiate the insults, the injustice, the mad accusations, the moral and physical tortures with which you have overwhelmed your crew during a year and a half, and you shall pay dearly for them! Captain, you have been judged by those whom you have offended, and you are condemned. Is that right, shipmates?"

"Yes, yes, death, death to the tyrant!" shouted the greater number of the seamen, threatening their captain.

"Captain Bligh," resumed Christian, "some have spoken of hoisting you dangling to the yard-arm, between sky and sea; others propose to make your back taste the cat you have so freely bestowed on theirs, until you die under the infliction. They lack imagination. I have a better plan than that. Besides, you are not alone guilty in this matter. Those who have always faithfully executed your orders, however cruel they were, would be in despair at having to submit to my command. They deserve to bear you company wherever the wind may drive you. Lower the long boat!"

Christian's last words were received with a murmur of disapprobation, which, however, did not seem to trouble him. Captain Bligh, who was not intimidated by these menaces, profited by the moment's silence to speak.

"Officers and men," he said, in a firm voice, "in my character of officer in the royal navy, commander of the Bounty, I protest against the treatment with which I am threatened. If you have had reason to complain of the way I have exercised my power, you might have had me tried by a court-martial. But, doubtless, you have not reflected on the serious consequences of the act you are about to commit. To lay hand on your captain is to put yourself in revolt against existing laws; it will render a return to your native country impossible, and will cause you to be treated like pirates! Sooner or later you will come to an ignominious death, the death of traitors and rebels! In the name of honour and the obedience you swore to me, I summon you to return to your duty!"

"We know perfectly well to what we expose ourselves," replied Churchill.

"Enough! Enough!" cried the crew, ready for any deed of violence.

"Well," said Bligh, "if you must have a victim, let it be me, but me alone! Those of my companions whom you condemn with me have only obeyed my orders!"

The voice of the captain was now drowned by a chorus of vociferations, and he was obliged to renounce the hope of moving those pitiless hearts.

While this was going on, arrangements for the execution of Christian's orders had been made.

However, a lively dispute had arisen among the mutineers, some of whom wished to abandon Captain Bligh and his friends without giving them a weapon, or leaving them an ounce of bread.

Some - and it was also Churchill's advice - thought that the number of those who ought to leave the ship was not large enough. They must get rid, he said, of all the men who, not being directly implicated in the plot, were not safe. They could not depend on those who contented themselves with merely accepting accomplished facts. As to himself, his back was still sore from the lashes he had received for deserting at Tahiti. The best, and the most rapid way of healing it would be to deliver the captain over to him! He would know well how to revenge himself, with his own hand!

"Hayward! Hallett!" exclaimed Christian, addressing two of the officers, without taking any notice of Churchill's observations, "get into the boat."

"What have I done to you, Christian, that you should treat me thus?" said Hayward. "You are sending me to my death!"

"Recriminations are useless! Obey, or else -! Fryer, in with you too!"

But these officers, instead of going towards the boat, approached Captain Bligh, and Fryer, who seemed the most determined, bent forward, saying -

"Captain, will you try to retake the ship? We have no arms, it is true, but the mutineers, if surprised, could not resist. If a few of us are killed, what matter! We can but try! What do you think?"

The officers were already preparing to throw themselves on the mutineers, who were now busily engaged in making ready the long boat, when Churchill, whose notice these words, brief as they were, had not escaped, summoning several well-armed men, forced them into the boat.

"Millward, Muspratt, Birket, and you others," said Christian, addressing some of the seamen who had not taken part in the mutiny, "go below and choose whatever you value most! You are to accompany Captain Bligh. You, Morrison, look after those fellows! Purcell, take your carpenter's 'chest, I will allow you to have that."

Two masts with their sails, nails, a saw, a piece of sail cloth, four small kegs, each containing twenty-four quarts of water, a hundred and fifty pounds of biscuit, thirty-two pounds of salt pork, six bottles of wine, six bottles of rum, the captain's wine case, were all the stores and provisions they were to be allowed to take.

They were given, besides, two or three old swords, but fire-arms of any description were refused them.

"Where are Peter Hey wood and Stewart?" asked Bligh, when he was in the boat. "Have they also betrayed me?"

They had not betrayed him, but Christian had resolved to keep them on board.

The captain now had a moment of discouragement and very pardonable weakness, which, however, did not last.

"Christian," he said," I give you my word of honour to forget all that has just occurred, if you will give up your abominable plan! I beseech you, think of my wife and family! Should I perish, what will become of them?"

"If you possessed any honour," answered Christian, "things would not have reached this pitch. If you yourself had thought a little more often of your wife, of your family, and of the wives and families of others, you would not have been so harsh, so unjust, towards all of us!"

The boatswain's mate, as he was embarking, endeavoured in his turn to soften Christian. All in vain.

"I have been suffering too long," he replied, bitterly. "You do not know what my tortures have been! No, it cannot last a day longer; and, besides, you are not ignorant that, all this voyage, I, the second officer of the ship, have been treated like a dog! However, in separating myself from Captain Bligh, whom, in all probability, I shall never see again, I wish from pity, not to take from him all hope of safety. Smith, go to the captain's cabin, and bring him his clothes, his commission, his journal, and his portfolio. Also, give him my nautical charts, and my own sextant. He will thus have some chance of being able to save his companions, and get out of the scrape himself!"

Christian's orders were performed, though not without many objections from the crew.

"And now, Morrison, cast off," exclaimed the master's mate, now the commander of the Bounty, "and leave them to the mercy of God!"

Whilst the mutineers saluted Captain Bligh and his unfortunate companions with ironical cheers, the unhappy Christian, leaning against the hammock nettings, could not take his eyes from the departing boat. This brave officer, whose conduct, loyal and open, had always, till then, merited the praises of all the commanders under whom he had served, was to-day no better than the chief of a band of pirates. He could never see again either his old mother, or his betrothed, or the Isle of Man, his native place. He had sunk in his own self-esteem, and was dishonoured in the eyes of everyone.

Chastisement was already following his crime!

Voyage of the Long Boat

With her eighteen passengers, officers and men, and the scanty provisions she contained, the boat which carried Bligh was so loaded that her gunwale was only fifteen inches above the level of the sea. Twenty-one feet long and six wide, she was a useful ship's boat for so numerous a crew, but for such a voyage as she was destined to perform, she appeared utterly unsuitable.

The sailors, confident in the skill and energy of their captain and officers, who were now all joined in the same fate, rowed vigorously, and the boat rapidly sped through the waves.

Bligh had no hesitation about what he was to do. He wished first of all to regain as soon as possible the island of Tofoa, the nearest of the Friendly Islands, which they had only left a few days before; they would there collect bread-fruit, and renew their store of water, and then run for Tonga-Tabou. They would there obtain a sufficient quantity of provisions to last them till they could reach the Dutch settlements in Timor, if, through fear of savages, they did not wish to touch at any of the numerous archipelagos scattered here and there on their way.

The first day passed without incident, and night was falling when they sighted the coast of Tofoa. Unfortunately, the shore was so rocky, and the cliffs so steep, that it was impossible to disembark that night. They must wait for day.

Unless it was absolutely necessary, Bligh did not mean to touch their provisions. The island would have to nourish his men and himself. That seemed difficult, for, on first landing, not a trace of inhabitants was to be met with. Some, however, soon made their appearance, and, being well received, others came, who brought them water and a few cocoa-nuts.

Bligh's perplexity was great. What was he to say to these natives, who had already trafficked with the Bounty on her last visit? At any cost it was necessary to hide the truth, so as not to destroy the prestige which the strangers had before acquired. Could they say that they were sent for provisions for their ship, which was out at sea?

That was impossible, for the Bounty was not visible, even from the tops of the hills! Should they state that their vessel was wrecked, and they were the only survivors? That was the story most likely to be credited. Perhaps that would touch the hearts of the natives and induce them to complete the provisioning of the boat. Bligh determined to say this, though it was dangerous, and he cautioned his men to adhere to the statement, so that they might all agree.

On hearing this, the natives made no sign of either joy or sorrow. Their faces only expressed profound astonishment, and it was impossible to guess what they thought.

On the 2nd of May, the number of natives from other parts of the island increased to an alarming extent, and Bligh soon guessed that they had hostile intentions. Some even tried to haul the boat up on the shore, and only drew back before the energetic demonstrations of the captain, who menaced them with his cutlass. Whilst this was going on, some of the men, whom Bligh had sent to search, brought back three gallons of water.

The time had come for quitting this inhospitable island. At sunset all was ready; but it was not easy to gain the boat. The beach was covered with natives, clashing stones against each other, ready to throw. The boat kept off a few fathoms from the shore, and only touched just as the men were ready to embark.

The English, really uneasy at the hostile look of the savages, walked down the beach, in the midst of two hundred natives, who were evidently only waiting a signal to rush upon them. However, all got safely into the boat, when one of the sailors, named Bancroft, imprudently returned to fetch some article he had forgotten. In a second, the foolish man was surrounded and felled with stones, his companions, having no firearms, being unable to help him. At the same time they themselves were attacked, and stones rained upon them.

"Come, lads," shouted Bligh, "bend to your oars and pull hard!"

The natives followed them into the sea, and showers of pebbles fell upon them. Many men were wounded; but Thomas Hayward (there were two midshipmen of that name belonging to the Bounty), picking up a stone which had fallen into the boat, took aim at one of their assailants and hit him between the eyes. The savage fell back with a cry, which was answered by a cheer from the English. Their unfortunate comrade was avenged.

By this time several canoes had left the shore and were giving chase. This pursuit could have only ended in a combat, the issue of which could not have been favourable, when the master had a bright idea. Without suspecting that he was imitating Hippomenes in his race with Atalanta, he stripped off his jacket, which he threw into the sea. The natives, leaving the prey for the shadow, stopped to pick it up, and this expedient permitted the boat to double the point of the bay.

In the meantime night came on, and the savages discouraged, abandoned the chase.

This first attempt at landing was too unlucky to be renewed; such at least was the opinion of Captain Bligh.

"We must now come to a resolution," he said. "The scene which has just passed at Tofoa will occur again, I am certain, at Tonga Tabou, and wherever else we may touch. So small a number as we are, without firearms, would be absolutely at the mercy of the savages. Having no articles for barter, we could not buy provisions, and it is impossible for us to procure them by force. We are reduced to our own resources; and you, my friends, know as well as I do, how miserable they are! But would it not be better to be contented with them, rather than at each landing to risk the lives of some of our party? However, I do not wish to hide anything of the horror of our situation from you. To reach Timor we have nearly twelve hundred leagues to run, and you must be satisfied with one ounce of biscuit and a quarter of a pint of water a day! Safety can be obtained at this price only, and also on the condition that you yield me implicit obedience. Answer me without reserve! Do you consent to attempt the enterprise? Will you swear to obey my orders, whatever they may be? Will you promise to submit without murmuring to these privations?"

"Yes, yes, we swear it!" exclaimed Bligh's companions, with one voice.

"My friends," resumed the captain," we must also forget our reciprocal wrongs, our antipathies, and our hates, in one word, sacrifice our personal grudges to the interest of all, which must alone guide us!"

"We promise."

"If you keep your word," added Bligh, "and if need be, I can force you to do so, I will answer for your safety."

A course was now steered to the W.N.W. The wind, which was strong, blew a regular gale by the evening of the 4th of May. The waves were so high that the boat disappeared between them, and could hardly struggle up again. Every moment the danger increased. Drenched and chilled, the unfortunate men had nothing to comfort them on that day but a glass of rum and the quarter of a half-rotten bread-fruit.

During the next and following days their condition did not improve. The boat passed by a few islands, from which several canoes put off.

Was it to give chase, or to try and barter? In any case it would be imprudent to stop. The boat, therefore, her sails filled with a fair breeze, soon left them far behind.

On the 9th of May again a terrible storm broke over them. Thunder and lightning succeeded without interruption. The rain fell with a force, of which even the most violent storms of our climate fail to give an idea. It was impossible to dry their clothes. Bligh then thought of plunging them into the sea, and thus to impregnate them with salt, so as to bring back to the skin a little of the warmth carried away by the rain. These torrents of rain, however, which caused so much suffering to the captain and his companions, spared them other tortures still more horrible, the tortures of thirst, which unbearable heat would soon have produced.

On the morning of the 17th of May, after a frightful gale, complaints became general.

"We shall never have strength to reach New Holland," cried the unfortunate crew. "Wet through by the rain, exhausted by fatigue, we shall never have a moment's rest! We are half dead with hunger; will you not increase our rations, captain? What matters it if our provisions do fail? We can easily replace them on arriving at New Holland!"

"I refuse," replied Bligh. "That would be to act like fools. What! We have only crossed half the distance we had to run when cast adrift to reach Australia, and you are already discouraged! Do you think, besides, that you will find it easy to obtain provisions on the coast of New Holland? You know neither the country nor the inhabitants!"

And Bligh described in a graphic way the nature of the soil, the manners and customs of the natives, the small dependence they must place on a friendly reception, everything, indeed, that his voyage with Captain Cook had taught him. For this time his companions listened and were silenced.

For the next fifteen days they were cheered by a bright sun, which dried their clothes. On the 27th they crossed the reefs which border the eastern coast of New Holland. The sea was calm behind this coral belt, and several groups of islands, covered with exotic vegetation, rejoiced their sight.

They landed, and advanced cautiously. No traces of the natives did they find, except some signs of fires. It was, therefore, possible to pass a good night on shore. But they had to eat. By great good luck one of the sailors discovered a bed of oysters, which furnished them with a regular feast.

The next day Bligh found in the boat a magnifying glass and a tinder-box. This enabled them to procure fire to cook game or fish.

Bligh then proposed to divide his crew into three parties; one to stay and put everything in order in the boat, the two others to go and search for food. But several men complained bitterly, declaring that they would rather go without their dinner than venture into the country.

One of them, more violent or more bold than his companions, went so far as to say to the captain-

"One man is as good as another, and I don't see why you should always take your ease! If you are hungry go and get something to eat! For all the good you do I could do as well!"

Bligh, knowing that this mutinous spirit must be put a stop to, immediately seized a cutlass, and throwing another at the rebel's feet, he exclaimed -

"Defend yourself, or I will kill you like a dog!"

This energetic attitude soon brought the mutineer back to reason, and the general discontent was calmed.

During this rest the boat's crew collected an abundance of oysters and other shell-fish, as well as a supply of fresh water.

A little further on, in the Endeavour Straits, of two detachments, sent out to chase tortoises and noddies (a species of sea-fowl), the first returned with empty hands, the second with only six noddies; but they would have taken many more had it not been for the obstinacy of one of the hunters, who, straying from his comrades, frightened the birds. This man acknowledged afterwards that he had managed to get hold of nine noddies, and had eaten them raw on the spot.

Without the food and fresh water they found on the coast of New Holland, it is very certain that Bligh and his companions would have perished. As it was, they were in a most pitiable condition, so exhausted and emaciated as to resemble skeletons rather than living men.

The voyage to Timor, through a little-known sea, was but a mournful repetition of the sufferings already endured by these unfortunate men before they reached the coasts of New Holland. The only difference was that the strength of all, without exception, was much diminished. In the course of a few days their legs became swollen, and while in this prostrate condition they were overwhelmed with an incessant longing for sleep. These symptoms, it was conjectured, foreboded a termination to their sufferings, which could not be long in coming. As soon as Captain Bligh perceived these alarming symptoms he distributed double rations to the weakest, and strove to inspire them with some hope.

At last, on the morning of the 12th of June, the coast of Timor appeared, after a voyage of three thousand six hundred miles had been accomplished under the most frightful and trying circumstances.

The English received an excessively sympathetic reception at Coupang; and remained there two months to recruit. Captain Bligh, having here purchased a small schooner, sailed for Batavia, which place was reached in safety, and thence he embarked for England.

On the 14th of March, 1790, the deserted men landed at Portsmouth. The recital of the tortures they had endured excited universal sympathy and indignation. The Admiralty almost immediately fitted out the frigate Pandora, of twenty-four guns, which, with a crew of a hundred and sixty men, was sent out in pursuit of the mutineers of the Bounty.

We will now see what had become of them.

The Mutineers

After Captain Bligh had been deserted in the open sea, the Bounty set sail for Tahiti. The same day she reached Toubouai. The smiling aspect of this little island, surrounded by a belt of coral rocks, invited Christian to touch there; but the demonstrations of the inhabitants appearing too threatening, a landing was not effected.

On the 6th of June, 1789, the anchor was dropped in the roads of Matavai. Great was the surprise of the Tahitians on recognising the Bounty. The mutineers soon fell in with the natives, whose friendship they had gained on a previous occasion, and to them they told a story, into which they took care to bring the name of Captain Cook, whom the Tahitians well remembered.

On the 29th of June the mutineers departed for Toubouai and began a search for some island out of the ordinary route of ships, where the soil was fertile enough to supply them with food, and where they might live in security. They roved thus from one group of islands to another, committing excesses of all sorts, which Christian's authority was rarely sufficient to prevent. Then, attracted once more by the fertility of Tahiti, and by the gentle and easy nature of the inhabitants, they returned to the Bay of Matavai. There two-thirds of the crew landed, but that same evening the Bounty weighed anchor and disappeared, before the men suspected Christian of any intention of going without them.

Left to their own resources, the seamen established themselves without much regret in different parts of the island. George Stewart and Peter Heywood, the two midshipmen whom Christian had excepted from the sentence pronounced against Bligh, and had brought in spite of themselves, remained at Matavai near the king

Tippao, whose sister Stewart soon afterwards married. Morrison and Milward joined the chief Peno, who received them well. As to the others they went inland, and before long took Tahitian wives.

Churchill and a mad fellow named Thompson, after having committed all sorts of crimes, came at last to blows. Churchill was killed in the struggle, and Thompson was stoned to death by the natives.

Thus perished two of the persons who had taken the greatest share in the mutiny. The others, on the contrary, by their good conduct, endeared themselves to the Tahitians.

However, Morrison and Milward, always seeing chastisement suspended over their heads, could not live quietly in an island where they might be so easily discovered. They, therefore, conceived the idea of building a schooner, in which to reach Batavia, there to conceal themselves in the midst of a civilised community. With eight of their companions, having only a few ordinary carpenters' tools, they contrived, not without difficulty, to construct a small vessel, which they called the Resolution, mooring her in a bay behind Venus Point; but the impossibility of procuring sails prevented them from putting to sea.

All this time, strong in their innocence, Stewart cultivated a garden, and Peter Heywood collected materials for a vocabulary, which, later, was of great assistance to the English missionaries.

Eighteen months had thus passed away, when, on the 23rd of March, 1791, a vessel doubled Venus Point, and anchored in Matavai Bay. This was the Pandora, sent in pursuit of the mutineers by the English Admiralty.

Heywood and Stewart hastened on board, declared their names and rank, and said that they had taken no part in the mutiny; but they were not believed, and were immediately put in irons, as were the rest of the men found on shore, without the least enquiry having been made as to the truth of their statements.

Loaded with chains, and threatened that they would be shot should they converse in the Tahitian language among themselves, they were shut up in a cage eleven feet long, placed at the end of the quarter-deck, to which some one versed in mythology gave the name of Pandora's box.

On the 19th of May, the Resolution, which had been provided with sails, and the Pandora, put to sea. For three months they cruised among the Friendly Isles, where it was supposed that Christian and the rest of the mutineers had taken refuge. As the Resolution did not draw much water, she was of great use in this cruise; but she disappeared near Chatham Island, and although the Pandora remained in the neighbourhood for several days, nothing was ever again heard of her or of the five seamen by whom she was manned.

The Pandora was on her way back to Europe with the prisoners, when, in Torres Straits, she struck on a coral reef, and went down with thirty-one of her own men, and four of the mutineers.

The crew and the prisoners who escaped gained a sandy island. There the officers and seamen sheltered themselves under tents; but the mutineers, exposed to the heat of a vertical sun, were obliged, in order to obtain a little relief, to bury themselves up to their necks in sand.

The castaways remained on this islet for some days, and then all reached Timor in the Pandora's boats, the strict watch kept over the mutineers, notwithstanding the fearful circumstances in which they were placed, never being for a moment relaxed.

Reaching England in the month of June, 1792, the mutineers were brought before a court-martial, presided over by Admiral Hood. The trial lasted six days, and was terminated by the acquittal of four of the accused, and the condemnation to death of six others, for the crime of desertion and carrying off of the vessel given to their charge. Four of the condemned were hung on board a ship of war; the two others, Stewart and Peter Heywood, whose innocence was at last acknowledged, were pardoned.

But what had become of the Bounty? Had she been wrecked with the last of the mutineers? This no one could tell.

In 1814, twenty-five years after the scene with which this narrative commences, two English ships of war were cruising in Oceania, under the command of Captain Staines. They found themselves to the south of the dangerous archipelago, in sight of a mountainous and volcanic island, discovered by Carteret in his voyage round the world, and by him given the name of Pitcairn Island. It was a mere islet, almost without a shore, rising perpendicularly from the sea, and clothed to its summit with forests of palms and bread-fruit trees.

This island had never before been visited; it was twelve hundred miles from Tahiti, 25 4' south latitude, and 180 8' west longitude; it measured four miles and a half in circumference, and only a mile and a half across in its widest part. No one knew what report Carteret had given of it.

Captain Staines resolved to survey it, and ascertain if a suitable place for landing existed.

On approaching the shore, he was surprised at seeing huts, plantations, and on the beach, two natives, who, having launched a boat and skilfully crossed the surf, came towards his vessel. But his astonishment was boundless when they addressed him in excellent English with the words -

"Hullo, you there! Will you heave us a rope, that we may get on board!"

Directly they reached the deck, the two sturdy rowers were surrounded by the wondering sailors, who overwhelmed them with questions. Brought before the captain, they were interrogated in form -

"Who are you?"

"My name is Thursday October Christian, and my mate here is Ned Young."

These names told nothing to Captain Staines, who was far from thinking of the survivors of the Bounty.

"How long have you lived here?"

"We were born here."

"How old are you?"

"I am five-and-twenty, and Young is eighteen."

"Were your parents wrecked on this island?"

The son of Fletcher Christian, for such the young man was, then gave Captain Staines the following narrative -

On leaving Tahiti, where he abandoned twenty-one of his comrades, Christian, who had on board an account of Cartaret's voyage, steered towards Pitcairn Island, the position of which appeared to him suitable for the plan he proposed. Twenty-eight men now composed the crew of the Bounty. They were Fletcher Christian, the midshipman Young, and seven seamen, six Tahitians, three with wives, a child of ten months old, and three men and six women, natives of Roubouai.

The first care of Christian and his companions on reaching Pitcairn had been to destroy the Bounty, so as not to be discovered. This, of course, prevented their leaving the island again, but it was necessary for their safety.

The establishment of the little colony was not made without difficulty among persons whose only bond of union was their common crime. Bloody quarrels soon broke out between the Tahitians and the English. In 1794 only four of the mutineers survived. Christian had fallen by the knife of one of the natives he had brought to the island. All the Tahitians had been massacred.

One of the English, who had discovered a way of manufacturing spirits from the root of a plant, became brutalised by drunkenness, and, in a fit of delirium tremens, threw himself from the top of a cliff into the sea.

Another, in a fit of madness, attacked Young, and one of the sailors, named John Adams, was obliged to kill him. In 1800 Young died from a violent attack of asthma.

John Adams was then the sole survivor of the mutineers. Remaining alone, with several women and twenty children, the offspring of marriages between his shipmates and the natives, the character of John Adams underwent a complete change. He was then not more than thirty-six; but during those years he had been present at so many scenes of violence and bloodshed, he had seen human nature under so many sad aspects, that, on looking back on his conduct, he became an altered man.

In the library of the Bounty, kept on the island, were a Bible and several Prayer-books. John Adams, who read them frequently, became converted, brought up the youthful population, who considered him as a father, in excellent principles, and became, in the nature of things, the legislator, the high priest, and, so to speak, the king of Pitcairn.

However, up to 1814, his alarms had been constant. In 1795, a vessel had approached Pitcairn, and the four survivors of the Bounty hid themselves in inaccessible woods, not daring to descend to the bay until after the departure of the ship. John Adams acted in the same way, when, in 1808, an American captain landed on the island, from which he carried off a chronometer and a compass, which he sent to the British Admiralty; but the Admiralty were not affected at the sight of these relics of the Bounty, there being something more important to think of in Europe just at that time.

Such was the narrative given to Captain Staines by the two natives, English on their father's side, one the son of Christian, the other the son of Young; but when Captain Staines asked to see John

Adams, the latter refused to come on board, until he knew how he was likely to be treated.

The captain, having assured the two young men that John Adams was safe, as twenty-five years had passed since the mutiny of the Bounty, went on shore, where he was received by a population composed of forty-six adults, and a large number of children. All were tall and strong, of a clearly-marked English type, the girls especially being remarkably pretty, the modesty of their manners making them altogether charming.

The laws in force in the island were of the simplest character. On a register was noted all that each one gained by his work. Money was unknown, all transactions being made by means of exchange; but there was no manufactory, as no materials were to be had. For clothing the inhabitants wore large hats and belts of grass. Fishing and agriculture were their principal occupations. Marriages were only made with the permission of Adams, and when the man had cleared and planted ground sufficient for the support of his future family.

Captain Staines, having collected much curious information relating to this island, thus long concealed from the civilised world in the most unfrequented part of the Pacific, put to sea, and returned to Europe.

Since that time the venerable John Adams has terminated his checkered career. He died in 1829, and was replaced by the Reverend John Nobbs, who then fulfilled in the island the functions of pastor, doctor, and schoolmaster.

In 1853, the descendants of the mutineers of the Bounty numbered a hundred and seventy individuals. Since then the population had increased and become so numerous that, three years later, it was decided to remove a number to Norfolk Island, which until then had been used for convicts. But the party of emigrants regretted Pitcairn so much, although Norfolk was four times larger, its soil remarkable for its richness, and living there was far easier, that after a couple of years' stay, several families returned to Pitcairn, where they continue to prosper.

Such was the issue of an adventure which had begun in so tragic a way.

At first, mutineers, murderers, madmen, and now, under the influence of Christian morals, and instruction given by a poor converted sailor, Pitcairn Island has become the fatherland of a gentle, hospitable, and happy population, among whom are found the primitive manners of the patriarchal ages.

In the Year 2889

In the Year 2889

Little though they seem to think of it, the people of this twenty-ninth century live continually in fairyland. Surfeited as they are with marvels, they are indifferent in presence of each new marvel. To them all seems natural. Could they but duly appreciate the refinements of civilization in our day; could they but compare the present with the past, and so better comprehend the advance we have made! How much fairer they would find our modern towns, with populations amounting sometimes to 10,000,000 souls; their streets 300 feet wide, their houses 1000 feet in height; with a temperature the same in all seasons; with their lines of aërial locomotion crossing the sky in every direction! If they would but picture to themselves the state of things that once existed, when through muddy streets rumbling boxes on wheels, drawn by horses—yes, by horses!—were the only means of conveyance. Think of the railroads of the olden time, and you will be able to appreciate the pneumatic tubes through which to-day one travels at the rate of 1000 miles an hour. Would not our contemporaries prize the telephone and the telephote more highly if they had not forgotten the telegraph?

Singularly enough, all these transformations rest upon principles which were perfectly familiar to our remote ancestors, but which they disregarded. Heat, for instance, is as ancient as man himself; electricity was known 3000 years ago, and steam 1100 years ago. Nay, so early as ten centuries ago it was known that the differences between the several chemical and physical forces depend on the mode of vibration of the etheric particles, which is for each specifically different. When at last the kinship of all these forces was discovered, it is simply astounding that 500 years should still have to elapse before men could analyze and describe the several modes of vibration that constitute these differences. Above all, it is singular that the mode of reproducing these forces directly from one another, and of reproducing one without the others, should have remained undiscovered till less than a hundred years ago. Nevertheless, such was the course of events, for it was not till the year 2792 that the famous Oswald Nier made this great discovery.

Truly was he a great benefactor of the human race. His admirable discovery led to many another. Hence is sprung a pleiad of inventors, its brightest star being our great Joseph Jackson. To Jackson we are indebted for those wonderful instruments the new accumulators. Some of these absorb and condense the living force contained in the sun's rays; others, the electricity stored in our globe; others again, the energy coming from whatever source, as a waterfall, a stream, the winds, etc. He, too, it was that invented the transformer, a more wonderful contrivance still, which takes the living force from the accumulator, and, on the simple pressure of a button, gives it back to space in whatever form may be desired, whether as heat, light, electricity, or mechanical force, after having first obtained from it the work required. From the day when these two instruments were contrived is to be dated the era of true progress. They have put into the hands of man a power that is almost infinite. As for their applications, they are numberless. Mitigating the rigors of winter, by giving back to the atmosphere the surplus heat stored up during the summer, they have revolutionized agriculture. By supplying motive power for aërial navigation, they have given to commerce a mighty impetus. To them we are indebted for the continuous production of electricity without batteries or dynamos, of light without combustion or incandescence, and for an unfailing supply of mechanical energy for all the needs of industry.

Yes, all these wonders have been wrought by the accumulator and the transformer. And can we not to them also trace, indirectly, this latest wonder of all, the great "Earth Chronicle" building in 253d Avenue, which was dedicated the other day? If George Washington Smith, the founder of the Manhattan "Chronicle", should come back to life to-day, what would he think were he to be told that this palace of marble and gold belongs to his remote descendant, Fritz Napoleon Smith, who, after thirty generations have come and gone, is owner of the same newspaper which his ancestor established!

For George Washington Smith's newspaper has lived generation after generation, now passing out of the family, anon coming back to it. When, 200 years ago, the political center of the United States was transferred from Washington to Centropolis, the newspaper followed the government and assumed the name of Earth Chronicle. Unfortunately, it was unable to maintain itself at the high level of its name. Pressed on all sides by rival journals of a more modern type, it was continually in danger of collapse. Twenty years ago its subscription list contained but a few hundred thousand names, and then Mr. Fritz Napoleon Smith bought it for a mere trifle, and originated telephonic journalism.

Everyone is familiar with Fritz Napoleon Smith's system—a system made possible by the enormous development of telephony during the last hundred years. Instead of being printed, the Earth Chronicle is every morning spoken to subscribers, who, in interesting conversations with reporters, statesmen, and scientists, learn the news of the day. Furthermore, each subscriber owns a phonograph, and to this instrument he leaves the task of gathering the news whenever he happens not to be in a mood to listen directly himself. As for purchasers of single copies, they can at a very trifling cost learn all that is in the paper of the day at any of the innumerable phonographs set up nearly everywhere.

Fritz Napoleon Smith's innovation galvanized the old newspaper. In the course of a few years the number of subscribers grew to be 80,000,000, and Smith's wealth went on growing, till now it reaches the almost unimaginable figure of $10,000,000,000. This lucky hit has enabled him to erect his new building, a vast edifice with four façades each 3,250 feet in length, over which proudly floats the hundred-starred flag of the Union. Thanks to the same lucky hit, he is to-day king of newspaperdom; indeed, he would be king of all the Americans, too, if Americans could ever accept a king. You do not believe it? Well, then, look at the plenipotentiaries of all nations and our own ministers themselves crowding about his door, entreating his counsels, begging for his approbation, imploring the aid of his all-powerful organ. Reckon up the number of scientists and artists that he supports, of inventors that he has under his pay.

Yes, a king is he. And in truth his is a royalty full of burdens. His labors are incessant, and there is no doubt at all that in earlier times any man would have succumbed under the overpowering stress of the toil which Mr. Smith has to perform. Very fortunately for him, thanks to the progress of hygiene, which, abating all the old sources of unhealthfulness, has lifted the mean of human life from 37 up to 52 years, men have stronger constitutions now than heretofore. The discovery of nutritive air is still in the future, but in the meantime men today consume food that is compounded and prepared according to scientific principles, and they breathe an atmosphere freed from the micro-organisms that formerly used to swarm in it; hence they live longer than their forefathers and know nothing of the innumerable diseases of olden times.

Nevertheless, and notwithstanding these considerations, Fritz Napoleon Smith's mode of life may well astonish one. His iron constitution is taxed to the utmost by the heavy strain that is put upon it. Vain the attempt to estimate the amount of labor he undergoes; an example alone can give an idea of it. Let us then go about with him for one day as he attends to his multifarious concernments. What day? That matters little; it is the same every day. Let us then take at random September 25th of this present year 2889.

This morning Mr. Fritz Napoleon Smith awoke in very bad humor. His wife having left for France eight days ago, he was feeling disconsolate. Incredible though it seems, in all the ten years since their marriage, this is the first time that Mrs. Edith Smith, the professional beauty, has been so long absent from home; two or three days usually suffice for her frequent trips to Europe. The first thing that Mr. Smith does is to connect his phonotelephote, the wires of which communicate with his Paris mansion. The telephote! Here is another of the great triumphs of science in our time. The transmission of speech is an old story; the transmission of images by means of sensitive mirrors connected by wires is a thing but of yesterday. A valuable invention indeed, and Mr. Smith this morning was not niggard of blessings for the inventor, when by its aid he was able distinctly to see his wife notwithstanding the distance that separated him from her. Mrs. Smith, weary after the ball or the visit to the theater the preceding night, is still abed, though it is near noontide at Paris. She is asleep, her head sunk in the lace-covered pillows. What? She stirs? Her lips move. She is dreaming perhaps? Yes, dreaming. She is talking, pronouncing a name his name—Fritz! The delightful vision gave a happier turn to Mr. Smith's thoughts. And now, at the call of imperative duty, light-hearted he springs from his bed and enters his mechanical dresser.

Two minutes later the machine deposited him all dressed at the threshold of his office. The round of journalistic work was now begun. First he enters the hall of the novel-writers, a vast apartment crowned with an enormous transparent cupola. In one corner is a telephone, through which a hundred Earth Chronicle littérateurs in turn recount to the public in daily installments a hundred novels. Addressing one of these authors who was waiting his turn, "Capital! Capital! my dear fellow," said he, "your last story. The scene where the village maid discusses interesting philosophical problems with her lover shows your very acute power of observation. Never have the ways of country folk been better portrayed. Keep on, my dear Archibald, keep on! Since yesterday, thanks to you, there is a gain of 5000 subscribers."

"Mr. John Last," he began again, turning to a new arrival, "I am not so well pleased with your work. Your story is not a picture of life; it lacks the elements of truth. And why? Simply because you run straight on to the end; because you do not analyze. Your heroes do this thing or that from this or that motive, which you assign without ever a thought of dissecting their mental and moral natures. Our feelings, you must remember, are far more complex than all that. In real life every act is the resultant of a hundred thoughts that come and go, and these you must study, each by itself, if you would create a living character. 'But,' you will say, 'in order to note these fleeting thoughts one must know them, must be able to follow them in their capricious meanderings.' Why, any child can do that, as you know. You have simply to make use of hypnotism, electrical or human, which gives one a two-fold being, setting free the witness-personality so that it may see, understand, and remember the reasons which determine the personality that acts. Just study yourself as you live from day to day, my dear Last. Imitate your associate whom I was complimenting a moment ago. Let yourself be hypnotized. What's that? You have tried it already? Not sufficiently, then, not sufficiently!"

Mr. Smith continues his round and enters the reporters' hall. Here 1500 reporters, in their respective places, facing an equal number of telephones, are communicating to the subscribers the news of the world as gathered during the night. The organization of this matchless service has often been described. Besides his telephone, each reporter, as the reader is aware, has in front of him a set of commutators, which enable him to communicate with any desired telephotic line. Thus the subscribers not only hear the news but see the occurrences. When an incident is described that is already past, photographs of its main features are transmitted with the narrative. And there is no confusion withal. The reporters' items, just like the different stories and all the other component parts of the journal, are classified automatically according to an ingenious system, and reach the hearer in due succession. Furthermore, the hearers are free to listen only to what specially concerns them. They may at pleasure give attention to one editor and refuse it to another.

Mr. Smith next addresses one of the ten reporters in the astronomical department—a department still in the embryonic stage, but which will yet play an important part in journalism.

"Well, Cash, what's the news?"

"We have phototelegrams from Mercury, Venus, and Mars."

"Are those from Mars of any interest?"

"Yes, indeed. There is a revolution in the Central Empire."

"And what of Jupiter?" asked Mr. Smith.

"Nothing as yet. We cannot quite understand their signals. Perhaps ours do not reach them."

"That's bad," exclaimed Mr. Smith, as he hurried away, not in the best of humor, toward the hall of the scientific editors.

With their heads bent down over their electric computers, thirty scientific men were absorbed in transcendental calculations. The coming of Mr. Smith was like the falling of a bomb among them.

"Well, gentlemen, what is this I hear? No answer from Jupiter? Is it always to be thus? Come, Cooley, you have been at work now twenty years on this problem, and yet—"

"True enough," replied the man addressed. "Our science of optics is still very defective, and through our mile-and-three-quarter telescopes."

"Listen to that, Peer," broke in Mr. Smith, turning to a second scientist. "Optical science defective! Optical science is your specialty. But," he continued, again addressing William Cooley, "failing with Jupiter, are we getting any results from the moon?"

"The case is no better there."

"This time you do not lay the blame on the science of optics. The moon is immeasurably less distant than Mars, yet with Mars our communication is fully established. I presume you will not say that you lack telescopes?"

"Telescopes? O no, the trouble here is about inhabitants!"

"That's it," added Peer.

"So, then, the moon is positively uninhabited?" asked Mr. Smith.

"At least," answered Cooley, "on the face which she presents to us. As for the opposite side, who knows?"

"Ah, the opposite side! You think, then," remarked Mr. Smith, musingly, "that if one could but—"

"Could what?"

"Why, turn the moon about-face."

"Ah, there's something in that," cried the two men at once. And indeed, so confident was their air, they seemed to have no doubt as to the possibility of success in such an undertaking.

"Meanwhile," asked Mr. Smith, after a moment's silence, "have you no news of interest to-day'?"

"Indeed we have," answered Cooley. "The elements of Olympus are definitively settled. That great planet gravitates beyond Neptune at the mean distance of 11,400,799,642 miles from the sun, and to traverse its vast orbit takes 1311 years, 294 days, 12 hours, 43 minutes, 9 seconds."

"Why didn't you tell me that sooner?" cried Mr. Smith. "Now inform the reporters of this straightaway. You know how eager is the curiosity of the public with regard to these astronomical questions. That news must go into to-day's issue."

Then, the two men bowing to him, Mr. Smith passed into the next hall, an enormous gallery upward of 3200 feet in length, devoted to atmospheric advertising. Everyone has noticed those enormous advertisements reflected from the clouds, so large that they may be seen by the populations of whole cities or even of entire countries. This, too, is one of Mr. Fritz Napoleon Smith's ideas, and in the Earth Chronicle building a thousand projectors are constantly engaged in displaying upon the clouds these mammoth advertisements.

When Mr. Smith to-day entered the sky-advertising department, he found the operators sitting with folded arms at their motionless projectors, and inquired as to the cause of their inaction. In response, the man addressed simply pointed to the sky, which was of a pure blue. "Yes," muttered Mr. Smith, "a cloudless sky! That's too bad, but what's to be done? Shall we produce rain? That we might do, but is it of any use? What we need is clouds, not rain. Go," said he, addressing the head engineer, "go see Mr. Samuel Mark, of the meteorological division of the scientific department, and tell him for me to go to work in earnest on the question of artificial clouds. It will never do for us to be always thus at the mercy of cloudless skies!"

Mr. Smith's daily tour through the several departments of his newspaper is now finished. Next, from the advertisement hall he passes to the reception chamber, where the ambassadors accredited to the American government are awaiting him, desirous of having a word of counsel or advice from the all-powerful editor. A discussion was going on when he entered. "Your Excellency will pardon me," the French Ambassador was saying to the Russian, "but I see nothing in the map of Europe that requires change. 'The North for the Slavs?' Why, yes, of course; but the South for the Matins. Our common frontier, the Rhine, it seems to me, serves very well. Besides, my government, as you must know, will firmly oppose every movement, not only against Paris, our capital, or our two great prefectures, Rome and Madrid, but also against the kingdom of Jerusalem, the dominion of Saint Peter, of which France means to be the trusty defender."

"Well said!" exclaimed Mr. Smith. "How is it," he asked, turning to the Russian ambassador, "that you Russians are not content with your vast empire, the most extensive in the world, stretching from the banks of the Rhine to the Celestial Mountains and the Kara-Korum, whose shores are washed by the Frozen Ocean, the Atlantic, the Mediterranean, and the Indian Ocean? Then, what is the use of threats? Is war possible in view of modern inventions-asphyxiating shells capable of being projected a distance of 60 miles, an electric spark of 90 miles, that can at one stroke annihilate a battalion; to say nothing of the plague, the cholera, the yellow fever, that the belligerents might spread among their antagonists mutually, and which would in a few days destroy the greatest armies?"

"True," answered the Russian; "but can we do all that we wish? As for us Russians, pressed on our eastern frontier by the Chinese, we must at any cost put forth our strength for an effort toward the west."

"O, is that all? In that case," said Mr. Smith, "the thing can be arranged. I will speak to the Secretary of State about it. The attention of the Chinese government shall be called to the matter. This is not the first time that the Chinese have bothered us."

"Under these conditions, of course—" And the Russian ambassador declared himself satisfied.

"Ah, Sir John, what can I do for you?" asked Mr. Smith as he turned to the representative of the people of Great Britain, who till now had remained silent.

"A great deal," was the reply. "If the Earth Chronicle would but open a campaign on our behalf—"

"And for what object?"

"Simply for the annulment of the Act of Congress annexing to the United States the British islands."

Though, by a just turn-about of things here below, Great Britain has become a colony of the United States, the English are not yet reconciled to the situation. At regular intervals they are ever addressing to the American government vain complaints.

"A campaign against the annexation that has been an accomplished fact for 150 years!" exclaimed Mr. Smith. "How can your people suppose that I would do anything so unpatriotic?"

"We at home think that your people must now be sated. The Monroe doctrine is fully applied; the whole of America belongs to the Americans. What more do you want? Besides, we will pay for what we ask."

"Indeed!" answered Mr. Smith, without manifesting the slightest irritation. "Well, you English will ever be the same. No, no, Sir John, do not count on me for help. Give up our fairest province, Britain? Why not ask France generously to renounce possession of Africa, that magnificent colony the complete conquest of which cost her the labor of 800 years? You will be well received!"

"You decline! All is over then!" murmured the British agent sadly. "The United Kingdom falls to the share of the Americans; the Indies to that of—"

"The Russians," said Mr. Smith, completing the sentence.

"Australia—"

"Has an independent government."

"Then nothing at all remains for us!" sighed Sir John, downcast.

"Nothing?" asked Mr. Smith, laughing. "Well, now, there's Gibraltar!"

With this sally, the audience ended. The clock was striking twelve, the hour of breakfast. Mr. Smith returns to his chamber. Where the bed stood in the morning a table all spread comes up through the floor. For Mr. Smith, being above all a practical man;

has reduced the problem of existence to its simplest terms. For him, instead of the endless suites of apartments of the olden time, one room fitted with ingenious mechanical contrivances is enough. Here he sleeps, takes his meals, in short, lives.

He seats himself. In the mirror of the phonotelephote is seen the same chamber at Paris which appeared in it this morning. A table furnished forth is likewise in readiness here, for notwithstanding the difference of hours, Mr. Smith and his wife have arranged to take their meals simultaneously. It is delightful thus to take breakfast tête-a-tête with one who is 3000 miles or so away. Just now, Mrs. Smith's chamber has no occupant.

"She is late! Woman's punctuality! Progress everywhere except there!" muttered Mr. Smith as he turned the tap for the first dish. For like all wealthy folk in our day, Mr. Smith has done away with the domestic kitchen and is a subscriber to the Grand Alimentation Company, which sends through a great network of tubes to subscribers' residences all sorts of dishes, as a varied assortment is always in readiness. A subscription costs money, to be sure, but the cuisine is of the best, and the system has this advantage, that it, does away with the pestering race of the cordons-bleus. Mr. Smith received and ate, all alone, the hors-d'oeuvre, entrées, rôti and legumes that constituted the repast. He was just finishing the dessert when Mrs. Smith appeared in the mirror of the telephote.

"Why, where have you been?" asked Mr. Smith through the telephone.

"What! You are already at the dessert? Then I am late," she exclaimed, with a winsome naïveté. "Where have I been, you ask? Why, at my dress-maker's. The hats are just lovely this season! I suppose I forgot to note the time, and so am a little late."

"Yes, a little," growled Mr. Smith; "so little that I have already quite finished breakfast. Excuse me if I leave you now, but I must be going."

"O certainly, my dear; good-by till evening."

Smith stepped into his air-coach, which was in waiting for him at a window. "Where do you wish to go, sir?" inquired the coachman.

"Let me see; I have three hours," Mr. Smith mused. "Jack, take me to my accumulator works at Niagara."

For Mr. Smith has obtained a lease of the great falls of Niagara. For ages the energy developed by the falls went unutilized. Smith, applying Jackson's invention, now collects this energy, and lets or sells it. His visit to the works took more time than he had anticipated. It was four o'clock when he returned home, just in time for the daily audience which he grants to callers.

One readily understands how a man situated as Smith is must be beset with requests of all kinds. Now it is an inventor needing capital; again it is some visionary who comes to advocate a brilliant scheme which must surely yield millions of profit. A choice has to be made between these projects, rejecting the worthless, examining the questionable ones, accepting the meritorious. To this work Mr. Smith devotes every day two full hours.

The callers were fewer to-day than usual—only twelve of them. Of these, eight had only impracticable schemes to propose. In fact, one of them wanted to revive painting, an art fallen into desuetude owing to the progress made in color-photography. Another, a physician, boasted that he had discovered a cure for nasal catarrh! These impracticables were dismissed in short order. Of the four projects favorably received, the first was that of a young man whose broad forehead betokened his intellectual power.

"Sir, I am a chemist," he began, "and as such I come to you."

"Well!"

"Once the elementary bodies," said the young chemist, "were held to be sixty-two in number; a hundred years ago they were reduced to ten; now only three remain irresolvable, as you are aware."

"Yes, yes."

"Well, sir, these also I will show to be composite. In a few months, a few weeks, I shall have succeeded in solving the problem. Indeed, it may take only a few days."

"And then?"

"Then, sir, I shall simply have determined the absolute. All I want is money enough to carry my research to a successful issue."

"Very well," said Mr. Smith. "And what will be the practical outcome of your discovery?"

"The practical outcome? Why, that we shall be able to produce easily all bodies whatever—stone, wood, metal, fibers—"

"And flesh and blood?" queried Mr. Smith, interrupting him. "Do you pretend that you expect to manufacture a human being out and out?"

"Why not?"

Mr. Smith advanced $100,000 to the young chemist, and engaged his services for the Earth Chronicle laboratory.

The second of the four successful applicants, starting from experiments made so long ago as the nineteenth century and again and again repeated, had conceived the idea of removing an entire city all at once from one place to another. His special project had to do with the city of Granton, situated, as everybody knows, some fifteen miles inland. He proposes to transport the city on rails and to change it into a watering-place. The profit, of course, would be enormous. Mr. Smith, captivated by the scheme, bought a half-interest in it.

"As you are aware, sir," began applicant No. 3, "by the aid of our solar and terrestrial accumulators and transformers, we are able to make all the seasons the same. I propose to do something better still. Transform into heat a portion of the surplus energy at our disposal; send this heat to the poles; then the polar regions, relieved of their snow-cap, will become a vast territory available for man's use. What think you of the scheme?"

"Leave your plans with me, and come back in a week. I will have them examined in the meantime."

Finally, the fourth announced the early solution of a weighty scientific problem. Everyone will remember the bold experiment made a hundred years ago by Dr. Nathaniel Faithburn. The doctor, being a firm believer in human hibernation—in other words, in the possibility of our suspending our vital functions and of calling them into action again after a time—resolved to subject the theory to a practical test. To this end, having first made his last will and pointed out the proper method of awakening him; having also directed that his sleep was to continue a hundred years to a day from the date of his apparent death, he unhesitatingly put the theory to the proof in his own person.

Reduced to the condition of a mummy, Dr. Faithburn was coffined and laid in a tomb. Time went on. September 25th, 2889, being the day set for his resurrection, it was proposed to Mr. Smith that he should permit the second part of the experiment to be performed at his residence this evening.

"Agreed. Be here at ten o'clock," answered Mr. Smith; and with that the day's audience was closed.

Left to himself, feeling tired, he lay down on an extension chair. Then, touching a knob, he established communication with the Central Concert Hall, whence our greatest maestros send out to subscribers their delightful successions of accords determined by recondite algebraic formulas. Night was approaching. Entranced by the harmony, forgetful of the hour, Smith did not notice that it was growing dark. It was quite dark when he was aroused by the sound of a door opening. "Who is there?" he asked, touching a commutator.

Suddenly, in consequence of the vibrations produced, the air became luminous.

"Ah! you, Doctor?"

"Yes," was the reply. "How are you?"

"I am feeling well."

"Good! Let me see your tongue. All right! Your pulse. Regular! And your appetite?"

"Only passably good."

"Yes, the stomach. There's the rub. You are over-worked. If your stomach is out of repair, it must be mended. That requires study. We must think about it."

"In the meantime," said Mr. Smith, "you will dine with me."

As in the morning, the table rose out of the floor. Again, as in the morning, the potage, rôti, ragoûts, and legumes were supplied through the food-pipes. Toward the close of the meal, phonotelephotic communication was made with Paris. Smith saw his wife, seated alone at the dinner-table, looking anything but pleased at her loneliness.

"Pardon me, my dear, for having left you alone," he said through the telephone. "I was with Dr. Wilkins."

"Ah, the good doctor!" remarked Mrs. Smith, her countenance lighting up.

"Yes. But, pray, when are you coming home?"

"This evening."

"Very well. Do you come by tube or by air-train?"

"Oh, by tube."

"Yes; and at what hour will you arrive?"

"About eleven, I suppose."

"Eleven by Centropolis time, you mean?"

"Yes."

"Good-by, then, for a little while," said Mr. Smith as he severed communication with Paris.

Dinner over, Dr. Wilkins wished to depart. "I shall expect you at ten," said Mr. Smith. "To-day, it seems, is the day for the return to life of the famous Dr. Faithburn. You did not think of it, I suppose. The awakening is to take place here in my house. You must come and see. I shall depend on your being here."

"I will come back," answered Dr. Wilkins.

Left alone, Mr. Smith busied himself with examining his accounts—a task of vast magnitude, having to do with transactions which involve a daily expenditure of upward of $800,000. Fortunately, indeed, the stupendous progress of mechanic art in modern times makes it comparatively easy. Thanks to the Piano Electro-Reckoner, the most complex calculations can be made in a few seconds. In two hours Mr. Smith completed his task. Just in time. Scarcely had he turned over the last page when Dr. Wilkins arrived. After him came the body of Dr. Faithburn, escorted by a numerous company of men of science. They commenced work at once. The casket being laid down in the middle of the room, the telephote was got in readiness. The outer world, already notified, was anxiously expectant, for the whole world could be eye-witnesses of the performance, a reporter meanwhile, like the chorus in the ancient drama, explaining it all viva voce through the telephone.

"They are opening the casket," he explained. "Now they are taking Faithburn out of it—a veritable mummy, yellow, hard, and dry. Strike the body and it resounds like a block of wood. They are now applying heat; now electricity. No result. These experiments are suspended for a moment while Dr. Wilkins makes an examination of the body. Dr. Wilkins, rising, declares the man to be dead. 'Dead!' exclaims every one present. 'Yes,' answers Dr. Wilkins, 'dead!' 'And how long has he been dead?' Dr. Wilkins makes another examination. 'A hundred years,' he replies."

JULES VERNE

The case stood just as the reporter said. Faithburn was dead, quite certainly dead! "Here is a method that needs improvement," remarked Mr. Smith to Dr. Wilkins, as the scientific committee on hibernation bore the casket out. "So much for that experiment. But if poor Faithburn is dead, at least he is sleeping," he continued. "I wish I could get some sleep. I am tired out, Doctor, quite tired out! Do you not think that a bath would refresh me?"

"Certainly. But you must wrap yourself up well before you go out into the hall-way. You must not expose yourself to cold."

"Hall-way? Why, Doctor, as you well know, everything is done by machinery here. It is not for me to go to the bath; the bath will come to me. Just look!" and he pressed a button. After a few seconds a faint rumbling was heard, which grew louder and louder. Suddenly the door opened, and the tub appeared.

Such, for this year of grace 2889, is the history of one day in the life of the editor of the Earth Chronicle. And the history of that one day is the history of 365 days every year, except leap-years, and then of 366 days—for as yet no means has been found of increasing the length of the terrestrial year.

An Express of the Future

An Express of the Future

"TAKE care!" cried my conductor, "there's a step!"

Safely descending the step thus indicated to me, I entered a vast room, illuminated by blinding electric reflectors, the sound of our feet alone breaking the solitude and silence of the place. Where was I? What had I come there to do? Who was my mysterious guide? Questions unanswered. A long walk in the night, iron doors opened and reclosed with a clang, stairs descending, it seemed to me, deep into the earth--that is all I could remember. I had, however, no time for thinking.

"No doubt you are asking yourself who I am?" said my guide: "Colonel Pierce, at your service. Where are you? In America, at Boston--in a station."

"A station?"

"Yes, the starting-point of the 'Boston to Liverpool Pneumatic Tubes Company.'"

And, with an explanatory gesture, the Colonel pointed out to me two long iron cylinders, about a metre and a half in diameter, lying upon the ground a few paces off.

I looked at these two cylinders, ending on the right in a mass of masonry, and closed on the left with heavy metallic caps, from which a cluster of tubes were carried up to the roof; and suddenly I comprehended the purpose of all this.

Had I not, a short time before, read, in an American newspaper, an article describing this extraordinary project for linking Europe with the New World by means of two gigantic submarines tubes? An inventor had claimed to have accomplished the task; and that inventor, Colonel Pierce, I had before me.

In thought I realized the newspaper article.

Complaisantly the journalist entered into the details of the enterprise. He stated that more than 3,000 miles of iron tubes, weighing over 13,000,000 tons, were required, with the number of ships necessary, for the transport of this material--200 ships of 2,000 tons, each making thirty-three voyages. He described this Armada of science bearing the steel to two special vessels, on board of which the ends of the tubes were joined to each other, and incased in a triple netting of iron, the whole covered with a resinous preparation to preserve it from the action of the seawater.

Coming at once to the question of working, he filled the tubes-- transformed into a sort of pea-shooter of interminable length--with a series of carriages, to be carried with their travellers by powerful currents of air, in the same way that despatches are conveyed pneumatically round Paris.

A parallel with the railways closed the article, and the author enumerated with enthusiasm the advantages of the new and audacious system. According to him, there would be, in passing through these tubes, a suppression of all nervous trepidation, thanks to the interior surface being of finely polished steel; equality of temperature secured by means of currents of air, by which the heat could be modified according to the seasons; incredibly low fares, owing to the cheapness of construction and working expenses-- forgetting, or waving aside, all considerations of the question of gravitation and of wear and tear.

All that now came back to my mind.

So, then, this "Utopia" had become a reality, and these two cylinders of iron at my feet passed thence under the Atlantic and reached to the coast of England!

In spite of the evidence, I could not bring myself to believe in the thing having been done. That the tubes had been laid I could not doubt; but that men could travel by this route--never!

"Was it not impossible even to obtain a current of air of that length?"--I expressed that opinion aloud.

"Quite easy, on the contrary!" protested Colonel Pierce; "to obtain it, all that is required is a great number of steam fans similar to those used in blast furnaces. The air is driven by them with a force which is practically unlimited, propelling it at the speed of 1,800 kilometres an hour--almost that of a cannon-ball!--so that our carriages with their travellers, in the space of two hours and forty minutes, accomplish the journey between Boston and Liverpool."

"Eighteen hundred kilometres an hour!" I exclaimed.

"Not one less. And what extraordinary consequences arise from such a rate of speed! The time at Liverpool being four hours and forty minutes in advance of ours, a traveller starting from Boston at nine o'clock in the morning, arrives in England at 3.53 in the afternoon. Isn't that a journey quickly made? In another sense, on the contrary, our trains, in this latitude, gain over the sun more than 900 kilometres an hour, beating that planet hand over hand: quitting Liverpool at noon, for example, the traveller will reach the station where we now are at thirty-four minutes past nine in the morning—that is to say, earlier than he started! Ha! Ha! I don't think one can travel quicker than that!"

I did not know what to think. Was I talking with a madman?--or must I credit these fabulous theories, in spite of the objections which rose in my mind?

"Very well, so be it!" I said. "I will admit that travellers may take this mad-brained route, and that you can obtain this incredible speed. But, when you have got this speed, how do you check it? When you come to a stop, everything must be shattered to pieces!"

"Not at all," replied the Colonel, shrugging his shoulders. "Between our tubes--one for the out, the other for the home journey-- consequently worked by currents going in opposite directions--a communication exists at every joint. When a train is approaching, an electric spark advertises us of the fact; left to itself, the train would continue its course by reason of the speed it had acquired; but, simply by the turning of a handle, we are able to let in the opposing current of compressed air from the parallel tube, and, little by little, reduce to nothing the final shock or stopping. But what is the use of all these explanations? Would not a trial be a hundred times better?"

And, without waiting for an answer to his questions, the Colonel pulled sharply a bright brass knob projecting from the side of one of the tubes: a panel slid smoothly in its grooves, and in the opening left by its removal I perceived a row of seats, on each of which two persons might sit comfortably side by side.

"The carriage!" exclaimed the Colonel. "Come in."

I followed him without offering any objection, and the panel immediately slid back into its place.

By the light of an electric lamp in the roof I carefully examined the carriage I was in.

Nothing could be more simple: a long cylinder, comfortably upholstered, along which some fifty arm-chairs, in pairs, were ranged in twenty-five parallel ranks. At either end a valve regulated the atmospheric pressure, that at the farther end allowing breathable air to enter the carriage, that in front allowing for the discharge of any excess beyond a normal pressure.

After spending a few moments on this examination, I became impatient.

"Well," I said, "are we not going to start?"

"Going to start?" cried the Colonel. "We have started!"

Started--like that--without the least jerk, was it possible? I listened attentively, trying to detect a sound of some kind that might have guided me.

If we had really started--if the Colonel had not deceived me in talking of a speed of eighteen hundred kilometres an hour--we must already be far from any land, under the sea; above our heads the huge, foam-crested waves; even at that moment, perhaps taking it for a monstrous sea-serpent of an unknown kind--whales were battering with their powerful tails our long, iron prison!

But I heard nothing but a dull rumble, produced, no doubt, by the passage of our carriage, and, plunged in boundless astonishment, unable to believe in the reality of all that had happened to me, I sat silently, allowing the time to pass.

At the end of about an hour, a sense of freshness upon my forehead suddenly aroused me from the torpor into which I had sunk by degrees.

I raised my hand to my brow: it was moist.

Moist! Why was that? Had the tube burst under pressure of the waters-- a pressure which could not but be formidable, since it increases at the rate of "an atmosphere" every ten metres of depth? Had the ocean broken in upon us?

Fear seized upon me. Terrified, I tried to call out--and--and I found myself in my garden, generously sprinkled by a driving rain, the big drops of which had awakened me. I had simply fallen asleep while reading the article devoted by an American journalist to the fantastic projects of Colonel Pierce--who, also, I much fear, has only dreamed.

About the Author

Jules Gabriel Verne (1828- 1905) was a prolific French author, whose writings have laid down the foundations of modern scientific fiction. An author ahead of his time, Jules Verne has written fictional accounts of space travelling, sea and air voyages .

Verne was born on February 8, 1828 in the seaport of Nantes, France as the eldest son of Pierre Verne and his wife Sophie. His father wanted him to follow his footsteps and become a lawyer but the young Jules was inspired by the fantasy of literature.

The birthplace of Jules Verne had a strong impact on his writings. During the 19th century, Nantes was an extremely busy port city with frequent visits from traders and sailors. Jules observed these things and his works reflect his own experiences at sea. He also worked as a stockbroker in Paris to support his family. But writing was a part of his soul and he never parted with his passion even during the toughest of times. He continued writing books till his death on 24 March, 1905.

Verne wrote some of the most amazing narratives merging the practical aspects of science with the imaginative concepts of fiction. His works have majorly contributed to the development of steampunk, a sub-genre in science fiction that deals with the machinery and industrial technological advances of the 19th century.

Jules Verne holds the reputation of being the second-most translated author of the world and ranks between the legendary playwright William Shakespeare and the prominent mystery-fiction writer Agatha Christie. He is often celebrated as the "Father of Science Fiction" along with the famous H.G. Wells.

Word Meanings

1. Burgomaster – the mayor of a Dutch, Flemish, German, Austrian, or Swiss town

2. Donjon – the great tower or innermost keep of a castle

3. Impetuous – acting or done quickly without any thought or care

4. Vivacious – attractively lively and animated

5. Congenial – pleasant or agreeable since it is suited to one's taste or inclination

6. Capricious – sudden changing in accordance with no particular rules or formats

7. Annihilate – to utterly destroy

8. Ineffable – too great or extreme to be expressed or described in words

9. Abomination – a thing that causes disgust or loathing

10. Belligerent – hostile and aggressive

11. Pusillanimous – showing a lack of courage or determination

12. Conjecture – an opinion or conclusion formed on the basis of incomplete information

13. Blockade – an act or means of sealing off a place to prevent goods or people from entering or leaving

14. Betrothed – the person to whom one is engaged

15. Appanage – a benefit or right belonging to someone

16. Physiognomist: A person supposedly able to judge character from facial characteristics

17. Adversary: One's opponent in a contest, conflict or dispute

18. Imperturbable: Unable to be upset or excited

19. Impetuous: Acting or done quickly and without thought or care

20. Gesticulations: Gestures used, instead of speaking, to emphasize one's words

21. Recrimination: An accusation in response to one from someone else

www.ingramcontent.com/pod-product-compliance
Lightning Source LLC
Chambersburg PA
CBHW060416030726
47495CB00003B/607